The KING'S LIZARD

A Tale of Murder and Deception
in Old Santa Fe
≪ 1782 ≫

A Novel By

Pamela Christie

Lone Butte Press
Santa Fe, New Mexico
2004

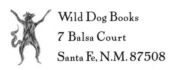 Wild Dog Books
7 Balsa Court
Santa Fe, N.M. 87508

WildDogBooks@att.net

Cover illustration: Christopher C. Clow & Pamela Christie

ISBN 0-9666860-4-7
Library of Congress Control Number: 2004109931

Printed in the United States of America

This book is dedicated to
Cleone Feir Stoloff
with love.

The characters in this story are entirely fictional,with the exception of Governor Juan Bautista de Anza and King Carlos the Third of Spain, each of whom was far too important to be overlooked or impersonated by another player.

A brief overview of the historical period and a glossary of Spanish words used in the text may be found starting on page 352.

Prologue

This is what my honored grandfather told me, all of it. Someone long ago taught him how to tell a tale, someone who knew what to do with the space between *En Años Pasados* and *Así Fué*. When we sat up together nights, waiting for babies to be born or for horses to foal, for travelers to return, or for news of the men who ran to the mountains after the uprising, he told me of those murderous times.

By the end of his life, the facts of the treachery had been revealed, the parts he had lived first-hand, of course, but also those they had kept secret from him, or that he had missed when he was away on his red Comanche mare doing secret business for the king. But by then, New Mexico was no longer Spain's, and there was no longer a king to serve and protect.

By then it was a new country called Mexico, and though still dangerous, it was a different place in many ways, where people were allowed to enter from anywhere, and rich and diverse goods flowed to us from all directions, no longer just from the viceroy's domain in the south.

Yes, it was different by the time my grandfather was old, but he remained who he always was, the strongest little man I ever knew, still able to ride his horse hanging upside down off the saddle to hide from Comanche arrows, and still able to hold his family with love, by the strength of his tough, small hands.

Santiago Sebastian Torres y Aguilar
Abiquiú, Nuevo Mexico 1838

I

From the map by Don Bernardo de Miera y Pacheco, 1779

The Padre

Santa Fe, Kingdom of New Mexico – 1782

*P*adre Miera levered his stocky body out of the wooden chair, marveling that he could be so fat in a colony known for drought and famine. He moved to the light of the doorway with the letter he had just written to his superior in Mexico. The breeze was warm this morning, the sky a perfect blue with only one white fish of cloud hovering above the peak called Chicoma.

For a moment his eyes scanned the long spine of mountains that rimmed the broad plateau. He lingered in the first warmth of spring, letting the brown ink dry in the sun. Then he bent to review his work, to make sure his outrage was only partly concealed by the polite rhetoric. "To the most benign and venerated Father Provincial. I kiss your Reverend Paternity's hand..."

Did his old and trusted friend realize that the impossible tax placed on every Indian and Spaniard in New Mexico for the war against England had proved too harsh a toll, particularly on top of the raging pox that had killed thousands last year? Would the Blessed Father agree that those burdens had caused

3

the alarming upsurge in the trafficking of Indian slaves, despite all regulations forbidding it? He was writing now in secret, trusting his report to an Indian's pack, to reveal that villainy to the Church, fourteen hundred miles away, because no official of the government here would lift a hand to stop it.

Miera grimaced as the one image he always tried to force from his mind rose before him: a young Indian girl, naked in the dirt at the Taos fair, men gathered around, one yelling, "Now she's not a virgin anymore! Now she'll be good for something!" And he, the fresh young priest in those years, standing there on the windy prairie below the bleak mountains, stunned by his own inaction, shamed by his fear and by the silence he kept.

Now, this bright spring day, from somewhere off in the fields, he heard the thin voice of a boy call out his name. The priest looked up and swore. "Damnation! Will I never have a private morning?" He could see an approaching rider momentarily detoured by the spread of water under the cottonwood trees where snowmelt rushing off the mountains had overflowed the riverbed. Miera hastened to add the mandatory closing phrases: "Our very Reverend Paternity, your least subject kisses your Reverend Paternity's hand . . ." He flung sand over the ink and hid the letter in the trunk at the foot of his cot, just as an urchin on a burro hurtled into the yard.

"Padre, padre!" the young boy cried. "You have to come to the plaza. Someone's been killed!"

"Who now?" Miera grumbled as he shoved his feet into moccasins.

"A soldier on guard duty, murdered at the palacio! They just found him!" The boy slid to the ground and offered the priest his mount. He helped the padre hoist himself onto the

4

burro, then tucked Miera's blue skirts under him to protect his legs from the scratch and fleas of the animal's back.

"Why all this hurry if the man's already dead?"

"They want you as witness, they want you to see how it was done!"

Another gruesome job for the padre, muttered the Franciscan, as he kicked the burro into a jolting trot. He resented the interruption of his letter writing. People died every day in this part of the kingdom. What else could they expect, these men who lived so cruelly and always by the sword? Why make a big commotion over one more death?

Miera turned onto the dirt road and headed for the dusty scattering of mud buildings called Santa Fe. He lifted his eyes to the steep green mountains that soared above the town, providing a protective eastern wall. Their higher reaches were still snow-covered, even though it was past Easter. He used thoughts of the cool forests and garden-like meadows up there to calm himself before he approached the tumult on the plaza.

A crowd had gathered at the corner of the mud building they grandly called the Palace of the Governors. The people were watching a fresh-faced guard who leaned sloppily against a huge cottonwood, his musket lying on the ground. Father Miera dismounted and moved in to get a closer look. A sergeant had pulled open the soldier's cape and was tugging desperately at a rough rope that bound the militiaman beneath his arms, but Miera could already see it wouldn't make any difference. The young soldier's head drooped forward. Streaks of crimson glistened on his leather tunic. The rope that lashed the man to the broad trunk of the tree was all that held him on his feet.

Off-duty soldiers, children, and women holding market baskets stood in silence while the padre walked up to the man.

Raising his hand in benediction he said a blessing for the dead, and then with the help of the sergeant, cut the rope. The lifeless guard crashed in a heap onto the dirt. The crowd fell back when they saw brains and bone fragments spilling from dark gouges where an ax blade had chopped into his skull. Then the stunned silence vanished.

"Murdered right here on the plaza!"

"Wasn't he with the militia, brought down from the north to fight the Comanches?"

"How horrible to touch a dead man, to tie him like that to the tree!"

Padre Miera turned away from the body. As a priest he had been summoned to officiate at many deaths, but this one made no sense at all; a young man doing routine duty in town, and someone bashes his skull open on a beautiful spring morning?

He helped lift the dead soldier onto the litter and pulled the man's cape over his face. The press of people began to disperse. Knowing his work was cut out for him for the rest of the day, he took just a moment for himself, bending to rinse his hands in the shallow runnel, the acequia that flowed at the edge of the street. He felt queasy from being so close to the victim and the sour stench of his brain. To get a grip, he tried to say a prayer for the man, but it kept coming out wrong. It kept being a prayer for this shabby little town whose peace had just been so violated, and for its odd and stubborn people, struggling for life on the farthest edge of the known world.

Nando

Abiquiú, New Mexico
Spring - 1782

The man standing above me on the ditch bank waved a stick five feet long and yelled curses that made me wince. He started out with Jesus and his mother and then went on to me: "Nando, you dirt-faced son of a slave! You skinny little half-breed!"

He was right so far.

"My donkey farms better than you do! Your water ruined my field. Look how your ditch bank broke!"

I didn't need to look. I stood still in the cropped field at the foot of the blue mesa, cast a longing glance at the wild mountains to the west, and tried not to pay too much attention to the man who shouted at me.

"It's been two years since your field paid its tithe! Two years no first-fruits to the Church, and now you're ruining mine, damaging me, the mayor's lieutenant!" He was thickset, red-faced and moving toward me. I pointed my shovel handle at his chest in flimsy defense.

"I never said I was a farmer, Teniente," I said quietly, but with an anger that matched his own. I doubted the mayor's assistant could hear me through the noise of his own harangue, but he may have, because he gave up trying to reform me and began to poke frantically at the ditch bank, trying to shove runny mud into the break with the end of his stick. Frustrated by all of it, he shouted, "Go back to raising your stinking sheep!"

In full agreement with his suggestion, I threw my shovel down on the grass, just missing his feet. "I would if I could!" I yelled and left my fields, climbing straight up the hill to town. I'd go back to the ranch in one minute if they'd let me, but our grant of land had been suspended after we'd been driven off by the Comanches. Now, without permission from the governor in Santa Fe, and the viceroy down in Mexico, and the king over in Spain, there was no way in hell I, or anyone in my family, would be allowed to set foot on it until we could re-establish our claim.

Abiquiú had turned into a different place since yesterday. All night I'd heard the squeak and jingle of harness and the movement of men and animals in the restless camps around the plaza. The long, cold winter had given up at last. Spring was here, and the traders were returning to put together pack trains and crews for the season of travel between the Spanish, the Utes, and the people on the plains. I figured fewer than a quarter of the outfits were legal, but that didn't concern the people of Abiquiú. The trade routes were booming business, and everyone, from our mayor to the lowliest Indian servant, found a way to profit from it.

Just as I reached the plaza, Anselmo started banging away on his drum. "What's your news?" I called out.

"The first pack train's coming in from the north!"

From the town's perch on the mesa we could see far up the river valley and follow the caravan's progress on the winding road that skirted the red cliffs. In less than an hour, the string of laden mules and horses clopped into the plaza and pulled to a halt beside the big wooden cross in front of the church. The reek of hot horse sweat overpowered the smoky stench of the crowd. Farmers and town officials, women in dresses and women in blankets, swarmed up to the incoming traders, bypassing for now the heap of trade goods and making straight for the more valuable cargo, ten bedraggled children.

The little Comanches, chalky with trail dust, stopped in a frightened huddle. The proud traders laughed and joked with the crowd, pretending the children didn't matter much, but a half-dozen sturdy men, bristling with lances and guns, stayed close to the captives. The older ones weren't allowed to dismount, so they sat there, heads down, tied to the saddles of Ute ponies. The toddlers tumbled to the ground and started to cry, reaching up to the village women for food. Two little girls clung to each other as the townspeople stared at them.

I'd be damned before I'd join the throng that poked at the captives. Instead, I took my time scanning the huge dripping baskets of tallow and piles of dressed skins the longhaired men had brought down from the mountains. Finally, I turned my attention to the children. Even if they did come from our enemies, they still were not much older than babies. It was hard to believe that children as filthy and sunburned as these represented such wealth to the Spaniards.

I watched the widow Montoya as she came out of her house, shielding her eyes from the brilliant sun. Wouldn't she like to have a slave! It wouldn't bother her that the children were terrified, being herded onto our plaza to be sold, or if no one here could buy, to be driven down the road and paraded in front of the church at the next village, and the next. She evaluated the dark-skinned children with a careful eye.

"Same old stuff, Teresa," someone ribbed her. As usual, the captives were in rags, their hair cut short against lice. "Maybe one of these little fellows you could afford?" A woman pointed to a tiny Comanche. I heard the widow sniff, feigning indifference. I knew her well enough to see her sharp mind calculating fast as an abacus. It would be years until these babies could do valuable work. Meanwhile, they would eat a lot of food. Old lady Montoya turned her back to the plaza and retreated into her home.

Our pious townspeople looked the children over and handled them like market vegetables. One of our better-off farmers, an old man with a perpetual look of gloom, started bidding for one of the bigger girls. It disgusted me the way the crowd spurred him on, so I escaped and made straight for my cousin Diego's place higher on the hill.

Diego had visitors. An older man, tough as a knot, who looked like he could still take on anybody and enjoy it, stood just inside the door, and sitting in Diego's only chair was the most handsome Spaniard I'd ever seen. He was about the same age as I, but right there the similarities stopped. The high-coloring in the man's patrician face was set off by thin, dark eyebrows and a crisp mustache that kept his florid lips from seeming effeminate. He wore expensive, tight leather breeches and a form-fitting jacket with silver buttons. There was money on the table between the Spaniard and my cousin, not much, but some. Diego stood with his arms folded, looking at the man's trim hands as they laid down several more coins. I wished I hadn't barged in. The old coot at the door eyed me like a pig in the auction pen, and his elegant master stopped dealing money to regard me coolly.

"Him too," he said, pushing over more coins. "Add him to your list, head-hunter."

Diego flung me a warning look, so I turned and headed back through the door. I hadn't gotten past the cedar posts before hard fingers grabbed my arm. "Hold on, son," the older man said. I shook him off and tried to keep on leaving, but it didn't work. His tough hands clutched my shirt as he tried to haul me back to his boss.

I was on the verge of driving a hard knee into his groin, when the patrón ordered, "Ease up, Lorenzo!" the way he would command a dog to drop his bone, and I was released. The rich man looked me over, smiling as he did so, showing off perfect teeth and except for that dark mustache, an uncommonly smooth shave. What he didn't understand was that I had no intention of being forced to work for a trader, no matter how beautiful he was.

It was beginning to dawn on me what I'd walked into here. I'd just discovered my own cousin busily brokering young men of the village into service with the caravans. Sure, the boys would be given a few pesos worth of trade goods at the end of the season and allowed to return home, but once the broker and the trail boss had cut their deal, the conscripts had no choice in the matter. I'd seen them seized physically, and I knew the traders held them by force until they were too far up the trail to make it back on their own.

Diego was waking up to what he'd gotten me into, so he pushed the pesos back to the Spaniard. "Ramón, you can't take Fernando. He's my cousin. His father was Don Benito Aguilar, may God keep his soul, and even though his mother's a Ute, Nando was raised in the Aguilar family."

Lorenzo almost hissed when he repeated, "May God keep his soul! So his father's dead, you say? Got himself a half-breed bastard, did he?"

While Lorenzo sneered at me, Ramón kept his eyes on Diego. My cousin was nervous under the stare, but he managed to go on. "I can't put Nando on the list, Señor. He has two older brothers who look out for him, and one of them's a lieutenant at the presidio. Nando takes care of the Aguilar property here and raises food for his stepmother's household down in Santa Fe. The family will not be pleased if you take Nando against his will."

Although Diego's speech was pretty enough and my flash of anger had dissipated, I was aware that no matter how important my father had been, I was still only a half-caste with few rights and little status. In these times, anyone but a full-blooded Spaniard could easily be picked up and might disappear altogether from the colony, aided of course by petty dealers like my cousin.

Lorenzo had his hand on me once more, but again Ramón signaled to let me go. Then he rose to his feet, picking up his gloves from the table. "Well then, you have a choice to make, don't you, Nando? Come north with me for reliable pay, or be put on the front line at the militia's next fight."

He could tell by the expression on my face that I didn't follow his meaning, so he took pains to fill me in. "We have received reports that government troops are riding north to round up more men. The call's gone out, and they won't bother to concern themselves with whether you want to be in the military or not. Is my meaning clear?"

Before going through the door he turned to me and extended his hand. I had no choice but to clasp it. "Ramón Duran. If you change your mind, we'll have a place for you riding with our caravans. We'll be leaving this evening." He was out the door. The older fellow was still there, retrieving the pesos that Ramón would have used to buy my services, and he lingered in Diego's room long enough to give me a look that let me know he wasn't done with me.

"Lorenzo!"

"Coming." The man pushed me aside and went out to join his boss.

Diego shut the door with care and took a breath. He was watching to see how angry I was at him. I detested what my cousin was doing to earn the coins weighing down his pocket, but at least he had the cojones to stand up for me when it counted.

I stood still, wondering which way to play this. Then, levelly, I asked, "Are army recruiters really coming up here?"

"Word has it the governor has put the pressure on, and this time they're so short-handed they're even picking up boys."

It appeared that one way or the other I was about to be forced out of my easy-going life in Abiquiú, but I hid my concern. "Who's the pretty one? This Ramón?"

"He's the son of one of the richest men in the province. His father's Tomás Duran, the alcalde of Santa Fe. Their company can't find enough men this year for the trade routes because so many have been commandeered into military service. Look, Nando, Ramón's outfits are all legal, travel permits, licenses, everything. He showed them to me. You could wind up with a worse deal. He was offering hard money."

"I noticed, and what percentage do you take for sitting here on your hind end and sending me off to do the work?"

"Look, I didn't initiate that. You just walked in at the wrong moment. But use your head, cousin. Under the circumstances, getting out of here could make sense."

13

I grabbed him and brought my face close to his, "How much?"

"Ten pesos," he admitted. I let go of Diego's shirt and turned away. Ten pesos, the price of a little burro. At last I knew my worth.

"If you're telling the truth and they're licensed, then presumably they can't be selling humans. Diego, you'd better understand that I'm not working for any slavers!" My cousin ignored my rising voice and shrugged. I thought about the older man, the one with the rough hands. "The other fellow, who's he?"

"Trail boss, named Lorenzo. Ramón doesn't go along, just sets the caravans up, waves them off, then outfits the next one."

"Sounds like a lot of work for a rich boy," I scoffed. If men were being pressed into the militia, getting out of Abiquiú would be a smart move, but there was no way I was interested in Ramón's offer, not with the disagreeable Lorenzo as boss. I was going to have to come up with some other solution: maybe a quick hunting trip into the hills, followed by a visit to my mother's people?

I was peering through the shutters down to the plaza, keeping my eye on Ramón and Lorenzo as they moved among the crowd, when I noticed a white plume billowing above the river road, coming from the direction of the capital. "Diego! Look!" We stepped out to his porch to watch because news always comes on dust. Sun glittered on metal, and then through the dirt cloud we could make out the bright blue cloaks of a presidio patrol from down south in Santa Fe. As predicted, here they came, galloping up the wide valley to force more men into the militia.

I had a horse and I owned a gun. Twenty-two years old, definitely unmarried, and only this morning called an incorrigible miscreant by the teniente, I stood out as ripe for recruitment. My cousin knew it too, and he taunted me. "O.K. Nando, what do you say? Do you want to be forced into the military to fight Comanches, or take Ramón's offer?"

"You little bastard! You're still drooling over ten pesos, aren't you?" I was cross, but mostly because I was faced with a miserable choice. As the horsemen took the turnoff to town, a prickle passed over my skin. Here came my future, riding in at a gallop. Still, I was too proud to tell Diego that travel with a trade caravan was looking more appealing.

For the moment my cousin was thinking in a more practical vein. "The army's riding in, and here's the town crawling with illegal traders!"

"Let them catch the sons of bitches," I muttered, knowing how stupid I was being since the majority of traders were our friends and the life-blood of this town. Diego gave me a sour look, then took off down the hill, sprinting to our local mayor-alcalde's house to deliver the news. I took the short cut to the plaza, through the shady slot between the church and the cold walls of the convento, to warn the traders. My words were few and I had to point toward the road only once.

The canny Lorenzo looked me over for a moment and decided I wasn't making it up. He snapped out orders, grabbed a lead rope and started a string of mules, still loaded with trade goods, moving away from the square. After he was gone, the captives were pushed out of a house and herded into a cluster. Men I'd never seen before picked up the young ones, clutching them tightly as they jumped onto horses, and in seconds they were moving in a fast, but quiet walk toward the hills. The last Appaloosa rump, with the last swishing tail, dis-

15

appeared between two long, low houses, and when the soldiers rode onto the hard-baked clay of the main square, there was no sign of any of Abiquiú's traders, much less a slavers' caravan.

Our mud-brown village, with white smoke rising from the chimneys, was a picture of peace, nestled against mountains. Three women ground corn on a porch and babies played bare-bottomed in the dirt. Old Tio Chano, wielding his crooked wooden hoe, broke up the hardpan and pulled out last year's shriveled stalks. A rich man and his friends knelt in the shadowy depths of the church, praising the Lord. The governor's soldiers took quick measure of the peaceful scene, then slapping dust from their breeches, dismounted and moved quickly toward the mayor's house under the trees. The village's young boys were proud to have reins thrust into their hands, proud to be told to water the king's horses.

Once the troop was inside the mayor's courtyard, Tio Chano decided it was time to chop the weeds beside the mayor's wall, but he hadn't worked up a sweat before he set aside his hoe and shuffled over to the women on the porch. With their quick mouths the news spread faster than if the drummer had announced it.

"They're demanding more men right away to fight the Comanches! Twelve altogether, but the king finally heard our need. They're going to pay this time!"

I had my doubts. Abiquiú's people had been mustered too often with empty promises of pesos for anyone to trust this. Our men had been lost in battles far from here and their widows had never received one coin. Yet now the government was requiring the village to turn over a dozen more mounted and armed men, and at the start of the growing season, too.

Diego had disappeared, so I lingered with the other towns-people while they chattered about the call-up. Then I was reminded how a small town can turn mean at times. My neck tensed as I noticed people already looking at me, deciding to put me on the short-list of those expected to go. My predicament was becoming serious and I still hadn't a clue how I was going to get out if it. To buy a little time, I slipped into the cool dark of the church, but before my eyes had adjusted to the gloom a hand fell on my arm.

"Thank you for coming," said Ramón. "I knew you'd see things my way. Ready?" Perhaps I gave some sign that I was, because his companions moved in close, their shoulders jostling mine. A firm hand took hold of my shoulder and steered me down the length of the nave toward the altar. I noticed that none of the men knelt or made the sign of the cross. Pushing me ahead of them, they turned abruptly into the sacristy, then we all exited through a door in the back. Their horses were hidden in the grove down the hill by the spring.

So, my rat of a cousin hadn't been able to resist a few extra pesos after all! At the last minute, he must have told Ramón where to find me, but now that the presidio patrol was fanning out through the village looking for "likely lads," I grudgingly admitted it might not be so bad that Diego had pushed this.

Whoever had me in his grip didn't let go until I was boosted into a saddle. Then the handsome Ramón came up to me with Lorenzo standing at his side. I was doing some quick reckoning. At least this caravan was legal, unlike the dirty pack of slavers displaying their child-captives this morning, and Ramón promised he would pay. A promise from him was probably less flimsy than a promise from the army's paymaster.

17

I looked at the alcalde's son, forcing myself to smile. "I'm with you," I said, then for good measure cheerfully added, "I've always wanted to see the north. Isn't that where we're going?"

He gave me a long, cold look. "You'll go where the trade takes you," he said. "If you don't ask too many questions and do as Lorenzo orders, things will work out all right." Then he seemed to relax, and waved away the trail boss.

"Very well, then. To the north! I hope the journey is all that you expected." He slapped the rump of the beast they'd put me on, and I found myself heading out with Duran's first caravan of spring.

The Taos Trail

1 was riding a shaggy white gelding all speckled with brown, mud most likely. The last thing I saw as we left Abiquiú was Rosinante, my own red mare, lifting her elegant head to watch the string of horses that cantered past, leaving her behind. Could she tell I left with them? I also noticed that the water from my broken acequia still poured into the teniente's pasture, gouging soggy ruts into his soil.

A crow flying to Taos from here would head northeast, but to avoid climbing over a range of chalky cliffs, we took the river road south. A few miles down, this valley would meet the larger one of the Rio Grande. Where the red stream of the Chama joins the cool green of the big river, we would turn north and soon be drawn into the deep canyon where the waters plunge down from the Taos mountains. The half-dozen crewmembers traveled in a cluster close around me, and Lorenzo rode where he could always keep me in his sight. They knew just how strong my urge to sign on had been. As we moved out, I sensed that the other group, the one carrying the captives, was not far ahead of us. Our horses had their scent, and some form of communication was going on between the animals.

I was trying to get used to the jerking gait of the horse, and also to figure out what had just happened to my life, when Ramón came up beside me, all animosity apparently behind us now, for he started talking as though I was already one of his boys. "The soldiers will assume we're going straight north into Ute country. They won't be looking for us on this route. When we get to the Rio Grande we'll take the Indian trail beside the river instead of the usual way over the hills. It's rough, but that way you won't be at risk from patrols."

I wondered if he was doing that just for my sake, or if he had reasons of his own. Thinking of who got me into this, I asked with some bitterness, "Does Diego still get paid?"

"You signed up voluntarily, as I see it," he said with a smile, "but he'll get a tip. Don't worry about that, Nando, we'll take care of it." So affable, this Ramón Duran, but still he watched me keenly. "You haven't heard the latest on the militia, have you?"

"I didn't have time to hear much news."

He ignored the innuendo and said, "Someone's out to get them."

"What's new about that?" I replied, thinking of the spate of recent attacks.

"No, not at the outposts. Right downtown in Santa Fe. Somebody sank an ax into a guard on duty outside the palacio. Too bad. He was really just a kid."

"Oh, come on, Ramón! Things like that don't happen in the capital. The governor's there, and the troops. People are around all hours of the day and night. Santa Fe's civilized."

"The governor's away, and the troops are spread thin. They say it's Indians, probably Apaches. They can come in easily at night." Ramón just rode along, letting me think about it for a while. Finally he said, "The killing's scared people. Word's getting out and men are deserting the garrison. This isn't a good time to be a militiaman."

"It sounds like someone's making sure of that," I said.

"Someone certainly is," Ramón replied. "Lucky for you the recruiters didn't pick you up." He shot me that engaging smile again.

"I'm sure I'm obliged to you," I replied with no smile.

Ramón said, "You'll do fine with us, Nando. So you're an Aguilar, are you? Did you ever visit their big ranch up on the Piedra Lumbre?"

"I lived there most of my life," I said with pride. This new piece of information made him turn to look me over. Then a more guarded look came upon him. So he knew about my family and was curious about our ranch. But Ramón covered up his interest, and instead chatted amiably about the good grazing in the valleys we were riding through. It seemed that the fine rico from the south was making an effort to be my friend. Ramón's friendship with me might be budding, but I wasn't at all sure how I felt about him. Too fancy for me, and too sure of himself, too certain that joining his outfit was the perfect thing for me. As we rode side by side, I decided to end this relationship the moment I heard the military was finished recruiting. It wouldn't be hard to find a way to ditch the caravan. Thanks to my Indian mother I didn't mind traveling alone cross-country, although most men wouldn't do it in dangerous territory.

Late in the day we stopped. Food was passed from hand to hand, but before I had more than a bite, Lorenzo made me loosen the panniers and then water the animals in the Rio Chama. By the time I got back, soaked to the shins, all the food was gone and, oddly, so was Ramón. No one mentioned his departure. His disappearance made me uneasy, because now it was just me, Lorenzo, and the six crusty men of the crew.

We let the horses graze for a short while, and then by the last orange light of the setting sun we mounted up and headed through the broad spread of cottonwoods, across the sandy delta to the Rio Grande. Our animals paid attention only to each other and to the boring business of putting one foot in front of the other. They'd settled down, so I figured the pack train carrying the slave children was no longer in our vicinity.

At the big river we rode in the shallows for several minutes, then crossed where the water ran two hundred feet wide so wasn't too deep. Then we turned north. Now we were heading toward Taos and the Ute territory, most likely to buy the piles of buffalo hides the tribes had cured during the winter months. Our party picked up speed, seeming to shake off the rules and restraints of the settled areas as we cantered along the river trail.

It might have been fun, but now that Ramón had left, Lorenzo began to needle me. I didn't ride well enough. I didn't keep my horse moving along like the others. I didn't need a break when I finally asked for one and he wouldn't let me stop. When at last we halted and made camp, I was given the watering job again and told to stand the first shift. Again I went hungry. The others had some food in their kits, but I had no kit, no blanket, not even my knife. Whether I ate or not didn't bother the trail boss one bit. It was a long, cold night.

The next day was a little better though, because one of the riders, Pedro Jaime, shared some bread and a piece of jerked meat with me. "He'll work you over for a couple of days, it's his way of teaching you who's boss," Pedro said, "but by the time we get past Taos he'll see you're outfitted. That is, if you don't disappoint him."

I planned to disappoint him first chance I got, but there hadn't been one yet. Lorenzo hadn't liked me from the beginning, and now he must be suspecting that I'd try to get away. I was watched all the time. Men slept inches from me. Yes, they had put me on guard duty, but there had been another man there as well. When I went into the woods to relieve myself, someone was waiting for me not far off. In short, they intended to hang on to me. Except for the one bit of kindness from Pedro Jaime, I traveled with a surly lot.

All the next morning we rode on a narrow trail between the swollen river and the steep pink cliffs that threatened to slide into it. In places, the banks had been undermined or cut away altogether by the rushing water and we had to lead the nervous horses along the precarious edge. When we were finally past that trick, we wound through mountains that would have looked utterly forlorn were it not for a lone cross, stationed on one of the pointed summits. Eventually, the trail lifted out of the river valley and ascended a pass. It was mid-afternoon when we stopped on the mesa top, just where the canyons and dark trees ended. The vista spread north as far as the eye could see. A great tawny plain was sliced through the middle by the black gorge of the river, and on the east it was bounded by an abrupt and solid wall of mountains. My worries lifted as we found the trail that descended into Taos. There I could surely find a way to leave this crew, but while we were still on the edge of the forest, Lorenzo threw a blanket near my horse's feet and ordered, "Come with me!"

The other men watched in concerted silence as I dropped to the ground to get the blanket, then started to remount.

"Leave the horse. You're walking now." Here it comes, I thought, as I followed the man on horseback. We retraced our route a short way to a thin creek that trickled down a side canyon. It was wooded in there, dank-smelling and dark even at midday, but a good place to hide if I needed one.

Lorenzo turned his horse upstream, then ordered, "Here now, walk in front of me." We had gone only a few hundred yards up the winding creek when we came to a furtive little camp under the fir trees. Nine men, one for each of the Indian children they were transporting, crowded around a dismal fire. The belief I'd fabricated that my new job didn't entail slaving evaporated, as I witnessed the greetings between Lorenzo and the very group of slavers I'd seen in Abiquiú. They guarded the same sorrowful children. Again, the younger ones were not tied, but around the neck of each of the older girls was a noose that could be tightened with a yank. None of the captives made a sound.

I cursed and turned on my heel, as disgusted with my own stupidity as with this horrible scene. I strode deliberately into the thick woods, knowing full well I wouldn't get past the closest tree. I ignored the first set of hands that reached for me and shook off the second. Then Lorenzo seized my shoulder, jerked me to a halt, and started roping my arms together.

"You'll stay with this camp today, Nando, until you get over your pretty notions. You'll be under guard until we clear Taos. After that, there won't be any more temptations." The way he wrapped my wrists, tight, and again, tighter, belied his matter-of-fact tone. There was no point in fighting, surrounded by men hard enough to buy and sell children. The stolidly silent captives watched me, too. Had Lorenzo just been waiting for Ramón to leave before he went about his real business?

Then a little boy erupted in tears. He couldn't have been more than six and the meat had fallen off his bread. A man leaned down, slapped the child and scooped up the food, flinging it into the trees. The boy howled. The trader clamped a dirty palm over the child's mouth and nose and held it there until I thought the boy would suffocate. I think he nearly did, for when the man released him the child slumped to the ground and lay there with his forehead pressed into the dirt, hoping to hide, trying to recover.

Though I was trussed and helpless, my own predicament was minor by comparison.

She Left By Stealth

*W*hen Lorenzo departed, half the men went with him, holding the older girls on their saddles in front of them. Having been thwarted by the arrival of the army patrol in Abiquiú, they would now try their luck at the fairground outside Taos, where people were gathering to trade goods and captives after the isolation of winter.

Afternoon in the hidden camp dragged on. The toddlers whimpered, ignored by their keepers, who intervened only when the crying got too loud. Mercifully, one of the traders finally untied me. They didn't seem to mind when I tended to the children, but that night they made me pay for it by tying me again, this time into the same length of rope that secured their captives.

I managed to scoot over to lean against the trunk of a small fir. I knew I wouldn't sleep, but this way I could rest. A little girl lay within reach. I put my hand on her shoulder and patted her. The boy who had dropped his food squirmed closer

26

to me, and I placed his small dark head on my leg to make him more comfortable. It relieved something in me to be able to reach out and touch gentle human beings. There wasn't much chance of that in the group I had been forced to join.

My brain was working hard on a variety of dubious schemes to get out of this. Now it looked a lot tougher than before, when I was sure I could break away whenever I chose. I'm not big, but I'm stronger than people think and I've learned how to fight. Being short I've had to, but the odds were stacked against me here. The traders were armed; and to make it harder, now I doubted that I would just sneak off and save my own neck, leaving these children to Lorenzo's schemes. In truth, it was probably too late to make much difference. The bigger girls had likely already been sold, and if Lorenzo got the price he wanted, he'd be back for the little ones in the morning. Hobbled at the ankles and tied into a lead rope, I couldn't even help myself just now, much less anybody else. I sat there getting mad, thinking, they can't get away with doing this to an Aguilar! Then I realized they probably could.

Sleep was impossible. There was something about slaves that wrenched my gut. With the boy's head on me, his cropped hair as thick and black as my own, and another child curled against my leg, I realized how similar our stories were, for my own mother had been captured as a child.

I was a number of years into my life, in fact I was already pulling whiskers out of my chin, before I found out that while I was indeed my father's son, I also was his slave. All the years on our family's ranch I was just another boy among many there who called him Papa, received his blessing on Holy days, got the edge of his tongue or the back of his hand when we'd broken a tool or couldn't find a sheep we'd let stray. Nothing in my life ever hinted that my mother was a slave. When she finally told me the truth, I was devastated. Though five years have passed since I found out, watching the children suffer that night carried a far deeper pain than Lorenzo or his cronies would ever know.

Ours had been a rowdy household far out in the country, nearly a full day's ride from Abiquiú. That was before the Comanche raids got so bad we couldn't stay. My mother, brother, sister and I had shared a room that we called our nest, where we whiled away stormy days in winter or curled up together to sleep. But there were also my half brothers from the other mother. There were cousins, too, living up there with my old grandmother, two aunts and an uncle. All told, more than twenty of us lived in the long, low houses that were built around courtyards where we baked or washed, and where the apricot trees could bloom in safety out of the northwest winds. There was work all the time, but I never minded it or thought of it as work, particularly once I was given my own horse and my father sent me out to the high valleys with a thousand sheep to watch over. One or another of my brothers came with me and we stayed for months.

The first summer up there, sometimes I missed my mother, missed her full round arms around me and the way she plucked and fussed at me. There was no doubt she loved me in a special way. I was her firstborn. After me came Segundo, and Nanna. Though she had three babies, my mother kept strong and stayed pretty. The pox never got her, not like most of the women who had suffered from it badly. You could tell by their skin. But Nan was beautiful, and I knew my father thought so too.

Benito would find her. When he returned from hunting buffalo out on the plains, or from chasing down our sheep when the Navajos raided, he'd find her wherever she was working, an hour or so after he got back. She'd carry the big leather bucket of hot water into his room, and the door stayed shut until morning.

My father was a strong man and a lively one. He was always figuring something out to make our ranch better, and he liked us all, every one of his kids. Not just me, Nando, third son to him, my long straight hair chopped to chin length when I was little, running all over the place, eager to be part of everything. He liked all the children, Diego, Manuel and Tobias, and the girls, who lived in the house across the yard with our aunt, and of course his "true" sons, Francisco and Carlos, who shared a room near the other mother, their mother.

She was Luz de Gracia, from Spain, tall and self-possessed, and she was the one who taught us how to read, and how to say our catechism. I remember she was often sick, something to do with having babies. At first she lived in another world from ours, staying indoors most of the time, "keeping her skin white," Nan and the aunts joked. Later I realized she always put that pasty white stuff on her face. It kind of smoothed her skin out, but I always wanted to scrape it off and see who she was underneath.

Even though she frequently stayed apart from us, Luz was never mean. Yet she was stern when we were reciting lessons, and it was hard to sit there in her shadowy room under her watchful eyes and try to make out the words. But in time I got it, and she let me come sometimes and read from the only book she had, her Bible.

She told stories to us, long ones that went on night after night. We learned about a girl who told these same stories to a king in order to save her life, and after those were done, she began another long tale about a man who fought with windmills. When I got my horse, just to let her know I'd been

29

listening, I named it Rosinante, after his. She described the king of Spain for us, and the palaces she had ridden past as a girl. Through her, our world stretched far beyond the wild plateau called the Piedra Lumbre, where we lived.

Now I know that Luz was my father's real wife, the one he'd married in the church, but we children hadn't figured those things out back then. It was also a long while before we found out that Benito's father had been sent back to Mexico. The governor had banished him and his first son from New Mexico forever. They had punished my father too, but not as harshly, sending him north out of Santa Fe to our ranch, a place too dangerous for most men to try to inhabit. But father loved it, and the success he made farming the bottomlands along the creek, and running sheep on the wide-open grasslands that unfolded beyond the steep-walled canyon where we'd built the house, redeemed him in the governor's eyes. Nevertheless, he could never obtain a pardon for the others in his family. All he ever heard about them was that they had returned to Spain.

The night I learned my mother was a slave, I had been out with the herd not far from the house, maybe just a mile up the canyon. We were holding the sheep close by, because it was the season when the Indios usually raided. I was lying on the ground, wrapped in my blanket, when I felt a hand on my forehead. I woke up, so surprised to see my mother's face that I must have sounded like one of the sheep when I bleated out, "Maaa!" She carried her own blanket over her shoulder. She flipped it open, rolled it around her and lay down beside me under the huge, starry sky.

"Nando. I have come to talk to you. I have to tell you a story." She used the talk we only spoke by ourselves alone in our nest, and I remember lying there happy to have her beside me, delighted she would come this far just to tell me a tale. "Nando, I have to go back to my people. They're nearby and have sent word to me."

"Ma, what people? We live at home."

"Be quiet for once, Nando, and just listen to me." And she told me, for the first time that night, the story of how they had stolen her when she was a child. She was nine, maybe, before she had become a woman. The men were Spanish and had horses. They had long knives and guns. They rode up to the edge of her village when no one but she was awake, and found her playing by the creek. They never even stopped, just scooped her up, and rode off fast across the grassland into the low mountains.

She had been taught to stay quiet. She had been taught not to complain, but she was hurting, tired and scared when the Spaniards finally stopped at a round meadow where other men like themselves were camped. They had good horses and more weapons waiting there, but no shelters or tepees, and no women. Yet, there were other children, four of them, Utes like herself. They were as sad as she. They wanted to go home, but at night the Spaniards bound them together in a circle, and the rope was tied to a man who tried to stay awake all night to guard them.

Nan told me how she had watched him fall asleep. She had chewed through the rope. She moved like a snake on her belly away from the other children. She reached the trees, rose to her feet and moved quietly through the sparse woods. She knew which way they had brought her. She would go back.

After a long time moving slowly without making a sound, the way she had been taught, she began to travel more swiftly, less carefully. She had watched these men, and she knew their ears weren't as good as the Utes'. She walked fast, emerging from the woods and onto the prairie. There were no stars. It was pitch-black. No moon. A sharp wind brought the first cold prickles of dry snow. She wore a good leather tunic and moccasins, but she had no blanket, no piece of fur. She didn't care. She ran through the night. Two miles. Two more miles. She was strong, but the wind came on harshly now, pushing into her face from the west. The snow was thick, blowing horizontally across the top of the grass, into her eyes, building up on her shoulders and in her hair. The sky was still dark, but the first glow of morning light was rising behind her. There were gray shapes of mountains up ahead, but for miles only this grassland to get across in the howling wind and the deepening snow. The men wouldn't find her in the storm, but to stay alive she knew she had to keep moving. She had traveled all night, hoping to catch up with her people. She scooped up a handful of snow and sucked the moisture out of it. That was stupid. It only made her colder.

The storm was a big one, with hard snow pellets deepening fast, up over her ankles. In places, because of the wind, it was as high as her knees. Finally she reached the pine forest, running between their heavy, dark shapes in the gray light of early morning. She came to a snow-filled arroyo with a dark hole in its bank. Coyote house. She tore at tree branches and gathered an armful of long-needled pine, the tips of the boughs. She crawled into the coyote's den. Good, he lived somewhere else now. She pulled the branches in around her. She was wet, cold, exhausted, but she was away from the Spaniards. Her heart was sad for the other children, but Nan was going home. She would see her mother again and her good father, who had just been chosen chief. This cave was little, and she could keep her heat here. Just beyond her pine boughs, the storm built and howled. She knew not to sleep. She sang her songs. She struggled to stay awake, but her mind drifted home, into the smoke of a warm fire. Her tongue tasted hot stew of buffalo and wild onions, and finally her head lolled against the wall of the coyote house. Her mother reached for her and wrapped her in her warmest blanket, the one made of feathers and fur. She snuggled into it. Sleep washed over her.

She woke up with her face jammed against the hard, new beard of a man. The metal buttons on his cloak pressed into her. The rough skins of the jacket he wore were in her mouth, and his arms locked her tightly in their circle of strength. He was asleep. She tried to slip out from his grasp, but at her first, slight movement his arms tightened. He opened his eyes and stared at her. He was one of them, the man who had first placed her on his saddle in front of him. Her dream was over, the warm food, her mother, a fire, the dream of seeing any of these again. He watched her eyes fill as she tried not to cry and he kissed her on the forehead, gently, like her father would. The tears she had learned not to give in to washed through her in waves, and still he held her. He didn't reprimand her. He didn't straighten her up and 'tut tut' at her and start wiping her nose. He just held her and let her cry.

"That was your father, Nando, who had left his companions to find me in that horrible storm. He had been traveling with a group sent out to recover the town's stolen horses. They never found their own herd so they went on a rampage, stealing whatever they could find from our people. What they found was me."

I had never heard any of this. My father kidnapped Nan? I was grateful right then that no one else was watching. I turned my face away while I thought this out, but then I snuggled in close against her blanket, needing to touch her, seeking her warmth. Even though I was big now, my mother wrapped me in her arms.

"We went through two days of that storm together. When it cleared and the sun came out on the snow, he was able to find his horse and his pack mule, but he never found his companions. They had given us both up for dead and gone on. There was no way I would survive in that hard time of winter without him, so I didn't fight him. We went back along the creeks, down to the big river and on for several days to Abiquiú. We were friends by the time we got there. Really friends. He didn't try to treat me like a woman. He knew I was still a little girl. When we got to his village, he gave me to his mother to raise. I lived in her house on Abiquiú's plaza for five years. I learned to weave, to cook their way, to speak their language. They took me to church and taught me the catechism, but they were not my real family and I missed my people badly. These Spaniards were very serious about their god, who didn't seem as big as our god, but I tried to love him.

"I was often sad, but seldom was anyone mean to me. No one misused me. I saw what happened to the other captive girls and I knew I was lucky, but I also knew I had my friend, Benito. Somehow he protected me. I thought someday he would marry me, because he had said he would, but I didn't dare tell anybody, and when he married Luz de Gracia I finally cried for the second time in my life.

"Then, when their third baby came, it only lived an hour. Luz was very sick and nearly died too. One day Benito came into his mother's living room, the sala, and I heard them talking. I had barely seen him since his marriage, when he had taken his wife to his ranch to live, and because it was almost a full day's travel between his hacienda and town, they seldom came in.

"I was weaving at the big loom out on the porch. He came and leaned against the doorpost, all brown and handsome, with his two braids down his back just like my brothers, and I could barely keep my fingers moving with the shuttle. Then he asked if I'd like to go for a ride and I looked up at him and then glanced toward the room where his mother was.

" 'I've settled it with her,' he said. 'You're mine once again.' So I wound the strand of wool around the shuttle and went to get my blanket. I wrapped my other tunic inside it, and my comb, and one or two small things that I owned. He took the bundle from me and carried it out to his horse. I went in to say good-bye to his mother while he tied my things onto the saddle. She held me in her arms and looked me in the eye in a way that let me know how much she liked me. Then she slipped a piece of silver into my hand, a heavy coin, and gave me a little push toward her son.

"He lifted me onto his horse in front of him, just like five years before, and we rode away off the hill by the back trail. I remember the padre standing in the doorway of the church looking at us, and Benito trying to get the horse to hurry up. Then we were off down the hill, away from the village and making good time on the road along the river. Before long he slowed and turned up the little creek there, Frijoles Creek.

"We could have gotten home that day, but it was two more days until we arrived at his hacienda. By then it was as though he was my husband, and I his wife. The next year you were born, and then Segundo, and finally Nanna. I worked hard to be a good wife to him, to learn how to help Luz de Gracia and so she wouldn't resent me. I was happy.

"Only three times in these years have I seen my people. When I lived with his mother I saw them once. They came onto the plaza, Utes all by themselves, without any of the traders. They were trying to sell three small children fast. One of the men was my cousin. He saw me standing in the door-way. I gave a little nod. He came back around to the other side of the house and, I know this sounds silly, but he asked if I was me!

" 'Of course I'm me,'" I said, but by then I looked different and it had been a long time.

" 'Are you all right?'"

" 'Yes, I'm all right here. My mother? My father?' "

" 'They live. They are sad because you're gone, but they'll be happy now that you've been found. Do you want to come home?' "

" 'Yes, I do. Can you take me?' "

He looked worried, then a little mean. " 'I can't take you this time. There's too much at stake here. It would make prob-lems, but I will tell them where you are and someone will come back for you. Not this year, it's too late for another run, but before too long. Can you wait?' "

" 'Yes, it's not bad. They take care of me.' "

But they didn't come back for three more years. That was just as well, because right after they left, Benito married Luz and I would have fled from that place in a heartbeat if there was any way at all. But by the time some of my people came again, I was in love, and you were in my belly, and again I told them I would wait."

I moved on my blanket but not too much, because I didn't want my mother to stop telling me this fantastic tale.

"I'm almost done, Nando. Stay quiet." She rolled away from me, lying on her back, looking at the stars. "Then there were wars again. My people from up there against my people here. The fighting was vicious, both sides trying to defend what they called "their country." I would see little children brought in and sold, and wonder if they were my sisters or my cousins. I would see terrified, starved, Spanish children bought back from being kidnapped, and I would wonder if my brothers did that. I looked among the dead, after battles on the Piedra Lumbre, to see if any were my family. I felt that some of the people on our hacienda and in the village started not to trust me. They didn't know if I sided with the Spanish or with the Utes. By then my heart was here with Benito, with you, Nando, and with all my children by this man I loved. But now it is time. Now you are grown, and I am going home."

"But ma! What about Benito? What about Nanna, Segundo and me?"

I thought she was going to hit me. Her hand came back and I expected it to crack across my cheek. We waited face to face for her to strike me. Then her hand came down gently, the anger out of it. She put it on my shoulder. She looked right into my heart and said,

"Nando, there's no way you would understand this, but I can't be a slave any longer."

My mother, a slave? She whom my father adored? I dragged my eyes out of hers.

"This is true?"

She didn't take her eyes off me, and she nodded.

"Does this mean . . . ?" She kept watching me, while it came to me for the first time, that I was my father's slave.

Oh sure, there were laws about this, and we were Christians, which was supposed to mean we couldn't be enslaved, but everyone ignored that law. Who was I? Just an illegitimate half-breed slave, or the loved son of Benito, a Spanish don? It was the first time I'd ever thought about these things. My mother couldn't just walk away, she needed to leave by stealth.

And I, would I be allowed to go if I wanted? Segundo and Nanna, were they slaves too?

"Ma!" I called out to her, and she turned back to me and put her arms around me once more.

"Ma!" I heard it again in my sleep. I sat straight up and felt the weight of a little head on my lap. The child was staring at me and babbling his mother's name.

"I'm not your mother, boy, but here," and I scooted him higher on my lap and held him close. Light drifted through the trees. There was a touch of warmth from the sun on my shoulders.

I shook off last night's memories and wondered how this would ever stop. I knew the Indians had always stolen women and children from each other, in revenge, or to replace dead children whom they had loved. When the Spanish came it didn't take them long to get caught up in the cycle. My father told me that at first the priests and the king sanctioned the taking of captives, because they claimed it brought more souls within their reach for conversion, but in time the Church had to protest the cruelty involved, and even the king agreed.

Thinking it kindness, he then provided money to purchase captives so they wouldn't be tortured or killed. He didn't realize that his benevolence had put a price on the head of every native woman and child in the kingdom. Slaving had become the latest cash crop, and groups like Lorenzo's were taking it to a new level of cold-heartedness.

I held the children still while a man untied the ropes. Just then Lorenzo, Pedro Jaime and the others come riding toward us through the trees. The girls were no longer with them. Someone mercifully untied the rope that hobbled my feet, and I stood up, using the tree to keep from toppling over.

Lorenzo was in a fine mood this morning. "We're moving out now! Never mind feeding them. They're sold."

"You struck a deal for all of them?" one of the traders asked.

"I got actual pesos and this horse here for the girls. The babies were tougher to move, but one fellow's agreed to take them all. I got a bushel of corn meal, and a good English gun, up front. There will be pesos coming, too. We're set. Come on, get moving!"

Even Lorenzo was saddling horses, throwing things in panniers, tightening ropes. With the thought that I would soon be in Taos where the possibilities to break away would be greater, I decided I'd work right alongside him like I'd always wanted to sell babies. From the smell of him I'd say brandy had been part of their price too.

A Matter for Chiefs

The gathering of people in the field near Taos wasn't the big fair of autumn, just a coming-together after the snows melted and the passes in the high mountains had opened up. People needed to see each other, pick up supplies and unload last winters' furs and hides. I was surprised at how many pavilions and tepees there were. Though people had come from different tribes, they mingled in peace. There was even a priest in the midst of it and I heard strange languages from faraway places. There was a small cluster of tough-looking white men, neither Spaniards nor Indios, though you couldn't tell that from their clothes. It was their voices that set them apart, because they talked in a way I had never heard before. As a rule, no foreigners were ever allowed to enter Spain's northern territory, and I'd been told such fairs were illegal without permits and government supervision. But the government apparently didn't know about this one, so people were light-hearted and relaxed.

Lorenzo and his men couldn't keep me tied up with every-body watching, but they still held me under guard. I kept busy at the edge of things, mostly just staying out of Lorenzo's way. Before long, he rode off with three men, each carrying a child. They cantered toward the edge of the field where a Spanish farmer waited with a wagon. He and Lorenzo talked for a while, staying mounted, eyeing the field from time to time. It seemed as though they were waiting for something.

Then a tall Franciscan left the fairground and walked across the open field toward the wagon. As a man of God, was he going to intervene? He approached Lorenzo and the buyer, but my hope sank when they showed no concern at all that this priest might put a stop to their transaction. In a few mo-ments it was clear, even from a distance, that the churchman was all about business too. I had heard that some padres kept slaves, though they called them servants. They justified it as a chance to convert more souls.

The Franciscan had money ready in his hand. He didn't even need to count it out, but passed it to Lorenzo. The children stood displayed in a line. There was the little one I'd become friends with, toeing the ground with his bare foot. After scru-tinizing them, the padre nodded. There was more talk, and more money passed hands. I didn't understand what was go-ing on, but the children were lifted into the back of the wagon, the padre climbed up on the seat with the farmer, and they drove north toward the village of Taos together, leaving Lorenzo behind holding his bag of coins.

I was ordered to stay with the horses, to guard them and our gear. I wondered if Lorenzo had lost his senses to leave me alone when I could so easily grab a sack of food, jump on a pony and be gone. But the boss wasn't stupid, and when he left I found he had made another man stay back from the fair to guard me. As our crew strode off to join the fun, I raised my hands apologetically to my sour-looking keeper, separated a couple of the horses who were hassling each other, and lay down on a saddle blanket in the shade of a piñon tree. Sun filtered through just enough to keep me warm. I worked a dry stalk of grass between my teeth, and while ruminating on a possible escape route up a deep creek-cut in the closest mountain's flank, I fell asleep.

The blast from a trumpet woke me up. I was on my feet looking where everybody else looked, at presidio troops streaming onto the huge meadow where the illegal fair hummed. The army looked good with its uniformed men and the pennants waving. I recognized soldiers from both the Light Troop and the Leather Jackets, sixty men if you included the foot soldiers, all their carts, wagons and the long strings of mules. The new recruits looked pretty seedy, but it didn't matter. All told, the force was impressive, and a lot bigger than they needed to be just to break up a casual gathering.

They rode right into the center of the tepees and pavilions, and everyone there, Comanches, Utes, Navajos and Kiowas, Spanish traders and the foreigners, stood stock-still, unable to flee without being noticed on the open field. Once the shock of the army's arrival was absorbed, people started moving about again, but carefully, and most began to pack up. Lorenzo and his gang walked nonchalantly over to our campsite and started gathering gear.

"That's Captain Valdez," Lorenzo told us. "One of Governor Anza's top officers. A man we definitely want to steer clear of. We'll slip out of here as soon as the captain gets distracted by something."

I hadn't started packing yet, because I was scrutinizing the soldiers and their horses, hoping no one among them would recognize me with this lot. Pointedly, Lorenzo leaned over and said, "You still want to join the militia, Nando? I'm sure they need you more than ever." I bent to my work.

Pedro Jaime sorted through ropes at my side, talking as he organized things. "Did you hear how this same Valdez dealt with the two Englishmen last year? People said they were easygoing and young, but just the same, we're at war with their country. Those boys were clamped into irons and hustled all the way to Chihuahua. Any minute now, Valdez will have his men combing the field to assess who's here. He's probably already heard there are French trappers on the field." In fact, a contingent led by a man on a big sorrel gelding, a horse I was thinking looked familiar, was already making the rounds of the outer campsites and had arrived at the one next to ours.

Lorenzo had his head down looking into a bag and everyone else was scrambling to get ready to leave. Now that I had experienced life in a slaver's caravan, a brief career in the military suddenly looked like a much better option for me. This was the best chance I'd had to break away since Ramón had laid his hand on me in the church in Abiquiú, so without any more thinking about it, I took off walking straight toward the soldiers. I was fifty feet out of our camp and approaching the neighboring one when the lieutenant leading the patrol noticed me coming toward him. He stopped and pushed his hat back a bit so as to see me better.

There was a shout from our camp. "Nando! Get back here!"

I didn't turn to look, but I heard men coming toward me across the ground. I picked up my pace, making for the officer on the sorrel. Lorenzo's thugs started to run. The lieutenant kicked his heels into the horse and nearly plowed into me as he whirled his animal around to shield me from the oncoming gang. He had his pistol in his hand when the first of my captors got a hand on me. "That will do, sir," the lieutenant said. "This man is under the protection of the military now."

Unfazed, Lorenzo began to argue with him, lying through his teeth. "He's my man. He's indentured to me and he's trying to run away, Lieutenant!"

The soldier made a gesture with his left hand, keeping his gun steady in his right and pointed at Lorenzo, while more horsemen rode in behind him. "That's not going to work this time, fellow. Do you think I don't recognize my own brother? Detain these men until we find out what's going on here," Lieutenant Carlos Aguilar commanded.

Lorenzo and his gang turned to run, but they didn't get far. The soldiers surrounded them and pushed them at gunpoint to the command tents that were just being set up. Carlos put his gun away and extended his arm to me. "Jump up, little brother," he said, and my career as a merchant slaver ended just as my stint in the military began.

I may have been only his half-breed brother, but Carlos was outraged. He swore out loud when he heard about Diego's sleazy profiteering, and showed no mercy to Lorenzo's party when their hearing was held in front of Captain Valdez a few hours later. Carlos had gotten the story out of me, and while I wasn't brought to testify, what I had told him was enough. They took all Lorenzo's booty from the sale of the children, and Carlos told me later that some of it was used to buy back the girls who had been sold to a rough lot. Lorenzo's gear was confiscated, and he and every one of his crew left Taos unarmed and on foot.

I wondered where they planned to hook up again. As long as there were Indian wars, Lorenzo could come across captives and start up somewhere else. A man could farm all year, and if it was a good year, make about as much as he could selling one strong female. Lorenzo was only going to go over the hill and catch his breath before starting up again. I protested when Carlos told me they had let him go, but the army was on a mission here in Taos and they didn't have time to deal with all the illegalities that a fair attracted.

Eventually we turned to my future. "Carlos, even though I'm damn glad you rode up just then, don't think I'm signing up for the army here."

The lieutenant scowled, but after a while he said, "All right then, we'll say you're my valet, Nando, as long as you're with the camp. No one will bother you, and if you're already in service, they won't think you're kicking around and ought to be recruited." So that I would fit in, he found a cadet's jacket for me that was only about three inches too long in the arms, and a wide-brimmed hat like the others wore.

After the first night there were no more foreigners on the field. They had sneaked off soon after the troops arrived. There were still many native people, though some had drifted away in the darkness too. Men of every tribe wandered in and out of the tents set up as wine shops, and Spanish traders camped at the edges of the field. If there were Indians being sold, the business was discreet, because while the official policy sanctioned the capture of natives in 'just wars,' it clearly prohibited the wholesale marketing of people.

My brother, the lieutenant, ordered dinner to be sent to his tent. Over stewed beef we talked. He explained that the army was up here on its way to a rendezvous with Comanches just on the other side of the pass. There had been indications that a group of them were close to terms of peace. Scouts were expected back any hour to tell where the meeting would be held, if, in fact, the Comanches had agreed to it. This was a matter only for the chiefs of the Comanches and Governor Anza, who would come to conduct the final parley if the preliminaries went well.

"That explains it. I didn't think you'd bring in all these men just to break up an illegal fair."

"We'd been told about it, but that's not why we're here. Let them think so, though. If the other tribes find out about our impending agreement with the Comanches, there'll be hell to pay." Carlos laughed, "I have to say, it was fun to ride in and crack a few heads."

"Find any foreigners? I was pretty sure I saw a few."

"They left. We'll send some scouts north to hunt them down after we're done with the Comanches. Captain Valdez isn't going to let anything distract him now."

"Carlos, I saw a priest buying children."

My brother looked up. "Franciscans aren't even supposed to have money."

"This one had plenty."

"Point him out to me if he shows up again," Carlos said.

"My pleasure." I forked the hot food into my mouth, thinking about the scant rations Lorenzo had provided. I was beginning to see some advantages to being in the military and to riding at my brother's side. In a while I asked, "Do you think I could travel over to Comanchería with you?"

"I thought you didn't want to join the army." He had me there, so I shut up for a while.

Realizing I was actually disappointed, he finally said, "I don't have permission to take you, Nando. Make yourself useful to Valdez, and maybe he'll decide you can go along."

"Do you think you'll get the treaty with the Comanches?"
Like a proper valet, I poured chocolate for my master.

"We're doing what we can. Some are ready, but too many
of them still delight in rampaging through our settlements, and
they all benefit from the trade in guns and captives. I'm not
sure the Comanches are ready for peace, but one of their
strongest leaders sent the message to Anza. The governor's
walking on eggshells, hoping nothing spoils his plan."

"Then why isn't he here?" I asked.

"In the name of Jesus, you ask a lot of questions!" Carlos
snapped, the big brother once again. "The man knows Indians.
He's staying at a distance until they commit. It's how he keeps
their respect. Besides, this whole thing could be a trap, or
strategically designed to mislead and divert us. The governor
needs to be sure before he gets in the middle of it."

"When do you ride?"

"When the word comes in. Tomorrow, hopefully." Carlos
leaned back against his gear and lit a pipe. Whatever was in it
stank. "When this is over, we'd better get you out of Abiquiú.
Lorenzo will be back, you can count on that, and before you'll
be safe there we've got to put a stop to cousin Diego's new
role as procurer. Go down to Luz, stay in Santa Fe with her,
and I'll see if I can find you a job."

It felt uncomfortable becoming my brother's charity case,
but I got over it by thinking about the alternative. His offer to
help me was attractive. While I'd always liked being in Abiquiú
because I was near the ranch, that was out for now, and Santa
Fe promised a lot more excitement than fiddling about in weedy
fields. It was almost a shame I wouldn't be around to irritate
the teniente anymore.

Inside a tent, smothered in blankets, I didn't sleep well. Carlos snored like a pig. Someone in a nearby tent started hawking and spitting about three in the morning, and if I'd been asleep at all, that finished it off. I figured there were two more hours of darkness left when Carlos got up and went out. I took a pee outside under the dazzling stars, then crawled back into my bed, waiting to hear from him. He must have been given a signal that this was the day to head into Comanche country. While it was still dark, he came back with a bucket of food. It was some kind of corn slop, but there was a chunk of dried beef floating in it. I was rolling up the blankets when my brother told me I couldn't go with him.

"Nothing feels right about this trip, Nando. It turns out we don't have the support from certain outlying groups that we'd been promised. There's talk of a much quicker foray, and it might turn into fighting instead of talking. If something happens out there, and you and I are both killed, Luz would be left alone. Francisco may get back from Mexico someday, but how long has it been since anyone's had word of him? The ranch would be lost for sure, and to the first man who offered the governor enough money." He looked at me gravely, hoping I wouldn't flare up. "We shouldn't both go on this mission— and I don't have a choice."

"You think I'll be better off traveling cross-country by myself? You think Lorenzo won't pick me off just to get even, the moment he spots me?"

"You need to stay away from Abiquiú. Too many slavers like Lorenzo go through there. Don't even get near it. You're smart enough to avoid trouble on your way down to the capital."

"Rosinante's in Abiquiú."

"So drop in at night, grab your horse and head for Santa Fe before anyone notices. Nando, please don't go near the ranch, and stick to the known roads every minute."

"And get a lashing for traveling without a permit. I'm not too sure about any of this." I was coming up with every excuse I could, trying to make him take me with him, but Carlos wasn't falling for it.

"The permit's easy. I'll write one for you before you leave." He tried to mollify me, but I just wouldn't give in yet. "That means I go sit on my hands in Santa Fe taking care of an old woman, while you get to travel over the mountains, meet the chieftains, negotiate a truce, have a big party and be the hero."

Carlos stayed gentle with his petulant kid brother. "If I thought it would be like that, I'd have you come along. Don't you get it? With Francisco in Mexico, forever maybe, and me riding into battle, you might be the only surviving son."

"I'm a half-breed, remember?"

Carlos brushed that aside with a gesture. "The family would die out without you."

"There's Segundo," I said, referring to Nan's other boy. "Carlos, I really want to ride with you!"

"Segundo wouldn't take over if you're gone. Thanks to you, Segundo's a Ute now," Carlos retorted.

I had to agree with him, particularly since I was the one who'd taken our youngest brother back to my mother's people. "For the time being he is, but he's Benito's son too."

"I know that, but because he went back to the tribe when he was so little, it isn't certain he'll ever live with us again. And anyhow, he's still young. Right now, it's you we need to protect— and I need to get moving and stop going on about this," Carlos said, putting a quick end to my wheedling. "I'll lend you a horse and you'll ride south when we leave. With the permit, you'll be legal all the way. You'll stay out of slave caravans, avoid inadvertent enlistment in the militia, and then you'll go help Luz. Those are orders, little Ute boy."

"I've always wanted to slug you when you call me that."

"Just this once let me get away with it. I saved your hide, didn't I?" Carlos smiled at me, hoping I might say something nice to him.

"I owe you one, Lieutenant. Write me that permit and I'll get your horse ready for you." We would have hugged, but we were being big men now, so we settled for thumping each other on the back, and then went to get ready for whatever was coming at us next.

II

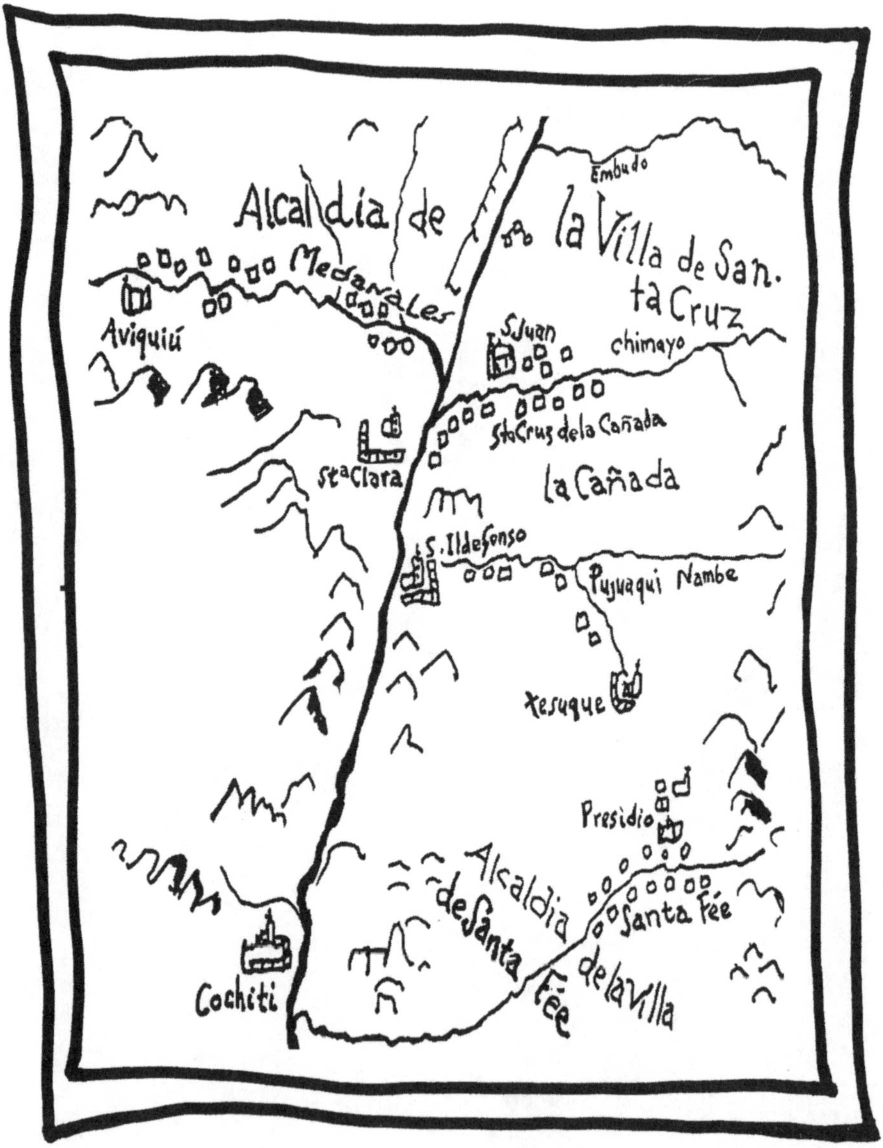
Embudo
Alcaldia de la Villa de San.
ta Cruz
Medanales
Aviquiú
SJuan
chimayo
StaCruz dela Cañada
StaClara
la Cañada
S. Ildefonso
Pujuaqui Nambe
Tesuque
Presidio
Alcaldia de Santa Fée
Santa Fée
de la Villa
Cochiti

The Militiaman's Wife

Medanales

*M*arisol's husband saddled his burro to go join the other new recruits of the citizens' militia. He sharpened his long knife and examined his lance, wishing to God he still had a gun. He tied the kit she'd packed behind his saddle. She was weeding the vegetable garden when he came to say goodbye. "How long do you think this time, Arsenio?" she asked.

"Ludi's saying about three weeks, and it's all for show. There'll probably be no fighting."

"Do you get paid then, if there are no spoils?"

"Not damn likely. I heard a rumor, though, that the army will put us on decent horses and we may get to keep them if we agree to show up again when they call. If that happens I could get something for the burro here. It's possible I'll get a gun."

"That would be good," she said, remembering how he had lost their old one crossing the river. "That could help us a lot." She looked downcast. Fear of being left alone was rising in her. Anything could happen to a woman on her own, and it some-

times did. But who knew she was out here anyway? And who cared? That could work both ways for her. No marauders would come this far off the beaten track, and certainly none would expect to find a lone female. They wouldn't even bother. Anyhow, once she'd put aside her fears, she admitted she liked it when he was gone. Her days became a gift to herself instead of a duty to him.

Arsenio rode off looking inadequate, bouncing on the back of the burro, his legs sticking out stiffly, his clothes coarse and shabby. She waved at his retreating form, but he didn't turn to see, riding as fast as he could away from their little valley that was rimmed by low black cliffs and shadowed by higher, forested hills. Once he was gone there was no one else anywhere near, no houses, no neighbors. The silence was big.

To distract herself, she half-heartedly plucked weeds out of a couple of short rows, not minding sitting on the dirt in her old dress. Then she laughed for being so afraid. What use would Arsenio be if trouble did come? He who lost their precious gun, and stabbed himself with his own knife when he was sharpening it? Besides, he left her often. Long ago she'd found hiding places she would use if she saw any riders approaching, places where she could wait until it was dark and then travel down to farms farther south along the river.

She was feeling better, and when the sun shone directly into her canyon, Marisol left her work, slipped through the bushes along the narrow cow path, and walked to the river at the bottom of their land. She took off her woolen stockings and stepped into the water. Today was the warmest so far this year and the chill was off. Willows had just leafed out bright sprigs, and the foliage was dense enough that she dared to slip out of her skirt and blouse.

She had scarcely been naked all winter. Holding onto rocks in the water, she lay in the stream and let it run all over her. She used soft silt from the edge of the river to scrub her face and hands, then scooped up a handful of the green clay in the bank and slowly massaged it into her skin. Once she had scoured herself with sand and clay, she stood up, and using her last precious piece of soap, washed her thick, black hair. Sinking back into the current, she rinsed, and then climbed out onto a warm stone, loving the air on her bare skin. There was new wild mint that she nibbled on. She combed her fingers through her hair, fanning it out in the sunlight, twisting it over her fingers so it would curl.

She hadn't had time for herself like this since he had gone away last year and then his old, sick father had been up in the house, so it had to be short. She hadn't looked at herself in a mirror once in all that time. Her body had become just a thing that worked hard all day, then lay down at night exhausted. Her husband would roll on top of her and then quickly with-draw, leaving her even more tired and somehow angry. She guessed she was still pretty, because the village men looked at her in their way, but she certainly didn't know it from living with Arsenio.

His father had finally died this winter, so for the first time, it was only she and Arsenio in the house. She didn't know why they didn't have children. She knew babies came from what took place in bed, but that didn't happen very often. It was just something he did once in a while, when he got restless and couldn't sleep. Marisol remembered something else, something much finer than that, but it was a long time ago, before all her troubles had started, and she had to let it go from her mind. But today there was a memory, and her body had life to it. Maybe it was the push of spring, or the freshness she felt from scouring away the soot and grime of winter; maybe it was from being by herself again, but she felt a sparkle and was happy.

The light moved toward evening, and deepened into long blue shadow as she went back up to the house. The corn in her kettle was beginning to soften, so she added meat and chili and a handful of wild greens she'd picked by the river. Salt. She hoped, at the least, he would remember to bring salt when he returned.

It was so nice to leave the door open. She had spent far too many hours in this dark, sooty kitchen. If she were the man on this farm, she would have built another room onto the house by now, but this husband of hers didn't seem to notice. It had been a long winter with lots of snow, good for watering the fields this summer, but she was aching for change.

She sat on the huge chopping block beside the door and leaned her back against the wall, looking up into the woods, watching the side of the hill go dark and the river turn into bubbling gold. When the darkness closed in on her she felt another twinge of fear, but she knew she had to put it aside. Everyone said she and her husband shouldn't live out here alone, that they should move in closer. The alcalde had even ordered them in one time, but how would they keep their animals and their garden? Besides, who would give them rooms, share a place? She was half Indian, even though all that was in the distant past. The people who had raised her in Abiquiú had returned to Santa Cruz years ago. If she moved into town whenever her mate left, she'd just be someone's unpaid servant again.

Marisol had always thought that if the Indians came she would simply talk to them. They would see that she was one of them. She would feed them, give them what animals they needed, and wish them well as they went elsewhere to live up to their reputation as marauders. It didn't occur to her that she had lost the words she would need, and that she looked very much like a Spanish man's wife.

She didn't know that a man had watched her all afternoon, that he had sat motionless on the hillside while she bathed in the stream. She couldn't see him, because he lay flat on the forest floor while she sat on the stump beside her door. She wasn't aware that someone thought her beautiful, that someone watched as her hair blew loosely and gleamed in the last light of the sun, that someone noticed she had put on a fresh white blouse, the kind of blouse a woman saves for dances. Marisol didn't know that he watched her carry water, close the gate to the garden and bring in her tools. Night came on fast now. She couldn't see that the man pulled his blanket tighter around him when she closed the door, and that he saw the small light in her window go out.

While she slept, he too went down to the river, drank and cleaned himself. He ate some food from the pouch at his waist. He took out his knife and inspected it for dirt or nicks, testing its edge. He moved closer in, alongside the corral. No dog barked or came toward him. She didn't hear him mutter, "Too bad the stingy bastard doesn't even get a dog to guard her when he goes away."

She was already dreaming when the man determined that he would climb through her window and began to walk quietly toward the house.

Like A Young Goat

It wasn't really a window, just a hole to enter the attic. There was only a piece of buckskin over it and I easily pushed that aside. I didn't know the layout of the house so when I dropped down into the room below I landed smack on her bed, and it wasn't soft. She woke up, shrieked, grabbed the covers and tried to get up, but I threw my arm over her and forced her down.

"Marisol, it's me! Be quiet! It's Nando!"

Her scream quit all at once and became the beginning of a giggle.

"Nando! Can't you knock? Can't you come in by the door?"

I'd only been here ten seconds and already she was lecturing me.

"One day you'll do that and I'll die of fright in my own bed. Or worse, Arsenio will be here and then *you'll* die in my bed."

She was clearly delighted to see me. I hadn't found a way to get near her since her marriage to that oaf, and we once had been best friends. And a little more. She lit a candle as I unlaced my moccasins.

"Food, food," I panted and she put a bowl of hot posole into my hands.

"This isn't as big as the bowl you had. You're holding back on me."

"Not true, and how do you know?"

"I watched you all evening. Sitting on the hill."

She blushed, thinking about her bath in the river. "And this afternoon?"

"This afternoon too," I grinned, remembering her lovely body covered with green mud. Marisol was small, strong, perfect. Her legs were sturdy, and from the hill I had noticed their pleasing shape. Now I looked into her broad, open face, tinged with today's sun and excitement. I put down the empty bowl. Cupping her head in both my hands, I pulled her toward me and kissed the top of her head. She snuggled in close.

"I had to make sure he was gone and no one else was here. I had to be sure you didn't have six children in this bed with you."

"It's only been three years."

"Two sets of three."

"Not likely. Oh Nando, hold me hard. I'm so happy to see you!"

"And you're clean," I muttered, my nose against her sweet skin.

"Not that that ever mattered to you."

I kissed her forehead, and then her mouth, and then I nuzzled at her breasts like a young goat. I picked her up and turned her over and nibbled on her backside, and then she got interested too and we had a race to see who could undress the other first. I won. We did it in that man's bed, and then on his table, and then outside under the moon on a blanket. In the morning we reversed the order, and then wound

59

up in the stream, cleaning each other up and practically licking each other dry. We ate more posole and even had a big glass of chokecherry wine before lunch. It finally got to where if we did it any more I would hurt too much and I could only guess at how she was feeling. Sometimes it got really slow and gentle between us, and maybe a little sad.

"Why did you go away so fast? Why did you marry him? He isn't much good, is he?"

"He isn't worth a damn." She leaned against my chest while she told me.

"They found out about us. The old witch saw you leave and I was hauled out of my bed and beaten, then sent to Ojo to live in her sister's house. I had to outrun that woman's ugly man all the time. After the last big raid, when everyone fled to Santa Cruz, she found this boy for me, probably to annoy her husband, and there I was miles from home, miles from you, stuck out in this canyon without anyone to talk to but the turkeys and a stupid man. I might have run away, but he wasn't all bad. I had enough food and this is my own house," she explained. "I'm nobody's slave any more, except maybe his. At least I'm smarter than he is, so I can pretty much get things my way."

"No babies? Surely he knows that much."

"Not one. He 'does it' but I only let him so I can have a child."

She leaned against my chest.

"Make me a baby, Nando. He'd never know."

"Maybe I already have," I said, tracing her face with my fingers. "I wonder if it will have a pretty Indian nose like yours or the arched snout of a Spanish don, like mine?"

"If it's a boy, he should look just like his father," she whispered. I snorted at that, but she was all over me again with little, soft kisses.

"Can you come back?" she pleaded.

"I'll figure something out. We'll have to get you out of here. But Marisol," my voice went quiet because I wasn't proud of this, "I can't take care of you yet. I haven't got a thing. We still don't have permission to go back to our ranch, and what would we do about the fact you have a husband?"

"Oh never mind all that." Gaily she was up on my lap, moving sweetly over me as I leaned back with sunlight on my eyelids, wondering how I could steal her away.

"I'll find a way, Marisol," I said to her, and I thought to myself, maybe the Comanches will give us a hand with this problem of her husband. "Marisol! How often can we just be where we really want to be?"

"Not so often anymore."

Stripped Down For War

I couldn't come up with any reason to leave for four days. For one thing, a storm blew in, giving us a parting shot of winter. What clear-thinking man would head out in driving snow, when he could curl up in Marisol's toasty blankets? I wondered how my brother was doing trying to cross the high passes in the Sangre de Cristos, but the next day the sun came out warm as ever. It melted the snow fast, everything dripped noisily and the mud deepened all day. I couldn't ask Rosinante to ride in that.

At last, though, there was no more putting it off. Marisol and I had struck a very cozy note. It was clear we should have been destined for each other, but for some reason it hadn't worked out that way. How could Arsenio ignore this beautiful gift of a woman? How could he turn his back on her, order up his food, work her like a slave on his farm, but never drift into the delicious torpor of being spoiled and coddled in her bed? Some people have all the luck and are too stupid to know it.

Midmorning on the fifth day I finally pulled myself away, actually starting out once, but returning to give her one more lingering hug. Then I turned, waved my last and kicked the horse up to a trot, hoping to convince myself I was a determined and purposeful man. On top of the hill, heading out to the main track, I gave up the pretense and bumbled along slowly, reveling in little purple flowers and the ornate whistling of the meadowlarks.

I'd dismounted to go into the woods for a minute and was in the trees with Rosinante's reins loose in my hand when I heard running horses on the road just thirty feet from where I stood. Through the screen of shaggy junipers I saw an Apache war party of twelve young men traveling fast, jubilantly shouting and laughing together. Blood from one man's head wound soaked his tunic, but even he looked pleased with the morning's work. The lead horses were double-mounted. Three of the Indians held captive Spanish children in front of them. Younger men pushed along a good-looking herd of horses. The Indios clattered by with sacks of pilfered corn bouncing on the backs of their ponies, and one man held a fistful of flapping chickens. They were gone before I could figure out any better hiding place.

My first thought was for Marisol, but because the Apaches looked like they were fully loaded with captives and spoils and heading home I wasn't too worried. I had just turned onto the main road, so after waiting a few minutes I tracked them back to her turn-off to make sure they had ridden past without making a detour. I debated riding back to her, but surely she was safe, and there would be many people down in Medanales who would be in desperate need of help. It was clear the raiders had prevailed.

My gentle mood of 'all's well with the world' evaporated. I pressed Rosinante hard down the last two miles into the green valley beside the Chama.

The first people I met had no further need of help. Two women lay in a heap in the road, both hideously scalped, one bare-breasted with her skirts fluttering high on her thighs and her blouse ripped down the front. There was no doubting they were dead, so I pulled the lady's dress down to cover her legs, made the sign of the cross and cantered on past a placita of smoldering houses. Adobe doesn't burn, but the roofs were gone and the wooden barns were smoking piles.

At last, a mile farther on, I found someone alive. He stood in a muddy farmyard bemused and motionless. I waved to him so he'd know I meant no harm and trotted down, swinging Rosinante around so I could talk to him still mounted. He was a boy, about a year out from his manhood, big as a man, but all skin and bones. He hadn't had time to take on meat yet. He told me his name was Miguel, then started to cry like a kid. He gestured toward the house to explain why. Two children and a woman lay broken and awkward among the logs of the woodpile, like so much tossed firewood themselves.

I had seen death: my father, babies buried right after birth, and the corpses of Indians left beside the river after battles on the Piedra Lumbre. It was part of natural law, but so far I had never killed. At this moment I knew I could, but the boy's grief overwhelmed my anger and I let out a quiet exhale of despair.

"Will you come to town? We'll see who's still there. We'll get you some help with these." I gestured to his family, silent and ghastly, not thirty feet from us. Rosinante in truth wasn't much bigger than a pony. Even though I'm small, she would be hard-pressed to carry two of us, but we would try.

The boy looked straight at me despite his tears and I knew he had just taken hold and would get through. He turned toward the house and his dead family, and said, "No. I can't leave. I have to bury them before the coyotes come. Then, maybe."

If he'd been any older I'd have left him to it, but he was too young to do this one by himself. I made the choice to help here where I could, and to go on to the village later to see what else was needed. I dismounted and we found tools and started digging.

One thing will never change about this land: if you dig, you'll always be digging in rock. We set the stones aside, one by one as we wrested them out, and in the end piled a considerable cairn on top of the grave where we buried his mother and sisters. It took hours, but we did it, and there's no doubt in my mind it was the right thing.

Late that afternoon, Miguel rode with me into the rough cluster of houses they called Medanales. There were still some people in the plaza, but they were leaving, pulling their carts themselves because their livestock was gone, taking a few last things, even metal hinges from the doors.

It wasn't the first time the people of Medanales had straggled back toward the bigger towns with whomever, whatever, they had left after a raid. But they'd been told the Indian wars were over, the Comanches now beaten by the Spanish, the other tribes weakened and driven away. This was the worst kind of grief, being dragged back into a horror they thought had finally ended. When Miguel slipped down off my horse I knew there was no relief for him here. These were as dejected and sorrowful a group of people as I had ever seen.

An elderly man noticed Miguel and came to him quickly. They spoke and the man turned to the tiny woman at his side. Her shrill scream caused Rosinante to rear in panic, and I had trouble holding my horse down as several women joined in the fierce keening for Miguel's family. Through their din I talked to the men who soon agreed that I should ride ahead to Santa Cruz and deliver the news: Medanales had been obliterated once more and its people were moving back to town. The Comanches had struck once again.

"Comanches?" I asked. Surely he was wrong. It was Apaches I had seen.

"Comanches! Who else? Long, flowing hair. Stripped down for war. Painted red all over."

This baffled me, because I am Indio too. After my father died and my brothers and I gave up the ranch, I went to live for a year with my mother and her people. They taught me carefully. While it was true that the warriors had ridden past swiftly, I don't think I was mistaken.

The people headed out now, unwilling to spend the night in their ruined village. I rode cautiously through the distressed crowd, careful not to look too relieved to be the only one sitting on a horse. Once free of the devastated town, I cantered south in twilight toward the garrison at Santa Cruz de La Cañada and the government officials who would begin to help these people.

A Hideous Mistake

I clattered into Santa Cruz the next day at just the same moment as a fast riding messenger from Taos. Rosinante and I had made good time and were both showing signs of our rapid trip down from Medanales, but this man was as lathered as his horse and his face was grim.

Outside the mud-walled garrison I saw Governor Anza, himself, greet the courier and then take him into an office, closing the door behind them. Someone went in with food and a pitcher of something. It seemed to me my news was pretty important too, and perhaps I might be offered a plate, but no one even noticed me. I resigned myself to wait, but in the end it was only a few minutes until I managed to talk to a sergeant and once he heard my news it didn't take long for me to be ushered into the room.

I was shown right outside again, only this time onto a sunny portál where the Taos messenger stood talking to Anza, who was taking the news sitting down on a garden bench. The governor was clearly a toughened old campaigner, weathered to cracking by the sun. Although he was getting old, his body was still taut, ready for anything. His long beard was pitch-black, but his hair was streaked with gray. It was clamped in a braid at his neck like that of most men of our region. I saw a lightening-white lick of scar on his right cheekbone. His dark eyes were as alert as any desert traveler's. He turned them on me, exasperated, clearly having no time for interruption.

"State your business," he said.

"Medanales, sir. It has been attacked and most of the farms along the river are in ruins." He was silent. I plunged ahead.

"I saw a half-dozen dead settlers, and children were kidnapped. The survivors are already on the road to Santa Cruz. They might get in tonight, but more likely tomorrow. They need protection and food."

He looked me right in the eye and apparently judged me intelligent enough, for he asked me to tell him everything. I gave details of the captive children on the horses of the raiders.

"Your name?"

"Fernando Aguilar of Abiquiú, sir. Called Nando."

Anza pushed the plate and the pitcher toward me and told me to finish them off. "Sit there and listen to what this man has to say. I think there could be a connection between your stories."

He called out to the guard posted at the door, "Get Sebastian over here." Then he turned his attention to the messenger, Leyba.

"What possible explanation is there for it?" the commander demanded angrily.

"The scout came back sooner than we expected. He said there were Indios waiting in the next valley, right above the trail. Apaches. Waiting to ambush us as we came through after the parley. It seemed like a stroke of luck that we found them, a perfect opportunity. Captain Valdez took a contingent up into the hills right away to surprise them from on top. The troop I was with went ahead on the main route. Down below, we pretended we had no idea the Indios were there, though we were expecting to draw the Apaches down onto us, but the captain's group got up there fast and attacked them from behind. It was right on dark when Valdez swamped them. It was a rout. They killed at least seven Apaches."

"Except?" The governor was terse.

"Except, they weren't. They were Comanches."

Anza groaned, then told Leyba to continue.

"It was one of the bands we had met at the parley. The scout was wrong. We killed our own allies. It was a hideous mistake. The people were just bedding down. They hadn't brought their tepees, because this was a fast-moving group of travelers. Many were only lightly clothed, lying beside the fires on their sleeping robes. Valdez found the Comanches' sentry and silenced him, so the captain was able to take them by surprise. Some of the people were trampled by the Spaniards' horses, others were killed by men slashing through the bedrolls with their knives." Leyba's voice had dropped almost to a whisper. "There were women killed and a baby."

He looked at Anza, who couldn't speak he was so enraged, but who gave a signal to continue.

"Those Comanches who survived got over the pass and alerted Red Horse. He must have swung into full battle mode within minutes. A hundred warriors rode out and by dawn were up the mountain and all over Valdez and his men. They pinned us down on the rocks and we couldn't fight our way out all day. I hold small hope for the men who were left up there."

My gut started to ache as I thought of Carlos, high in the mountains, taking the heat from a hundred seething Comanches. It was for just this reason that my brother had refused to let me ride with him.

"Some smaller groups got away in bits and pieces, but I know we've lost men. The Comanches were furious, like an overturned beehive. There was nothing to do but fight as hard as we could to get out of there."

"Who was the scout who made the initial error?"

"Perea."

"Is he alive?" Anza sounded like he wouldn't mind if he weren't.

"I'm not sure. He was detailed to Valdez's group, so he might have been where they took the hardest hit."

"With your permission, sir." I was too worried to stick to protocol any longer. "Is there any word of Lieutenant Aguilar, Carlos Aguilar?"

Leyba answered, "I don't believe he was in the detail that went up to the Comanches' camp, but in the end everyone was in the fighting."

Anza spoke, his lips tight with worry. "Sub-Lieutenant Carlos Aguilar, young, but one of my best men. If anyone can get out of there he can, but who knows what they're up against." He was silent, thinking, then he exploded, "I can't believe they could be that stupid!"

I had to say it. "That's my brother, sir. He knows the Indios well. If he could see them at all, or hear them, he could tell the difference between a Comanche and an Apache. Carlos couldn't have gone with Valdez and the scout, because my brother wouldn't have made that mistake." Anza looked at me appraisingly. He probably knew about my father, because Benito had been an important man.

Now Sebastian and others were on the portál with us and Anza was giving orders for increasing the defenses at the Santa Cruz garrison, for a small contingent to ride after the stolen children and to give aid to the farmers fleeing Medanales. The governor himself would head north toward Taos to meet his returning army, what was left of it anyway. There was no time to call out the pueblo auxiliaries, though he issued orders to put them on alert. He sent a rider out to increase the levy for the militia yet again and to warn all the northern towns of the likelihood of more hostilities.

As everyone went into action, Leyba turned to me and asked, "Didn't I see you at the camp when we first got to Taos?"

"I was helping my brother, but before you went up the pass he sent me away to look after our mother. It wasn't my choice to leave."

"Probably a good thing you got out of there," Leyba muttered, then there was silence until I asked again the name of the man who had wrongly identified the Comanches.

"It was Perea, Géraldo Perea. He's normally a good scout. Comes from Bernalillo."

"I think I remember him," I said. "Light eyes?"

Leyba nodded. I could picture Perea's square, flat face. He was a mixed-blood too, though his mother wasn't Indio but some kind of European. He was fair-haired, always peeling from sunburn, a short, strong man. He didn't look much like us, even though he talked like any Spaniard here.

"Hasn't he been around a long time?" I asked. "For him to make a mistake like this doesn't make sense."

The man gave a shrug by way of agreement.

I had to ask it. "Do you think my brother is alive?"

71

Leyba shook his head, but more from doubt than certain knowledge.

"I was sent out of there around midnight by Valdez. It was tough to slip through. I went over a cliff face to do it. We split up into small groups, fighting from separate pockets in the rocks. I'm sorry, I never saw Aguilar. If he lives or not, I haven't a clue."

Something tightened up in me. I knew it would stay that way until I found out. Sometimes my big brother irritated me, but I couldn't imagine life without him.

Anza was getting ready to leave, but he had been listening to us. "We're never going to get that treaty now." His dejection was palpable. "The Comanches feel they've been betrayed, and rightly so. We murdered at least four of their warriors and apparently women and children too. They won't take that lightly. Two years ago we would have been overjoyed. Today it's a disaster."

The governor was, at this moment, an unhappy man.

"Nando, join us if you can. Will you go on to Santa Fe with the news? I'll put it in a letter. Ask Alcalde Duran to send me whatever men he can find and tell him to be ready for anything."

"Yes sir, I will," I responded, secretly pleased that I'd found my own job without Carlos's intervention. I thought of Rosinante tied up out in the sun in the paddock. "But my mare's spent, sir."

"Sebastian, set him up," the governor said, and he left.

It's a pain in the backside in every sense, but you can get from Santa Cruz to the capital in just one day, riding over sand hills up a wide valley and then through the forest. In the end Leyba came along with me and I was glad of his company. I let him rattle on, because unlike me, he'd been in the thick of things. He told some more about how it had gone after I'd left the troop in Taos, then he was quiet for a while as we negotiated a series of steep-sided arroyos. Back on even ground he said, "Three years ago I rode with Anza when he smashed Cuerno Verde."

"You did? That was the big one. I'd like to have been there!"

Leyba drank this up and went on, more the know-it-all than before. "Since we beat them up, the Comanches have definitely been more peaceable, but Anza insisted from the beginning that he won't finalize the treaty until they bring in every last one of their renegade bands. They have to come together as one people if they want to deal with him.

"He really plays it up around them; wears his best uniform draped with galloon, his fancy hat and all. 'Governor of the Kingdom of New Mexico! Representative of his Majesty, King Charles the Third of Spain!' " Leyba let his voice boom across the sand hills.

"Even the Comanche chiefs agree some force must be brought to subdue their wilder members. We always expected more fighting, but before we really got into it, Anza wanted to try this parley because we actually do have a lot in common. Everyone's had it with the Apaches." I let him babble on, because it was good to catch up after being stuck in Abiquiú all winter.

"Anza figures that if we finalize an alliance with the Comanches, then the whole Ute nation might fall in with us. Then it happens, a giant pincers movement against everyone's enemy, the Apaches."

It sounded like one of Luz's fairy tales to me. "We're not so naïve we think that will really happen, are we?" I asked.

Leyba shrugged. "Right now it's only a dream. What they're praying for is that every damn Indian who's ever been hurt by Apaches will finally come out and help us. It's the only way to get them off our backs and make some headway in this struggling province. It'll take time, but if it works then the settlers won't always have to look over their shoulders for hostiles riding in from the north. Everyone can concentrate together on stopping the Apaches."

That would be amazing. For the first time in two hundred years the farmers and shepherds could go about their work without listening for the whistle of arrows. Wasn't it only a couple of years ago a boy had been snatched from the family cow pen right in Santa Fe?

As a Ute, at least half of me anyway, I didn't know whom I liked least, the Comanches or the Apaches. Our huge Ute tribe was usually easy-going and interested in trade, though I had to admit that gentleness was being kicked out of us. The Comanches had swarmed in from the northeast and were pushing up against our territory, steadily getting tougher, richer, and better armed and mounted. They had already finished pushing the Apaches all the way out, and they were looking for a fresh group of people to harass and exploit. The Apaches used to roam the buffalo country, tough in their own right, but the Comanches didn't care what it took, they wanted command of the plains. Now those Apaches who had survived were jammed up against the western mountains, fighting tooth and nail to hang on to the desolate country they'd wound up with. Raiding constantly, they were making a comeback. The poor Pueblos, civilized and gentle, were suffering horrendous attacks.

Leyba started talking again, echoing my own thoughts. "The Apaches are on the rampage in the south and the Comanches are getting stronger, looting our towns, pillaging and enslaving anyone weaker than they are. Thank God the tribes keep beating up each other," he added. "It's the only way the Spanish have survived, that and our truce with the Pueblos."

I was thinking how the Comanches had bellied into Ute territory, then turned south into the upper Chama valley and moved onto the Piedra Lumbre where they started attacking our ranch. It was the beginning of the end for us, hastening my father's death and the loss of our home on the high plateau.

"Take that peace with the Pueblos," my companion went on. "That's held most of the time since we got back into the territory. What's that, ninety years now? It's always been good for us. This alliance with the Comanches that Anza's trying for could work for us like that. If we get it, we can finally stop worrying whether we'll still be here in the morning."

We had just begun the gradual climb up to the royal city. We took it easy, as it had been a long day for the horses. I handed Leyba some dusty jerky. He chewed and talked at the same time.

"By the time you left the fairground in Taos, when the troops were getting ready to travel to Cimarron, Valdez was pretty excited. He'd had spies out, mixing with old contacts. I was in on that, mingling as a civilian. Torres and Trujillo were detailed to ferret out foreigners. Perea was working with us too. I remember he talked a long time with a friar, that skinny one who usually stalks the barrio in Santa Fe."

I remembered that padre. I'd seen him buying children.

"We hadn't been at the fair long when Valdez started getting back positive reports that the Comanches were ready to talk. He was ecstatic. Being instrumental in this would be a big boost to his career. So we headed out, made it to Cimarron,

75

met with a group of important chiefs, and seemed to make progress on the groundwork for the treaty. But then, when we left, well, damn it, the rest you know.

"It's been more than two years since Anza started out to achieve a truce with the Comanches. The parley went well, and if it hadn't been for Perea's mistake, the fighting could have been over before the end of May. It didn't happen."

"Blown to hell," I said and we rode along a good half-mile before either of us said another word. I always liked this part of the road, with the Sangre de Cristos flanking me on my left, lofty, and this evening, glowing almost blood-red as the sun threw its afterglow into the sky. Riding along beneath the mountains, I wondered if the failure of Anza's plan would send our people back out of this country a second time? We had a lot more invested in it now.

Leyba parted from me near Tesuque, so I did the last three miles alone, riding over the hill into Santa Fe in darkness. I went straight to the plaza to Tomás Duran's house, as I had been instructed, and knocked on the carved wooden door.

This time I got a much quicker audience because I had a letter from the governor and was riding an army horse. Tomás wasn't just the alcalde mayor in Santa Fe, he was the richest landowner in the area. A good friend of Anza's, he acted as head of the villa while the governor was away. Duran was short but handsome, and always welcoming. He knew me a little through my stepmother and tonight he was friendly with me.

He read Anza's letter while he finished his supper, calling for another plate. I immediately set to the remnants of a venison roast and corn pudding. He actually let me eat about half of it before he started to ask questions. When I was through relating details of the failed parley, the mistaken identity of the attacked Indians, and the destruction of Medanales, he pushed his chair back from the table and got to his feet.

"And I thought we were on the brink of peace. Who on earth is going to be able to convince the Comanches we just made a mistake? 'Sorry, we didn't recognize you in the dark!' Damn!" He was busying himself with pen and ink and asked me to build up the fire so he could see better. I was wondering whether I should mention that I'd met his son Ramón up north, but I still wasn't clear how I felt about the man, nor what he was doing exactly, so I let it wait.

"Nando, did you ever hear about the time we made the same kind of error and took out a whole village of Utes?"

I shook my head.

"They'd come down to Santa Cruz to sign a peace treaty, but we misread their intention. Our soldiers took the sword to a camp of a hundred tepees before we recognized the error. In revenge, the Indios tore through the northern settlements killing or capturing everyone they could get their hands on. It took years to get them to trust us again."

Actually, Nan had told me this story, but from the Ute's point of view. It was easy to understand how the Comanches were feeling now.

"How did you come to be on the road above Medanales, Nando? I thought you were living in Abiquiú." It pleased me that this important man knew so much about me, but I couldn't exactly tell him the truth.

"Not much going on at home. Planting hasn't started up north and they didn't need me for the last call up. I just wanted to see a friend so I took off."

"Four excuses," Duran laughed, "so it must have been a woman. Spring fever?"

I gave him a smile. When the alcalde winked back at me he looked like a kid. Then his face became grave.

"Comanches back on the warpath and Apaches supposedly everywhere, but actually nowhere at all. Anza is going to be up against it this summer. It looks like I'll be stuck in town for a while yet."

He looked as disappointed as a cat who's just swallowed a bird. Duran owned a huge ranch along the Rio Grande down by Bernalillo and a smaller one in La Ciénega, not so far from Santa Fe. His haciendas were smooth-running operations, thanks to the many pueblos nearby where he obtained free labor for his fields and household. But Tomás liked action, he was a gambler, and he liked city life. I suspected he dearly loved being in town, particularly when the governor was gone. Many opportunities could come his way. This duty was no hardship to him.

"Walk me to the palacio," he said.

We took off into the cool, spring night, going across the plaza now the mud had dried. That way it was less than a hundred yards to the sprawling palacio where the governor lived and where all the offices, barracks and storerooms were. Its adobe walls shone in the moonlight, but from where I stood it looked more like a farmyard than a palace.

I noticed it also smelled like a barn as we walked under the portál. The stench of animals and manure that usually emanated from the palacio's courtyards was heightened by the presence of the elk Anza was sending off to King Carlos's menagerie. I had heard of these animals and the amazing fact that while we had to stay and gut it out here, the elk were getting free passage to Spain. We'd also heard that Anza's soldiers hated having to sleep next door to them.

When we got to the gates the alcalde stopped. "Have you heard about the murdered militiaman?" Hedging, I shook my head.

"Killed with an ax right under that tree there. Shook this town up and scared the other volunteers plenty. To my mind, another inexplicable event, like the others you told me about tonight."

"When did it happen?" I asked, to make it seem like the first I'd heard of it.

"Early last week. They're interrogating a couple of Indios, but they haven't made any arrests yet."

Before he went inside he asked, "Do you have to go back up north right away, or will you stay with your stepmother?"

"Sure, I'll be with Luz, unless she's away doing her good deeds, cleaning up old churches or something. I'd go back to Abiquiú tomorrow, but I've got to stay until I find out about Carlos."

"Here, take these," and he dropped some coins in my hand as we parted. One felt like it even had a little weight to it, but I was too well brought up to inspect it in front of him.

Shape Shifting

I was walking away when a friar loomed out of the dark of the empty plaza. He crossed swiftly over the rutted road and grabbed me, swinging me around to face him square on. Beyond a doubt, I was face to face with the padre who had been in Taos. I'm about a head shorter than he, and he glared down at me, gripping my shoulder. He must flatter himself that he's the kind of man who can peer right into a man's soul. Let him think so. I'd known for a while that my soul doesn't speak his language, but I endured his scrutiny in silence. I wondered if he knew I'd seen him buying children? He uttered a few words in Latin, assuming correctly I couldn't understand them, and then whirled off in his gray-blue robes. I noticed he walked right into the palacio unchallenged, and then candles were lit in the governor's office where Duran had just gone. How anyone could endure that padre's presence was beyond me. I shook myself to get the memory of his sharp fingers off my skin. Nasty old fart, I thought, as I went off through the shadowy streets to my stepmother's house.

80

For a moment I was tempted by the light coming through the shutters of the two-story adobe on San Francisco street. It was Rosa's home, in the evening a wine shop, and a little later at night more of a hotel, or what friend friar might refer to as a whorehouse. I heard that he once stormed through the doors and went into every bedchamber, pushing the couples in the beds apart with a stick. I also heard that later that month he got very sick with stomach troubles. The whole town thought it a pity.

The temptation to go in didn't last long, as I was still well satisfied by my sojourn beside the Chama with Marisol and I knew my stepmother would have wine that would be a lot better than Rosa's.

The pious Luz de Gracia, widowed since the death of my father four years before, was alone at home sitting by the fire, fairly guzzling a mug of wine. When I barged in on her, I saw her try to hide it on the hearth behind the logs, but she was too late and she knew it, so she reversed herself and offered it in salute. I took it from her and happily downed all but a last taste.

"I suppose you think there's more where that came from."

"I know very well there is. Madam, that is disgusting wine!" I imitated the prancing grandee fop I'd seen once when I was down in Santa Fe before. It was actually quite good wine and I winked at her.

"I've found a connection," she beamed proudly, "someone near Socorro who has finally learned to make it well and to get it here without ruining it. Your father really shouldn't have died so young. Nando! Welcome!" And then we hugged. I brought in more logs and got the fire roaring. She lit two real candles in honor of my visit.

"Luz," I asked, not having shaken off the incident with the cleric, "who is that friar who looks like a buzzard? He just jumped me on the plaza."

"Father Baldonado. Such a blessed man that no one can stand to get near him. The whole town went without confession for two months when he was the only priest here. Fortunately Miera returned and we all managed to come back to grace."

"It's funny I never realized how wicked you could be. You were different when you were bringing us up."

"Thank you!" she said. "I was too busy with a house full of children, the majority of them half-breeds, and your father introducing me to a new wife every few years. Raising the ladies was hardest of all. Except for Nan. I swear she raised me." My stepmother had been surprisingly pragmatic, particularly for a woman who spent a lot of time on her knees in church.

I had to tell her about being pressed into a slave caravan, and how Carlos had rescued me. But now that had been eclipsed by the necessity of telling her that her son was missing after being on the wrong side of a raging battle. I had to tell her about Medanales being sacked; I had to tell her about the failure of the treaty. I would in a few more minutes, but right now it was a joy to see her, proud, upright and, through some transformation I had not previously been aware of, naughty. I used to think her stern, but she had always been the wittiest one of the family, smarter even than my father, and here she was, fifty at least, and much shorter than I remembered her. She was skinny, losing teeth, and with the thinning hair on her head pulled back so severely that her face would be intimidating if you ignored the sparkle in her eyes.

We chatted and laughed, and I put off my news as long as I could.

She took it fairly well. She had complete faith in Carlos as a fighting man with brains. She poured more wine, but sensibly into two cups this time, lest I further deplete her share. Luz can get very organized when she is worried. I could see her mind working on plans and contingencies and I knew that I was becoming a distraction, so I went to bed, leaving her with a kiss on her high forehead and a promise to stay in Santa Fe until we had word of Carlos.

I only had a few minutes to think, because a real bed had claimed me and sleep was pressing in fast. The night before, I'd been hurrying down from Medanales and had only snatched a couple of hours in a flat spot between two bushes alongside the road. The half of me that was Ute made do, the half that was Spanish gentry wished to hell for at least one more blanket.

Lying there at Luz's, adjusting to sheets, pillows and warm covers, I finally had time to wonder at myself for never having told Anza or the alcalde that it hadn't been Comanches on the road north out of Medanales. I had only told my father's widow.

"Shape shifting," she had said, knowingly. "In Medanales the Comanches are Apaches and up on the mountain the Apaches are Comanches. Horse gear, clothes, paint color, hair cuts, they differ by a mile. Anyone living here for more than a month would know the difference. And yet, twice in one day, the mistake was made by whole groups of people."

"Or maybe just by Perea and me," I suggested. She gave me her famous 'You little idiot' look, one I had tried to avoid over the years. Actually, as kids we had called it 'the dumb-bastard look' but Luz wouldn't have known the word, and from her treatment of us as children, she didn't have the concept either.

Talking it over, we found we both suspected that no mistake had been made. Both cases of confused identity might well have been part of a strategic plan.

In the morning word was out, the Comanche peace was over, local militias were being pressed for even more men, and we heard that the refugees from Medanales had arrived in Santa Cruz. They were destitute and in mourning for their dead and the three children taken prisoner.

I hung out on the plaza for a good hour picking up news and frankly reveling in being back in Santa Fe. The array of two-wheeled carts, wagons, oxen, strings of mules and horses, and workers loading, shifting and organizing gear, fascinated me. Braying donkeys and screeching cartwheels drowned out the shouts of men. There was the stench of mule piss, old tallow and stacked hides. I loved browsing through the assortment of pottery, blankets and food that women sold under the portáls. It was a spectacle I hadn't seen for a while, so I lingered, taking it all in, but when I noticed the contentious friar enter the scene, I felt it was time to give my stepmother a hand. Rather than buy more wood, I took her mule up onto the mountain and cut her a toppling load. We weren't poor, but we were never rich either, and any coins we saved for this elderly lady were important.

By the time I returned, there was still more news, in a way even worse. Riders had hurried in ahead of our annual supply train that had been rumbling north to us from Chihuahua and had finally reached Socorro. The caravan had suffered the worst Apache attacks ever and fully three-quarters of the wagon train had been looted. The supplies reaching the colony, the first after the winter, would be desperately few. Rumor had it that for some incomprehensible reason, the accompanying armed guard had been considerably smaller than in previous years.

A young friar on his way to New Mexico was among those slain. Almost all the Franciscans were natives of Spain; rarely was one recruited from the population in Mexico, so new padres were scarce and for one to be killed was a serious loss. We were still going to be at the mercy of Father Buzzard and have a ridiculously small number of missionaries elsewhere in the province to tend to our souls. I didn't care much, having inherited my religion from Nan, but I knew that it worried our people to have none of the sacraments for years, even that of marriage.

It had become a cranky day of hard wind and no sun. Luz and I sat inside, gloomy and dull. The gray sky made the bare, dirty streets and the crumbling houses of the old town of Santa Fe look even more decrepit than usual. Hopeless, I would call it. It was almost two hundred years since we'd started a colony here and once again we were hanging on by a thread, but were forced to remain because there was no place else to go.

The gentry, like Luz de Gracia, were by now so far removed from their old life in the south that they would have no families and no connections should they return. They might own enormous grants of land here, but unless it was in the river valleys, like Tomás Duran's, they always were hard-pressed for money. If Luz, for all her wit and character, got off an ox-cart in Mexico City after six months on the trail, she would

85

look like the lowliest of drudges, ragged, sunburned and pock-marked. Life under the hot blue sky on our ranch had aged her far beyond her actual years and she would always be poor, relative to the gentry of Mexico or Spain. No one would know she was full-blooded Spanish and an educated woman of gentle birth. Her estate was now a three-room mud brick house and a couple of small fields along the Santa Fe River. Her few animals rustled in a barn attached to the outside of her bedroom wall.

In theory she owned nine thousand acres of land above Abiquiú, but none of us had been to the ranch in years. I remembered our father, already sick when the Comanches started raiding in earnest. He lay in his bed, his thick silver hair plastered against his tanned face. His body was helpless, but he still gave the orders. My brothers, cousins and I fought hard, but the Comanches forced us out. The authorities told Carlos and Francisco that while the grant to the ranch was temporarily suspended, the future rights would rest half in Luz's name, half in theirs, but meanwhile they must come into the capital and do the governor's bidding.

My brothers still owned sizeable farms and a small house in Abiquiú, but I was the only one who stayed up there, raising some crops and a few animals to help supply the family in Santa Fe. Part of Luz's plan was for me to be handy to the ranch. We were wary that someone else would make a claim upon it, calling us deserters. It had happened before. After she outfitted Carlos to become a cadet at the presidio and sent Francisco to Mexico to study, she gave me two fields and a shovel. Not that she didn't like me, but Luz was struggling, a widow in a war-torn country. If you were a pureblooded Spaniard, you were somebody. If, like me, you weren't, you just had to figure something out.

86

This colony had fallen apart a hundred years ago. We'd built it back, but in recent years so many settlers had been killed or taken captive that once again towns all over the north were abandoned. No one had been able to farm much, or raise horses, because of the Indians' continuous attacks. Unfortunately, before the governor was able to retaliate effectively, he had to beg Mexico to send our presidio a whole new herd. As usual it took three years to get what we asked for. And even though they recently sent fifteen hundred horses up the Camino Real, they may have come too late. The colony was on the brink of collapse again. If it happened, people of "broken-color" like me, which means most of us on the frontier, would be back in Mexico begging in the streets. We northerners might be sturdy and unique, but it was certain that if we left New Mexico, no one in the outer world would want anything to do with us.

Sleuth of the Northern Province

I heard the shriek of wooden-wheeled carts rolling into town and ran toward the plaza, surprised to find it packed with people. From the bedraggled look of them, I figured many were the refugees from Medanales. I was surprised; I had thought they would stay up in Santa Cruz.

The newcomers and the Santa Feños watched, horrified, as the beat-up army limped in. Soldiers were wedged into the oxcarts, most bloody, listless or barely conscious. Men lay prone on the floorboards, and I wondered how they could possibly have survived the jolting over the miles of dreadful roads. Drivers hurried the carts through the gates into the palacio's courtyard. I tried to squeeze through beside them, but an armed guard held me back.

I glimpsed Luz inside though. If I knew her, she had just walked right through the main entrance unchallenged. She would get to Carlos first and snatch him out of the hands of the army medics. I positioned myself where she would see me when she came out of the compound.

Father Miera stood beside me, also watching, as the gates started to close behind the awful caravan. I kissed his hand and was beginning to introduce myself when he recognized me. He knew me back when I was a boy and he was a young, eager padre in Abiquiú. When I told him that Carlos might be on those carts, he took me by the elbow and pushed me ahead of him into the belly of the palacio.

This was not a good day in the City of Holy Faith. The courtyard was mayhem. Soldiers, women and pueblo servants were lifting men out of the carts. Luz noticed me come in and I moved over to her quickly. Her sharp eyes picked through the carnage and in a few moments she had located Carlos. Of course, being a lieutenant, he was in the first cart, but it wasn't clear whether he was living or dead.

Within minutes she had him out of there, with two pueblo men carrying him in a crude litter as gently as they could through the slop of the narrow street that led out of the plaza. As soon as we'd cleared the crowd I ran ahead to the house and threw my belongings off the bed. I yelled at the two servant girls to force the fire up fast with aspen kindling so that the kettle would be boiling when they brought him in.

He was alive and he let everyone know it with such ungodly language that even I, a devil worshiper (or so that skinny priest thought), was looking over my shoulder hoping none of the pious in our neighborhood could hear.

He had a bullet hole in his upper arm and his ankle was smashed. Clearly no one had taken the time to do more than wrap a rag around his arm, so we all set to work. Luz handled the worst of it with determined fingers and an angry look about her that softened only for a moment when she looked down at the filthy face of her eldest son.

The first mug I gave him was of water, and the second was water mixed with wine. Before she began on his ankle I got a half mug of brandy into him. I didn't dare do more, because Carlos was lousy at holding his liquor.

You don't live on the frontier without knowing a lot about bones, both yours and those of all the animals you've killed and pulled apart for the pot, and Luz put this knowledge to use. Luckily for Carlos, she had the ankle set as best she could and was wrapping it fast, just as the so-called surgeon showed up with his tools. Carlos was by this time unconscious, so he never knew what he missed. We sent the surgeon back to the palace, but politely, in case we needed him to come back tomorrow.

When Luz finished and was scrubbing her hands and arms, I slipped the other half mug of brandy into her. That helped her decide it was now all right to fall apart, and so she did, in full view of the servants, collapsing in tears into her chair and wiping her nose with the back of her hand like a little girl. She unwrapped her bloody apron, and the maids had the sense to gather it up and get out of there. I took the bony old girl into my arms and let her wail.

The storm didn't last long, but it was a powerful one. Tough as nails, our Luz de Gracia, yet so soft inside. She probably missed my father terribly, and I began to see how wretched her life must feel, alone here in the villa and growing old, far from the ranch we had all lived on, and much farther still from her native Spain. Sons, yes she had good ones, but they were both gone a great deal of the time. I wasn't much good, and I was only partly a son to her, but as she sobbed in my arms I knew it was right that I was there.

When everyone settled down, and Carlos seemed to be asleep instead of dead unconscious, I slipped out to Rosa's with Tomás Duran's jingly silver in my pocket. Again her shutters were closed, but lines of light leaked through them onto the dark street, and I knew the wine drinking crowd was carrying on inside.

Not exactly carrying on. Our town had taken hard hits this week and the mood was dark. Men drank sourly, numbing the pain. There was none of the usual levity. The news of the ransacked caravan hit the high-living ones the hardest. Most of us made do with what came out of the ground, usually just mud and stones, but some of these men had real expectations.

At one table I recognized Ramón Duran, whom I hadn't seen since he disappeared from the caravan by the river. He was holding a low-voiced conversation with two other men of his class, all of them clearly in their cups. I wondered if he would recognize me? Probably not, since he associated me with a different part of the world, and pictured me a few hundred miles north of here. If I got a chance, I would try to talk to him, to figure out if he knew what Lorenzo was really up to. If he didn't, he ought to. With a man like Alcalde Duran for his father, and thousands of acres of some of the best bottomland along the Rio Grande, there was no need for Ramón to be inadvertently mixed up with a slaver. For now, he was becoming comfortably drunk in the company of other ricos.

There were soldiers too, more than the usual handful, and tonight Rosa seemed to be overlooking the debts they had accumulated while they waited for their pay to crawl up the Camino Real from Mexico. Most likely the Apaches had gotten their hands on the paymaster's silver too. Rough wooden furniture wobbled on the flagstone floor. The few low candles drooled their wax onto dirty tables and the fire in the corner smoked awfully. It was a disheartening scene. A girl passed through, trying to look cheerful and ready for business, but no one seemed to care. Libido sinks fast in the face of misery.

I took advantage of the sullen inattention and passed through the curtain to the kitchen without having to talk to anybody in the bar. Rosa, a big, handsome woman, was there at her table comforting an armful of weeping girl, a pretty one too, if her face hadn't been all swollen and wet, and her eyes panicked with loss. It was one of the bar maids, in some sort of breakdown. Rosa had me sit at her side while she went on stroking the girl's hair, crooning to her, encouraging her to let it all out, but meanwhile looking up at me and with her free hand silently making the motions of an ax chopping into a head. This must be the girlfriend of the soldier who had been murdered outside the palacio. I hadn't known he'd been seeing one of Rosa's serving girls. Maybe she was only a wine shop girl, but it was obvious, if she was crying this hard weeks later, that she had given her heart to the man who'd been tied up dead to the cottonwood tree.

"The padre told him not to. He told him not to be a fool and join up." She choked out the words through her balled-up fist. "But it meant so much to him. Marcos finally had his own job. If we were ever going to marry, he needed to get away from his family, their farm was nothing and he thought the army, . . . he thought now that the Comanches were on our side, . . . " She fell apart again, wetting Rosa's blouse with her tears.

Rosa gestured to the wine jug and indicated I should make the rounds. I was glad to help out. Soggy emotion is not easy for me and this was the second time in an hour. So I went and filled mugs and collected little coins or made marks on a tablet, trying to be a tavern wench for the one and only time in my life.

I escaped the depressing place within the hour, after helping myself to a cup or two for my labors. Rosa at last had gotten out from under the unhappy girl and actually brought out brandy for the gentlemen in Duran's group. This only made the atmosphere worse and I was eager to leave, sensing a crazy anger in the air, and in no way wanting to confront Ramón Duran in his current condition.

I do like to talk to God, despite appearances to the contrary, but I like to do it away from a church, nearer the Spirit. So in total darkness I left the plaza by the north road and felt my way through parked wagons and across the swampy garden behind the palacio's stables. Then I climbed onto the Martyrs' hill. There is a solitary cross up there and you can kneel and have a chat, pass on ideas and information that God might like to know, say a few thank-yous and ask for additional favors if you feel you might be in line for some.

The spring windstorm was over, and the night air was lovely and light now that we'd reached the first of May and winter really had departed. I stood there looking down on the town's few specks of candlelight, smelling the cedar and piñon smoke from the dozens of hearth fires. Straight out ahead of me, and then arcing all above, were the thousand stars, messengers of the god my birth mother Nan had given me. She always said there were two gods: the Spaniards', to whom one must be polite and do all the proper obeisance, particularly if the priests were looking, and then there was the Great Spirit, evidenced in this wind, who held the priests and their God in the small of his hand, cradling and protecting them until they learned the larger truth. It used to confuse me, but now I think I had it straight.

So I knelt and prayed at the foot of the cross, prayed for Carlos and Luz de Gracia and for the dead soldier's soul. Then I stood under the stars and prayed for the Comanches who had been killed just because of a mistake, and even prayed for the Apaches, some of whom I had known, who only wanted to be left alone on their own lands. I prayed for the people all over this territory. It was a lot to think about and I hadn't had much time to think of late, what with Marisol, Carlos and all. So I stood there quite a while.

My head finally cleared, and my spirits were beginning to rise above the sadness of the beleaguered town, so at last I kissed the earth beneath the cross, blew a second kiss to the sky and plunged down the face of the hill, not even taking the trail.

I was climbing through the bars of a small corral when I heard the scuffling and muttering of angry men. A gang of soldiers, looking more like ruffians than members of the army, had driven a stocky, fierce-looking man back against the cedar rails. A half-dozen were advancing, their hands out-spread, twitching to seize him. Just beneath me, one of the attackers held a long, steel knife low by his thigh. I had barely avoided plunging into the brawl. I slipped to the ground and lay hidden there in the dark.

Like a pack of dogs running together in winter, the soldiers moved as one and at some signal they all sensed, leapt upon their prey, hurling him to the ground and pounding their heavy boots against his tough frame. Grunts, cursing and a ripping sound came from their work. Then I heard men running, more voices. There was jittery light from a small brand. The watch? The attackers pulled back, and in the little bit of available light we all saw the gleaming leather pants, tight jackets and white shirts of rich men. The ricos rushed at the pack of soldiers, swinging at their heads with polished oak staffs and scattering them. They were more effective than I would have thought possible for men of their station, as scrappy and streetwise as the soldiers. One of them seized the fallen man by his tunic and tried to drag him to his feet. The others followed the soldiers at a punishing run, out through the corrals and into the alleys behind the palacio.

"Perea! Get up! Get moving!" The man below me pulled on him urgently. Perea finally started to respond, but not fast enough for the other, who hitched an arm around the fallen man's middle and hauled him out of there. Perea, half-dragged, partly conscious, stumbled along, trying to get his feet under him.

It was over in a minute, all the men gone, and the corrals so quiet now that I could hear oxen munching and rumbling in the dark. I didn't want anyone to know that I had witnessed that piece of work, so I backtracked up the hill to pick up the proper trail and to come down the way one usually would to return to the plaza.

I was nearly at the top when I saw that somebody else was up there now, standing by the cross, someone tall and swathed in long robes. A Franciscan. The man was in a state of great glee, his smile huge, his eyes shining with delight. It was Father Baldonado, the dread buzzard, laughing his head off. He had to sit down on the bench under the cross, so he could catch his breath while he slapped his knees at whatever pleased him so.

Two days later I had Carlos sitting outside in the sun with his foot up and a blanket over him. My brother was the fairest of all of us, his hair brown, not black, and the skin beneath his clothes was white, but after his ordeal, all of him seemed bleached. We needed to get him pinked up. So we'd moved his chair to the garden, and now he could see the river and watch the corn shoots grow, which was far more exciting than lying inside the dark house. Luz had gone to Mass, so we finally were going to get our chance to talk.

I could tell he was not only hurting, but in low spirits. He wasn't ready to talk about the battle yet, so I planned to tell him about sneaking up on Marisol. Then I thought better of it, as her husband might be one of his men. Maybe I could ask later if he knew Arsenio and if the man survived the battle.

For the moment, we were relieved to be out in the spring air and to see new green leaves fluttering above us in the blue sky. There was real heat in the sun now and I began to consider how I could build Luz a summer ramada, a long portál on this side of her house. But, before we got down to talking, we were interrupted by a three-foot-tall urchin with filthy face and nose, a fresh smile, and trusting brown eyes. We knew him as Baz, and had yet to find a way to discourage him from either our kitchen or our hearts.

Baz moved in beside Carlos carefully and reached out a grimy finger to touch my brother's bandaged foot. Carlos snarled and Baz leapt back, amazed. Then he saw Carlos smiling at him and shaking his head.

"Don't you dream of getting near that, Baz. Don't come within a yard of it." Baz stepped back three feet.

"Come over here, kid. You can paw at me." I scooped him onto my lap and held him locked inside my arms. He tilted his head back and tried to put his mouth to my ear. I ducked the nose, but then decided to wipe it for him. Cleaned up, he whispered his news to me.

"Mother of God, Carlos! The governor's coming. He'll be here any minute!" Carlos looked impressed that the province's leading man was coming here to our mud house in the corn-field, but he couldn't do much about it. I dropped Baz and told him to run to the church, find Luz and get her home.

I jumped up, grabbing loose shirts and sheets drying on the bushes in the yard as I called for the serving girls. They showed up so fast they must have been right around the cor-ner, to overhear whatever Carlos and I hadn't gotten around to talking about yet.

Once again they made the fire roar under the kettle and I flung things out of the chest looking for the silver mug and the good candlesticks.

"Here, get these lit," I shoved the last wax candles at Estrella. "Quick, spruce this place up." She and Feliz were running.

I set Luz's clean apron where she would find it as soon as she got here and hurried out to Carlos with our comb and a clean washrag for his face. I managed to get him into the jacket of his uniform, though his wounded arm couldn't go through the sleeve.

Luz hurried into the yard and disappeared inside. It was clear she knew, because I heard the clatter of things falling, and sharp commands. I don't think five minutes passed be-fore the governor's carriage pulled to a halt at the head of our lane, and Anza emerged to walk the rest of the way, be-cause the street was too narrow. There weren't many car-riages in New Spain for just this reason. You couldn't get any-where in them.

Despite being on foot, he looked regal enough with his broad-brimmed hat and the feather curling down from it. A beard and mustache covered his lower face, and his eyes were bright with intelligence. He strode right into our humble courtyard, and ignoring the chair we'd just brought outside, seated himself on the chopping block close beside Carlos. Luz offered him wine or chocolate, and he agreed to the latter.

"Would you object if I give your lieutenant here a mug of wine? It helps his disposition considerably," my stepmother asked.

"Give him whatever he needs. Believe me, the man deserves it."

I have a way of not being very noticeable if I want, being short and always plainly dressed. I can even be quiet when it serves. So while the women went to prepare drinks, my brother and the governor talked privately and neither seemed to care that I was sitting on a stone under a cottonwood, carving a new stock for an old pistol.

Of course Anza asked after my brother's injuries, and Carlos reassured him that he'd be back to serve him. Then Carlos inquired about various men who had been in the battle and learned that Colonel Valdez had wounds he probably wouldn't survive. They had only transported him as far as Santa Cruz.

"I need you back quickly, Aguilar. If Valdez doesn't make it there will be a promotion for you. With Valdez gone, and six other men dead up there, my ass is in a sling. I've been given five years to get the Comanches and Apaches off our backs. Three have passed, and we're in a worse mess than when we started."

The man was discouraged. He did, however, pause for a polite moment with Luz when she brought his steaming chocolate. From the way she pretended, he wouldn't know that this was the last of the chocolate and the sugar, maybe for a year, since the wagon train had been ransacked. "In a few minutes there'll be a cake, too, Señor, but it isn't quite out of the oven."

He had no idea she was lying. She must be rustling up cake from a neighbor.

The governor was clearly disheartened. Carlos reminded him that he had vanquished Cuerno Verde, "And surely that goes on the plus side of your record."

"Yes, but there'd better be more than one victory in three years, or I'm out of here. Even the governors who succeed in Santa Fe often go to jail the moment they get back to Mexico."

Carlos acknowledged that with a sideways shake of his head. "You're the best man we've had here in years, sir. I think this was a temporary setback. If anyone can sort the mess out and put us back on our feet, it will be you."

Good old Carlos. His loyal, devoted temperament made him perfect for the army.

"So many different things have gone wrong," said Anza, "and the trouble is so widespread, that I'm beginning to feel someone doesn't want us to succeed."

"Yes sir, some ten thousand Comanches and almost as many Apaches."

Anza let the remark slide. "I mean someone among us. Maybe there are still people here whose interests lie in this colony being on the point of collapse, but since we regularly chase out any stray French or English who show up, other than them I can't imagine who it could be. The Pueblos? They need us. The Church? Sure, we argue with them, but we're all attacked by the same enemies."

Carlos tried to sit up a little straighter, to be part of this conversation like a man instead of an invalid. "Is there any word of Perea?"

"None. No one even remembers seeing him on the field. Once he told you there were Apaches up on the mountainside, he vanished."

I thought of a man with that name being dragged from the cattle pen, but it wasn't time to speak up yet. Anyway, Carlos was forging ahead.

"How could anyone in the north, for that matter, anywhere in New Spain, not want peace with the tribes?" he asked.

Anza looked at Carlos thoughtfully before replying. "I've been puzzling over this. The Franciscans are the weakest they have ever been. They can hardly get anyone to come up here any more. I think they're totally exasperated with the limited effect they have on the Pueblos and their complete lack of success at converting the nomadic tribes. The lure of unsaved souls isn't calling to them like it used to. I wonder if they believe they could make themselves seem more necessary, recreate "the calling" by purposely weakening the secular government? Doubtful, though you never know how a cleric thinks."

I thought of how eerie Father Baldonado always seemed, and how he had been busy on the field in Taos just before the battle. The governor might like to know about that. He went on, still considering the Franciscans' stance.

"Time and again I've begged them to forbear with the pueblos and then watched them undermine their own position by bullying and punishing the people. If it weren't for the garrison and the soldiers, they would have been run out of here a second time, and this time for good, decades ago." There was silence for a moment. "But still, I don't think this current trouble lies with them."

"I'm wondering," said Carlos, "even though the French have been sent packing, could there still be Europeans working against us, not just individuals, but allies of the French, or other governments entirely, using the Indios to gain position?"

What, did my brother have an imagination after all?

"As infiltrators?" Anza asked. "I have little doubt foreigners are trying to get into New Spain. They'd love to gain control of our Pacific harbors and the minerals in these mountains, but I know that at present the British have their hands full with the uprising in the east, and it wouldn't be the eastern seaboard rebels either. Those Yankees can barely wage their own war. Spain's had to bail them out, even help them meet their payroll. Remember the tax that our people here had to pay to support that effort? I was just barely able to exempt the poorest pueblos from it. No, I believe the English army and the eastern colonists are too busy fighting each other to be making a move on our lands, though when they finish with that war we'd better start looking sharp. That leaves some Russians on the northwest coast, and a few French, though I thought we'd taken care of them."

So that angle was discarded, but Carlos kept working through the possibilities. "What if Perea is just loco? Or has his own agenda? I mean here's a man who should know the difference between an Apache and a Comanche, but he obviously forgot whatever he knew. And then disappeared."

Anza went on. "And Valdez, trusting the man's word, dashes up the hill and kills seven of our allies."

I judged that it was now a good time for my entrance, so I walked out from under the tree over to my brother and took off his blanket. I folded it carefully, standing there in front of Anza for a moment. He noticed me for the first time.

The governor looked me over. "Where have we met, young man? I remember you, but not the circumstances. Forgive me, there's a lot going on."

"I'm from Abiquiú. I brought the news to you of Medanales being sacked, sir."

"Yes, sorry. You are Carlos's half brother, then. Stupid of me." He hesitated, as though that was done and now I should leave, but I lingered and ventured, "About Perea, sir."

"What?" Anza was cross that I hadn't gone away.

"I saw him the night before last." The governor looked like I was still an annoyance. It was hard to go on.

Carlos helped me out. "Where'd you see him, Nando?"

"Tossed on his back in the corral under the Martyrs' hill, with six men working him over." I had their attention now. Anza started to quiz me. I made him drag it out of me.

"And then?"

"And then a number of men rushed Perea's attackers, drove them off and lugged Perea away with them."

"How did you know it was Perea?"

"The man who hauled him out of there kept calling him that."

The governor looked at Carlos and asked, "Are there many Pereas around here? Do you know of any other?" Carlos just shrugged. "Where'd they take him? Was he hurt?" Anza pressed.

"Hurt, yes, but sort of walking, with help. I have no idea where he went."

"But the men, who were they?" he asked, eager for my information now.

"The first group I took for soldiers, sir, from the garrison. The men who saved Perea looked like men who'd been at Rosa's wine shop earlier. Ricos."

"So this was a street fight, a drunken brawl?"

"I'd say not sir, I'd say this was a well-timed, successful attempt to rescue Perea from a savage beating."

I couldn't tell if Anza was more taken aback by my news or my choice of words. Half-breeds weren't supposed to be adept at the language, but sometimes the don's son just had to put in an appearance. Behind Anza, I could see Luz hovering in the doorway, close enough to overhear the conversation and secretly cheer me on.

"Could you identify any of the men, from either group?"

"Possibly. Some of them anyway. I'm not sure it would be a good idea just yet." Why on earth did I say that to the governor? Maybe I wasn't ready to implicate the alcalde's son before I had figured out what was really going on.

He lowered a black eyebrow at me to let me know he didn't appreciate being told how to do his business.

"What was your role in this, Nando?"

"My role was to lie in a cow pen, flat on my face in the dirt, and pray no one noticed me."

"How did you happen to be in that particular position?"

"I'd been praying up at the cross on top of the hill. I was there catching my breath after we patched up Carlos."

"Do you not pray in church, then?"

"Yes, sir, I do." Damn Carlos, he was going to make me laugh if he didn't get that look of phony disapproval off his face. Well, anything for a job, I suppose. "I had the company of a friar though."

"What? Speak plainly, Nando. In the cow pen? Face down in the dirt?"

"Not exactly, sir. I came upon the padre after they rescued Perea. I didn't want to be seen by any of them, so I ran back up the hill, and this man was standing under the cross, slapping his knees and laughing his head off."

"What?"

"A tall, blue-robed padre, who looked a lot like a skinny bird, flapping his wings in the dark."

This got them. Carlos and Anza looked at each other in amazement and started talking on top of each other.

103

"Nando! Why haven't you told me this?" Carlos sounded like the authoritarian big brother that he rarely was.

"Because you've been asleep or in misery ever since it happened. I was just about to when Governor Anza came to see you." Carlos yielded to this. I saw Luz make a gesture from the doorway that looked sort of like, "Well, go on." It was apparent she approved of me for the moment.

"There's more," I said, turning toward the governor. "Up in Santa Cruz, when I told you about the raid at Medanales, I left out something. Another mistake of identification was made."

"Please, tell me there was no raid, that settlers aren't murdered, and children haven't been stolen."

"I can't tell you that, sir. When I first encountered the survivors, they were all worked up about the Comanches, and down on our plaza it was the same lament: Comanches, Comanches. But you might remember sir, that I myself got a glimpse of the raiding party just after the massacre."

This next part was a little awkward to explain.

"Well, in fact, I was just off the road a little, in the woods. You know. The men I saw were not Comanches, they were Apaches. I saw the raiding party clearly and heard them speak. It didn't come to me until afterwards, when things had settled down and I'd had time to think, that everyone was convinced they were attacked by the Comanches, but they were wrong."

"Was this just a mistake the settlers made in their terror, or was this an act of trickery on the part of their attackers?" Anza was no fool.

I shrugged, like it was beyond me to figure stuff like this out, though Luz and I already had.

Anza pulled at his mustache and turned to my brother. "Two cases of mistaken identity within a day of each other, possibly on the same day. What do you make of it Carlos?"

Carlos clearly wasn't making much of it. He was slumped over in his chair, weary with pain. He had held himself together as long as he could. Governor Anza saw this and rose to leave. Luz came out and put the blanket back over my brother and kissed the governor's hand. I walked with him to the edge of our yard, where he invited me to walk along beside him up the lane.

"Twice you've helped me, Fernando Aguilar. I've a job for you, if you don't object, and anyway, I forbid you to. I don't want you to tell a soul, not even Carlos. The first part of this job is to stay close to him and keep him safe until he recovers. The second part is to report to me in the palacio tonight, right after Mass, and to make sure no one sees you come in. Enter by the wagon gate. You will not be barred. Cover your head so you're not known. I'll come for you as soon as I can, but be close by the south offices. There's a tree near the old well there. That's where I'll look for you."

And so, unbeknownst even to my family, I became a functionary in the army of the King of Spain and, dressed in shabby buckskins, my career as sleuth of the northern province began.

An Honest Man

$\mathcal{H}$e found me soon enough, skulking around behind the well. It was after dark and I'd made sure no one noticed me, either when entering the palacio courtyard or now, slipping through the side door into the governor's quarters.

Obviously the guard had been alerted and given some description of me, because he simply pretended not to see me walk through the gates. No inquiry, no permission to pass. Just ignored. I wondered what he'd been told to look out for? Light-skinned half-breed, shorter than some, with extra-high cheekbones, the failed attempt at a beard typical of a person half-Ute, half-Spanish, and, oddly, wrapped in his stepmother's shawl? I suppose it would be preferable to ignore a man of that description as he slipped through the gate.

Inside, we bypassed the governor's office and went right into his private rooms. I didn't know what to do, call him sir, bow, kiss his hand, stand up tall, kneel or prostrate myself. So I stood there nervously, eager to unpeel the engulfing shawl.

"Can I come out now?"

He looked at me and laughed. I started unwinding the fabric, and in so doing became uncomfortably aware of how dirty my clothes were. Anza, at one time a fighting soldier in Sonora, didn't give them a glance. He sat in a chair and offered me one, which looked far too delicate to be sat upon, but I tried it and it held.

"Nando Aguilar, is there any chance that you are a truly honest man?"

What a question! I began to organize my reply.

"Well, if you have to think about it, I suppose you have some doubt. Repeat for me, please, the details of the Medanales raiding party."

So I did.

"And your observation of Perea from the cow pen."

That I told him over again too, this time disclosing the names of the men I had recognized. I saw a flicker of concern in his eyes.

"Now the encounter with Padre Baldonado."

I went over that.

"I take it you don't have fond feelings for this friar?" I hadn't fooled the governor.

"No sir, I don't."

"Explain these feelings please."

I wasn't sure how honesty would serve me here, but I'm not a complex man so I plunged in. "That friar's scary. I don't think he likes me, or any of us. Any chance he gets he tries to shame or intimidate me, and I don't think I'm the only one he does that to."

"Were you at Rosa's the night he asserted his moral authority over her patrons?"

"No sir, I was in Abiquiú, but the story reached there in two days."

107

Anza smiled at the efficiency of communication in his province. "If Padre Baldonado were the only father confessor in Santa Fe, would you confess your sins?"

Oh dear. "No sir, I wouldn't."

"You'd rather risk dying and going to hell with stains on your soul?"

"Yes sir, but maybe only because I'm not dying at present."

Anza laughed. "I take it you'd plan the timing of your death to correspond to the arrival of a different padre?"

"If given the opportunity."

I could tell he was toying with me, but by now I had enough respect for him to know it was with purpose.

Finally he leaned back in his chair, filled his pipe, with punché to my surprise, and the air became acrid with the aroma of illegal, homegrown tobacco.

"I'm going back up north tomorrow," he said. "This last parley was so thoroughly botched that I don't trust anyone else to try to make the next contact. I've got to find the right men among the Comanches to meet with. There are one or two I think could help, and I've got to convince them to talk to me. We're going to put this back together, and I have to let them know that it matters enough that I'm going myself.

"Alcalde Duran will be in charge of Santa Fe while I'm gone, but I need my own eyes here, Nando. I need to find out more about Perea, and I need to know why he led Valdez up that mountain to kill the wrong men. And to be killed. I heard this evening that Captain Valdez died early this morning. With him gone and your brother weeks away from recovery, my staff is gutted. Watch for Perea and keep your eyes open."

"Yes sir, I can do that."

"There are other problems, some of which you seem to have stumbled onto yourself. One of the biggest right now is that your brother is a sitting duck. He'd be helpless if attacked. Keep a close eye on him. Another thing I've got to root out is why are the Apaches disguising themselves as Comanches, as they apparently did when they raided Medanales? You've lived up north, how many years?"

"I'm twenty-two, sir, and I've lived near Abiquiú most of my life."

"Have you ever heard of an Apache being anything other than an Apache? Would an Apache ever deign to look like a Comanche?" he asked.

"I've never known an Apache to pretend to be anything other than he is, except maybe when one makes himself look like a wolf, or like a sheep in a herd. I've never known any to fake being Comanche."

"Who was your mother?" His questions came fast, as though he'd like to catch me off guard.

"My mother is Nan, daughter of Cedro, chief of the Capotes. Ute. She went back to her people five years ago."

"Do you speak that language?"

"I do."

"Any others?"

"Ute's close enough to Comanche that I can follow that too. I have some words of Apache. Navajo is beyond me. So's Latin." I got the feeling from the wry look on his face that he agreed with me there.

"Have you ever lived with your mother's people?"

"Three years ago. After my father died I went to my mother with the news, and I stayed there a year. I took my younger brother back to her. He's still there."

Anza was musing out loud. "This helps. All of this might be very useful to me. You don't, by any chance, read and write?" He looked at me like it was a wild hope.

109

"Only Spanish, sir."

He looked frankly amazed. "Easily?"

I thought of Luz, years ago, in the cold winter rooms of our hacienda, fixing me in her patient gaze as I struggled with words.

"Not at first, but you know my stepmother. She taught me."

He nodded his understanding, then out of the blue, asked, "Do you believe in original sin?"

I snapped my eyes into his, looking directly at him, something we Indios don't often do. I took a chance.

"No."

He scowled at me with such intensity that I wondered if he would summon the padre to punish me. I'd never been flogged, and flogging certainly wouldn't be unheard of for this, but after a long pause he said,

"Good, Nando. I have found an honest man."

So he gave me some instructions, offered me a much better pistol than the antique he'd seen me fiddling with under our cottonwood tree this morning, and set my pay equivalent to a soldier's at thirty pesos a month. In short, I was to get a handle on this mess for him while he was away: the dead palacio guard, the whereabouts of the errant scout, and while I was at it, would I please figure out why his colony was falling apart at the seams, north, east and south. West was still in relatively good shape, but only because so few people lived out there.

"Damn it, Nando, I'm the governor. I can't hang out in the wine shops. I can't loiter in the market. I can't lean on a wall and smoke punché with the soldiers. No one is going to drop little pearls of interesting gossip into my ears by mistake. Do it for me." He pointed with his pipe at a blue-tailed lizard perched on the mantle above the adobe fireplace. "Be like that cagey fellow, Nando, someone nobody notices, but who shows up everywhere. Be my eyes and ears, and listen to the colony for me."

I almost felt sorry for the man. Besides, who'd ever heard of a governor who smoked punché like the rest of us? Maybe he couldn't afford the king's highly taxed tobacco either. He'd grown up on the frontier too, so maybe he just preferred punché.

"Aside from Sebastian, who, by the way, let you in tonight, I'm only going to tell one person for now that you are in my employ, and that's to make it easier for you. Not Carlos, not while he's still laid up anyway. He'd just worry about you. Not Tomás Duran, not either of the padres. Only Luz de Gracia."

I was reassured by the astuteness of his choice. Anybody else I could fool, but not that woman.

III

StaCruz de la Cañada
la Cañada
Sta Clara
S. Ildefonso
Pujuaqui Nambe
Tesuque
Presidio
Alcaldia
Santa Fée
de la Villa de Santa Fée
la Ciénega
Cochiti
Sto Marcos
Galisteo
Sto Domingo
S. Ph.
St Lazaro
huertes
frontera y en
tradas delos
enemigos
Cumanchis

The Patrón

A Hacienda near Santa Fe

He planned to have her this night. Everyone knew it and no one was speaking to him. His wife had withdrawn to her end of the house. The servants were slipping quietly off to their huts, and some had walked all the way back to the village the moment the sun had set. There was a gloomy air of sober judgment and disapproval in the household. The man was disgusted.

Who should care? Why should anyone have a bleeding heart about one Indian girl? Everyone knew that his wife was never well. What was a man supposed to do? Lie with another man like that priest they caught last year over at the mission? The patrón didn't think of himself as a brute. He wasn't going to rape her, but she did belong to him, didn't she? He could demand in good conscience that she submit. Anyway, once she'd had it done right she would come back for more. They all did. They liked it, and they liked getting the babies from him too, the strong, handsome boy babies that the patrón always threw, like any good stud.

He banged his mug down on the wooden table, expecting it to be filled. No one responded. Angrily he rose and went into the kitchen. There wasn't a person in sight. A little warmth still came from the hearth, but the coals were mostly white and no water had been left to heat over them. He picked up the wine jug, but found it empty. It was the last straw.

He went out to the corral, yelling for a stable boy, but no one was there either. Thoroughly cross now, he caught his horse by himself. Even the damned animal was skittish tonight and it took him extra time to force the bit between its teeth. The man's strong thighs clenched the side of the horse as he bent low and whipped it with his quirt. He headed away from his ranch, down the river road toward the pueblo. It was time people discovered what happened when they refused to do the patrón's bidding.

Knowing it was an insolent act, he rode right across the ceremonial ground and then pulled up in front of a multi-storied house near the center of the pueblo. He threw his reins over the rail in front. Without knocking or hesitating, he strode through the door.

The girl sat with her family in the dark beside a small fire on the corner hearth. The man crossed the room and stood in front of her impatiently, his heavy thighs just inches from her face.

"You work for me now. It is the payment. Get your things."

She kept her face down. He saw only the top of her head. Her old grandfather was supposed to be someone important among his own people, but the patrón was pleased to see that he just sat there on his bench like an impotent fool, without seeming to look at the Spaniard. There was total silence in the room and no movement from the girl.

Sick of this, the man grabbed her thin arms and pulled her to her feet. His strong hand seized the hair at the back of her head and pulled her face toward his, so she couldn't avoid looking at him.

"Now!" He yanked her around and walking behind her, pushed her through the door. "Send her things tomorrow!" he ordered as he left.

Lifting her roughly, he set her in front of his saddle. Then he mounted, and clutching the girl by her tunic, turned the horse with his knees and rode out of the pueblo. Galloping up the road, he clamped her young body against his. People watched silently from their rooftops or from inside the dark doorways, but no one intervened. They were all old, or very young. All the healthy men, all her brothers, were away, laboring for Spanish landowners.

He avoided the main house. He certainly wouldn't go near his wife's room. He was angry there was no dinner laid out for him, but he found a jug of wine. He grabbed it in one hand, held fast to the Indian girl with the other, and ushered her roughly to the empty cottage where travelers sometimes stayed, and there, throughout a long night, he taught her everything he knew about love. Which was nothing.

Pamela Christie

Worth Two Good Horses Each

Sunday I went with Luz and the girls to Mass at the parish church. This was one of the special days of procession and the governor, in full parade dress, was flanked by his officers and a smartly turned out squadron of presidial soldiers, some of whom held a silk canopy that shaded him as he walked between the churches. They had the tall cross out, and along with both friars, the sacristans and altar boys, and a parade of young girls, they were bringing the icon of The Virgin, Nuestra Señora, to the old chapel in the field where De Vargas first camped when he retook the capitol.

The procession was impressive, the musicians almost in key, and we all lined the sunny street, eager to catch a glimpse of La Señora and of Anza, a governor we actually liked. Sticking to the tradition of this parade, despite the recent assaults, made us all feel a little better, and I saw that the Medanales people were on the sidelines too, enjoying the spectacle. I couldn't believe I'd sat and sparred with this elegant commander

118

in his living room last night, and certainly he showed no sign, as he walked by without giving a flicker of recognition.

When the ceremony was over, the women and I went home for our luncheon, a young, roast goat today. I had seen Sebastian leaving our house last night, just as I returned from the palacio, and a slightly elevated deference toward me from my stepmother indicated that she knew of my employment. Finally I would become a productive citizen. She also was celebrating the additional thirty pesos to our household, judging by the feast that awaited us.

After lunch, when the rest of the family drifted off for siesta, I wandered back to the plaza, thinking it was time I started leaning on posts and overhearing gossip. I got there just as Anza was leaving on his conciliatory mission to the north. He was taking advantage of the plaza being nearly empty on the warm Sunday afternoon when most people napped.

He was considerably less ostentatious in his campaign clothes and he'd gotten rid of the fancy hat. His cohort was pared down for efficiency, just five men for now. They left by the Santa Cruz road, looking purposeful, and were obviously eager to let their horses run once they were past the town. For a moment I wished I were going with them. This would be an exciting mission, and besides, I needed to get up to Santa Cruz and get my horse back. It was no small honor, however, to be Anza's "eyes and ears," so I ignored my usual urge to rush for the country.

Realizing there wasn't much point in being a spy right now, since everyone was sleeping, I went back to the house, got my fishing pole and some hooks and, borrowing the mule from Luz, rambled out along the river. There were a few pools about a mile below the plaza and it might be warm enough for a swim if the fishing didn't pan out.

I'd been there an hour, maybe more, waiting for a trout to notice the worm I'd dangled into a deep hole. I think I slept some, lulled by the sun and the newborn insects humming around me, but I woke up when I heard horses coming. I shoved my hat low onto my brow, pulled the edge of my manta across my face and sat spraddled there, for all the world like a dozing fisherman without a thought in his brain.

A string of loaded mules came at a fast trot down the trail beside the river, led by several men on horseback. On the backs of the mules rode Indian women and children, their hands bound with rawhide. There was also a small group of Indian men being run behind the mules, horsemen lashing at them with their riding crops. This party was in a hurry and was not traveling by the main road that would have taken them through town. The captives were hot and harried and the running men neared exhaustion.

Talk about being in the wrong place at the wrong time! I tried to look innocuous, but a Spaniard rode right up to me and poked his quirt into my shoulder. I had my manta up over my face so he only saw my eyes. Just as well. I was once again face to face with the handsome Ramón, but this time he had sweat streaming down his face and patches of moisture staining his leather vest. There was no way he wanted to be seen by me or anybody from town right now. He pulled his arm back and struck me a stinging blow across the face with his quirt.

"Keep your mouth shut!" he commanded, then satisfied by my instantly cowering manner, pulled his horse back, glared at me once more, then cantered to catch up with the now disappearing slave caravan.

My manta saved both my identity and my face. Ramón hadn't recognized me at all. There was just a sharp lick of pain at the edge of my cheekbone under one eye. I found a streak of blood on my hand when I reached up, but it didn't seem important, because now I knew the truth about Ramón, and also I had seen that one of the Spaniards, a fat, unpleasant looking one, was riding Rosinante. My horse was supposed to be stabled with the military up at Santa Cruz, and yet here she was, being ridden way too hard, miles from where I'd entrusted her to the garrison. This was foul, all of it, and my red mare was a captive too, being driven south down the river trail as fast as she could go.

My sadness for the Indians welled up again, as it had in Abiquiú when I saw the slave children brought in, and a quick, hot hatred flared in me at the Spaniards who perpetrated this. Yet, I had seen the women raped and scalped by Indians, lying naked in the road above Medanales, and I was part Spanish, part native, myself. What in God's name was I supposed to think?

The only thing that was clear to me was I wanted my horse back. I gave them ten minutes, dabbed some mud on my face wound, retrieved the mule from the thicket, and rode off, having no trouble following their tracks.

There are rules about enslaving Indians and people at least pretend to follow them. I doubted this was the case here, since these men were avoiding the village and in such a rush. I was pretty certain where they were heading. Ramón's father had a small ranch in La Ciénega, just above the swamps. It was only one of his holdings – the main one was down by Bernalillo – but this ranch was convenient to Santa Fe and his family sometimes used it in the summer to escape the pestilence the heat brought to the town.

I rode behind their dust a good way along the trail, then cut west to the base of the hills and approached their hacienda from behind, through a short canyon. At first I lingered high above the house, looking down onto the wide roofs, figuring out how to steal my own horse. I'd left the mule at the top of the canyon and hid myself in the scrub oak. Its thin, transparent leaves, just out this week, barely offered shade. On the other hand, they didn't impede my view.

The Spaniards had penned the Indios in a corral. Men on horseback patrolled with guns and whips. The late afternoon sun burned down on the exhausted prisoners. Some slept on the ground, while others leaned against the rails, motionless. They had shared a pot of food that now lay empty on the dirt. A boy went over to the wooden trough and drank from the muddy water. A baby cried.

I saw Ramón come out of the long adobe ranch house and shade his eyes from the lowering sun. He scanned the yard and the corral. Seeming satisfied, he went back inside. There was no longer the faintest doubt in my mind that the alcalde's son was a slave dealer. I realized I had been expecting to see Lorenzo here too, but there was no sign of him.

Was this Ramón's own operation? His father couldn't possibly know. Certainly there was no sign that the alcalde was here. No doubt Ramón's men were only waiting until dark to move the slaves on to the south. Whether they were headed all the way to the mines of Chihuahua I didn't dare guess. Nobody would live long in the mines, even if they did manage to survive the journey.

I tried with little success to find comfort in the thought that probably only the males were headed for the mines. A young Indian woman was worth at least two good horses in trade, so the women and their children probably would be sold nearby, in Albuquerque, or Socorro. I recalled that the Durans operated a mine over by Cerrillos that was just beginning to prove out, but I doubted Ramón would be so stupid as to use these slaves close by, because this was definitely illegal.

After sunset the action picked up. I kept my eye on Rosinante grazing with the other horses in the curved field between the house and river. Here was a dilemma. I was perfectly entitled to my own horse. She had been left in care of the garrison when they changed me over to an army horse last week, but how she'd come into the hands of a private citizen moving slaves through the territory needed explaining.

Could I just sally in and say, "Hey that's my horse. I'll be taking her home now?" My hand moved to the cut on my face. Best to wait for dark, slip in, steal her back and cut out of there, but then what would happen when Duran recognized me riding Rosinante in town? I decided that could be a problem for another day and I got ready to sneak down and liberate her as soon as it was dark. It would give me a chance to get near the captives, too.

I had time to work out a plan while the slow business of shutting down the hacienda for the night went on beneath me and the sunset irradiated the sky. Just before nightfall, Ramón's men rounded up the horses, including my own. They tied them to the outside of the corral where the Indians were held. Protected by twilight now, I felt my way down the hill and crept in, mingling with animals in the field. There were enough men loading pack mules, retying prisoners and watering horses, that a few moments after the darkness became total, I was able to walk to the corral, lean on the bars and start stroking my mare. When the signal came to move out, I jumped up on Rosinante's back. Dear Jesus, let it work!

In the dark they thought I was a member of their party and I took hold of a rawhide line that someone thrust at me. To avoid drawing attention to myself, I grabbed the rope and jerked it hard to get the mules moving.

Our direction was south and the caravan moved without haste now; even the slavers were tired after their rush to the safety of the hacienda. In a few minutes, I had my end of things under control and was able to look around for the fat Spaniard to see if he'd been inconvenienced by my reclaiming my own animal, but he was nowhere in the group. That was one piece of luck.

I was going to need more to get away with this. When the caravan had settled in and was moving well, I let Rosinante drift back until I came alongside one of the captive Indian women. I rode next to her mule for several minutes. She kept her head down, her hate palpable, but that helped my plan.

"Keep looking down, I need to talk to you," I whispered in Ute. She gave no response.

"Do you understand me?"

I saw her head nod, just slightly. "Ute or Comanche?"

She whispered the word for Comanche in that tongue.

"Be ready," and I leaned over as though I was checking the knots and drew the blade of my knife through the rawhide loop that bound her wrist. I held the severed ends and slipped them into her hand so no one could tell she was now cut loose. Gradually, I did the same for two other women who were tied this way. There wasn't much more I could do without risking being noticed by the men around me, but in time I returned to the first woman and slipped the haft of my long-bladed knife into her hand. I felt a little pressure from her fingers, which I took for thank you.

We were entering the narrow part of the river canyon where it begins its steep, rocky tumble onto the plains below. Our party was spread out in a thin line through the black gorge.

I was on the lookout for a side-canyon that I knew entered around here somewhere, and as soon as I made out its boulder-filled mouth, I started a ruckus. I let loose a high-pitched scream like a man hit by an arrow, whirled around and slapped at the mules' rumps to drive them into the side-canyon, then tugged sharply on Rosinante's reins until I was practically hoisting her up the canyon wall. Scared to death, she leapt up the thin band of rim rock and opened into a gallop, stretching herself to the maximum.

I could hear the commotion of stampeding animals, yelling men and musket fire reverberating inside the canyon. I had little doubt that the Comanche prisoners would make good use of the confusion, and that at least some would get away in the night. The women had a fair chance, being mounted and unbound and in possession of a knife. They'd have to keep their babies quiet, but Indian women are good at that.

As I sped away, I wondered what had come over me. Was I possessed? Maybe these were legitimate captives, truly heathen, maybe they even belonged to my new boss and I'd just ruined my position with him. But damn it, hadn't I learned all I needed to know about Ramón by now? I hoped to God that I wasn't the only person escaping from that bastard as fast as possible across the plains tonight.

Rosinante was pleased to have me back on top of her again, though probably because I weighed a hundred pounds less than the last man who had been riding her. I hadn't forgotten that I had Luz's mule tied up above the hacienda, so I rode back there and, from then on, with an animal in tow, made slower time. I wondered if what I'd done would fit the governor's concept of the work he wanted me to do. He might not be pleased, but I was feeling good after my first full day on the job.

I got home just before light cracked the horizon and the town's burros started to bray. After putting Rosinante away inside the shed, I lay down on the bed beside my injured brother and fell asleep at once.

I woke up falling down the gap between the bed and the wall. I had been shoved farther and farther over until half of me was in the slot. I pulled my numb arm out, pushed myself up and looked over at my greedy, thoughtless brother. He was still asleep, squished into the middle, because now there were three men in our bed. The newest lifted himself onto his elbow and grinned at me.

"Francisco!"

I couldn't believe it! He was supposedly in Mexico, studying. We hadn't had word of him in a year. I leaned out over Carlos and slugged Francisco on the arm. Though I would have liked to sleep until noon, now I was too excited to even consider it. I crawled off the end of the bed, restored the covers to Carlos, and with my long-lost brother following me, went out into the bright May morning and watched him give his mother a heart attack. Or so she pretended.

We got Carlos up and helped him hobble into the sunlight, and while wolfing down eggs, chile and tortillas at the table in the garden, Francisco began his tale. He had run out of funds at the University. Moran, who had backed him in his studies to become a surveyor, had died unexpectedly, and that put an end to his education. No loss; he hated the school anyway. This all sounded very typical of my dazzling, changeable brother.

He didn't have enough money for his supplies and a horse, so he'd gotten his passage up here by assisting the new mapmaker, who traveled with the caravan as far as Chihua-hua. It didn't take long for the man to find out that Francisco hadn't gotten the hang of surveying yet, but they kept him on as an able-bodied, armed man. The caravan was sorely under-protected, the usual twenty soldiers reduced to eight, plus a half-dozen barely trained Indian auxiliaries.

"It was a horrible trip. The attacks were constant, even below El Paso. At first they ran off livestock. Twice we had to travel ahead to the next outpost and borrow animals to bring the carts on farther. Near Robledo there was a vicious battle. That's where the new padre died. I felt sorry for him. He was younger than I, still sort of soft inside. He actually went out from our group to try to talk and they just cut him down."

Luz shook her head. Francisco's voice had become quiet. He had looked pretty good to me at first glance this morning, but now I could see he was exhausted.

"From then on we only had the animals that were under us, a short string of mules and just four carts out of the twenty three that had started! Fortunately some of these had food, but all the hard goods, most of the provisions, and the wag-ons with the steel and weapons were lost to us. The Apaches driving them away looked like drunken charioteers. I doubt they'd ever handled a team before."

This was horrible news. I realized I was lucky to have this half-brother of mine sitting here with us, as the young padre's wasn't the only death among the people traveling north. Two of the auxiliaries had died in the same attack as the padre, and also a woman died giving birth. The baby hadn't survived ei-ther. Our colony sometimes waited a year between shipments of its vital supplies. I wondered why this one had been so undermanned.

"Was it always Apaches?" I asked.

"Always, and madder than ever. Once we got to Socorro the violence ended, but because we failed to bring much of anything to you, we were miserable this last week coming up the road."

"God brought you here safely, Francisco," said Luz, "And we're used to doing without. Maybe the grandees aren't. They'll miss their Belgian linens and their imported shoes, but we've become pretty good at getting by."

That prompted Francisco to lift from his bag a linen package that he handed to his mother. We knew what it was: chocolate! Many egg-shaped balls of it. We weren't going to be reduced to drinking brewed weeds every morning.

"Thank you, thank you!" she twinkled at him. "Don't tell anybody, or they'll all be coming over."

"No. You'd even get the governor. Most of his supplies went west with the Apaches too. Here, I've got a little sugar, not much, but enough for a while."

Then he proffered a flat wooden box, solid, just over a foot square. He pulled it out of a sheepskin wrapping. "Somehow this made it," he said, putting it carefully in his mother's lap. "I know you like miracles."

She held it awkwardly between her hands, wondering how to open a present that was nailed shut. I borrowed Francisco's knife and pried off the narrow top board. Francisco took over then, and with utmost caution pulled something flat, hard, and delicate out from another skin wrapping. We watched, fascinated. It was a piece of glass.

Luz took it from him and held it to her face, peered through it, turned it over and over in her hands, and then went over to the wall of her house and held it approximately at the place she would like it. On the wall facing the river, looking south toward the sun, we had placed pieces of translucent mica into spaces we'd left between some adobes. They gave enough light that we could see a bit in the room when the door was closed. Now there would be good light, lots of it, and we could even look out. There was only one other building in Santa Fe with real glass in its windows and that was the palacio, which had just three windows on the side of the governor's office.

"Some glass was being shipped up to Duran for his home. I bought this single piece off the merchant just as we were leaving, and kept it with my things, nursing it all the way up here. Then Duran's whole load went west with the Apaches. As far as I know this is the only piece that made it." He smiled. "Who needs glass in a tepee? The way the raiders were driving, it shattered within a mile, anyway."

Luz chuckled. "Better than the mayor. As good as the governor. We Aguilars are something!" She turned to me. "Nando, can you make a frame for it? We'll cut out a hole in the adobe wall and put it in. We probably need to make a grill for it; we wouldn't want it to break."

"Sure," I said, knowing just how lousy my carpentry was. I watched as she rewrapped it carefully. I was deciding whether I should tell them about last night. After all, I was only fishing and then trying to get my horse back. I wasn't out on king's business, so this wouldn't necessarily have to be kept secret.

"I need a little help," I finally said to my brothers. What a luxury to have them here to say that to! In spite of the condition each was in, they tried to look willing, so I told them about my trip south on the river, about watching the captives in the corral, and, in the end, ruining the slavers' plans.

"I have to come up with a reason to have found Rosinante. It has to be a good one, and I want everyone in town to hear it. Ramón Duran's got to know I stumbled on my horse here in town. No way do I want that arrogant bully to find out I'm the one who turned his slaves loose."

Francisco leaned back on his bench and began to weave this yarn about how a little red pony had attached itself to their worn-out party last night, running loose, and apparently aiming, on its own, generally in the direction of town. It had wandered into the stables at the palacio in the middle of the night, following the remnants of the caravan.

"In fact, I'll drop her off after dark," he offered.

"I think there's a man in there who can help see that it gets done right," I added, thinking of Sebastian.

That arranged, I went to feed my fine red beast and pulled more rails up, so she would stay hidden in the dark seclusion of the shed for the daylight hours.

The Cold and Tumbling River

*L*uz insisted it would be grand if we celebrated Francisco's safe return by attending Mass together at mid-day and I acquiesced, thinking that it would do little harm to have the town see me behaving properly, and that Father Baldonado might even back off a little on his assumption about me. We didn't want anyone to know the shape Carlos was in, so we got Baz to stay with him while we went to church. That way the servant girls could come along with us.

More people than usual were at Mass, including the alcalde and his wife. People had lost so much in the caravan, I think they felt they'd better put more effort into praying for the future.

The sun blinded me when I came out of the dark church. I was achingly tired after my wild night freeing slaves, so I took a moment and leaned against the church wall. I found that I was sharing it with the soldier's girlfriend, whom Rosa had comforted in the bar the other night.

Paulina was doing better now, though it was a thin veneer of strength. She was shy, but I could tell she recognized me, so I started some small talk and in a few minutes she opened up a bit. She remembered I'd been in Rosa's kitchen. Then I, too, recalled something she'd said that had been bothering me.

"That night you said something about the padre, like he'd told your soldier not to join the militia."

She looked wary and dodged the question in the best Catholic tradition. "Oh, Baldonado, he has an opinion about everything."

I laughed and for a moment wondered if he'd pried them apart in one of Rosa's beds. I think she read my mind, because she shook her head, no, and then luckily for me, decided to talk.

"Before Marcos joined up, he went and saw the priest. Baldonado had been the padre in the village near his farm for a short time. Marcos told him he wanted to join the militia, particularly now that things were coming to a head. All I re-member is the padre told him to forget it, to stay on the farm."

"Sounds like a padre. Did Marcos pay any attention to his advice?"

She shook her head. "Baldonado told him the peace treaty would never work and any man signing up now would surely be thrown into the worst battles our colony's ever known. I know it made Marcos think his decision over again, because he already was having a hard time believing the Comanches could be our friends. But Marcos really needed to get away from home. Their farm was too small, he had older brothers who'd inherit long before he would, and all the work he did never got him anywhere."

Tears flooded her eyes, as she remembered where joining the militia had gotten him. "Normally the presidio soldiers stand guard and they're used to it. They know what to look for, but most of them were out in Santa Cruz or up by Taos. The militia was asked to help out, just for a couple of nights. I know Marcos talked to the padre again that day, and the priest got really mad and told him he was a fool if he went on guard duty, and he was right because Marcos wound up dead!"

Now tears ran down her cheeks and I looked around to find a girlfriend of hers, my stepmother, anybody, to help her out. But there was only me, so I put my arm around her and got her settled down a little. She slumped against me, crying against my shoulder. I found once more that I had a knack with weeping women.

Damned if the big padre wasn't striding toward us over the packed dirt in front of the church.

"Fornicating dog!" I let the girl go and faced him, steeling myself, while still trying to look appropriately deferential.

"Right here in front of the Holy Cross!" He grabbed Paulina by both shoulders and shoved her away. Then, concentrating on me, he exploded with rage.

"Always this one! This little half-breed bastard! No regard for the laws! No respect for the righteous rule of the Mother Church! This is holy ground!" He had my manta in his hands and was trying to wrench it off me, as though to reveal my evil soul to the whole world. Why me? All I was doing was comforting an unhappy girl.

"On your knees! Beg forgiveness!" He shoved me down, making a spectacle of me in front of the dozen people still talking quietly near the church. I was embarrassed to see that the alcalde watched too, but he soon turned and departed, clearly not wanting to become involved.

This priest was a lunatic! But he held power here. He could make life very difficult for me, for Luz de Gracia, for all of us. I went down on my knees, begged his pardon, began reciting the Creed as fast as I could, and wondered where on earth Francisco was when I needed him. I grabbed the man's knotted fist and kissed it, then scrambled to my feet, pulling back from him as fast as I could in case he kicked me. Clearly I was anathema to him, but I had no idea why. I hurried through the churchyard gate. I didn't need to look back to know he was standing there, self-righteous and enraged, glaring after me.

I ran past the soldier's girlfriend, who had the decency to linger behind the wall to make sure I was all right. I rolled my eyes back toward the priest, twiddled my finger around my head so she'd catch my drift, and then made haste for home.

I was barely at the turn to our road when Luz came flying at me, her skirts at her knees, thin arms grasping for me.

"Where have you been? Carlos is gone!"

Carlos gone? A rush of hot fear melted my muscles and stopped me in my tracks. I looked down at her, stunned.

"Gone? How can he be gone? He can't even walk!"

I ran beside her back to the house. The yard was a mess, his chair overturned, our belongings strewn on the dirt: bedding, plates, our few precious books open on the ground, their leaves turning in the breeze. I cast a look into the gloom of the house. Inside was chaos, everything flung out of chests. Carlos was absolutely not there.

"Francisco ran to the palacio for help." Her voice was nearly a shriek. Horses' hooves had churned the ground, but a quick glance at the shed showed me a gleam off Rosinante's eye.

She was still hidden away. Oh my brother! I was supposed to be protecting you, but hadn't I left Baz with him?

"Baz? What about Baz! He was supposed to be watching!"

"He's nowhere," Luz asserted. "Something bad has happened! No seven-year-old, not even Baz, could stop it!"

I cut for sign like a good dog, quartering the ground of our garden. Twenty feet out near the corn patch, I noticed grass bent down, shining a paler green. I ran over and there at my feet black blood pooled on the ground among crushed spring weeds. Luz was right behind me, knowing I had caught a trail. Terrified of what we would find, we followed the marks where something had been dragged along the dirt path, down to the river. Right there at the edge, among little round stones, the trail ended. Beside it was a scrape of mud, the print of a man's boot and nothing more. Obscenely sparkling water moved rapidly in front of us.

"You go up, I'll go down!" I waded into the river, mindless of my church clothes. Luz hitched her skirt above her knees and ran in and out of the water, using the hard ground wherever she could to make time. The servant girls caught up with us.

"One of you run, get Francisco here, and you, stay with the Señora!" I called out as I moved away from them down the stream.

Oh my beautiful brother, Carlos, where are you? Please be alive. Be alive! I prayed hard as I climbed over fallen branches, around tumbled rocks. The prayer words poured out of me, audibly, on top of my straining breath. I passed two other farms, still staying by the river, ignoring a chance to get onto the cart path. My brother had been heaved into the flowing stream, now made faster and deeper than its usual puny self by the spring runoff. In the shadows, it was gray-blue with snowmelt, and churning. Yesterday I had tried to swim, but it had been brutally cold. My mouth was dry as a communion wafer. Choking on fear, I ran on and I found him.

He lay belly down at the river's edge, his arm swaying gently in the moving water, so that he seemed to be pulsing, breathing. Sunlight and moisture gleamed in his long brown hair. He looked peaceful, his cheeks soft like a sleeping boy's. I was scared to come near. I knew my brother was dead. One side of his face lay in the mud and the shallow water lapped at his mouth and nose. Blood spread out on the little waves.

I was on my knees at his side, crying in the sunlight. I reached down to move his face away from the intruding water but I was afraid to touch him. Perhaps I had cried out when I spotted him, I don't remember, but all at once everyone was around me – Francisco, three soldiers, the girls and Luz.

"Get his face, get his face up!" She shouted commands, still running toward us. What use, dear mother, I murmured, but she'll know all too soon. Yet I obeyed her. I did reach down then and took his head in both my hands. A sense of life sprang into my fingers. He had warmth still and his neck was supple. Now I bent to my task, arranged him anew, carefully inching his face back from the water. My tears streamed. This miracle, this miracle of life, here, when I had thought him gone!

His head had a jagged cut above the ear. Blood oozed red and sticky down my hands. Luz knelt beside me in the mud. Then she sat down half in, half out of the water and we rested his head gently in her lap.

"He lives."

The quiet certitude of her voice awoke me. I came back from the realm of terror.

"Friends, get a litter. Is the surgeon in the garrison?" People started to move. "Blankets!" Francisco was also on his knees, feeling the broken body of his big brother. Carlos' shoulder was knocked out of its socket. He had a vicious blow to his head and his earlier arm wound was bleeding, his bandaged foot akimbo.

"I hope he'll stay unconscious for a while," his mother prayed.

"Hopefully he'll regain consciousness. This is a hideous wound." These words I delivered privately to Francisco, who nodded agreement.

It took over an hour, but we got him home. The surgeon came and worked with Luz, sewing and wrapping wounds. I had to admire how she handled the surgeon, making him feel like the man in charge when she only used him as an assistant. The neighbors watched us, some standing right inside the house, others staying out in the garden. Women gently picked up our things and set them beside the door.

No one could believe an injured man had been attacked resting in his own garden. It had the appearance of a burglary gone awry, but I hadn't had a chance to see if anything was missing. Then I remembered Baz.

The cry went out again, "Where is he?" People spilled out of our yard to search for the boy. Some thought he would be hiding; others expected the worst. I would join them as soon as Carlos was stabilized, but I took aside some men from our street and spoke to them hurriedly. They moved off toward the river the way we had just searched.

Two people showed up at our gate simultaneously. First came Baz's old grandmother, scared to ask, scared to know. She trembled all over when she came into the room where they were doctoring my brother. Right behind her was the alcalde, Tomás Duran, who showed his concern by hurrying to our house. He appraised the situation – the torn-up rooms and my unconscious brother still bleeding from his head.

"I am so very sorry, Señora." He tried to address my stepmother as a friend, but being a politician he couldn't help but make a speech.

"I will see that the resources of our government are turned immediately toward apprehending your son's assailant. This is a terrible deed, to attack a convalescing officer in the king's army. These are hard days for our town."

He turned to Baz's old grandmother and even took her hand.

"We will find Baz. From what I know of him, the boy is not likely to be subdued!" Fortunately the alcalde's visit was short, for he was irking me and there was much I had to do.

Right after he left, Carlos mercifully regained consciousness, spoke a few words, then fell into what seemed a deep sleep. The whole household relaxed a notch, but I couldn't. I had to find Baz. I needed to track the horses and find out which bastard had done this. Francisco, Luz and I would have to post a continuous guard against further hurt to Carlos. I had no idea where Perea had gone, and that had been Anza's specific charge to me: find him, keep an eye on him. The governor wanted to know why his whole suffering colony was under attack. By now I had the same question, but about my own family. This had gotten personal.

Was it yesterday, could it have been only last night, that I watched illegal slave traders sneak around the outskirts of town? That good-looking rich boy, who busted up the soldiers at the corrals and extricated Perea, also bought and sold human beings. There was no longer any doubt that Ramón was the man to watch if one wanted to learn what was going wrong around here.

Soon now, I needed to spirit Rosinante back into the palacio so that I could stumble innocently across her tomorrow morning and make sure that whip-crazy slaver didn't link me to last night.

My big brother, whom I was supposed to have protected, was smashed up and in agony. My normally tough stepmother was nearly done in with the terror of the afternoon, and I was wretchedly tired after only two hours of sleep last night and the wild undertaking along the river. Furthermore, a mean and angry priest had manhandled and humiliated me in front of half the town at lunchtime today, and if that wasn't sufficient trouble, I was hungry enough to eat a skunk and no one in our house had given a thought to cooking dinner.

Rosa solved that last one in five minutes, when she and the soldier's girlfriend came right into the house without knocking and set a big bowl of stew and a napkin full of hot tortillas on the table. I knew Luz didn't associate with Rosa for obvious reasons, but she looked up from where she sat beside Carlos and said a genuine thank you. I think we all looked pretty beat up, because the two women filled our plates for us and put them into our hands. A bowl still lay on the floor, and Rosa just wiped it off with her apron and loaded it up for me with stew and a tortilla to soak up the juice.

Just before dark, Francisco came back from looking for Baz. We brought him his dinner and listened while he explained. The conclusion was not good. Three horsemen had entered our yard; one man stayed mounted the whole time. Baz's footprints were scattered among those of the two who had attacked Carlos. One wore leather boots, the other moccasins. They found prints of Baz's bare feet right up to where Carlos had been thrown in the water. Then there were no more signs of the child.

The horses were shod in the Spanish manner, and while they'd found where all three rode out of the river upstream by the first mill, their tracks mingled with too many others on the road there. So they returned to search the river by our house in case Baz had been treated the same way as Carlos. The men walked the banks far below where we'd found my brother. Baz, smaller and lighter, would be carried much further downstream. They found no sign of him.

They finally decided that the attackers must have taken him away on horseback. Baz, having his own special charm, might convince them to let him go, but I feared not, as he had been a witness to the attack on my brother. Prisoner, hostage, no matter, it was better than being a body washed up on a riverbank. I planned to spend a lot more time in search of that boy, but night had fallen and I needed to be here guarding Carlos.

While Rosa was still at the house, I left for a few moments and hurried up to the palacio, where luckily I found Sebastian at the gate again. He caught my drift at once and I got Francisco to take Rosinante up there in the dark.

It was all I could do to stay awake to make sure it went all right, but when Francisco got home he told me that Sebastian took the horse from him as though it was routine, leading Rosinante away to the stables at once. I was glad to have that problem solved. Anza told me I could rely on Sebastian. I wondered, how much did he know about me?

We had relinquished the bed to Carlos, so I unrolled sheepskin mats on the floor. Luz wanted to sit up with him, but I talked her out of it, insisting I'd be right beside him all night. I practically had to carry her to the rickety bed in her own room.

We'd picked up most of our scattered possessions. Only a few pieces were broken and it seemed nothing had been taken. Just before going to bed, Luz opened the chest in her room and found the silver goblet still there, along with our brass candlesticks and miraculously, the precious windowpane, safe in its sheepskin package. She looked at me and said with conviction, "They didn't come here to steal. They came to murder Carlos." Her assessment was the same as mine.

We may have been on duty, but we certainly weren't awake. It was still pitch black when Carlos fixed that. He woke up with a curse and a yell of pure terror. He tore off his covers and knocked a water jug onto the floor. Soaking wet, I woke up fast. Francisco got hit too, so both of us were at Carlos' side, holding and calming him. I scarcely knew where to grip him for all his bandaged parts. Francisco lit a candle and we managed to settle our brother down. I was so relieved to see him awake that I didn't realize how awful he must feel, suddenly aware of the shape he was in. We brought him more water and I used some to wipe his face. He lay back on his pillow, wincing as his head made contact. Then he babbled, "Three men. Rode in. Knocked me out of the chair. Boots, kicking me. I tried to fight. Foot didn't hold. A rifle, swinging at me. Dragged me toward the river. Stuff crashing in the house. Baz jumped them, crazy, yelling."

Francisco looked at me meaningfully. Good one, our Baz.

"An old man grabbed the horses, pulled them right over me, stepped on me. Baz kicking and fighting. Indian grabbed him. Rifle butt clubbing me. I remember . . ." here he stopped and didn't go on for a while. Then his voice came back to him.

141

"Cold water. Tumbling. Couldn't stop, couldn't grab hold. Baz screaming. Where's Baz?"

I knew we shouldn't be letting him talk. Luz would kill us, but her room was on the other side of the sala, so maybe she wouldn't hear us.

"Carlos, enough. Enough. Take it easy. You're alive. You're here with us." Francisco held his hand and soothed him.

I leaned over. "Carlos, *why* are you still alive?" Francisco looked at me like I was crazy.

"Weren't trying to kill me. Trying to tie me, trying to haul me off. Baz wrecked their plans. Where's Baz?" His voice was so low I could barely hear him, but he was coherent.

"Indians, or Spanish?" I pressed.

"Yes," was what he replied just as he lost consciousness again.

Whatever You Want With Her

After the grueling night taking care of Carlos, it was hard to want to playact, but I had no choice. While it was still early morning I made myself as conspicuous as possible, lolling about the sunny plaza, chatting with the women selling goods under the portál, as though yesterday's events were the last thing on my mind. It wasn't long before I heard my name called.

"Nando! Get over here! I've got something you're going to want!" Big Sebastian was bellowing across eighty feet of marketplace.

"What could you have that I'd ever want, Sebastian?" I yelled back at him and grinned for all the world to see.

"Your poky little horse is here!" He was calling out the news so at least thirty people heard it. "Came in the other night, tagging along behind the caravan."

We were closer now, but still blaring at each other.

"Glad to know the government can hold up its end of a deal! What kind of shape's she in?"

"Tired as heck, looks like she's been dragged all over the province." And so the whole town was informed I'd just been happily reunited with Rosinante.

In a moment, we were inside the palacio's main courtyard and no longer on stage. Much more quietly he said, "And Perea's back. He was behind you on the plaza, sitting on a bench under the east portál."

"Thank you and thank you," I said. "Don't you need to pee too?" I veered toward the latrine.

At first he must have thought me rude, but the light dawned, and he chuckled as we meandered over to the corner. So we got some minutes alone and I told him about Ramón and the slave train, and the action the previous night south of the alcalde's hacienda.

"That puts him out of range of your brother the next day."

"Who?"

"Ramón and his cronies."

I thought about that for a minute.

"You'd think so, but I suppose it still could be possible, particularly if the slaves did get away and his mission was aborted. Do you think he would dare do that to Carlos?"

Sebastian was pensive. "I don't know. I can't imagine why anyone would do that. All I can figure is there's at least a chance he suspected it was you out there in the canyon, but why that would make him brutalize your brother I don't know. From what you told Anza before he left, it looks like there's a connection between Perea and Ramón, and we already know we don't trust Perea. Those two bear watching."

"I'm beginning to gather that's my job," I said. "It's been hard to get around to doing it though, with all that's happened."

"Whether by mistake or on purpose, you seem to keep running into all the players, Nando. Let's go get your horse."

Rosa's wasn't the only wine shop in town. There was another one that no rico like Ramón would ever dream of entering. Its clientele was mostly transient, the best of them the Mexicans who came up with the caravans. Soldiers would go there too, because the rotgut they served would, for the price, speed through the bloodstream much faster than Rosa's. You could get your gourd or wineskin filled to carry out. Men just stood up at a counter. There were no amenities like tables and chairs. I think the proprietor didn't really want anyone staying too long.

I tried to act like I was just out "taking the air," except I was holding my breath. I watched where I put my feet in the smelly side alley as I walked by the place. I was looking for Perea, but I'd been unable to turn him up all day. It occurred to me that he probably suspected he was being watched, so I lingered here and there, back tracked, and walked in circles for a while, trying to locate him. No luck.

After sneaking around all day I realized I'd overdone it, because when I found him at dusk he was completely careless of who might spot him and certainly had no interest whatsoever in me. He curved out of the bar clutching a wineskin and headed for the river. An unappealing looking militiaman stumbled along beside him. He reminded me of a lost puppy trying to attach himself to a man who wasn't at all sure he wanted a dog.

Perea remained self-assured. Without looking around or waiting to see if anyone followed him, he strolled down to the river, took the little path that started at the ford and sat down on a boulder. He leaned back on a shelf of rock and began his drinking. It was easy for me to wait and watch him from a pile of brush and fallen trees at the edge of the river. The man seemed arrogantly at ease and it was clear he intended to put away a fair slug of wine on this pretty May night. He occasionally allowed the lost puppy a squirt.

"I'll pay you back," the recruit whined. "As soon as they pay me."

"You'll wait a while for that," Perea asserted. "Your money went west with the Apaches." Then he gave the man another shot at the skin to show he was big-hearted after all.

"When are you heading out?" Perea asked the young soldier.

"They say we're here for a while. To back up the presidio, do guard duty for them."

"The presidio can't even post its own guard?" Perea asked with a sneer.

"A group of soldiers were detailed south to see if they could pick up any remnants of the caravan. The ones that weren't shot up near Taos are still in Santa Cruz. I guess all that leaves them short-handed enough so that they promised us actual money if we stayed."

"You believe them?"

"What else can I do?"

"You can go home and get your crops going. The bosses are just stringing you along."

"Hell, I'd rather hang out in town, be around the garrison. Can I have some more of that?"

Perea passed him the skin.

"Are the other volunteers staying on?" he asked.

"Just about everybody. It's too rough now for farming up north, and it looks like under Anza things are about to get good for the militia. He's giving out horses, he's promised pay. I think this Comanche thing is a big deal to him. I heard he thinks he's actually going to pull them in this year."

"Who told you that?" Perea asked.

"Everyone here knows it, and word's getting around. More men are coming in to join up every day."

"So it doesn't scare them that the volunteer got killed?"

"Most of the new ones hadn't heard, but my crew figured it was just a one-shot deal. Someone had it in for Marcos. He gambled a lot."

"Everyone in Santa Fe gambles a lot. What difference does that make?"

The volunteer shrugged. "Marcos was green at it. Got lucky once and then thought he couldn't lose. He was going under fast."

"Well, I guess that could explain it," Perea said, "but you don't usually get an axe in your skull for gambling." He slumped lower onto the ground and took another long pull from the skin. Then he extracted a second wineskin from under his jacket.

The militiaman's eyes brightened. "Someone's paying you pretty darn well. Where are you getting all that money?" he asked.

"None of your goddamn business." Perea's wine was making him surly, but the puppy kept nipping at him.

"I heard you called it wrong up there on the mountain. I heard some of the soldiers were trying to get you."

"You don't know shit, man. They didn't get me, did they?"

The young man looked at Perea admiringly. "Five men on you and you got away."

"News travels fast," Perea said dryly. "Don't you have anything else to talk about? Or maybe you could just shut up? I came out here to have some peace."

Obediently, the militiaman lay on his back and looked up at the stars through the new leaves of the cottonwoods. Perea kept at his wine and then, after the soldier had behaved himself for a while, Perea relented and passed along the skin.

"You've got a farm?" Perea asked. "Any family?"

"Yeah. I've got the last place north of Medanales."

"On the east side of the river?"

"That one. Got a bitch of a barren wife, turkeys, one cow. Not much to go home to. My father died last winter. He was the only reason I kept going on the place."

I stood motionless, in deep shadows in the creek channel, with an eerie feeling. It was dawning on me that this militiaman was Marisol's husband, Arsenio. Bitch of a barren wife! Any last twinge of remorse I had about cuckolding him disappeared like snowfall in May.

"You left your wife alone in Medanales? You know they were attacked last week. A bunch of settlers were killed. The raiders took some kids too." Maybe this man Perea had a conscience?

"No problem. My wife's half Indian. She'd get along fine if they took her. Them Comanches could solve a big problem for me. I never should have married her."

"Wasn't Comanches. It was Apaches," Perea said. I was surprised to finally hear someone who agreed with me on that, and who said it so definitely.

Arsenio smirked, "Well, Apaches could be harder on her, if they got her. But they don't usually raid up there. I believe it was Comanches, that's what they say."

Perea muttered something I couldn't hear from my place by the creek. Then he offered, "I'm going up there pretty soon. You want me to check on her?"

"On Marisol? You can do any damn thing you want with her," Arsenio said.

I winced.

"When are you going up?" the militiaman asked.

Even Perea was disgusted by this man. He pushed himself up onto all fours and worked his way to his feet. "Not exactly sure. I have to go down south tomorrow. Check out some horses. Find me a good one so I'll be ready when the word comes to go north, and when it does I'll be passing by Medanales." Perea climbed up the riverbank, talking all the while.

"Marisol, you say? I used to know a woman named that up in Abiquiú. Never knew where she took off to. I was thinking about her just the other day."

Arsenio interrupted, "So what?"

"You might not be worried about her, but a woman probably shouldn't be left up there alone. I'd be glad to drop in. What's your name? I'll let you know when I'm going."

The little shit didn't even notice the threat to his manhood in Perea's message. "Arsenio Archuleta. Everyone at the garrison knows me," he said proudly, "this is my second tour."

"Good night, Arsenio. Forget what you heard about me, 'cause damn little of it's true."

"Gotta go myself," said the nasty little rat who was married to my love. "Got guard duty later tonight. Need to sleep some first."

It was easy for me to picture an ax blade dropping into his skull.

They plowed off in opposite directions, making so much noise on last winter's dead leaves that I didn't need to wait more than a minute before I could hurry out of the damp cold by the water. I had to restrain myself from going after Arsenio and wringing his dirty neck quietly in the dark, but having managed to hold back, I got up on the road and despite the gravity of the situation, I allowed myself a little leap, clicking my heels in the air. This was the kind of information we needed. Someone was paying our errant scout, and he was spouting information only an insider would be privy to. With this we had Perea nailed.

"Lend me your horse. Nando, wake up, I need to borrow Rosinante." Francisco was shaking me in the gray morning light. I sat up and looked at him severely.

"I only got her back yesterday. What do you need a horse for?"

"A message came. I've got to go see someone." Francisco wasn't usually this discreet.

"Which someone?" I wasn't going to let him off the hook.

"I can't tell yet. I don't know if she's 'someone' until after I see her."

Was my freedom-loving brother becoming interested in a woman? Or thinking about it?

"How far are you taking my horse?" I asked.

"Thank you! I knew you'd say yes! Just a little way out of town. I'll tell you all about it when I get back."

He was already dressed and reaching for his cape. I was buck naked, so he had a good head start. I draped my manta around my middle like a woman's skirt and followed him out to the shed.

"Damn it, Francisco, don't go hurtling off like this. The town's seething, people are getting killed every time you turn around, and there could be war parties within a couple of miles of here. You've got to be straight with me. You probably shouldn't go alone."

"Jesus, is this Nando talking, or my mother?"

"I just don't think it's a good time to be taking off, so if you want Rosinante, stop a minute and let's discuss this." I guess I still sounded like Luz.

"All right, all right, but you were the one who was gone all day yesterday, leaving me at home to knit socks and spoon soup into my brother. I can't just sit around in that dark little house all the time. What were you up to, anyway? It's not like you're exactly open about things with me."

Apparently Francisco had been letting this build up, because he was mad.

I tried to figure out what I could tell him and still keep my pact with the governor. Surely, finding Carlos' attackers and Baz was as much Francisco's problem as mine. It was not, strictly speaking, government business, though I wasn't sure the attacks on my family and the governor's problems weren't connected.

"O.K. I told you about fishing, and finding the slaves, and winding up in the canyon past Duran's hacienda. I saw Ramón Duran heading the slave train, and I think he may be connected to a person I've become curious about, a scout named Perea."

Francisco watched me closely as I spoke. I think maybe he didn't quite recognize his little half-brother, dead serious and rattling off facts.

"Duran plucked the scout out of the middle of a fight, saved his ass. Not many people would help Perea right now. I'm getting curious about why Ramón cared."

"What's Perea's story?"

151

"You're probably the only man in town who doesn't know it, because you just got back from Mexico. He was the scout who mistook the Comanche party for Apache raiders up on the pass. Whether it was a genuine mistake or a calculated move, we don't know yet. But if it weren't for him a lot of evil wouldn't have happened, and our brother wouldn't have been wounded in the first place."

Some of this wasn't making any sense to Francisco and I could see why.

"So if he blundered so badly why isn't he in irons? Why is he free?" he asked.

"He's been keeping himself scarce. He was only glimpsed in town once, in the middle of that fight, just before Anza left. When I was getting Rosinante yesterday, Sebastian – he's the big man who often guards the gate – pointed him out to me sitting all by himself in the gloom under the portál. Sebastian thought someone ought to try to figure out what he was up to, so that's what I did yesterday."

"Were you successful?"

"It took me all day. I finally overheard him talking to a militiaman down by the river last night. He says he's riding south today, down to La Ciénega. That's where the Durans have their place. So my hunch about him being in league with Ramón is holding."

Francisco looked worried. "You think Ramón's a bad one?"

"He hit me across the face on Sunday while he was smuggling slaves around the edge of town. Just for starters." I pointed to the cut on my cheek. "So where are you going?" I pressed.

Francisco let out a long, slow breath as he decided how much he was going to tell me. "I made friends with a woman who came north with our caravan. A young woman."

"An attractive woman, I gather?"

Francisco glowered at me and went on.

"During the two months getting up here we spent a lot of time together. It's not like being in town where you have to live by rules. On the trail we saw each other, at meals, doing chores, crossing rivers, whenever. I told you, some of the trip was terrifying. I think I was a support to her. I was hoping that it wouldn't be over once we got home."

He looked pretty forlorn for a man in love.

"She sent a servant with a message yesterday. She's at home now in La Ciénega."

I was starting to catch on and I didn't think I liked it.

"Her name's Luisa. Luisa Duran. She's the alcalde's niece, and, hell yes, Nando, I think I'm in love." Here was irony served up on a fancy plate. We stood there in silence, neither quite looking at the other, not sure what this meant.

I went into the house and came out with Rosinante's gear. "Just keep your wits about you." Then I handed him the pistol the governor had given me.

He eyed it admiringly. "Where'd you get this?"

" I didn't steal it, if that's what you think. It was entrusted to me. And I want my horse back here by dark tonight. Sebastian needs more help and you're babysitting."

Francisco was busy saddling Rosinante. I helped him get the bit in her mouth. A chilly wind had blown up and I could tell we were in for a spring storm.

"Keep your eyes open, brother. You might come across Perea, and I have no idea where Ramón is right now," I added, pointing to my cheek. "And don't forget about Baz. You might just find him, or at least someone who's seen him."

Francisco thanked me, then cantered off toward the river road. I was glad that Rosinante had a proper rest. I could use one myself.

Street Mutts Hoping

For a Crust

I huddled in the house all day. A ragged little wind was picking up the dust of the streets and zinging it down the alleys. When the sky is gray and the wind brutal, there is little to be said for Santa Fe. Even the best houses look like sinking hovels, the streets and stark plaza become blowing desert wastes and you can't even see the mountains. During storms, smoke from the household fires barely clears the chimneys and hangs low, choking the town. There is gray in the sage, the juniper trees and the dirt. When the sun goes away here, the whole place turns to dullest lead.

I spent much of the morning tossing wood onto the miserably smoking fire in the corner of the sala. My job was to watch over my brother, and I was doing that, but I couldn't keep myself from brooding. None of us had been up to our old hacienda in four years. Were our houses, barns, and corrals even there? That was Comanche country now. Our horizon seemed so contracted sitting in this dark, smoke-filled house, I wondered that we ever had those good years living on the plains of the Piedra Lumbre.

Carlos was severely injured, his career as a sub-lieutenant probably over. Francisco, no matter what excuse he gave, had basically dropped out of school and come home to rustle up another scheme. Luz still appeared spry, but when I took time to really look at her, I saw she was tiny, weather-beaten and at the edge of old age. Like our prospects, she had withered.

I hadn't seen my own mother and her other children in over a year. With the constant warring everywhere, I had no idea whether she was alive or not. I wanted to be with her. I didn't like being here in the capital with the constant badgering of the government and the church. Their rules, levies and taxes on everything were onerous. Of course, an occasional governor, or alcalde, got rich working the system, enslaving Indios or pushing the common folk around, but it seemed very few people in New Spain thrived.

And, as the wind blew smoke out of the fireplace into my eyes, I finally had to admit I was missing Marisol. That had been a grand four days we'd spent together, but it had been blasted out of my mind by the destruction at Medanales. I was beginning to realize that my visit with her had been more than a couple of kids stealing a weekend for horseplay. That woman was tucked up under my heart and seldom far from my thoughts. I hoped to God she had moved in closer to other people, particularly after overhearing Perea's remarks about her, but I doubted she had. I wasn't even sure if there was anyone else still alive near her.

I'd gotten stuck in town by duties to king and family. It would be impossible to leave for a trip that would take two long days each way. Perea would likely "drop in" on her long before I could get back to her farm. It sounded like he'd had designs on Marisol from years back, but there was no way I would leave Carlos again until he could defend himself.

Looking at him, either sleeping fitfully, or lying flat and listless on the wide banco we called a bed, I could barely forgive myself for having gone to Mass the other day. I knew, too, that a woman wept over the missing child named Baz. I was supposed to be working for the governor, yet I couldn't even leave the house. Nevertheless, Carlos was improving. Today he was sitting up sometimes and had eaten a little.

Sitting here, feeling stuck, it finally occurred to me how dumb I was. Right here at my side was the one person able to provide the information I needed. Carlos had been an officer at the battle caused by Perea's misinformation. If he was up to it, I might be able to get him to talk about it, but right now he slept, so I sat there poking moodily at the fire.

It was a relief to hear someone knock on the door. Here was Rosa again, apparently emboldened by the fact that Luz de Gracia had treated her with respect the other day, coming back to bring us a little cheer in the form of baked custard.

The mood in our house lifted like a flock of birds when that solid woman proffered her treat. Even Carlos woke up and moved into more of a sitting position than he had yet tried. I found some drier wood and made the fire behave, while Luz got out spoons and brought a chair near the hearth for our visitor.

Rosa brought news, too. A lot of the militiamen were suddenly going home. They had been given some pay, not enough to be sure, but as a result, several of them were preparing to leave and had felt flush enough to come into her wine shop last night.

"They're using the excuse that their farms need work, but I also heard them talking a lot about Paulina's boyfriend. They

156

said they don't mind fighting Indios, but if they get murdered right outside the palacio, that's a little much. That really scared them."

Luz said, "I'm surprised they stayed as long as they have. Are there many in town?"

"Maybe forty still. Others went south with the troops trying to recover the wagons."

To our surprise, Carlos spoke, adding to the conversation as he normally would.

"The governor's counting on the militia being here when he gets back. Believe me, he knows exactly how many men he has at his disposal. It took three weeks for them to come in after his call for aid," Carlos said. "Nando, how long's Anza been gone?"

"Six days. That's all."

"Great, he's at least another week out and every last one of them will have drifted off by then. What's the matter with them? They're getting fed. They're being paid. That's pretty remarkable, since it's been a year since an intact caravan came through. What's the matter with these men?"

It was Rosa's turn. "There are rumors, mean ones, that Anza's no good, that he shouldn't have been sitting in Santa Cruz while he sent the rest of you to get ambushed in the mountains. People think he knew something and stayed away."

Carlos shook his head, denying it. Rosa went on.

"They talk about your injuries and Captain Valdez, as though the governor's trying to get rid of you both. They say that as only rural militiamen they're nothing to him, so they were the ones sent off on a suicide mission, instead of the regulars."

Carlos wasn't too weak to get angry.

"It wasn't like that at all! We were making our first good contact in years with the Yupe Comanches. They knew, everyone knew, that Anza was coming up once they were assembled. It was his way of holding to his word, that he wouldn't treat with just any ragtag band. He insisted that they get together, that they come to him as one people for this. It *was* a set up, but not the one everyone thinks. We went ahead, out in the lead, to preserve the impact of his authority. It's what the Comanches needed to believe about him. They admire strong men. Remember how Cuerno Verde was."

Luz and I exchanged looks, glad Carlos was sitting up and talking like a soldier. I turned to Rosa, "Do you have any idea what it would take to keep these men here? Does the alcalde know what's happening? Could he stop them from leaving?"

"Well, let me just drop in and have a chat with him!" Rosa laughed. She was, after all, madam of the best whorehouse in Santa Fe.

My stepmother's lively eyes let us know that she got it, but she sounded serious when she offered, "I think I'll go try to talk to the padre. He's always going over to Tomás Duran's, comforting his soul, I suppose, while he drinks his sherry. If I tell Padre Baldonado, it'll be a way to make sure that Duran is in the know."

Carlos asked, "Who's on duty at the garrison right now? Surely he can count, though it will be subtraction he needs."

"Technically, I think it's down to Sebastian," I said. "He's good, but as a corporal he's pretty small potatoes. Everyone of importance is out in the colony dealing with one crisis or another, or is laid up in bed," I added looking over at our invalid. I turned to Rosa and said, "You know how to keep a man in town."

Luz de Gracia cried. "Nando!"

I scrambled to retreat. "I meant wine, you know, the enticements of city life. Sorry Rosa, I'm sorry Luz." Chagrined, I backed out of the conversation for a while. Carlos watched me make an ass out of myself and let the impact sink in for a minute. Then he backed me up.

"Do what you can, Rosa. I'll see that the governor knows and pays you back for anything you have to give away." Luz gave a little shudder, but stayed quiet. I was never quite sure these days which side of her we were going to get.

"Ma, you should go to the padre, but go to the good one, Miera." I said. "Talk to him first, see what he thinks. I'll go with you if you want." We had polished off the pudding. Luz was gathering up the spoons and had started to clean Rosa's bowl.

"Rosa," I asked. "Have you seen a little creep in your place named Arsenio? Best described as callow?"

"I had to kick him out last night." Her comely face was stern.

"That doesn't surprise me," I said. "What happened?" Rosa looked over toward Luz cleaning the dishes and let me know with her eyebrows that we wouldn't talk about it in front of my stepmother.

"Some people I just don't want in my place. He joined that club last night." Something to do with the girls, I figured. I remembered how he was starting to get drunk when I left him at the river. Another couple of drinks and that slime could try anything.

Luz put the clean bowl in Rosa's hands and thanked her with a hug. "Let me know what else I can do," Luz offered. "I'll find you if there's any news after talking to the padres."

"It'll be better if I send Paulina over later. I think you need to stay home as much as you can," she added with a look, "though I can understand you may need an excuse to come out to a wine shop now and then."

Our Luz was ready for her. "How's your Monte?"

Sweet Jesus, here was my pious stepmother challenging the local madam to a card game. Interesting times in the colony.

Rosa laughed at her as she patted Carlos on the hand and sailed out the door, calling back, "Probably not nearly as good as yours, Señora. We'll try it soon!"

As soon as Luz left to get a bead on the padres, I poured myself a cup of her wine and flopped down beside the fire. Carlos reached out for his share and while we passed it back and forth he said, "I know that fool, Arsenio. He was in my detachment once."

"What do you suppose he did to make Rosa kick him out?"

"Rosa doesn't tolerate anyone being rough on her girls," Carlos said. Then he filled me in on the man. "I remember watching him arrive when he joined up. Arsenio was so typical of what we were usually sent that Valdez got really depressed when he rode in. He said Arsenio and his crew reminded him of street mutts hanging around hoping for a crust. Valdez asked me for the count of Arsenio's group.

" 'Seventeen,' I told him. Valdez looked like he was sick of it all. 'And all told? What are we up to now?'

" 'Sixty-three, and fully a quarter of them have teeth,' I said, but that day Captain Valdez was in no mood for jokes. I remember him with his head in his hands staring at the planks on the table.

" 'Cull the best,' he told me. 'Christ, Aguilar, you know what to do. If there's anyone too old, give them to the commissary.'

"I laughed out loud.

" 'Not to eat, Aguilar! Just to help with the cooking. We'll wait one more hour and see what else crawls in . . .' I tell you, the man was morose."

Carlos turned toward me, bringing himself back to the present. "Your Arsenio was what provoked him. He was useless in the field. Mostly I had him help the packers. He certainly couldn't cook. The way he handled an animal, I was scared to give him a gun. Thank God he wasn't on the mountain with us during this last fiasco."

"Carlos, when did you get hit?" My brother was getting tired, but he seemed to want to talk so I didn't stop him.

"At dawn the day after the slaughter, when Red Horse overran us. I knew as soon as I caught up to Valdez that we were in for it. Once I saw the carnage and who we'd killed, I hurried the men back toward Taos a good three miles. We were looking for any spot we could defend.

"I was ready, in the unlikely case that someone would talk before attacking us, to make apologies, offer food, horses, weapons, do whatever penance it would take. But I never got a chance. They smashed into us at first light. They were on every side and we took a beating. Finally we drove them back enough that we were able to climb down off a cliff into the creek bottom, but once they figured out our move they made another push and I got shot in that one. Fell off the rocks, ten feet or so, when the bullet got my arm. Some of my men covered long enough to get me over the creek, and I know one of them took a hit at the very end.

"That scout, Perea, wouldn't have been my first choice. He was good in his way, but there was always an edge to him, an unpleasantness. Torres or Trujillo would have been a better choice, but Perea clearly wanted the duty. I heard him outline his plan to Valdez very convincingly, and when he came back Valdez was gloating at our good luck and clapping Perea on the back. Valdez wanted this one too badly. Within minutes his troop took off, following Perea into the hills. I remember feeling let down, like I'd gotten the boring part of the duty."

"Yeah, but you didn't get a bullet in your throat, like Valdez."

Carlos nodded slowly. "I've been wondering if I was meant to, if whoever set up that fiasco wanted me out of the way too, and came back to do it right two days ago."

I was interested that Carlos was piecing it together much the way I saw it, but at present I was looking for some way to cheer him up. "Whoever it might be isn't very good at killing you, Carlos. They miss every time." Neither of us laughed. We sat there in silence for many minutes.

His thoughts must have returned to the attack in the garden, when he said, "It felt more like they were trying to intimidate me. Or maybe take me hostage? If they wanted to kill me they could have done it. I mean, a lame man dozing in a chair can be picked off pretty easily."

"Maybe they were cheap. Throwing you in the freezing river saved bullets," I offered.

Carlos wasn't moved to play along with my joke. "I think," he went on, "when Baz flung himself into it, things went wrong for them. All of a sudden here's a witness, a furious little kid making a whole lot of noise. They had to wrap him up fast, and dispose of both of us. Baz could be slung onto a horse, but I'm too big. The river looked simple."

I sat there in silence, giving him all the time he needed to remember the details. Carlos scratched at the wound on his arm, then said, "Come to think of it, even though they were dressed like us, they must have been Apaches. Funny I didn't recall that until now. Two Apaches and one strung-out looking white man, an old guy, who ran the show. You know when Nan used to mimic how the Apaches talk? They sounded just like that."

I was thinking that's how it was for me up near Medanales, how once I heard them talk I recognized them as Apaches even though they were dressed like Comanches.

"I want Anza to know this," I said. "Apaches are into everything right now. Francisco says they got most of the last caravan. The wagons have been traveling up from Mexico for almost 200 years, but they've never lost the whole load: hard goods for the colony, soldiers' pay, everything, right down to the governor's chocolate. Sounds like maybe they've got a big plan they're working on right now, and I'll bet attacking Medanales dressed up like Comanches was part of it too."

"There's been a shift for sure," Carlos said. "It seems a lot like the last time they threw us out of here." We were silent, thinking over that ignominious part of our history.

"We managed to return though," I said. "But can you imagine having to wait in El Paso for twelve years?"

I built up the fire again, then went and stood in the open door. Now that the afternoon was getting on I began to wonder about Francisco and how his love affair in La Ciénega was shaping up.

"Carlos, do you think we'll ever get our ranch back?" I asked.

"If we get the treaty we will." Carlos was certain of that. "Without it we can kiss it all good bye."

Luz came back just then with news. "Baldonado's not in town today, but if we hurry we can catch Father Miera in his office behind the chapel. Are you coming?"

I wasn't sure why I'd suggested Miera, since Baldonado was the man with connections to the alcalde. Why not just visit the alcalde himself? When I protested, Luz looked at me like I was a royal pain in the neck and pushed me ahead of her through the door.

"It's always good to start with the proper channels," she preached. "Anyway, you can learn a lot from Father Miera, if you shut your mouth and listen."

Just as we arrived outside the priest's private garden, an old pueblo man came out through a cedar gate in the stone wall. He held his blanket tightly around him and never seemed to see us. I stood aside to let him pass. He had a look of anger, or maybe even disgust, on his face but I could tell his demeanor was forced, because as he tried to close the gate his hand shook too badly to make the latch work.

Father Miera, looking worn out, watched him from the doorway. He waved us to enter, but stood on the step for a moment, looking at the Indian walk off down the lane. Then he joined us inside.

"Señora Aguilar? Fernando? What can I do for you?"

"I think the question had better be reversed, Father. You look exhausted." Luz missed little.

Father Miera sat behind his plank table. It was littered with papers, a broken quill, and an overturned pot that drooled brown ink onto the floor. His gesture displaying the mess was almost frantic.

"It's always the same, and there is nothing I can do. That man's granddaughter was violated, and by a person of considerable rank. She has been used as a concubine and relegated to the role of kitchen slave, yet she is the daughter of a cacique!"

Luz sat straight upright on the hard bench and I stood behind her, watching the exasperated priest.

"There is no way we can combat it! There is no viable means by which we can restore this province to morality and peacefulness. When our leaders abuse the natives in this manner there is nothing to do but prepare for a second revolt. It's coming, and while I write urgently to Mexico, protest to the governor and confront the perpetrators, I am, in truth, powerless to effect the slightest change."

He looked at us pleadingly and through a scrim of tears. I saw that the chaos on his desk was not from the pueblo man having attacked him, but from the padre's efforts to communicate his desperation to the authorities.

"What will you do?" Luz asked gently.

Miera shrugged. "All that I can. Require that the man return the girl with sufficient payment to offset the deed and wait to see if he complies. Go get her if he doesn't. I could threaten to excommunicate him, but he'd laugh in my face. Anza might bring pressure to bear, he knows how delicate everything is, but he's not even here now." He sighed, and then seemed to remember that we must have come for a reason. "Please, what brings you here this windy afternoon?"

"The alcalde, father."

Miera looked at Luz sharply. "Yes?"

"Do you talk with him? Do you have his ear?" The padre searched our faces trying to get a clue as to the nature of the request.

"Certainly. On those occasions when he's in residence in Santa Fe."

"We have learned," Luz went on, "from the person who perhaps would know best, that men from the militia are quietly deserting. My son, Lieutenant Aguilar, was most concerned that Anza will be deprived of important military support that he was counting on, and he was hoping to get word to the alcalde, so that he'll take action to keep the men in Santa Fe."

Miera nodded his understanding. "I'll be visiting him tonight. What more should I tell him?"

I stepped forward. "It has to do with the dead soldier, father. He was one of the citizens in the militia, filling in for the regular guard. The men are terrified. Carlos says it's crucial to stop them from leaving, and the alcalde's the one to do it since the governor's gone."

"I see. Yes, there is almost no one left at the garrison to oversee things. I will pass the word to Alcalde Duran. But, Nando, why did you come to me, why not to Father Baldonado? He is the priest of your parish and is quite close to the alcalde."

I shrugged. Miera kept his eyes directly on mine.

"Did I hear something about Padre Baldonado and you, in the courtyard, after Mass?"

"Perhaps, father." I lowered my eyes. "Padre Baldonado mistook my actions for something else."

"He is quick to anger," the priest agreed, "but whenever I think he might not be the best man for the Order to have sent us, because of that difficult temperament of his, I try to apply understanding and to realize that he is as dedicated as any to the advancement of Christian ideals. He came to us highly praised by the priests from the seminary." Then Miera shook his head. "It is unfortunate that his manner is so off-putting."

Luz was still as a stone. Finally she asked, "Could he be, well, slightly deranged? Perhaps the stresses of the frontier have worked to his disadvantage?"

Miera stood up and started pacing the room. "I will tell you the little bit that I have heard. As a child he lost his parents when they were arrested in Mexico and returned to Spain.

166

The priests of a rural monastery took over his upbringing from a very young age. His was a peculiar childhood, isolated from all children, brought up by kitchen slaves, and then subjected to the strictures of the Order long before he was able to voluntarily seek them. To everyone's amazement, he took to it precociously." The padre grimaced. "We have seen how avid he can be." The room had become dark. Now that the wind had died down, Miera opened the door to let in the last of the light.

"I hold him in my prayers that he will soften and be congenial like other men. Meanwhile, you must honor him as your priest and do what you can to make him comfortable in the company of ordinary people." This, Miera addressed to me. To Luz he said, "Your son Carlos, Señora? Is he recovering?"

"Better than we had hoped. Praise to God, he is sitting up and talking plainly now, and it's only been three days."

"And I hear Francisco's back?"

"That's right, and already chasing a lady!"

The priest smiled. "I remember Francisco well. You will have your hands full, madam, but your heart must be full as well."

"Indeed, it is!" We both knelt and kissed the priest's hand, and then he relaxed and gave us a hug. When he said, "God be with you!" I could tell he really meant it.

A Cruel Relic

I decided to make a quick tour of the town before night, and hoped that while I was at it, I might encounter Francisco coming home.

The wind had died down and it was lovely and still, though the young leaves were dried out and bedraggled, and dust in the air made the last of the sunset livid. The streets were completely empty except for the guard posted outside the palacio gate, walking slowly back and forth. I could hear animals munching in their stalls behind the crumbling adobe walls. I circled the plaza, noticing that the lights were out at the alcalde's and only a few burned in the governor's quarters at the palacio. The church was locked up tight. I looked up to the hilltop cross where I'd encountered the crazy friar, but there was nobody about. I decided I'd go to Rosa's.

So that's where everybody was! The place was lit up like there was a fandango and every table was full. The girls were serving wine so fast there was no time for dalliance. A quick glance told me the customers tonight were soldiers and militiamen. Neither Ramón nor his rico buddies were around. And look, Arsenio was back!

Why would Rosa let him return? She must have a more forgiving nature than I thought. I popped my head into the back room, but it was empty. I thought possibly Francisco might have returned and dropped in before coming home. Disappointed, I wandered into the kitchen to see if my new friend Paulina was there. She wasn't.

It started as a scuffle between Arsenio and a tall soldier. It was earnest fighting, eerily silent, though all the patrons were on their feet. The two antagonists slugged knotted fists into each other, tight and dirty, trying for a groin shot, catching at whatever clothing, body part, or hank of hair came within reach. Then someone flung a chair from a side table and it caught the smaller man on the head, flipping him over backwards and tossing him into the crowd. Showing no mercy, the onlookers shoved the stunned militiaman back to the center of the floor, into the grip of his attacker.

Rosa emerged from behind the curtained door and stood there sternly. Knowing her rules, the gathered men moved toward the fighters and as one body shoved the two of them out of Rosa's domain into the street, where both men instantly plunged back into the fight. Arsenio went in low and fast, but the soldier grabbed him by the hair and began to yank him fiercely from side to side. Then he kicked the smaller man's legs out from under him, toppling him to the dirt. He jumped astride Arsenio, seized his head and began pounding it against the ground. Everyone stood back, Rosa too, watching justice being meted out. Was this part of her plan?

Arsenio didn't have a chance, knocked nearly unconscious by a man far larger than he. His assailant was in a blind rage. As little as I liked Arsenio, it was awkward to stand there watching someone try to beat him to death. Rosa looked over and caught my eye. I hated to do it, but I knew what she wanted. I walked into the street, past the gawking onlookers. Rosa parted the crowd and moved toward the fight from her side. Thank God! Sometimes it feels fine to hide behind a skirt.

I grabbed the kneeling attacker by his shoulders and tried to pull him off Arsenio. Rosa stood in front and reached out to grasp his face, as though she would calm him, talk reason to him. The big soldier resisted my own pulling, oblivious in his rage, but Rosa's hands caught his attention. When he stopped thrashing Arsenio for a second and looked up at her, I tightened my grip and pulled hard, dragging him off.

With a yelp the enraged man was on his feet. He delivered a brutal kick to the writhing Arsenio, yelled again, and plunged into the darkness down the street. Two of his companions ran after him. Instead of the usual sullen letdown, there was relief among the crowd. A member of the garrison could have been jailed for months and marched all the way down to Chihuahua with the next caravan, to be tried for murdering another soldier. It didn't matter whether his victim was only a militiaman. It would be a miserable end to the soldier's arduous career.

I shook my head to clear it, unable to believe I had actually saved Marisol's pathetic husband from his just desserts. I took several steps backwards into the crowd, then turned and went inside, not caring one bit whether the stupid ass died out there in the night. Rosa stuck a cup of wine in my hand, but I couldn't thank her. I drank guardedly. No one would look at me or talk. Just as well, because I felt murderous. Finally, I had enough of it all and went back to the street. I was going to leave my unfinished cup beside Arsenio, but he wasn't there. There was no trace of him at all.

Neither Rosinante nor her rider was home when I got there. Everyone else was asleep so I put up the bar on the door and lay down beside Carlos, certain I would worry all night. Sleep caught me before I pulled the blankets up.

At first light I headed south on the mule, but I hadn't gotten far when I saw my brother riding dejectedly up the road. From the way he looked, I'd say the reunion hadn't gone well.

"Sorry," he said with a faint smile. He had leaves all over the back of his coat and twigs in his hair. I decided he wasn't so much down, as bemused.

"Are we still in love?"

"Hush, brat." Francisco pulled Rosinante to a halt, turned to me and moaned, "It's horrible and yes, we're in love."

Then he tried to cover up his misery by kicking Rosinante and cantering noisily away. I meandered along behind, letting him have his mood, then I dropped down to the sparkling river, dismounted and sat on a grassy bank, ostensibly watching the water. It worked. Francisco soon sat beside me and spilled out his story.

"It was perfect. At first, perfect! Alcalde Duran, himself, was there, greeting me at the door. They were preparing luncheon and invited me to stay. We went through the little formalities: he pretending not to know why I was there, I pretending to have dropped in just to be sociable. I sometimes glimpsed Luisa in the back room, but she acted like she didn't see me. Finally I inquired after his niece and watched the light seem to dawn on Duran's face. Señora Duran brought Luisa into the sala, and she was looking much prettier and not exhausted, as we all had been after the trip. She took my hand so properly! No one there would have guessed that I'd lain right on top of her, firing at Apaches, just three weeks ago."

I grinned at that. "Any excuse at all, eh Francisco?"

He pointedly ignored me and went on. "Lunch was a feast. I've never seen anything like it in New Mexico. Duran, his Señora and another ten people sat at the long table. We dined inside with candles, even at midday, and fires burned at either end of the room. They had a dozen servants waiting on us. Tomás was affable. He started smiling at us both, like he was beginning to think I might be a good idea, enough so that I dared to touch her hand. Her cousin Ramón was polite, as was the rest of his family. I think your Perea was one of the men sitting at the foot of the table. Ramón asked him if he'd picked out his horse yet and when he was heading north, but Tomás interrupted them, as though they weren't supposed to talk business at the table."

"Stocky? Thirties? Not too tall?" I checked.

"Yeah, that describes the man. Somewhat of an accent."

"I've never noticed that, but it must have been Perea."

Francisco went on. "Luisa and I were allowed to take a walk together after lunch. There was a maid of course, but she knew her place. Everything is perfect between us. I think Luisa will marry me, but what do I have, Nando? She knows about the ranch, says she wouldn't even mind living out there, but I don't know how I can ask for her hand until I have either that, or a job, or something more than a corner of Luz's house to offer her. I guess there's still the little farm near Abiquiú, but it would never support us." He didn't sound happy. Neither was he sounding like himself. Was the mercurial Francisco about to settle down?

I reflected on the difference between his situation and mine. Any woman I might ask to marry me would help me build a little mud house and call it home. Francisco, being patrician, had to find a woman suitable to his station, then convince her parents that not only was his blood-line impeccable, but that he had the money to back it up. And if he managed to pull that off then he needed the governor's permission as well.

"What does she look like?" I asked, to indulge him.

"She looks a damn sight better than she did last week! You'll see her. I can't really describe her, but her face isn't pocked; it's smooth. Her hair was bound in ribbons today, but on the trail it fell free, and there is some copper in the black of it. Her eyebrows are thick—I guess that sounds weird, but somehow they're perfect. She's nearly as tall as I am, but she looked almost dainty today in silk shoes and a new linen dress." He considered this. "Do you think she knew I was coming?"

I started picking leaves off Francisco and he caught on and found the twigs in his hair. "Where did you sleep?"

Francisco sagged. "I don't think I did sleep. I think I was unconscious."

"The effects of love?"

My brother shook his head. "This isn't a joke. I left at dusk. I knew that was pushing it, but I was glad for the time with her. I was nearly to Agua Fria when they came at me. Men riding hard out of the west."

"What? Oh shit, Francisco!"

"At first I thought it was someone coming to warn me of raiders, so I waited while they crossed the river. When I saw they had their mantas over their faces it was already too late. I was a love-struck idiot and didn't realize, until they had me completely in their grip, that I was being attacked. One grabbed me and pulled me backwards off Rosinante. Two others started alternating punches, with me in the middle. There were more men watching from their horses. They threw me onto my back. A man stood above me, threatening me with his whip and shouting,

"'Stay away from the woman! She is not for you! Come back and you're dead.'

"I rolled over to protect my face and the blows began. I was kicked and whipped. I can't tell you any more.

"I woke up near dawn. Sitting up was a sickening nightmare, but by some miracle, Rosinante was cropping grass down by the river, dragging her reins, and there was the water, so I crawled down, washed my face and drank, then started home. I swear I didn't remember the man's words until about an hour ago. I still can't figure out what happened. It was like I was the prodigal son down at the alcalde's."

"Remember the other brothers didn't care much for the prodigal son."

"That hadn't occurred to me." He looked dismal.

"Do you still have my pistol?"

"The pistol? Mother of God, I hope so!" He got up and went over to Rosinante, opening the saddlebag.

"Not here. All gone." This wasn't going to please the governor much, but maybe I could somehow get it back before he'd know. Meanwhile, I'd have to get my old gun working fast, because it seemed like we Aguilars were coming under constant attack.

I shrugged, trying to pretend that losing the weapon didn't matter much. "Let's get back. Your mother's all alone with Carlos."

"How's he getting on?"

"Not great, but well enough to sit up and talk like an officer once in a while."

"Anything I should know?"

"Not until your own head's better." We mounted and rode quickly toward the town, each of us immersed in our own thoughts about the reception Francisco had received when he went to court his lady.

When we rode onto San Francisco Street, we got caught up among townspeople hurrying toward the plaza. They'd left their cooking on the fire and their doors wide open, and were running to the palacio. I saw Padre Miera in his blue robes in the midst of the crowd in front of the palace gates. Everyone stood with their necks craned toward the sky, peering into the high branches of the cottonwood. We moved in close and looked up too, and saw the swaying body of last night's guard, garroted by a rusted iron collar, a cruel relic from the Inquisition. They had used it to hang him by his neck from a fat limb of the leafy tree. After one glance at the bloated, grotesque face of the corpse, I dropped my eyes to the tattered soles of his boots. I turned to Francisco and said, "That makes two."

The Other Man's Wife

That did it. The volunteer militia fled from the villa, so that only a handful remained by Monday morning's roll call. There were not enough regulars left in town to give pursuit, and without the governor, there was no one to organize it effectively anyway.

Carlos demanded that we carry him to the palacio, where he sat all afternoon deliberating with Sebastian, the other officers still at the garrison, and the alcalde. Francisco and I literally carried our brother between us in a 'chair' made of our arms. When we set him down in the office, everyone gathered at his side and the alcalde had to be restrained from seizing Carlos' hand and pumping his arm, in his delight at having him back among the men. We waited out in the courtyard while our brother did what he could in the absence of the governor.

Becoming bored sitting outside, I started going over what I knew and suddenly remembered a question that had popped in and out of my brain since hearing Francisco's tale. "Francisco, did you hear anything at the table that night about when Perea might be heading north?"

He thought for a second, and said, "Not really, but I sensed he was getting ready. He'd gotten to La Ciénega ahead of me and he'd already picked out his horse for the trip."

"And Ramón?" I asked. "Tell me about him. How did he act toward you? Did he seem friendly with Perea?" Francisco thought out his response before speaking.

"Nando, I think it was Ramón who beat me up, but obviously I have no proof. The viciousness, the air of the man standing there, his raised whip, it all was an awful lot like how you were attacked beside the river last week. It's just a feeling I have."

"I've got the same feeling, Francisco, but what about earlier, down at the hacienda?"

"He was decent enough. Very serious and polite. He seemed busy though. I spent most of the time with his parents and Luisa. He only came into the house when it was time to eat. I'd say it was all business between Perea and him, except the scout was seated at the foot of the table, so it was unusual that Ramón spoke to him from way up at the other end. That was when his father asked him to stop."

I could picture the alcalde seeing to the decorum at his table. "Tomás is a gentleman," I said. "I know he's helped out Luz more than once since Benito died. His ranches thrive and the governor respects him for that. But, going back to yesterday, is there anything else you can remember? Anything about the slaves I saw Ramón transporting?"

"Not really, other than there were a lot of pueblo women waiting on us at the table and working in the house. There were many Indios out around the barns and in the fields. It was really bustling and it looked like the Durans are sitting pretty down there." He was shaking his head. "I don't know if they sent someone to warn me off because I'm far too poor for them, or because my manners stink."

I could tell I'd brought him back down into his misery. "Your manners *are* horrible, Francisco, but you are one of very few pure Spaniards still in the colony. Your lineage can't be challenged by anyone, and if the ranch is restored to us, no one could call you poor, either."

"Sympathy at last," said Francisco.

"Also that wasn't a mild little warning," I added. "That was a brutal attack. They had no idea if you were left for dead, and obviously didn't care."

Francisco nodded. "Just like they did to Carlos. You know, whoever is doing this doesn't seem to mind if we go on living. They just want us thoroughly frightened; maimed, but not necessarily dead. It means we don't pose a serious enough threat. We just need to be moved aside." My brother was talking sense.

"Someone who is sure of his strength and is just tying up loose ends," I added.

Francisco nodded and asked, "But how are we in their way? What are they running that we could possibly muck up for them? Particularly since we're too stupid even to know what game they're playing here?"

While I mostly agreed with him about the latter, I had a few ideas and they were starting to braid together in my mind. "Did it seem like anyone down in La Ciénega was trying to push you away?"

"Not Luisa!" Francisco said adamantly. "When lunch was almost over, I could tell the alcalde was ready for his nap. That worked in my favor, so I could get her to myself. Everyone else went right out to the barns after lunch and back to work."

"Who saw you off when you started home?"

"Ramón, with a polite handshake. His mother. Luisa of course. The alcalde had departed for Santa Fe while we were on our walk. Ramón was the one who suggested we stroll up the canyon a little. 'The wind's calming down' he said. 'Stay over in the creek canyon, it'll be warmer in there.' Sweetly solicitous, I thought, of two people who had just survived the Camino Real."

"And out of character for a man who is about to threaten your life if you continue to court his cousin."

"True, but he's smooth. That could have been for the benefit of his parents or anyone else listening."

"Directing you up the canyon also kept you away from the barns."

Francisco was nodding in agreement when the door to the meeting room swung open. Sebastian came over and told us it was time to pick up our brother, literally. Before we went to get him, Sebastian filled us in. The guard was to be doubled at the palacio, and extra men posted on the roads south and north of town, in an attempt to round up deserting militiamen. A courier was heading north to tell Anza, assuming he could be found, of the second murder. They were suggesting a special Mass be held for the soldier, and that it be made public that his widow would actually receive a pension, along with his back pay. Word of this unusually generous arrangement was to be leaked to the garrison at once, in hopes the remaining militiamen would reconsider their decision to turn tail.

Word had also just come in, Sebastian said, that the cohort that had pursued the Apaches to retrieve remnants of our caravan had indeed found several of the wagons abandoned in the hills. They'd even won a small skirmish against an Apache war party. The troop was returning in two groups,

179

one right behind today's courier, and a slower contingent bringing back the recovered goods. This would revive spirits and restore some strength to the garrison. Finally a smidgeon of good news.

As soon as Francisco went inside to bundle up Carlos, Sebastian gave me surprise orders. "Perea's headed north. I want you to follow him."

"Wonderful. Has he drawn me a map?"

Sebastian chuckled. "You're lucky this time, Nando. He's tanking up at Rosa's before he leaves. If he doesn't overdo it, he plans to go in the middle of the night. Listen carefully, here are your contacts," and he instructed me who to look for when I got to Santa Cruz.

How on earth Sebastian knew Perea's movements was beyond me, but I paid attention to what he had arranged, then said, "What about Carlos? I'm supposed to be protecting him."

"He's more or less on his feet now, and Francisco can take over the job."

That's debatable, in both cases, I thought as I hauled my share of Carlos down the road to Luz's, mentally packing my bag, and sorely lamenting the loss of my pistol. It was exciting, though, to think about traveling again, and I had the feeling I'd be seeing Marisol soon.

My brothers went straight to bed and I wandered into the sala, where I found Luz praying in front of the Virgin. I could feel the intense buzz of communication between her wiry little body and the statue in the niche. When she got up from her knees, I let her know I was taking off and why. She started at once to fill a pouch with food and to put together my fire kit.

"Where's the governor's gun?" she demanded.

"They took it when they beat up Francisco."

"You loaned it to him?" Her disapproval was stinging.

"I didn't like what he was getting himself into. My old one still works most of the time."

She muttered something about Anza while she filled the water gourds and rolled my blanket, then she disappeared into her room. I heard her slinging things out of the old trunk and kicking objects around, from which I gathered that my stepmother was thoroughly upset.

'Why not?' I thought, as I shoveled chile and venison into my mouth. I was her only family member left who hadn't been thrashed and left for dead. Now I was burdening her with the whole sad lot of them and heading out on a lark of my own. From her point of view, anyway.

In fact, things were a little better. The only thing damaged in Francisco was his hope for an easy marriage to Luisa. His heart couldn't possibly be broken, given her clear enthusiasm for him. He still limped and looked exhausted, but there was nothing a few more nights in a bed wouldn't clear up. Carlos had surprised us all by insisting on joining the leaders at the palacio this evening. If he treated his foot gingerly, and used a stick or someone's shoulder, he could walk across a room now.

Once Luz was through beating up her possessions, she came out of the bedroom and plunked herself down in front of the Virgin again. She refused to be distracted by anyone else's needs, and in the gloomy light of one candle, she prayed fiercely, rattling away at her beads. I had the feeling that she had a thing or two to say to Our Lady, and not exactly as a humble penitent.

I stashed my kit by the doorway and, as instructed, went over to Rosa's bar. When I ducked my head under the low door, I found it quiet in the main salon. It was still early for business, so I looked for her in the back room. Rosa sat in there with Paulina and another girl, idly shuffling cards. She looked up at me from beneath her blackened eyebrows and raised her eyes to a corner of the ceiling, indicating that Perea was above us in the corner room.

"Paulina," she said matter of factly, "take this gentleman up to the green room and show him what a good girl you are."

I opened my mouth in surprise to protest, but Rosa was no longer looking at me. Her face was inside her fan of cards, her concentration on them complete.

Paulina came to my side, her eyes also down. She took my hand and pulled me into the back hall and up the thin stairs to the bedrooms. I doubt anyone would believe that I'd never been up there before, but it's true. Commercial sex doesn't tempt me, probably because I don't have any money.

Paulina put her fingers to her lips as we walked past several cubicles. She let me into the last one, followed me in, and shut the door. We were alone in the little cell. She got on her knees and pulled off my high moccasins. This wasn't exactly what I'd been expecting, but I could see there was unexpected potential in my job.

Then chastely she sat down on the bed beside me. With the rustling of her skirts stilled, I knew at last what was going on. Through the thin lath walls of the brothel, I could hear a man grunting out the last few strokes of his lovemaking, and the pretend sigh of the lady underneath him. I heard their mattress crunch and the covers shift, as they finished their tryst and leaned against the wall that separated us. The acrid smell of punché from his cigar circulated in our air as well as theirs.

Paulina put her mouth right next to my ear and carefully whispered, "Perea."

I pulled her alongside me and we leaned against the partition, comfortably shoulder to shoulder, snuggling just a little while we waited for further action from next door. I realized my own density at not knowing where Sebastian got his information. Clearly he, Rosa, and possibly even my stepmother, were all part of the intelligence network in our tight-knit villa. I was beginning to appreciate the caliber of the company I had been invited to join that night in Anza's office. And, I was at last coming to understand my own role. Nando, half-breed, was the vector, the player who could travel anywhere without restriction. I was the only one of them who could move freely, not only across the territory, but also up and down through its different social strata. I liked that.

I also liked having a warm, good-smelling female cuddled up beside me, but I understood I was at work, for none other than King Carlos, I reminded myself. So I limited my hands to just slowly stroking Paulina's rich, black hair, and listened as best I could through the daubed slats.

Francisco was right. Perea did have an accent, just a slight off-note on a vowel or two, a softer way of using a consonant. Was he from a different part of Mexico, or maybe one of the Caribbean islands? Anyhow, it sounded strange to me, and odd I hadn't noticed it that night listening to him goad Arsenio under the bridge. But then he'd been drinking heavily, and the river's noise had been competing with his voice as well.

"You'll be here next week?" Perea's voice came through the wall.

"Mmmhmm." Sounds of additional seduction. I took it out on the curly strands of Paulina's hair.

"You'll be here when I get back? You want to see me then?" he asked. No further spoken language, though reassurance was obviously offered. Then Perea muttered,

"I've got to go up by Abiquiú to see about a ranch. Meet some friends. Then I'll come back."

"Women friends?" Petulance in a feminine voice.

"Not exactly." Avoidance, dissembling. "Just checking up on someone's wife."

My fingers stopped combing through Paulina's hair.

"Where's her husband?" the girlfriend asked.

"That's the problem. He doesn't know if she's all right, and he can't leave, he's in the army. She used to be a friend of mine."

The lady was no fool. "Just doing a pal a favor, right?"

"Ouch! You bit me!" Giggling. Playful wrestling noises from next door. To my surprise, Paulina leaned over and bit my upper arm ever so gently. I bent and kissed the top of her head, still listening carefully.

Perea's voice again. "Can I sleep here for a while, do you think?"

"Rosa told me I could let you stay. I think she knows you're special." Good acting or true love? I would have to check the identity of this girl when I got a chance, to see which team she was really on.

"Can you wake me up in a couple of hours?" Perea asked her. "I've got to get to Santa Cruz to meet my companions by noon."

Murmur of assent.

Companions? Was this going to be a party? I needed to tell Sebastian about this development before I left.

There was whispering and the gentle realigning of body parts, then the room next door went silent, but only for a minute. Stentorian snoring soon shook our wall, and we tip-toed out with no fear of being overheard.

My Father's Gun

$\mathcal{B}$ack at Luz's, I saddled Rosinante, hoping she had the stuff to hold out for another strenuous journey. I wondered about asking my stepmother for her mule as back-up, but I didn't like leaving the family without a single mount. I tiptoed into the house and stuffed some leftover tortillas into my mouth while I gathered my kit.

"Nando."

I jumped. Luz sat in her chair in the dark, waiting for me like any good mother. Now that I knew she was there, I could just see her outline against the paler light coming through the open door.

"This belonged to Benito." She passed into my hands a beautiful pistol, its fine steel shining, the smooth curve of its handle molding neatly into my hand.

"It's yours." She couldn't see the expression on my face, but she heard me say softly,

"That's amazing. It fits my hand perfectly."

The KING'S LIZARD

"Why not? He was your father. Take it on your journey. There's powder here, some extra flints and shot enough if you're careful. She handed me the leather bag of tools and supplies for the flintlock.

"Luz, you've had this all along?"

"It seemed like a good thing to have around. There used to be two. I gave one to Francisco when he went south. Carlos, of course, has arms provided by the military. Francisco didn't bring his gun back. I haven't had time to ask him why."

"That's two he's lost then, and each, I suppose, carries a tale. What will you use now if the need comes?"

"Francisco, Carlos and my wits. I've never needed that pistol yet, and I think you might. So take it and may God stay close to you. I believe that this man you are following is guilty of the death of many people, both New Mexicans and Comanches. He won't be happy to have you on his trail."

"I intend to keep him from knowing that I am. Luz, I just found out he's meeting more men in Santa Cruz. I won't know who they are until I see them at noon tomorrow. I need to leave at once in order to be well placed in the town before he arrives. Will you tell Sebastian that the party increases? It's now Perea and companions."

"I'll find Sebastian on my way to Mass. Is that soon enough?"

I strapped on the holster and tested the draw of the pistol. "Tomorrow will be fine. My guess is whoever is attacking your sons will be gone from here for a while. I think you can concentrate on healing them. Get them rested and put some meat on their bones. In a few days I'll be back, and then I plan to take my turn."

"Will you be on the Taos or the Abiquiú road?"

"Abiquiú, I think, but I'm not the person calling the shots here."

187

She put her arms up and drew me down into a loving hug. She held me close, made the sign of the cross over my heart, and said softly, "God speed."

After my long, fast ride to Santa Cruz, I went right to the army's stables, as Sebastian had instructed, and even though the sun had barely risen, there was one small man already starting to work with the horses. He could tell at a glance that Rosinante had a stone bruise. He came over from where he'd been pouring water into a wooden trough, and bent down over the horse's leg, tapping her to pick up.

"You'll need another mount, I can tell." He had the deepest voice I'd ever heard. I agreed, but reluctantly, because last time I'd left Rosinante here, Ramón had stolen her.

He gestured to the handful of ready-looking animals in the paddock and said, "Take your pick."

I looked at him in question, and he replied, "Orders. Just come to me. My name's Juanillo. Any animal you want."

I took a chance. "Any word of the governor?"

He ignored that completely but said, "And you'll be needing sleep. Over there in the hay barn it's quiet and dark. I'll let you know when Perea arrives." This was an entirely new world for me. I pretended not to be amazed that this groom knew my secret business. I was trying to get up to speed as fast as I could.

"Pick my animal, will you? You'll know them better than I. The country will be rough and the days long."

I heard Juanillo rumble, "What's new?" He limped, because of what seemed to be a short leg, over to the barn and threw a blanket into a corner on the hay, then said, "Go to sleep. You have a few hours."

I must have trusted him because I dropped off immediately, having short little dreams in which Paulina and Marisol became mixed up in my mind. Then the scene switched to a dog snarling and snapping at my legs, leaping at my face. I reached out to fend it off and found myself pushing at the crippled groom, who shook my shoulder with one hand and set a pot of food beside me with the other.

"Nerves on edge, looks like. Ought to be. The quarry's arrived and having lunch two doors down from the plaza."

"Lunch! God, man. Good thing you woke me. I'd have slept 'til tomorrow."

"Looked like it," he said. "You want more of that I can get it for you." He pointed to the pot.

"How many men?" I asked, starting in with the spoon.

"Perea, Duran's son, and one other. Not sure who he is."

Ramón. No surprise, really, but not good news, and some unknown person. Were my hunches holding? Could I be about to meet Lorenzo again?

"They've got two pack mules readied, and fresh horses for each of them. I'd say gear for a week."

I looked at my own small sack of supplies and wondered if it would do.

"There's more ready for you, but we want you light. It's hard to conceal yourself on that road, so you may have to take the long way round. I've picked out a mule for you, descended from the best stallion in the garrison's herd. We need to get you off that animal of yours anyway, in case you're spotted. It's easy to disguise a man, but not his horse." I'd been thinking that myself, but wasn't aware I'd be so well taken care of.

Now that Juanillo was good and ready he answered the question I'd asked six hours ago. "The governor's made good contact with the Indians he was hoping to talk to. It's been patched up. He's taking a chance though, going deeper into Comanche territory. He needs to push his advantage. Two more bands are meeting with him on the other side of the mountains. Essentially he's completing the work that was started at the parley, before everything went awry. We heard he had to eat a little crow, but he's a tough man and he can give a lot without being weakened by it. Five or six more days probably, until he's down from there."

I was waking up, eating, thinking and talking all at once. "How come Ramón's mixed up with men like these, Perea and the like, when his father is the governor's friend?"

"Wait 'til you raise kids," the groom offered laconically. "It makes Anza's problem a lot more delicate, but if Ramón's truly a bad one, the governor will do what he has to in the end. My guess is he's put the alcalde in the picture. They're too close to have avoided it, but Anza would be diplomatic."

"Any idea where they're heading, or when I'm taking off?" Might as well ask, I thought, because this little man seemed to know just about everything.

"We think you'll be going northeast toward Taos, rather than along the Abiquiú route. At dusk most likely. We'll station a man to watch until you get past the junction, to learn which direction you end up traveling. We're sending someone along with you too, so you'll have a way to get word back if there's anything we need to know."

This came as a surprise. Did I need to be watched? I think he saw my discomfort because he quickly added, "You know the boy. His name's Miguel. You brought him down from Medanales after the raid. They gave him to me to help with the horses, but he was so quick and eager the sergeant thought he might do for a scout. He's just in training, but all he'll really need to know is how to get back here."

That makes two of us just in training, I thought. However, I never minded company on the road; the journey went by much faster. Besides, who was I to argue? Someone clearly had this whole mission planned down to the last loaf of bread.

The groom spoke again. "If you need to contact us you have one chance, and that's Miguel. From then on, you've got to figure it out for yourself, though at least we'll know into which corner of the province you've been drawn. Once you send Miguel back though, you're on your own. You, one mule and a pistol—I oiled it for you while you slept. That's a hand-some piece." He ignored my blush at my obvious lack of caution.

Great, I thought, rolling up to my feet and shaking out the blanket in a great flurry of glistening hay. "Let's get on with it!"

IV

The KING'S LIZARD

The Chieftain's Daughter

In Ute Territory, Above Saguache

*T*he light, the grass and the trees, all the way to the bottom of the meadow, were faintest blue, and moisture beaded the tall bushes. Nan sat in the aspen grove listening to the creek running noisily after the night of rain. Her blanket kept most of her warm, but her feet were cold, soaked by the wet grass. Behind her, at the top of the meadow, the people slept in their lodges, buffalo skins pulled tight across the doorways.

The woman had risen early because she was afraid, and she needed time away from everyone to let her thoughts develop into more than just vague, but persistent, worries.

It was odd that she felt this way, because her father's people were happy. This place at the edge of the mountains was one of the best in which they'd ever lived. They had plenty of food, and no babies had died last winter. The horse herd was healthy and many now were fast, impressive animals. In this high valley no enemies had found them. She realized that as a people they had never been this strong.

195

She had sat with the men last night while they talked with her father. Though it was five years now since she had come home to her parents, she was still pleased to spend as much time as she could beside them. For twenty years they had been lost to her, and now that she was home she was still drinking them in. Partly it was because a piece of her was lonely for her man who had died, and for her oldest son whom she hadn't brought back with her to the People. She recognized there was an empty place left within her, so she stayed close to the family she still had.

Last night's gathering had been tumultuous. The young men wanted to ride south. There was promise of a good fight and more guns for the people, good guns, not the cheap, easily broken ones the Spanish offered in trade.

All of the men, not just the younger, restless ones, spoke of their worry about this coming arrangement between the Spanish and the old enemy, the Comanches. Some wanted to ride to Santa Fe right away and demand to be part of the treaty that was being made, but they weren't the majority. Most pushed to destroy the Comanches right now, before they entered into the coward's alliance with Spain that had been rumored for months among all the people in the foothills.

The arrival of yesterday's visitors had taken their peaceful village and turned it upside down. Incredibly, they had talked of joining the Apaches! Nan spat the piece of grass she was chewing onto the wet earth. She knew enough about life not to go to bed with Apaches.

Smoke began to rise from a cookfire at the camp. The woman laughed. It would be tough to get that one to burn this morning. When the sun moved to the foot of the grove, she untied her moccasins and wiggled her bare feet in the warm light. She set the shoes on a stone and turned them so they would dry.

Her father's face had been troubled. He had worked hard with the younger men, but he wouldn't say no to them, not at this point anyway. She could see he had been worried though, and she noticed that he kept checking the face of his grandson, her youngest boy. Would he, too, be eager to travel south look-ing for guns and booty and the chance to prove himself? Of course he would, but she took comfort knowing the men wouldn't invite him, since he was still so young.

A squirrel started bickering at her from high up in a spruce. The sun's warmth pulled moisture from the wet world and the mist rose like smoke. Something in her settled. She would ask her father to let her travel south, and she wouldn't resist when he insisted that men accompany her. It was a good way for the chief to get information and to let some young ones travel without jeopardizing anything. She wouldn't be afraid, now that so much time had passed, to visit the old family. She could find out from them more about this threat that loomed over the future of her people. If the Comanches were becoming the friends of the Europeans, that could make the Utes the new number one en-emy. Would the Spaniards come to revile her people and try to eliminate them too, like the Apaches and Navajos? The Utes had almost always held a special place with the Spanish. Would that be lost now?

She could hear the camp waking up and someone moving the horses. It was time she got back; it wasn't all right to leave for so long when there was work to be done. She lingered a moment though, looking into the sunny woods, while she put on her wet moccasins.

Nan knew her father would say at first that she couldn't go, but after a day or two he would give her permission and whatever she needed to travel safely. There was no hurry. She wouldn't be leaving right away, because he would wait long enough to make her think it was his own idea. Even with his favorite daughter he had to keep his power as the chief, but she was counting on how much he missed his oldest grandson and how he would welcome the chance to get news of him and to urge him to come back. He also knew she spoke the languages and even had a stepson inside the government she could talk to. She would learn about this treaty, and then she could help. Her years among the Spanish would now serve her people, to keep them from being driven from the strength and comfort they had only so recently achieved.

Gully Lizard

1 knew we were headed for Abiquiú after eavesdropping on Perea. I figured I'd just lead out a bit on that road, wait until he came along, and then move in behind him. But now that I had Miguel and also some mysterious escort on my flank, I decided I'd better play it by the book, so when Perea and his two friends pulled out at dusk, we gave them a half a mile's lead, then followed.

They could have made a fool out of me right then, when they ignored the Abiquiú cutoff.

I knew they had a second, sneakier chance to switch to it at San Juan, so Miguel and I rode up there and waited in the cottonwoods while the threesome had their supper. A left-hand turn after dinner would take them over the river and up to Abiquiú, or they'd go straight north toward the haciendas on the Rio Grande, which meant we were off to Taos.

We took turns hanging back with the mules in the woods, or crouching close to the Y in the road. Maybe they wouldn't come at all, because it was also possible they'd spend the night in San Juan.

Perea didn't let us down, and within half an hour they clattered out of the pueblo. It's hard to conceal three men on horses, two pack mules and extra mounts, but contrary to what Perea had said earlier, they took the right fork and headed straight north. Did Perea lie even to his girlfriend? In the night we couldn't watch for tracks, so we had to move in pretty close and keep alert for sounds. All my senses told me that, after they took the north road at the junction, the groom's invisible observer had left us and returned to Santa Cruz, to report Perea's choice of direction. Taos!

Miguel dropped behind to lessen the chance they might overhear us. A sliver of moon rose into the opening at the tops of the overhanging cottonwoods, providing the faintest light that gave us glimpses of the three men ambling along at a pace safe for night riding. I had to hold us back time and again, trying to overcome my urge to be right on top of them. I wanted to figure out who the third man was and to listen in.

Moonlight glancing off a piece of steel was my only warning that they had stopped abruptly in the center of the road. Then I heard branches breaking and animals moving through deep leaves. They were slipping into the forest.

Miguel came up to me quietly. Together we listened as Perea and company sneaked off the Taos road and fumbled in the woods for a trail they knew would secretly take them west, over the Rio Grande. They must have found it, for they became quieter, just one snap of a branch telling me they were on the cleared path that wound through the bosque and back to the Abiquiú road.

I let them go. Miguel and I waited until they were out of earshot, then we turned and walked our mounts back to San

Juan, on the softer ground at the edge of the road. At the pueblo we turned west and looked for a way to cross the fully flooded river. It was going to be a deep, wet crossing so we stripped naked. Good thing, as we couldn't ride it, but had to swim beside the mules. I had no idea if Miguel had ever done anything like this before, or even if he could swim, but he managed, and I could just make out his relieved grin when we stood on the west bank and shook the water off us.

Now that I knew where Perea was going, we rode flat out a good couple of miles toward Abiquiú in order to position ourselves. There were farms in here and we started the dogs barking, but I couldn't afford to care.

We easily forded the smaller Chama, then holed up in a willow thicket not far from the river, and chewed on some toasted corn before we rode on. As I'd hoped, I heard those same dogs bark again, letting me know that Perea had now made it across the Rio Grande and was behind us. I liked it better that way. I'd ridden this road all my life and even if I lost them for a while it wouldn't be for long, because I knew the best places to stop for feed and water. I had a fair idea where he might hide during the day, though I couldn't be sure that he'd do so. No matter, Miguel and I rode along ahead of them, easier now that we weren't always in danger of tripping over them.

I could see there wasn't enough night left to give us cover before we crossed the wide, dry bed of the Arroyo del Oso. So we dismounted and, being careful to brush out our tracks where we left the road, we walked the mules along the arroyo's south bank into the ever-thickening trees by the river. I found a place to hide in the willow underbrush. Then, leaving Miguel and the animals, I walked quietly down to the Chama.

The sun was just breaking over the craggy top of the red mesa that jutted up immediately in front of me. Now that it was light, I was no longer free to move about, but for a moment I stood in the bushes on the bank, taking in the bright colors of my own country. I was thinking how much I loved this fast, red river, when I was startled to see a man getting up from a crouch on the beach. He was a lean, smooth-limbed Apache whom I hadn't noticed washing in the water, just over the roll of the sandbank.

Slowly, I lowered myself into the brush, hoping my old buckskin clothes would look like one more drab bush. The man rose, stretched and began plodding through the mud up the beach. Staying in the trees, I followed until he joined a dozen of his people around a small fire. They were chatting, sharing food and unwrapping themselves from their blankets, as the sun's rays found the floor of the forest where they camped. This wasn't a casually traveling family; they were all men of warrior age. Their handsome horses were tied to a long, fallen tree not far from where I'd stopped.

I needed to return to Miguel and move him and the animals back, then try to get myself close enough to find out what the Indios were doing here. Mostly Apaches don't come in so close to the villages and when they do they are a lot more secretive than this.

I was backtracking to Miguel, thirty feet inside the bosque, when I heard Perea's group approaching. He and his friends rode nonchalantly over the open ground alongside the groves. They had the air of kids just let out of catechism class. I suppose Perea thought he had outwitted any followers with the quick maneuver in the woods last night. Ramón, I was glad to see, was soaking wet, his leathers dark. He must have gotten dumped in the river. I hoped his pants dried on him too hard and too tight.

I caught my first up-close glimpse of the third man. He wore a greasy hat and leggings. It took a lot of leather to cover him. He was tall and rode a strong horse that he handled well. He was older than the other two. His long, stringy hair blew wildly awry so I couldn't see his face.

I lay on the ground while they passed, praying Miguel had his wits about him, though I don't know how you make mules lie down flat. Perea's group was heading right into the band of breakfasting Apaches, but I certainly wasn't kind enough to warn him. The colony's troubles could be over in the next five minutes.

Perea rode past me and soon I heard a faint rustling, maybe a squirrel in the leaves. I turned and there was Miguel, grinning at me from behind a shaggy juniper and pointing toward the back of Perea's group. I waved at him and with my hand indicated that there were several men up there and he should stay put and low. With his nod of acknowledgement I was free to wiggle into Apache territory. I moved warily toward their camp, expecting to hear musket fire at any second, but to the contrary, it was very quiet.

Using a dry creek bed to hide in, I crawled toward them. When it rained, water would pour from this arroyo onto the beach near the Indian camp, but now it was bone-dry. I had a short wand of leafy cottonwood tucked into the back of my pants and when I got close enough to hear, I used it as a blind. When a sharp-tailed lizard scurried across my path, I chuckled, remembering Anza's words to me, but as I inched along with warm sand on my belly, I was actually scared spitless. If any one of the fifteen men spotted me, I'd be a squashed skink for sure.

There was an odd air of merriment down below. Perea and Ramón were off their horses and the Indians had gathered around them. There was much brotherly grasping of shoulders and Ramón even ruffled the hair of one of the Apaches. The third man was slower to dismount. Age maybe. After Perea introduced him to the group, the lanky stranger walked right over to the cut bank beneath me and took a lengthy leak. He wasn't eight feet away and I learned a lot about him right then. Including the fact that he was Padre Baldonado.

He took off his hat and wiped his brow. The padre's pate was clean-shaven in the typical Franciscan tonsure, but with his hat on no one would know. The sickly looking hair I'd seen turned out to be a fake fringe, courtesy of someone's scalp probably, sewn or glued into the brim. It must have plagued him though, because he brought up all ten fingers and scratched. He was so close that I heard him sigh as he put the hat back on and went over to the group.

I could tell Perea was fluent in Apache, and Ramón followed along pretty well. Padre Baldonado stayed close but didn't say anything. He was unpacking one of the mules, temptingly laying the wrapped bundles out on the sand. From my perch on the wooded riverbank, I couldn't hear all that much, but I caught words and gestures. They spoke the governor's name many times and I saw the Apaches separate into two groups.

They couldn't conceal their excitement when Ramón unwrapped the two packages, one of gleaming new guns, those much-coveted lighter ones with the shorter barrels, the other of efficient-looking pistols. Ramón handed each of the Apaches a new weapon and bags of ammunition, which the men hung from their belts.

The first and larger group of Indios was traveling light and they packed and mounted within minutes. No Spaniards accompanied them as they rode straight east into the sunlight, taking the cold river at breast height and then moving swiftly up through the broken talus at the mesa's foot. Clearly they were seeking higher, rougher ground to avoid farms and pueblo people. They barely made a sound, although they traveled on loose rock. There was no doubt in my mind where they were going: due east and slightly north, to ambush Governor Anza as he returned from his meetings with the Comanches.

Perea and Ramón would have picked up the same news in Santa Cruz that the groom had given me, of Anza's successes and of his timing, though his return route was anybody's guess.

The three Spaniards and the remaining Indians stood side by side on the rocky beach, watching the Apache war party ride out of sight. Seeing them chatting and grinning there, it was clear to me that anyone who armed Apaches was also crazy enough to send them in pursuit of our governor. I itched to get Miguel back on the road to Santa Cruz with the news.

Now all the gestures of the remaining Apaches and Perea's group pointed upriver, to the north and west. After the distribution of arms, one mule was left with all the weight, so Perea and Ramón pulled it over into the shade not far from me and transferred some of its load to the other animal. I heard Ramón ask Perea, "Do any of these Apaches speak Ute?"

Perea clenched a leather strap between his teeth while he worked on a lashing. He could only nod until his mouth was free. "Two of them, and the padre says he can speak it some. We should be all right. We'll have to go behind the Sierra Negra to get past the narrows at Abiquiú without being seen, but I don't think we'll have any trouble. We'll still get to the Piedra Lumbre by dusk. Someone will lead us in when we get there.

I'll send the Indians ahead by the same route. I've learned it's too damn hard to go around Abiquiú through the mountains."

"You're the scout," said Ramón.

"When we cross the river again," Perea was looking down, concentrating on a clasp, "I've got someone I need to visit in Medanales."

"Not allowed!" Ramón ordered.

"It's a pretty important favor someone asked me."

"I said you're not going. No one's to know we've been anywhere near here."

"I told you it's important." Perea's voice had an edge to it as he persisted. "There's a woman who needs attention." The bastard actually laughed when he said, "You could consider it part of our militia intimidation process, a little additional twist, to keep the business of the dead guards right up front in every-body's mind."

Ramón was interested now. "What's her name?"

"That doesn't matter. Let's just say this is unfinished business."

Ramón observed him closely, then yielded. "If the Utes go for our deal and agree to help us, we're set. Then you can take a detour on the way back down."

Perea had a mouthful of leather again. His bristly brows gathered together in annoyance, but he gave a curt, obedient nod.

The four Apaches took off first. A few minutes later Perea, Ramón and the priest led out, moving upstream a few dozen yards before they kicked their horses up the sharp, red face of the river bank and disappeared into trees. I gave them five minutes in case they had forgotten anything, then rolled over onto my back and exhaled forcefully. I think I had held my breath for an hour and a half.

I expected Miguel had moved our animals by increments deeper into the woods, to get away from the men at the river, but I turned and found him crouching right behind me, watching the scene below as avidly as I. He was a sneaky one, all right. I would make sure the army knew just how good he was. Then I gave him his marching orders.

"Get back to Santa Cruz and tell Juanillo there's an Apache war party looking to intercept Anza. Eight men, newly armed, thanks to Perea and Duran. Best looking weapons I've seen in a long time. They can be over at the Rio Grande and twenty miles upriver by the end of the day. It'll take some convincing on your part, but tell them there's no doubt the third person is the crazy padre, Baldonado, dressed as a trader, with a phony hairpiece sewn into his hat. Only God knows what the man's doing here, but I plan to stick close enough to find out."

"A padre? Traveling with these characters?"

"Yes, and when he shuffled his gear I spotted his habit rolled up in a bundle. He's set up to play both roles on this trip. Tell Juanillo that."

"What do I tell him about you?"

"It looks like they have a rendezvous with some Utes out on the Piedra Lumbre. I'm heading up there. Heck, I might even get to see my family's ranch again, but don't tell anyone that. They're traveling with four Apaches and the padre speaks Ute, so they've covered the translating. Also, they don't plan to be seen anywhere in the valley."

"The padre knows Ute? I thought all padres think everyone speaks only Spanish or Latin? Why would he have learned Ute?"

"I have absolutely no idea, but everything about the man's a mystery to me. Can you repeat the message?"

"Yes."

"Then tell it back to me."

He did, nearly perfectly and without benefit of any training by Luz. Then Miguel looked at me, worried. "Nando, you've already got enough evidence to hang them as traitors, seeing them arming the Indians and plotting to attack the governor. It hasn't been safe to go above the rim onto the Piedra Lumbre for four years, and now you're doing it alone?" He pleaded with me. "You don't have to go up there. You should come back with me and give first-hand information."

"Sorry Miguel, but my orders are to stick with these men. Go now. Santa Cruz needs to hear about this."

He shrugged like he'd tried, clasped my hand and took off. I watched him riding to the south, picking his way through the leafy groves that bordered the river. I hoped he'd make it down there in one piece, and I was glad to see he kept to good cover. His were awfully skinny shoulders to be carrying the future of the colony.

The boy was smart and his advice wasn't bad, but if I played this right I could learn who among the Utes might be hooking up with the Apaches. I might even know them personally, after that year living with my mother's tribe. I also had another reason to stay up here. Perea seemed particularly intent on finding Marisol, and I planned to see that it was the last thing he ever did.

Moonlight On Barns

*I*t was approaching dark and it had been another long day, but I was on top of the rim now. I rode slower, mindful of the noise I made, traveling the same road that had taken me home all the years of my childhood. At the bottom of the vast, tilted slope, the river glittered in the dwindling light. Soaring sandstone cliffs protected these plains, lifting above them like gold and purple castles. Ahead of me rose the towering, flat-topped Pedernal, casting its final shadow long and deep all the way to the river below.

How I would find the rendezvous on this huge plateau eluded me. Night was about to close in. I was near enough to the ranch that I decided to return there, protected by darkness, and maybe even to sleep in my old home. I would feel safer there than anywhere out in the night. Possibly. The inky crone shapes of the twisted cedars, and the dense shadows under the piñons, were making me as nervous as a girl about to shoot her first gun. I was scaring the animal under me too. When I knew from the road's turn uphill that we were almost at the ranch, I slid off the mule, took it to the creek and tied it. I went on by foot.

I got there the same time the moonlight did. The long shadows of the houses reached across the farmyard to the low barns. This place had existed for so long only in my head that I had trouble reconciling these crumbled buildings with my memory of the lively plazuela where we had once flourished. I crept up to the rear of the main house. The silence scared me. I hadn't the courage to face the ghosts inside, so I quietly prowled the exterior of the compound, not too sure in the eerie light if this was truly my old home. Then I found a bench I had made, a split log on two posts that I had dug into the earth beside the door, a ten-year-old's triumph. Our three, long houses still stood, but their plank doors were gone.

Finally I went into the smallest house where my cousins had lived. Moonlight glared off the heap of fallen earth that had crashed down when the roof caved in. A shelf sagged, bearing blocks of tumbled adobe. I smelled animal urine, like wildcat, and I backed out of there, wary.

The barns were in ruins too, cedar fence rails lying askew, roof beams rotted out, the dirt that once covered them washed away. Deep in the barns' shadows, heaps of debris, prickly with cactus, bespoke the new inhabitants, packrats. The little well-house, with its pointed roof and delicately carved arches, lay broken in the dirt of the courtyard. The apricot tree was twisted and small. I stroked it and saw there were a few tiny leaves sprouting on its dried-out limbs.

At last I went into the main house. Except for a long crack in the wall at the corner of the sala, deep and wide enough to leak moonlight all over the floor, it was intact. The floor was still solid, the roof had held. We once had oiled skins in the windows, but now only shreds flapped.

The kitchen floor had been flagstone. Some of that was pulled up, awkward to move across in the pitch black, but I made my way. I realized I had become desperate to see the room we called the nest where we'd lived with our mother. Its interior door was still in place. I pushed at it and felt it sweep debris back as it opened.

Sipapu, womb, hearth, nest, home. I sat on the edge of the wooden bed frame built into the corner and wondered how a world could be so changed. Where was my mother? Why had my father died so suddenly, going from vigorous health to bones in the ground in a few months? All the people of our little plazuela had scattered, pressed to lonely and bare existences on their own. Maybe my brothers and I would rebuild. Maybe we would come back.

I climbed up onto the wide, raised shelf above the fireplace where I had slept when I was too big to share a bed with Nan. I set my pistol beside me, pulled my manta over both it and me, and decided I would stay here a few hours and sleep. For just a little while I needed not to be the king's saddle-sore sleuth. I just needed to be Nando at home.

I dreamed of a house full of lambs that lay all over the floors of the sala, the kitchen, the sleeping rooms. Men hurried in from the storm, carrying newborn sheep under their cloaks, and handed them to dark-haired women who worked to clean and dry the precious animals in front of the roaring fires. In my dream I was sent out in the night, into the wet, dripping snow, to find more, to keep looking. "There is blood on the snow, they are easy to find," voices assured me. There were so many lambs, and Luz standing in the middle of her sala, smeared with mud, exclaiming over the filth in her house, bending to tend another one. I was told to bring in more wood and was allowed to stack damp logs right inside, to get them dry enough to burn.

I dreamed of my father calling out for water, of hoof beats, of a rattlesnake floating at me through the air, flying level and direct toward my face. I dreamed of the smell of smoke.

I rolled onto my pistol and woke up. I still smelled smoke. I could see the red glow of fire on the ceiling of my room. It crackled and shot sparks into the sky just outside my window. With a firm grip on my father's pistol, I slid down from the hearth-bed and silently made my way to where I could see out.

In the wide courtyard a bonfire blazed high into the night sky. Men in blankets sat around it, piling on more wood. Firelight gleamed on the shiny coats of the horses that were tied to posts in front of our old barns. There were men wearing wide-brimmed European hats. There were men with mantas pulled over their heads. There were men whose long hair was decorated with strung beads on leather thongs. I realized I no longer had to look for the rendezvous. It had found me.

I knew there were two ways I could get out of this room, through the window smack into the circle of men, or using the door, through the kitchen, the sala, and out the back window there. Who else might be in the house by now? Who might have spotted my mule and started looking for me? I thought about the chimney, but I remembered it as being too narrow.

But why leave? My vantage was perfect, even warm and out of the wind. I couldn't hear them very well, but there was no way was I going to get any closer than this, and I could catch some of the words. Their gestures told me plenty about how their negotiations progressed. Clearly the Spaniards and

Apaches were trying to overcome old feelings of mistrust and to convince the Utes to join them in some venture. I didn't recognize these Utes, but from their clothes, I knew they were from a tribe west of my mother's people. The Spaniards sat together on blankets, with the Apaches on their right and the Utes to their left. Across the fire, there was still a wide gap between the traditional enemies. Clearly, they weren't ready to close the circle.

Yet it seemed relaxed. No one gripped a weapon or was itching for a fight. The men roasted meat on long sticks, venison, from the rich smell of it. They passed a gourd around. Surely Ramón wasn't dumb enough to bring liquor up here? Not if he wanted cooperation.

It was clear that he was the one running this meeting, while his companions translated, Perea for the Apaches, the padre for the Utes. The Indians had their spokesmen too. The Apache was calm and studied in his presentation. The man who spoke for the Utes was younger than the other leaders, but backed up by a dozen fighting men, two of whom waited by the horses. Was another man now patrolling the property, keeping an eye on the flanks? I sensed a tension in the Apaches, who were wary because they were outnumbered.

I'd say for a man trying to bring oil and water together, Ramón had a good night of it. He was handsome and affable. He spoke with deference to the other leaders. Food was passed and it moved from hand to hand with equality through the group. The barriers were breaking down.

The discussion seemed to be mainly among the three leaders, then was translated for everybody else. I couldn't hear the actual words, but I understood the drift and I could tell, too, that most of the Indians understood the other languages without benefit of either Perea or the padre's help.

The moon disappeared and the fire burned down. They stopped adding wood to it and sat there in silence. A pipe was passed; all the men smoked, even the padre. It didn't smell like our rank punché. It was some sweet herb. There was a sense of closure, but I wasn't sure if an agreement had been reached.

As the night ebbed, I worried again about how I would extricate myself. I knew the Indians wouldn't come inside the house, but Perea's group might welcome a roof. The old phrase, *mi casa, su casa* wasn't too appealing. There was no way I wanted to be sharing my house with them.

Before I had come up with a plan, the circle began to break apart. The men stood, stretched, wrapped their blankets tighter and started drifting away from the fire. It was time for me to get moving and find a way out of here. Gun in hand, I slipped around the half-closed door of my bedroom and crawled on hands and knees through the kitchen. Then, out of some old memory, probably tweaked by being on all fours, I remembered the wood chute where we threw kindling into the house for the cook fire. I used to exasperate the women by climbing in and out of it when I was little. I found it easily, but wiggling into it as a man was another matter. Somehow I squeezed through and fell out on the back side of the house. From there it was easy to sneak into the woods and down to the creek. I grabbed the mule's reins and tugged it straight up a side gully, directly away from the houses. I needed distance fast before the beast started braying, and I got it by climbing straight up into the ever-thicker forest above the ranch.

I had maybe a half hour of darkness left, which I used to get the mule stashed in the next canyon, and then I climbed onto the sandstone bluff that formed the back wall of our ranch. By sunrise, I was lying half way up the red and gold cliff in a yellow dish of stone, encircled by tiny, newly budded oaks.

When I pushed myself up on my arms, I could peer down onto our houses.

The Apaches had slept by the fire and the Spaniards were folding their blankets on the portál. Going into the abandoned buildings had been too eerie a proposition even for them. The Utes had camped by the creek. They were rising, scooping handfuls of food out of pouches, and gathering their gear. Two of them walked back up to the buildings and talked with the others for a while. They showed no fear, confirming my impression that an agreement had been struck. The Utes rode off first, heading down onto the plateau, taking a northward route across the Piedra Lumbre. It looked like they were going home to talk this over with their tribe.

Utes and Apaches together? That would be a formidable alliance, one that would offset any gain made by Spaniards befriending the Comanches. Surely it would drive any and all Comanches out of this area along the Chama, which would give the Utes a deeper inroad to the south, to the main caravan route and the farms of the lower Rio Grande, places that until now had been the Apaches' sole domain. Those two tribes linked together could devastate the Spanish colony.

Ramón and Perea were having one last friendly talk with the Apaches who'd traveled with them. From above, I watched Padre Baldonado walk alone toward the edge of the forest. In a few minutes, he emerged from the trees into a sunny meadow where he stopped and knelt, facing the morning sun. Who was this man who looked so pious at his prayers, but whose actions were so devious? Was he just confused, or crazy? Or was he simply evil?

When he returned, he hastened over to his horse. Ramón and Perea were already mounted, ready to go, but at the last moment Ramón seemed to have an afterthought, for he waved the other two on down the road, dismounted, and walked back to my family's old home.

He explored as I had last night, examining every building. He peered into the dusky barns. He walked across the portál and then finally entered our house, spending some time in there. From my perch I couldn't tell what he was doing, but long minutes later, when he emerged, he stood on the porch like a man at home. He shaded his eyes with his hands and admired the view of the plains to the north. Then, to my surprise, he dragged poles and timbers from a barn over to the house and sealed the doorway in a rough, but practical, way. Ramón worked with a proprietary air, and to my annoyance, he walked on my ranch like a man would on his own.

What a nice location this would be for a person whose business was illegal and who operated in the forbidden lands to the north. His only problem in taking possession would be the prior right of the Aguilar men. The images of Carlos bleeding in the river, and Francisco regaining consciousness after a long night in the open, entered my mind.

Finally the intruder left and I climbed down the cliff and went back to the houses. I was afraid he might have noticed my footprints and realized that someone else had roamed the buildings last night, so I went back inside to see what evidence there might be of my earlier visit. I decided, looking around, that I'd been lucky. There was nothing obvious.

I spent a few more minutes in the house, remembering the tiniest details of our former life. In the rubble of the room that my father had shared with Luz, I found the rain-soaked, faded book that she had taught me to read, the sad remnants of their Bible. I stuffed it in my leather bag to take back to her. In the kitchen I found a big piece of broken crockery and went down to the creek three times, carrying water up to the apricot tree.

Next I studied the prints at the fire ring, noting types of footgear and then kicking through the dust for any bits of evidence the men might have left. A dull coin flipped up from under my moccasin where Ramón had been sitting. When I wiped the dirt off I saw that it was gold, and not like any coin I had seen before. I turned it over, trying to make out the writing, but it was unfamiliar to me. Carefully I put it in my fire pouch. Less than two weeks on the job and I was richer than I'd ever been!

Then I went over to where we had buried my father. The mound was there, the rocks still piled tidily on it, though the wooden cross was gone. I went down on my knees to pray to the man I had loved with all my heart, and as my eyes cast across the ground to his grave, I saw the prints of another man's knees in the curdled earth. Apparently not only I, but someone else as well, had been moved to pray for my father, Don Benito Aguilar.

Rare Peso

I didn't realize I had beaten them into Abiquiú. I entered the plaza via my private route up the back of the hill and through the tiny alley. It was the best way to get to cousin Diego's house and remain unseen in the nosy village. I wasn't sure if I could trust him after he'd almost sold me, and for sure he'd lied to me about Ramón not being a slaver. I held my knife hidden up my sleeve so he couldn't see it, but I'd wait to hear his story before deciding whether to use it or not. He jumped a foot when he saw me step onto his porch.

"Holy Mother of God, Nando, I thought it was your ghost."

"You figured they'd killed me?"

For a minute my cousin tried to act tough. "I wasn't counting on it until they read me your will." I glared at him until he knocked it off, and when he spoke again I realized how scared he actually was. "I knew you'd be back to straighten this out," he said. "Are you all right? Where did they take you?"

"Not far. I got away in Taos with the help of Carlos. Since then I've been in Santa Fe mainly. Carlos got hurt, and I helped

Luz take care of him. Francisco made it home too, after a disastrous trip up the Camino. I've been playing nursemaid to all of them. Diego, why in God's name did you lie to me?"

I swear he hung his head in shame. "It happened so fast. There they were spreading money around and you walked into the room. You saw me retract the deal, but then when the recruiters rode in, I figured going with Ramón wasn't so bad, it would save your hide."

"You little shit!" I had him by the collar and was gathering energy to slam him into the wall, when below us I saw Perea and company ride onto the plaza. They looked for all the world like caballeros out for a spring jaunt, fresh and full of their own importance. I needed to see where they went, but right now I was busy. I couldn't let Diego get away with this.

I backed into the house to concentrate on my cousin who slumped in my hands, willing to be punished it seemed. "You acted like you were protecting me and then you went and told them where they could grab me. What did they pay you, Diego?" I shook him like I was extracting money from a bag.

"In the end, all I got was five pesos worth of trade goods. I still have most of the stuff. You can have it if you want." He looked up at me pleadingly. I pressed his head hard against the doorjamb, barely holding back from knocking him a few times against the sharp corner of the wood.

"Damn right I'll take it, and for now you're going to do everything I tell you, and fast. See those three men out there? I can't let them know that I'm here. My life depends on it. Did you realize, when you handed me over to them, that you were risking my life, Diego?" He shook his head and gave me such a pathetic look begging forgiveness, that I almost let go my grip.

"Jesus, Mary and Joseph!" I gave him one good crack against the wall, then pushed him away from me. "Get my mule and hide it quick. Then get your despicable self back here."

Diego caught my drift, because he convinced that mule with one tug to go around the corner of the house. I guess he tied it to the old tree back there, and I even heard him getting some water. When he returned he looked at me forlornly and said, "Nando, I didn't mean to, but they made me."

I wasn't having any of it. "When you went to work for Ramón, were you thinking about the others?" He looked at me, not knowing what I meant.

I glared at him, wanting to yell, but I had to keep my voice down. "You worked for a slaver and you knew it! Did you think about the tiny children you helped tear from their parents to be sold into a lifetime of misery? What about the girls, not even women yet, *little girls*, Diego, you caused to be raped by half the men at the Taos fair?" I was shaking worse than he was. This wasn't going to get me anywhere.

"I'll finish with you later. Right now I've got to watch out for those men down there. But cousin, you owe me, and you owe something to a whole lot of innocent children."

Diego's house was a hot little adobe box, but the sweat that dripped down his face wasn't from heat. He sank onto his rolled up sleeping mat and rubbed his neck. He looked thoroughly whipped. I knew my cousin. He wasn't truly a bad person, and I couldn't hold a grudge for long, but it would be a while before I'd let him off the hook for profiting on the misery of children.

Through the open window I kept my eye on Padre Baldonado, back in his faded blue robes now, with their swirling skirts and the long belt with the cross hanging at the bottom of it. His shaved pate gleamed in the sun. He parted from his friends and went into the priest's office next to the church. We watched Perea and Ramón disappear into the alcalde's walled garden.

"Diego, what possessed you to join the trade?" I asked while I looked over the plaza. I could maneuver the swinging shutter to keep an eye on anyone who left either the church or the mayor's compound.

My wiry little cousin shrugged noncommittally. I sat down and put my gold coin on the table between us. Diego looked at it and then at me. Coins were rare, gold ones rarer still. He didn't want to take money off me, but it was hard to pass up. I saw the indecision in his eyes. We both left it there, dull but suggestive on the wood.

"What do you know about your business partner, the rich slaver Ramón, who just went over to the mayor's?" I asked.

Diego said, "He's been through here a lot recently. He's got a damn good connection going right now."

"Does he do the running or just set things up?"

"He doesn't work the actual trail much any more, though he did in the past. Lorenzo travels for him now."

"How about you, did you ever pick up children for him?" I had my fingers on the coin and I turned it over a couple of times.

Diego looked bleak. "The truth is Nando, I'd rather do anything than work for that son of a whore."

It was clear my cousin didn't like Ramón much at all. "So why do you? For the money?"

"He rarely pays me. He owes me. But I'm not moving to collect, that's for sure."

I let that lie for a moment. "Where does he get the captives? Do the Utes bring them down?"

Pamela Christie

"I think so." Diego was being evasive. Spain insists traders be licensed and doesn't allow them to work beyond the borders of the kingdom, because any small mishap could ignite violence that would threaten the whole colony. But there was no way the government could shut down access to all the lands beyond New Mexico, and Abiquiú was the jumping off spot to the northwest and the wealth it offered. Illicit trading was what fed this town, my cousin included, and no one here wanted to risk losing it. So I had to press.

"Has he started getting slaves from the Apaches?"

"Possibly, because the Ute trade got really slow after the pox last year when a lot of children died. I think that's when he branched out and started working with Apaches too."

"Have you seen many Apaches around? Heard of them being up here recently?"

Diego stuck out his lower lip while he thought. "Just rumors. No attacks."

"Not even that one down in Medanales?" I probed.

"Those were Comanches and they hit hard," he said. There it was again.

"Anybody left down there?" I tried to sound like it didn't matter to me.

"I heard everyone who lived on the plaza moved south. A group is still hanging on down river from there. I haven't heard of anyone above the plaza making it through. Makes sense, since the Indios came in from the north."

I sat there and fiddled with the coin, this time not to tantalize, just thinking and worrying about Marisol. Her farm was north of the village.

"Before today, did you ever see that scout who's with Ramón?" I asked.

"The short, thick one?"

222

I nodded.

"He rode through here with the Domínguez expedition in '76, but he was only out with them about a week. Left them and came back down on his own. Too churchy for him, was how he put it."

"That fits," I said, "but then what's he doing traveling with a friar?"

Diego grabbed the gold piece out of my fingers and shoved it over to me. "Stop fiddling with that damn thing, will you! I'm not going to take your money. You're pretty worked up, Nando."

"Do you blame me? You've got me feeling as brittle as a week old tortilla."

Diego blurted, "You sound like a god damn government interrogator! I'm your cousin, remember?"

"Yeah, the one you tried to sell for five pesos!" I retorted, but his words put me on notice. I returned the piece of gold to my pouch and slid down in the chair.

"You still don't trust priests, do you?" he asked, quiet once more.

"You're right, Diego, and that friar scares me. He tried to kick the shit out of me down in Santa Fe, in front of half the town. He busted up my friend's house. I found him laughing his head off up above town one night, like the devil was tickling him all over. He's crazy as a loon and he's somehow mixed up with Ramón, slaving, and everything else that stinks around here." I stopped for breath, then told him, "I was at the ranch last night."

Diego's thin eyebrows shot up. "You went all the way out there and you're still wearing your hair?"

"I followed those three right to our home, and damn if Ramón wasn't stomping about like the lord of the manor and rearranging the furniture to suit his taste."

"There's still furniture up there?"

"No, that was a joke, Diego. The place is gutted, but Ramón acted like he owned it and like he'd been up there before." There was no way I was going to tell Diego about the rendezvous, not yet anyway. I didn't want him guessing I really was a spy. I had a job to protect.

"Your weird padre's been here a couple of times this year," he told me. "He seems to be friends with Father Martín, but he usually travels in and out with Ramón. I guess he uses his party for protection on the road."

Ramón and Perea I had nailed, but I still couldn't figure out why Baldonado was running with them. I could prove he was as guilty as the other two if anybody would believe my testimony. But why was a priest arming Indians and running with a slave trader? I didn't get it.

"Diego, I've had three hours sleep in the last two nights. I've got to follow Ramón and Perea when they leave. Until they do, can I sleep here, and can I beg you not to tell anyone you saw me?"

"No problem, primo." Diego was eager now to please me anyway he could, and I noticed he looked at me differently than usual, with respect, and concern too. "You want some food?"

"Absolutely, Diego. And keep the mule fed and out of sight."

"You first, mule second," he said, putting beans and beef in a tortilla in front of me. As a single man he'd become a pretty good cook.

"What would it take to get you to sneak up to the ranch now and then and see what's going on? See how come Ramón's interested?"

"I know I owe you, primo, and I'm going to make good, but I wouldn't go up there for all the money in the king's purse. I can't believe you risked your ass on the Piedra Lumbre."

"It actually seemed very peaceful up there."

"I doubt that, but it doesn't matter because I won't go. I'll keep my ears open though."

"How come Ramón's got you in his pocket?"

"You don't want to know." Diego's face went dark.

"Tell me," I insisted.

Diego hesitated at least half a minute before he unloaded. Very quietly he said, "The rico's weird. The slaves weren't doing it for him. He tried to force himself on me." Diego's eyes were down on the table, but then he looked up at me pleading that I understand.

"Nothing happened, but the man's sick. He keeps trying, and now he's threatening to tell, to let people think it did happen. Going along with him in the trade is the only way I can shut him up."

I felt sorry for my cousin, though I guess I wasn't surprised. Diego is softhearted, and because of his size, almost delicate looking, but underneath he's rugged and a rancher. The attempt, or assault, whichever it was, must have been supremely offensive to him. Yet my cousin didn't attack Ramón, he tried to placate him, which was proof again of the fear Ramón instills in men.

"I'm sorry, Diego," I said, and I meant it. "That son of a bitch. Was he after women too?"

"Anything that moved. I was worried for the animals."

I looked at him with my nose wrinkled in question.

225

"That was a joke, Nando." He threw my own words back at me. "Forget about it. Go back in there, and get some sleep." He lifted the woven curtain that divided the room. After taking one last look out onto the plaza, I went over to the soft pile of sheepskins and lay down, hoping to sleep.

"Quit worrying, I'll wake you if anything changes." Nothing did for five hours.

"Nando! They're gone! Nando! Nando!" I woke up in the pitch black of the room with Diego shaking me until I rattled.

"O.K., O.K.! Ease up! What? Is it night already?"

"Primo, they left hours ago! I didn't see anything! After I took care of the mule, I didn't go anywhere, I didn't stop looking out the window. When it was almost dark, I got worried. I went out to the plaza. I wandered around the mission. The padre was still in there with our priest. I could see them out in the garden, so I wasn't too concerned yet.

Finally I found old Chano. He went on and on, spitting at me through his teeth before he told me they only stayed at the alcalde's fifteen minutes! Before you even ate your dinner they were out his back gate!"

I pulled on my pants and moccasins while he spoke. He hurried away into the sala, calling, "I'm sorry! I'm sorry!" He was packing me food and filling my gourd with water.

Sleep jumped out of my brain. "They must know someone's onto them. They figured it out. Get the mule while I tie this stuff together." Diego ran out the door.

As I settled into the saddle, I leaned over and clutched my cousin's shoulder. "You did fine. It's not your fault they sneaked away."

"Oh shut up, Nando, you don't have to be nice to me, after what I pulled on you. Listen, cousin, whatever you're doing may be a big mystery, but I've got a feeling we're all in it together." He was tying a blanket onto the saddle for me, and just like the old Diego whom I remembered and loved, he said, "When you get back to Santa Fe, send me some of that new corn seed. I'll try some of it out in your lower field." He slapped the mule hard, and it took off before I could say thank you or farewell.

Her Once Beautiful Face

I was out of there making all kinds of racket as the mule kicked up stones and the dry dirt of the road. Never mind stealth; let me be known as the mad rider of the night.

I crossed the river right away at the Abiquiú ford and galloped south toward Medanales. Compared to the cross-country treks of the last few days, this was nothing, an hour at the most, but that was true for Perea and Ramón as well, meaning they could have been at Marisol's for several hours. Of course they'd have to find her farm, but that's probably what the visit to the mayor was for; that, and a little something or other about slaves. Wondering if she was still alive, thinking of what they might be doing to her, I whipped at the mule.

At the turnoff to her canyon, I dismounted and crawled around on the dark road trying to discern prints. They were there and easily read under my fingertips, so I left the road and took a route across the face of the hill. That put me in the woods on the south end of her farm and lined me up with that little upstairs window.

Ten minutes away from her place I left the mule, and taking only my weapons and my manta, plunged down through the soft pine litter on the side of the hill, careless about noise at first. When I could make out the house, I eased up and became the part of me that is Ute. Ute on the prowl. There was light coming from her cabin, and the men's horses and one of their pack mules were brazenly tied to the garden rails. I heard a scream.

I had to keep from running. I had to move in slowly. I couldn't let my palms become too sweaty to wield a knife. It seemed like five miles across her garden patch, and another ten across the dirt of the side yard leading up to the wall with the attic window in it. Marisol screamed again, and this time it was cut off short and ended with a choking sound. In seconds I was where I could see through the lower window that she'd left casually unshuttered in the warm May night.

Marisol crouched on the corner of her bed with blood streaming down her face and along her smooth, brown arms. She was naked from the waist up, trying to maintain her clutch on a blanket to shield herself. Perea knelt on the bed in front of her, his pants unfastened and the tip of his knife resting dangerously on her left breast. Ramón leaned against the rough cedar-post wall, arms folded across his chest, and leered.

I knew I could get in through the upper window as I had before. I could get a shot off at Ramón, and drop down onto Perea and open his neck with my knife as I fell. Perea's threats and Marisol's anguished pleading covered the sounds I made getting to the back and climbing up the logs. It was a route I knew. Flat like an ascending lizard, I headed up the wall. When Marisol cried out, I knew Perea had cut her again. I had climbed ten more inches when I heard hoof beats clattering down the road.

Whoever it was must have heard her last scream. He hurled himself off his mount and in the same movement was through the door and moving toward Perea. I don't know if he even saw Ramón. It was Arsenio, being a man for the first time in his life. In his right hand he carried a large, old-fashioned pistol and one step inside the door he brought it up and shot point blank at the man attacking his wife. Even through the swirling smoke and sulfur that clouded the room, I could see Marisol's mouth fall wide open. She dropped the blanket and fairly flew off the bed, making for the door. In the same second, Perea's body crashed onto the mattress. Blood poured out of a gaping tear above his heart. He had been less than a foot from Marisol. It was amazing Arsenio hadn't shot his wife instead.

I think three seconds had passed. Here was Perea, dead or dying, and Arsenio with a hot pistol in his hand. Marisol barely reached the door when Ramón stepped out and grabbed her arm. He swung her naked body in front of him, and turned to face the dazed Arsenio. By the light thrown off the fire, I could see sweat mingled with blood streaming down Marisol's skin. A sheet was tangled about her feet. Her dark hair flew wildly and terror flared in her eyes as she tried to wrest herself from Ramón's clutch. His eternally handsome smile had twisted into a mean snarl.

Arsenio drew his knife from his boot and lunged toward the pair of them, but Ramón caught him with his heel hard in the groin and Arsenio dropped with a moan. Marisol slammed the back of her head into Ramón's face, knocking him off balance, until he caught her hair and yanked her down onto her knees. He slapped her hard, back and forth across her bleeding mouth, then thrust her face down to the stone floor. He took off his belt and quickly lashed her hands together. Keeping an eye on the fallen Arsenio, he jerked her through the door and dragged her on her knees across the dirt yard to his horse.

He used the dangling ends of the reins to tie Marisol to a rail nearly under the feet of his animal. Then he slammed her head against a post, tested the knot that held her wrists, grabbed his crop off his saddle and went back inside to deal with her husband.

Perea's death and Arsenio's ill-fated lunge I witnessed while I clung to the ledge just below the high window. By the time Ramón began slapping Marisol I had jumped to the ground and was running toward the house, but when he dragged her through the door I threw myself flat behind the wide cottonwood chopping block. I lay only a few feet from where he had tied her.

Inside, Ramón started working Arsenio over with his quirt. I stayed low and crawled nearer my girl. Marisol was too quiet. "Marisol?" It was such a soft whisper I doubted she knew if it was real, but her head lifted a little.

"Marisol?" I reached her, using the horse as cover, not that Ramón was paying attention. Enraged, he was working Arsenio over with whip, fists and boots. I had my pistol. I could try to shoot him through the confusion of two fighting bodies, but it would be a tough shot, so I decided to get the woman out of there first.

Gently I reached over to Marisol's face and ran my hand down her cheek. She looked up and started to say my name, but I pressed my finger on her lips in warning. Ramón was only a dozen feet away. I sliced the reins easily and unwound the belt from her wrists. Clasping her hand, I pulled her into the darkness away from the savagery. Her back was to the house, but I could see inside and was glad she couldn't.

We probably moved too fast and made too much noise, but if I reached the woods I was pretty sure I could get her away from this brute. We heard Arsenio scream just as we got to the edge of the clearing. I was ready to carry Marisol if I had to, but she was moving well on her own.

In the pines I recovered my manta, wrapped her in it, and whispered, "My mule is in the oak grove downstream. Can you get there on your own? I need to go back to help Arsenio and see if I can get us another mount." She reached up to me and put her arms around my neck in a precious hug of gratitude, but she remained silent as she gathered the poncho around her and headed toward the river.

"Stay with the mule. Keep low. I'll be back in minutes." Or I won't be back at all, I thought.

It was awful to walk away from her in the night, but I made myself hurry back to the house. Before figuring out how to do anything for Arsenio in the hands of this madman, I got down under Ramón's horse and slit the cinch. That done, I loosened the rope that tied Perea's horse. I hoped it would wander away, but not while Ramón might hear it take off.

My line of sight through the door showed me Perea's once sturdy legs, hanging limply off the side of the bed. On the floor before the fire, Ramón's body curved hunched on top of Arsenio, who was face down, smashed into the dirt. I couldn't be sure what Ramón was doing, but I thought I knew, and there was no doubt at all from the empty way Arsenio lay there that he was dead.

I raised my father's pistol to kill Ramón. I took aim at his tensely arched torso, but then I lowered the gun again. I needed a horse. I only had one shot and if it failed to hit Ramón we would be easy prey for him unless we had two good mounts. Reluctantly, I lowered the weapon, turned Ramon's horse loose

232

and, grabbing Perea's by its bridle, I walked it slowly over the loamy ground of the garden. First things first. If it all worked out right, I would come back a third time and shoot the bastard.

But maybe it was better not to kill him. That would be the governor's job. I just needed to get us out of here and back to Santa Fe. Ramón was the son of one of the most important men in the colony. I could be sorely used if the evidence didn't go my way

I got her to the river, about two miles from the farm. We curled up in a hollow out of the wind. The sand was still warm and we had the saddle blanket and my manta. I held her all night. I couldn't bathe her wounds until daylight. She would be too cold if I did.

In the morning we woke up and looked at each other. I was as bloody as she. It was then I told her Arsenio was dead. It was all a shock; the assault, Perea shot to death right in front of her, Arsenio's burst of glory that could have killed her as well. I could tell by her eyes that she was submerged in horror.

She didn't speak, but wept silently the whole time we were down at the river treating the cuts that criss-crossed her skin. They were mostly superficial, but there was a nasty gouge on her left breast that was deep and could become infected. The lacerations on her arms looked bad at first, but turned out to be relatively shallow. Her face was a mess. There was a long, thin cut across her brow, and rapidly purpling bruises. Cuts on her mouth bled when she tried to talk or eat. I didn't have much to work with, but I got her into the river and rinsed and rinsed her wounds. Then I mixed up the rest of my punché with river mud and made an ointment out of it. Dabbing it on her cuts, I wondered if punché worked as well as real tobacco to keep the wounds from festering. I had to hope so, because it was all we had.

I was pretty sure I had slowed up Ramón for a while, freeing his horse and wrecking his saddle, but I knew he wouldn't waste any time to bury either Perea or Arsenio. There was really no way he could have any idea who had stolen Marisol from him, but I knew he would do his damnedest to hunt us down and eliminate us before we reached civilization. Thinking of him pursuing us, I knew I'd been dumb not to kill him when I had the chance. Could he possibly think that Marisol had escaped on her own? The man wasn't stupid. My tracks were all over the place. We needed to beat him to Santa Fe, get to the governor, and eliminate this monster.

Marisol was still in shock. I decided it was best to stay hidden here for the day and let her rest and maybe Ramón would go on by. I needed to get her down to Luz, but I had a serious problem, the Godiva problem, something I had learned about in one of Luz's better tales. Marisol had escaped with no clothes whatsoever. I would have to figure out how to cover her before I took her down the road.

We would travel by night. We'd move in closer to the farms around San Juan Pueblo. There I would try my luck with clotheslines and head for town.

An Incredible Throw

*T*here are places all over this country where a man can hide and be sure no one will find him, but once we got near the farms and pueblos I was having a hard time figuring out how to conceal not only a man, but also a horse, a mule and a cut up woman. I'd already had to do it once when I slipped into someone's barn to borrow whatever rags I could find.

With reluctance I had left Marisol and the animals alone for a few minutes deep in the bosque, because there was no way I wanted us all chased by dogs and a sleepy farmer with a spear. By then Marisol was in my shirt with my manta wrapped around her like a skirt, and I wore leggings and nothing more. In the barn I got lucky and found a rotten chunk of old blanket they must have laid sick animals on. I had no qualms about slitting a hole for my head through the thing. When I belted it with a hunk of rope it had quite the air.

We had been making for Santa Cruz. If I could get there and into Juanillo's hands before daylight without Ramón discovering us, we'd be all right. Food wouldn't be turned down either; what still rattled around in the bottom of my pouch wasn't too appetizing. Marisol rode along behind me with her head lolling, half-asleep in the saddle, but we were only about an hour out. I was hoping to find a better ford than the one Miguel and I had used the other night so we could manage to stay reasonably dry.

From time to time I thought someone was following us. Once, I waited on a side trail for almost an hour. I'd let Marisol lie down on the leaves and get some rest in more comfort than a mule's back offers, while I watched the road. But no one came near us and after a while I heard no more sounds.

The only people traveling at night would be sneaky ones like us; Indians moving through, not wanting to be seen, maybe illegal traders or slavers, though there'd be a whole band if it was any of those. Night travel wasn't for the innocent. It wasn't too smart to be out here alone, but right now I preferred it that way.

We moved steadily on, not setting any record for speed, heading in carefully. Perea was no longer a threat. That debt to Carlos was settled, thanks to Arsenio. Arsenio was dead too. Judging by what I had seen in the dim light inside the cabin, the woman I rode with was a widow now. Leaving aside Apaches, Utes, and Comanches as possible enemies, that left Father Baldonado, presumably playing his priestly role up in Abiquiú, and the mad predator, Ramón. I shivered.

I couldn't figure him out. Yes, he was a slaver. Yes, he was brutal, but why? He had it made. His father was the richest man in New Mexico and he had no brothers. Why wasn't Ramón sitting down at one of the family haciendas with a wife and babies, smoking a pipe? One with real, government-approved tobacco in it? He already had everything, rich farms, horse herds, mines and slaves galore. What on earth would drive him to the cruelest occupation in the land? One that put him at risk for everything he had?

I supposed he could be at odds with his father, competing against him, or for some reason trying to make it on his own. Sons do that. But no matter what that relationship was, Ramón clearly got along fine with the great scout, Perea, who'd lied about which Indians were in the camp above Taos, causing needless slaughter. And that freakish padre? Surely the Father Custodian of the Franciscans didn't issue hats with scalp hair sewn in them to his ordained priests.

My horse began to drift and I gave it a reminding kick. We were all falling asleep. I'd done my part by identifying the conspirators. Bringing them in wasn't part of the job description. The best I could do now was to get back to Anza, if Ramón's Apaches hadn't picked him off, and tell him all that I'd learned. Undoubtedly there was plenty the governor knew that I didn't, so the padre and the clandestine meeting with the Utes just might make sense to him. I knew I was only a small player in his plan.

Tonight I was the slow-rolling player. I only wanted to make it back to Santa Cruz, get enough help to limp into Santa Fe, and unload my information on someone who'd had some sleep and could figure out it's meaning. Once I got us over the Rio Grande, it would be only minutes until we started up the road along the banks of the Santa Cruz river. There'd be tree cover along there, or an old shed where I could leave Marisol while I rousted Juanillo.

It was a damn good thing that about then my brain kicked in. "If Ramón wants to stop your mouth, he's going to do it right now," it said, "before you reach anyone at the garrison."

"But," I argued, "he doesn't know who I am, remember?"

My brain was adamant. "All he has to do is watch the road into Santa Cruz. There won't be a whole lot of boys and girls traveling into town together at four in the morning. Even fewer in possession of his dead friend's horse."

I skipped the crossing near the mouth of the Santa Cruz river, and pulled us on south. We'd eat a rabbit or roots or something, but I wasn't heading into that trap. We crossed the river where it braids and never gets too deep. I kept us off the road and found cover under arching cottonwoods where later in the day we'd be in the cool shade. There was no way I was going to light a fire, so for food we made do with the sorry remnants in my bag.

Marisol was starting to be able to talk about it. I was supremely relieved to hear that Perea hadn't gotten her. They'd both scared her to death, handled her roughly and forced her to kiss them, but it had only become truly nasty a few minutes before I'd gotten there. We sat apart from each other on the thick grass and slapped at insects. She wasn't ready to relax her guard with any man, including me, but at least she talked.

"It seemed like they were playing with each other as much as with me," she said. "One would do something and the other would take it a step further. Ramón pulled open my blouse, but he wasn't looking at me. His eyes were on Perea, watching him get mad."

They'd made her cook for them. They'd sat at her table with their weapons beside their hands and ordered her to bring food while they emptied the wine jug. They wouldn't let her go outside. She had no idea what happened to the cows and her turkeys that evening. Perea made her heat water and soak a festering wound on his arm.

"It was a bite, it looked like a human bite, something he'd gotten a while back, and it had become infected. Someone's teeth had torn out a piece of his arm. It took ages to get the rags hot enough and I kept changing them."

"That's probably what bought you some time," I murmured, remembering all too vividly her being cornered on the bed.

"Ramón watched while I doctored Perea. 'Some kid!' he said. 'It was probably lucky for you the brat got away.'

" 'Spitting out my skin as he went! Too bad we lost him, but none of us knew what we were in for when we picked up that little devil.' Perea added, 'Normally, I don't like to kill kids, I'd rather make some money off them, but if I get another chance at that one, I'll do it.' "

Could they be talking about Baz? The description suited him perfectly, but Marisol had more to tell.

"That was when I knew I was in real trouble. Even though they were rough, they still had been holding back in a way, and after all, I used to know Perea a little when I was younger. I thought I might be able to get out of it, but once I heard Perea say he was eager to kill a child, I knew these were truly bad men.

"Ramón started to handle me, reaching up my skirt, egging Perea on. Then Perea suddenly felt like he'd been doctored enough and he started to get really nasty." She shuddered. "I was trying to get to my knife, but they were throwing me down and fondling me, sticking their tongues in my mouth, kneeing me between the legs. I played weak and scared. I knew that if I fought them I'd be dead, and I didn't want them to have any idea I was working on a plan.

"Then Ramón found Arsenio's hidden jug. It was the only thing my husband ever spent money on. For a while there was a break, while the two of them sat there drinking and pretending to ignore me, but one of them always kept his eye on me."

239

Painful as it must have been for her to tell, I needed to hear all of this. It had to be good for her to talk it out, but also, Marisol probably had learned more that would be useful to the kingdom in those hours than I had in the past month. I pulled her close to me and carefully rubbed her shoulders. I considered it a good sign that she let me. We had all day to waste, not much energy to spare, and I wanted her to go on talking as long as she could.

"Perea looked up at Ramón and said, 'We've got the Utes with us now, don't you think?' Ramón apparently thought so, because he poured more liquor in his cup and knocked it against Perea's.

" 'The whole trade's going to get a lot easier,' Ramón said. 'This'll open up the north. We'll be the first up there in years. That ranch is perfect. No one anywhere close, plenty of buildings, corrals, and right on the edge of the whole northern territory.'

" 'I think the Indians have visited it before and camped there, from the looks of it,' Perea said, but I could tell by the look in Ramón's eyes that he knew more about it than Perea.

" 'The Aguilars have only been off it for about four years. It's fallen apart fast, but it can be brought back. They won't be around much longer. We're working on that.'

"I remember Ramón laughed then." Marisol turned to me. "Isn't your last name Aguilar, Nando? Isn't that your ranch?"

I was sullen. "It's my ranch. Mine and my brothers. Perea lost his crack at it, and you can bet Ramón's never setting foot there again either."

She turned and studied how serious my face had become. "Can you stand to hear more?"

"I want to hear all of it, Marisol. Some of this you'll never be able to tell anyone, but it's best if you tell me all you can."

She was near tears, but she went on. "When they'd been through most of the brandy, they started a game. Draw straws. They got very intense. 'Two out of three,' they said, looking into each other's faces. It was then that I got hold of the knife. I hid it in my skirt until I could slip it under the pillows. I already knew this would end up on the bed.

"By then the fire was low and it was getting dark in the room. Ramón told Perea to go get wood. Perea told him to get it himself. Ramón didn't like that one bit, and he rose up out of his chair and leaned over the table and said not at all nicely,

" 'Get the god damn wood. I'm not going to touch her until you're here watching.'

"Perea was mad, but he went out and I heard him breaking apart some of the dry branches I'd brought in this week. Ramón started making me kiss him. I almost choked. I figured I had to fight right then, because in ten minutes I'd be dead. I had my knife and I got it up behind Ramón, but Nando, I've never stuck anything but a pig before! I couldn't do it. I was being forced down by Ramón, still trying to get up my courage to stab him, when Perea came in and threw the wood on the floor. He yanked the knife out of my hand, shoved Ramón off me and showed him what had almost gotten him. Then he pushed me onto the bed. I fought, but Perea sliced me down the arm fast, and then he cut the other one very slowly. I hardly remember the rest."

Her hand went up to her face and traced the cut on her brow. She burst into tears. "I must look horrible!"

I pulled her in tight and looked right into her sad, brown eyes. "You've been cut, you've been beaten, you've fought off rape, and still you're beautiful, Marisol. Your face will heal." She put her head on my chest and broke down completely.

We sat in the flickering sunlight of the grove, so deep in the bushes that we barely felt the day's heat. While she cried, sniffed, wiped her eyes and then pulled herself together, I just held her and waited. I heard the river nearby and I planned to go down there in a few minutes to fill the gourd again. I listened to the horse and mule rustling their muzzles through the grass. Insects spun past.

I also kept thinking I heard something else, something moving steadily and quietly in our direction, but whenever I paid close attention there was nothing after all, and I knew for a fact my nerves were on edge. We slept some. Later in the afternoon, getting on to the time when the light slants deeply, I did finally hear a whinny somewhere by the river.

I jumped up and grabbed Perea's horse, covering its nose with the palm of my hand. It tried to lift its head to respond, so I pulled its ear into my mouth and bit down hard. That animal never let out a sound. Marisol got the mule's lead rope and held its head in close against her belly. We both knew who was most likely to be out there. Neither of us moved. Hell, we didn't even breath as we listened to slow hoof beats on the river's edge and then, whoever it was, rode on.

Try as we might, we couldn't make it all the way to Santa Fe that night. Traveling with Marisol was slow and, purposely, I kept us off the road in the trees most of the way. Then to top it off, Perea's damn horse went lame. Barefoot, like most frontier horses, it wasn't doing us much good at present. I wanted to leave it, but how? If I tried to drive it away it would surely come back and follow us. I couldn't tie it up in the woods and leave it to die. If I tethered it near the road, I would be

announcing our place and time of arrival to Ramón. I'd like to
shoot it and eat it, we were that hungry.

Somewhere on the creek near Tesuque Pueblo, I realized
we weren't going to get all the way into Santa Fe before first
light, so I decided to quit trying so hard and to hole up until it
was well into the day and we could travel on the road alongside other people. While I liked to think I'd been discreet and
no one was following us, it wouldn't have taken more than
ten minutes for Ramón to learn we'd by-passed Santa Cruz
and were heading for home. I just needed to be smarter than
he was for five more hours and about as many miles.

I compromised and gave the horse to the pueblo, whether
they wanted it or not, looping its reins around a cedar limb
where we crossed their road. I liked traveling with only the
mule, though it meant I was on foot. I let us all have a drink at
the creek, then pushed up a tiny side canyon, went around a
few tight turns between sandy rocks, and made a burrow in a
little slot where the canyon cliffed out at our backs. I could
guard the approach, sitting up by Marisol with my pistol at the
ready while she slept. Myself, I was beyond it.

It was still dark when I woke up. Marisol jerked upright as
Ramón's long fingers grabbed her hair. The pistol in his other
hand was aimed directly at my forehead. He managed to hold
it without wavering as he pulled Marisol up to her feet. Then
he trapped her in an arm lock and shifted the gun so it was
pointed at her face. My stomach contracted into a hard knot
of self-loathing and despair.

He did not offer his glittering smile. He was ready to kill.
"On your feet!" he ordered, and I obeyed.

A storm had moved in while I had so stupidly fallen asleep. Light rain was picking up speed and the arroyo bottom was slippery with slick, wet clay. There was a desperate plea in Marisol's eyes when she dared to look at me, but there was nothing I could do.

"Start walking." He motioned for me to move in front of him and held the pistol tight against Marisol's temple. We walked single file through the arroyo in the wet dawn. His horse and pack mule were a little way down, around two tight, steep-walled corners. He'd already tied our own sorry mule into his string.

"Get the irons out of my saddle bag." With Marisol as his hostage, no further command was needed. I reached into the leather bag and pulled out a fourteen-inch chain with an iron cuff attached to either end. Each leg clamp had a hinge and a lock. Ramón threw a heavy key toward me. It landed in the mud at my feet.

"Put them on." I must have made a gesture in question. Ramón sneered, "On you, Nando. Slave!"

Marisol twisted against his grip, but impatiently he repositioned her tighter against his body, with one arm under her throat, still jamming the pistol against her chin.

I fumbled on the ground in the thin light of early morning, groping for the key. How to delay, how to fake the lock, how to dive for the man's legs and bring him down with the chain? Marisol was gagging from the pressure on her throat. There was a whimper as he rammed the pistol barrel hard against her jaw. I picked up the key, opened the first cylinder, and clamped it over my ankle.

"Lock it."

I did.

"The other one. Hurry up!" Another cry came from my girl.

I put my left ankle in that one, locked it and became the man's possession. I straightened up, took a tentative step, and fell over in the mud. There was a hissing laugh from Ramón. I figured out how to bend my knees into the fetal position and get my legs under me. I struggled to my feet. He came over and took back the key.

"Start walking."

I shuffled down the twisting arroyo in the gray light. Rain streamed off my hair and through the opening in my make-shift shirt. I couldn't see Ramón or Marisol, but I heard him lift her onto the mule. He must have tied her to the saddle some-how. That took several minutes. Then he was up on his horse, tugging at the lead to get his pack animal and Marisol's mule moving. There was no point in hurrying. I could only lurch forward in slow, jarring steps.

The short chain tripped me at every move, hanging up on sticks and brush in the arroyo. Twice more I fell. Ramón, on his tall horse, threatened to run me down where I lay rolling in the red clay, trying to get enough purchase to lever myself back up. Marisol and I were both going to die and I knew it, but how long would the torture go on?

He was in a hurry now. He needed to get us across the main road while it was still storming and barely light. I already knew he had a secret route that bypassed the town. Hadn't I seen him run the Comanche slaves along it?

He broke out his quirt and slashed my back. The pain was fire on my skin. I could feel cold air and water trickling down my back where the whip had ripped opened my shirt. At least I was moving better now, finally getting the hang of the leg irons. He hit me again when I tried to turn and look back at Marisol. It took everything I had to keep moving fast enough to avoid his whip.

245

We were nearly at the road. It was light, lighter for sure than Ramón wanted. We paused in a thick cluster of dripping junipers while he listened for other travelers on the route. I managed a glance at Marisol. She was shivering and rain and tears streaked her face. Ramón decided that the murk of the storm meant we could cross and remain unseen.

"You first. Make it quick, Nando." He was right beside Marisol again with his pistol on her. I crossed, doing a shuffle-slog through the sloppy mud. The rain came down so hard that in minutes our tracks would disappear, not that anyone was looking for us.

I leaned against a piñon tree catching my breath and getting some protection from the streaming water. Ramón and Marisol were gray shapes rushing across the road. Holy Mother, where was my pistol, my father's fine weapon? It had been in my hand when I sat down to guard us. It had probably tumbled to the ground when I slept. In the darkness Ramón missed it. Never mind, it was long gone now.

Ramón pressed on, pushing me and pulling Marisol's mule. Soon it was full daylight, though as gloomy a morning as we ever got. Fog churned in the valley and clouds hung dark. The ankle irons cut through my leggings, the wet, cold metal opening wounds on my bare shins.

Once we were a half-mile beyond the road, he pulled to a halt. Despite his hat, water ran down the grooves on his angry, determined face. He dismounted and signaled me to sit on the ground. "Stay down. Don't get up." I sank into a puddle, eager for respite from the rubbing iron.

Ramón walked back to Marisol, who sat huddled on our mule and, using a four-foot strip of rawhide, tied her wrists more tightly, lashing them to the saddle horn. She shook in rough spasms from the cold. He must have felt sure of his prisoners then, because he turned his back on us and moved toward the trees.

Then, in the gloomy light I saw him pitch forward. I saw water splash where he hit the soaking ground. Instantly he lay still, face down in the pooling mud. Quivering between his shoulder blades was a long knife with a dull metal handle, deeply imbedded in his spine. His lean, patrician fingers clutched the earth and let go.

I stared dumbfounded at Ramón's suddenly inert body. Marisol's eyes widened with horror. In one movement we both turned to the woods from where the miraculous knife had come. We heard a crackling of branches and then, to our relief, muted footsteps running away through the wet forest. Ramón's killer wasn't after us, but neither was he going to let us see him. It was a smart move. It would not be wise to be known as the murderer of the son and heir of the most powerful alcalde in the province.

We were stupefied. I rose to my knees and by tipping back managed to get on my feet. The chain clanged against itself as I did. I looked toward Ramón. There was still no movement from him. I began to believe he might truly be dead. Whether he was or not, I had to use whatever time this offered to get to Marisol and untie her frozen hands. It was done in a minute, though the lashings were slick from rain. Fortunately my arms were free, and though my balance was precarious, I got her off the mule. We both looked down at my chains.

Marisol whispered, "He's got the key."

"Let's get you out of here first. He may only be unconscious. Maybe he isn't really dead." She looked at the irons in doubt.

"Lead the animals, head that way," I pointed back toward the road, "but don't let yourself be seen. As soon as you're hidden, raid his bags. Get yourself a poncho. See if there are any weapons, an ax, something that might bust these off me. But get out of here, now!"

She wanted to argue. She didn't want me to risk going near Ramón while I was still shackled, but I think she was too cold to put it into words. I quickly tied Ramón's horse onto the lead and sent them off. I hadn't once let the fallen man out of my sight and he hadn't moved.

I took what I hoped were my last twenty steps, hobbled by iron, over to him. I waited to see if he still breathed. There was no sign. I got on my knees beside him and struggled to turn his long, limp body onto its side, carefully avoiding looking into his open eyes. I didn't know where he had put the key, so I felt under the dead man's belt, down his cold legs to his boots, and up his tight cuffs for it. It wasn't there. I flopped him onto his back in the mud and laid my hand on his pistol.

In a sudden spasm, the dead man jerked, arching bolt upright into a sitting position, his arms stretched forward, and he stared straight at me. I screamed like a girl and scuttled backwards on all fours. Then Ramón twisted himself nearly in two, shook with another spasmodic contraction, and fell flat on the ground, rigid and motionless. Blood gushed from his mouth.

Thank God Marisol wasn't watching as I crouched in terror, mouth open, trembling like a sick dog. Though I waited long minutes, Ramón never moved again. Fearfully, I approached him once more. There was no breath. No heartbeat. With shaking hands I resumed my search for the key.

I drew his pistol out of its holster and got lucky when it pulled the key up with it. Even though the gun was too wet to fire, I laid it close beside me just in case the man came back to life a second time.

I stabbed the key into the lock on the right leg iron. The keyhole was full of grit and I could barely make it work, but at last it did and I pried the iron ring open. I withdrew my bleeding ankle, shook it and went to unlock the other one. Nothing I did made it open. I got the key in, but could only turn it a quarter of the way. I yanked, twisted, and tried to knock dirt out of the lock, all without success. I quit trying, picked up the loose end of the chain and held it out of the mud. I quickly checked out the gun before I shoved it into the waist of my pants. It really shouldn't have been a surprise. It was the governor's pistol, the one Anza had given me the night I was first employed, the same one someone had taken off my brother on his return ride from La Ciénega.

Francisco would get a kick out of that.

I stood up then and looked at the once-gorgeous Ramón, motionless and soaked with muddy water. Rain made a pattering noise on the hard brim of his hat that lay a few feet away. Water thinned the blood that oozed out of him.

That was one hell of a throw. Judging from where the trees edged the clearing, someone threw that knife from at least twenty feet away so it severed the top of Ramón's spine, someone who had no qualms about killing the alcalde's son. Whoever saved our lives was a master of the knife.

Though the chain and remaining ankle iron were a pain, I could carry them and still move almost freely. I was back with Marisol in minutes, just as she pulled a woolen poncho over her head. She wrapped Ramón's blanket around my shoulders. Then she turned, searched frantically through his bags, and finally extracted a round of the hard, thick bread often carried by travelers. She cracked it in two over her knee and we fed ourselves greedily, standing in the slow rain under a juniper tree.

Pamela Christie

By God's Grace

𝓜arisol took over because I was a shaking wreck. She got me on the mule and, with considerable determination she mounted Ramón's horse. She led me, stupid and out of it, onto the road. I began to protest that we shouldn't risk being seen, but she gave a snort of impatience and jerked the lead line so my head snapped back when the mule stepped out. There was no fight left in me. I let her take over, following behind her in the stupor of after-shock. Just once, I managed to take notice of the beautiful, small figure riding upright on the strong gelding that had so recently belonged to Ramón, but mostly I kept my head down and clutched the saddle for support. Eventually I recovered enough to take the reins myself, and then it was like pushing and pulling. We traded off, with one, and then the other, being overcome with weariness and not willing to go on. Whoever of us was stronger at the moment would goad us both forward.

The storm started to clear just as we came over the top of the ridge and looked down on the town. Below us I could see our three large churches rising above the little brown houses of the capital. It was Marisol's first time ever here, so I roused myself and pointed out the huge, flat roof of the palacio and the alcalde's mansion. I showed her the streets leading in and out of the main plaza and told her which one was the Camino Real that started here and led fourteen hundred miles to Mexico City. We could make out the river by the tall, leafy trees that followed the water. It was a brave village tucked against the high wall of the Sangre de Cristos. Billowing clouds were breaking apart in the wake of the storm, revealing fresh snow on the mountain peaks.

I didn't much want to be seen returning to the villa with a chain on my leg, alongside a wounded woman of unknown origin who sat atop the horse that belonged to the dead son of the alcalde. We'd been lucky on the road; no one was venturing out of town in the rain, and we only passed one group of people on their way in from the pueblo. But, no matter how ready we were to collapse at Luz's, I made us wait until it was nearly dark and then we hurried down the hill and skirted the plaza. We entered Luz's yard from the river path, and before I even let my family know we were home, I hid the dead man's horse in our pole barn.

Luz and my brothers came to the doorway when they heard us. Clearly they'd been listening for me all week. Francisco took over with the animals while I bundled Marisol into the sala and started to unwrap her like a present in front of the fire. The whole family stared as a woman with a battered face emerged. She was bleeding, bruised, and swollen, not to mention smeared with mud and tobacco juice.

Marisol waited, wondering what would happen to her now. She still wore my manta for a skirt and my stinky leather shirt. She was barefoot and filthy, but she shrugged and turned her

251

arms akimbo in a gesture of supplication. My brothers stared, speechless.

Luz threw up her hands and said, "My God! Get going, boys. Heat water. Bring blankets." Marisol was finding her smile again, and now that the introduction was safely over, I sank onto a bench and pulled my leggings off. Luz watched with apprehension as I separated the leather from the oozing wounds on my legs.

"Jesus, Mary and Joseph! What happened?"

I was struggling to get out from under the stolen animal blanket and she helped me pull it off my shoulders. My back must have looked like sliced meat. The exclamation that erupted from Luz's mouth made both my brothers turn their heads and look at her.

The serving girls came running in with more wood and blankets and got the fire roaring under the kettle. Luz pulled the stopper from a jug and put a cup of wine into Marisol's cold hands, then gave me one. She forgot Francisco and Carlos, but they quickly corrected the oversight.

"Estrella, get the fire going in my room. I'm taking this girl in there." She turned to me. "What's her name?"

"Marisol. She's from Medanales. She's been attacked and widowed, just three days past. She's also my friend."

Luz looked at me quizzically, then turned and snapped at Francisco and Carlos. "What are you doing just standing there? I've waited on you both long enough! Take care of your brother, and feed him, for God's sake. Look at those bones." She took Marisol's hand, led her into the bedroom and slammed the door.

"Francisco, can you go to the palacio and find Sebastian? Please, now, fast," I pleaded.

He pulled on his boots and left. Carlos and one of the girls started cleaning me up. The servant didn't seem to mind that I was standing stark naked in the living room. She rubbed some herb into my cuts and obviously enjoyed my pain. Carlos gimped over to the fire and, as unmanly as the work was, got the pots to boil and brought me a bowl of soup. He knocked on the door to Luz's room and passed a bowl in without being invited inside.

"The governor's back," he said to me matter of factly. I stopped dabbing at gore and looked up at him.

"No kidding? Is he hurt?"

"He's fine. He rode in yesterday. I haven't met with him yet, but I heard it went well. Perea's treachery at the battle has basically been undone."

"Perea's been undone too," I murmured. Carlos looked at me in question. "Totally undone," I said to reassure him.

Estrella came out and started braising a chunk of meat over the fire. She chopped meat, greens and dried chili, working furiously at the wooden counter. Luz apparently thought the soup wasn't enough for people in our condition. She was right.

By the time Sebastian got over to our house, we were eating hot, broiled venison and warm tortillas. Luz heard him enter and came out of her room, waving the servants back into it. She shut the door on the three women. Francisco had told Sebastian about the slave-iron on my leg, so they had brought a huge metal chisel and a mallet. They laid me out on the floor and began pounding away on the thing.

Their blows jarred my leg and sent fresh pain shrieking up my body. "You bastards! Hold on!" I yelled. "Maybe you can get the key to work."

Francisco found it in my bag. Luz poured dirty, but warm, bath water through the mechanism and with three men and an old woman working on it, they opened the galling thing.

Sebastian examined it and said, "This is as old as that garrote on the soldier in the tree. I didn't know there were still any of these left in the colony. No wonder it didn't open."

Luz seemed to have forgotten that my role with the government was secret, because she perched herself above me in our one chair, waved to indicate that the rest of them should sit on the rolled-up bedding, and said, "Tell us, Nando."

They had me stretched out on the floor on sheepskins in front of the fire and thankfully they kept my cup full. I tried to give Luz a meaningful look: was it all right to be talking? She caught it, but still nodded for me to start.

I told them where to find Ramón's body. I told them about our mysterious savior with the ten-inch knife. I confessed I had lost Benito's pistol, but that I thought I could find it.

I explained about Perea's death and Arsenio's, casting a warning look toward the bedroom so they wouldn't ever tell Marisol the details, and I even told them what Diego had said about Ramón and his predilection, though I kept my eyes far away from my stepmother when I spoke of it.

I asked them if Anza had been attacked by Apaches. In fact he had, but he had outfoxed them and little harm was done. I explained why the Indios' weapons were so modern and so numerous, something, Sebastian said, the governor had also noticed.

"Well, that's one mystery solved," Sebastian said, while Carlos looked furious.

I'd forgotten, frankly, about Francisco and Luisa, but the forlorn look on my brother's face when I told him about Ramón let me know he wasn't sure how he was going to be able to court her now.

Finally, I told them I'd been to the ranch, and about how I thought I'd just spend the night, but wound up eavesdropping on a clandestine rendezvous. The family leaned forward, rapt with curiosity about the gathering and our home. I told Luz I had been to Benito's grave. I told them the apricot tree was still alive, and about crawling out the wood chute.

Sebastian brought me back to the point by asking more about the rendezvous. I told him outright that it looked like the Apaches, at Ramón's instigation, were on the verge of joining up with the Utes.

"Holy Mother!" Sebastian exploded, forgetting about the woman in the room. Then he added, "But of course that's what they'd do. How else can they possibly stand up to us once we unite with the Comanches? Do you still have any connections up there in Ute country, Nando?"

"My birth-mother's there, and I have a brother and sister, and of course all the rest of her family."

"How would you feel about a little trip?"

"For the love of God, not tonight!" I said and I flopped down on the floor. I bounced up again with a yell, because I'd forgotten about my back. Francisco solicitously filled my cup again and Luz held hers up for some too.

I think Sebastian was actually embarrassed. "I don't mean now. I just have to tell Anza what our resources are. We may need you later. Sorry, Nando." I nodded at him.

"What ever happened to Padre Baldonado?" Carlos asked.

"I never saw him after Abiquiú. Diego said he was talking to Father Martín when I left. The man's a conundrum. He's got all kinds of games going, and he was hanging out with the worst men in the territory."

Pamela Christie

"Father Martín is a good man, though," said Luz, "A very fine priest."

I looked at her, wondering if I agreed with that. "You're probably right. I just haven't figured out Baldonado yet. Remember, I watched the man put weapons into the hands of Apaches." The wine was creeping up on me. "How's Máhri?"

"Who?" Luz asked.

"Marisol. I always used to call her Máhri."

"Always used to?" Luz wondered at that. "How long have you known her, Nando? I assumed you just . . ."

"She was in the Martinez household in Abiquiú. She was the little girl who lived with them, the one they bought on the plaza. Don't you remember her?"

Luz was amazed. "The poor woman in there used to be that chatty, funny, little girl? I do remember her. You two were friends."

I was getting past words. It had been a devil of a day, and a long, long month since I had become an employee of the governor. I hoped he thought I'd earned my thirty pesos.

"Is Marisol going to be all right?"

"She's been cleaned, bandaged and fed. I put her in my bed. She can sleep with me tonight. You'll see her in the morning."

There was one more thing. "Francisco," I said, "Shove my saddlebag over here." He got up and carried it to me. Together we undid the straps, and I rummaged through. They watched, wondering, as I pulled out a thick, dirty bundle.

"Here Luz, this is for you." I passed it to my stepmother. She held it and turned it in her hands, just as she had handled the packaged windowpane.

"By God's grace, Nando!" Excited, she turned through the ragged pages of her own Bible. "Thank you!"

We looked over her shoulder while she ran her finger lovingly down all our names that had been carefully written in red ink on the flyleaf.

Providing Temptation

*S*ebastian must have thought I looked pretty puny, because he gave me two whole days of rest before I was called to meet with the governor. In the evening, after supper, the summons came.

Anza glared at me through the blue smoke of his cigar and said, "So every one of our suspects is dead."

Was that true? I had to think for a minute. "Yes, except for maybe the padre."

Anza nodded. "Has anyone seen him?"

"Not since Abiquiú, as far as I've heard."

"If indeed Perea and Ramón were at the core of this, things should be a lot quieter now," Anza declared with some satisfaction. He was right. With those two dead, the troubles had to be behind us now.

"What happened at the battle sir, when the Apaches attacked you?"

"Not a problem. Only a minor skirmish. We'd gotten word just in time to be on the lookout, by only a few minutes, to be exact. That boy you sent down to Juanillo, he got us the message."

"Miguel, himself? All alone, he found you?"

"No, they sent him with Leyba, but the kid's good. He's getting experience fast. We were coming down the Rio de Pueblo, keeping right on its banks. There's that tight spot in the canyon where you often have to ride in the water. It's running high right now, and at this time of year we usually climb out of the river bottom and ride up on the plateau."

I told him I'd seen the place. Anza went on.

"Leyba had checked out the upper route on his way to us and noticed tracks. When he warned us, we just stayed down in the canyon, though we had to swim the horses a couple of times. I had Leyba and Miguel go back on top to keep a lookout, and sure enough when the Apaches figured out we weren't using that route, they started down toward the mouth of the canyon, ready to pick us off at the waterfall there, but that's where they ran out of luck. Because of the warning, we'd moved through in double time. When they came, we were already past the canyon and positioned in a small wood. Our first shots took them totally by surprise and they only fired a few potshots on their way out of there.

"We took off in pursuit and exchanged fire. I noticed every one of them was armed with new rifles. Apparently though, with the chance to surprise us eliminated, they knew they were out-manned for a full-on fight and it ended pretty fast. A couple of them got nicked."

"You heard about Ramón and the weapons? Down by the Chama?" I asked.

Anza's whole face was a scowl. "I did. Sebastian led a party out by Tesuque and they recovered Ramón's body, by the way. I've got your testimony, and Miguel's, and the corroborating evidence I saw myself of the new weapons on the Apaches. I hope that's sufficient to make a convincing case in my reports."

"You could always ask Padre Baldonado for testimony. He was there opening the panniers with the weapons in them."

"So I understand, but it's always been tricky getting the Franciscans to let us torture one of their priests to obtain evidence. We're definitely looking for him though." This sounded appealing to me.

Anza shook his head. "Ramón's father is going to have a hard time believing this. I haven't figured out how to tell him yet."

"Where's Ramón's body?"

"Wrapped in a blanket, locked in a cell. I've got him in the cold north one so he doesn't need burying so fast. I want to see who gets worried and misses him, who else might be concerned about how his slave business is going."

"What about the mess up in Medanales?" I asked, thinking that would be a filthy job for Marisol to undertake if she ever decided to go home.

"I'm sending a couple of soldiers up there. I need verification of Perea's death. They'll clean up. One of them's part Ute, like you, and when he's done he's going up farther to see whether he can get a different kind of message to the Ute tribes, one from our point of view this time. Who's the woman you brought back?"

Word gets around, I thought. "Marisol, the wife of the militiaman that Ramón killed. Luz is taking care of her."

"Was she raped?" The governor didn't beat around the bush.

"She says not. I think it was close though. They cut her up and tormented her, but she stayed on a horse all the way down here and survived Ramón's last attack. Hell, in the end she practically carried me in."

He looked concerned, but hurried on. "What kind of knife killed him?"

"High-quality steel, long blade. Whoever threw it knew how."

Anza pressed, "What's your guess?"

"It could have been an Indian, one who didn't even know who Ramón was, but who saw the situation. It could have been any slave who'd gotten away from him, maybe someone Ramón once tortured, someone who'd been looking for a chance for revenge and got lucky." I really had no clue and I'd been thinking about it for three days.

"It's obvious to me that it was you whom God was looking out for that day. Here." Anza passed me a cigar and ordered my cup refilled. "I'm going to let you in on our plan, but you've got to keep your mouth shut. Things are going to start moving fast now. If there's still anyone dangerous lurking out there, we'll know right away."

Smoke from our cigars circled high against the dark ceiling of the room. A servant came in and added logs to the fire. The wine in my silver cup was like velvet. Thick sheepskins padded my chair. The governor leaned back in his armchair chatting comfortably with me, Nando, son of Don Benito Aguilar and the Ute Princess, Nan. This was the good part of the job.

"We're going to do a test run with the Comanches," he confided, "by conducting a joint action against the Apaches, and anyone else who thinks it's to their advantage to join up with them. In order to draw them in, we're moving the horse herd, the 'caballada'. All thousand animals are going to be driven out of the Pecos Valley across to the far end of the Galisteo Basin. We're going to dangle the herd there on the western boundary and make it look irresistible to rustlers. We'll make it easy for their spies to discover that we're cutting the guard by half. We think that's bait any normal Apache will rise to, and at the same time we're going to learn just how well we get along with our new brothers-in-arms. If the Apaches really did get all our cargo off the last caravan, they'll be caught with enough loot to satisfy the Comanches' love for Spanish goods, though I hate to think of anyone else getting my ration of brandy." The governor grimaced. "Anyway, we're running out of grass over by Pecos. The Galisteo's been rested for a while."

This was neat. A practice run. "So without Ramón and Perea to arm the enemy and misinform the commanders, you think you'll get a pretty good crack at this?"

"That's the hope," Anza replied without much conviction. "Sebastian's heading out to alert the caballada to start moving. The Comanches are moving into position on the big mesa just south of Pecos, and will watch for our signal. I think we'll finally be able to put this colony on a safe footing, now that the treachery that's been undermining us has been put to rest."

Thinking of Ramón lying dead in a dark corner of the palacio, I said, "Some of the treachery, anyway, will definitely be put to rest, as soon as he gets too warm for storage." Anza, trying to relight his cigar, somehow let me get away with this.

"How in God's name am I going to tell Tomás and his wife that Ramón is dead? They'll be back in town tomorrow." Anza sighed. "We're supposed to play chess in the evening." Concern for his friend showed in the governor's eyes.

"Gently, I suppose. Maybe they already know about Ramón? Maybe this won't be such a surprise to them?"

Anza looked sad. "Ramón was the apple of his father's eye; he could do no wrong. This is going to be tough."

I wished I could feel more sympathetic, but I was having trouble getting there. "Sir, have the men already gone north to Medanales?"

"Not yet. They leave tomorrow. Why?"

"When you were gone, during the attack on Carlos, a little boy was stolen. Marisol told me that a child bit Perea, and she heard him say that the boy ran away. Could you ask your men to be on the lookout for a seven-year-old? I think he might be wandering around between Santa Cruz and Abiquiú somewhere, very ready to come home."

"Absolutely. I heard about Baz disappearing. Does this further convict our dead suspects? Battery on an officer and kidnapping a Spanish child?"

"Only if the bite marks on Perea conform to Baz's teeth, or if the boy's still alive and can tell his story. Mother of God, I hope they find him! I just crossed that country, and I hate to think of a seven-year-old alone and on foot up there."

"I'll alert those two and everyone else as well. This Baz sounds like a feisty Spaniard and we need all of those we can get." He paused. "Is there anything else you can think of?"

With a little reluctance I handed him the coin I'd found. "I dug this out of the dirt by the fire, after the rendezvous."

Anza examined it for a moment. "Never seen one of these before. I'll show it to Padre Miera and see if he recognizes it. He was in Mexico the most recently of any of us. Maybe it's something new." I watched as my bonus disappeared into the governor's vest pocket.

With this, the formal part of the interview was over.

"Take a couple of days off, Nando. Go fishing. Lie in the sun. Have you got a girlfriend?"

Now the governor was getting personal. I thought about that. Did I have a girlfriend? In a flash I decided that I did. "Yes, I've got a great one."

"Go spend some time with her. Things are out of your very capable hands, Nando, at least for a few days."

He walked me to the door. I slipped across the courtyard and out of the palacio gates, realizing how quickly I had become adept at stealth. I made my way home and, after begging Luz for mercy, was allowed an hour sitting by the fire with my arm around my girl.

I did just what the governor ordered and lay about indolently for a couple of days. When that got old, I went over to Rosa's one night and got drunk. My wounds skinned over and some of the terror was beginning to fade.

Finally I got bored with myself, and got Francisco to go with me up into the foothills to cut some poles to build Luz a decent porch. The house was getting crowded with all of us at home, and a wide portál would make another whole room for us, at least for the summertime. My brothers and I could sleep outside and the girls could get out of Luz's room. I knew we'd better start making adobes, too, and thinking about adding a real room before winter.

Carlos was well enough now to put in frequent appearances at the palacio. The governor had him help with the endless paperwork of the required reports to the viceroy. With Perea and Ramón silenced, it seemed safe enough to leave the house, and Juanillo had sent Rosinante back down to me.

There are worse things than heading into the woods with your brother and a pair of animals on a summer's day, particularly when there is an enormous and hypocritical funeral going on at the parish church for a man you have known to be consummately evil. A tired-looking Father Miera was handling the details, because there was no sign of Padre Baldonado.

We got out of town early and worked hard for hours. We fashioned a travois and dragged the poles back. Luz was pleased and the next morning put up with the mess while we peeled off the bark out in the yard. Even though it was Sunday, she let us start building, and we had the frame notched and lashed together by dark. The next day, still in a domestic mode, we took the windowpane up to the carpenter's and had him measure it to make us a frame.

"Shouldn't be too hard, when I can get to it. I've got a big job ahead of you so it will be a week or two." Francisco and I looked at each other, wondering whether this was acceptable, but since he was the only carpenter within three hundred miles, it would have to do.

Summer was starting to roll now, with long hot days and cicadas grinding away in the trees. Before we'd even finished roofing the porch with poles and brush, the women were sitting under it doing their work. I figured I'd have to borrow an adze and start making planks for benches, and splitting junipers for a more solid roof over at least a portion.

Francisco was a big help, but unusually quiet. I could tell he was trying to hang on until he could somehow manage to see Luisa again. The day of the funeral, he had used Estrella to deliver a message and a little silver cross to his girlfriend.

Estrella giggled when she returned. "She thought I was being forward, getting close and taking hold of her hand, but when she felt what I pressed into it, I saw a smile on her face even though she was veiled. That girl likes you, Francisco!" the serving girl announced.

"I should have gone, she won't understand," Francisco tormented himself. "But after all that Ramón did to you, to Marisol, to everybody, I just couldn't go. How will I ever get close to Luisa again?"

We'd heard that the alcalde and his family had returned to La Ciénega in their carriage and were in seclusion, avoiding contact with the villa while they recovered from the loss of their son.

I went up to the palacio one afternoon to help Carlos walk home. Every day he insisted he could do it on his own, but it was a lot easier if he had a brother to lean on, so Francisco and I took turns.

He wasn't out in the street where we usually met. After a while I went in through the big gates and hovered around the open door to the governor's office. Carlos, Governor Anza, two other officers, and an aide were in there. I could tell there had been news. They were picking up their weapons and slapping their hats on as they moved quickly out to the stables. Carlos looked after them forlornly.

"What's happened?" I asked when I got to him.

"Sebastian's down! Coming in from the new grazing grounds. His horse threw him. For some reason he was all alone. Soldiers returning to town found him unconscious. He's been lying out in the sun most of the day."

"Sebastian?" The ground tipped under my feet. "Is he going to die?"

"I don't know. They're riding out to meet the cohort that's bringing him in. He's the most useful man the governor has."

I wasn't thinking about Carlos' feelings when I said, "That's how it seems to me."

I wanted to race home, leave my disabled brother to make his own way, get Rosinante, and tear out after the governor. I needed to see for myself what had happened. It seemed maybe the villainy hadn't ended after all. They'd struck down Captain Valdez, then Lieutenant Aguilar, and now the Corporal, the number one aide to the governor. These were important men. By comparison, it seemed the two murdered militiamen were mere decoys.

Carlos recognized the urge in me to charge off. "You can't go, Nando," he pleaded with me. "He needs you to stay apart. You can't be seen with him. Trust that he knows what to look for."

I dropped my head and anxiously ran my fingers up through my hair. My brother had just revealed that he was aware of my role. "How much do you know?" I asked.

"Everything, I think. While you were up north, Sebastian gave Luz permission to tell us. When Anza got back and heard about the attack on Baz and me, he decided we all had to be on the team."

I let out my breath. "That helps, I guess." Sometimes, with my own family, keeping my role secret had felt devious.

"Could Sebastian's fall just be an accident? Tell me it's possible, Carlos, that I haven't been chasing the wrong men all month?"

"It's possible. Go out tonight. Act like you don't know anything. Chat with the ladies, have a few drinks. There may be more you can learn."

As we were walking home on our own bumpy lane, I was thinking how much our lives and our roles had changed since Carlos had pulled me onto his sorrel at the Taos fair. I squeezed my big brother's arm affectionately and he said, "Ouch!"

A Small Circle of Informants

I made my way into the hospital section of the palacio shortly after dark. A serious-looking soldier guarded the room, but I begged pardon and asked if Sebastian was still alive.

"Not by much, but he's looking a little more possible now. Who are you?"

"Nando. I'm a friend of his." I tried to be a congenial nobody.

"No one's to enter, kid. Sebastian's to get absolute rest. Besides, he's unconscious." This was not good news.

"O.K., but if he comes to, will you tell him Nando came by? To check on him?"

The soldier was not cooperative. He was starting to tell me how in a few more minutes he wouldn't be the one standing duty and that I'd have to try again tomorrow, when we heard a coughing sound from inside the room.

The guard gestured for me to stay where I was, as he hastened through the door. He was gone several minutes. I heard his voice and a few words from Sebastian too. He was awake, alive!

The guard came out. "I've got to tell the governor! Stay here. Don't let anybody in." He took off quickly down the corridor.

I popped my head into the room. By the light of a single tallow candle, I saw the broad-shouldered Sebastian lying prone on the narrow bed with an awesome bandage around his head. His face was ashen, and blood leaked out of the dressing onto the sheet. I disobeyed the guard and went to my friend, picking up his clammy hand.

"Sebastian?" I whispered.

"Nando? How'd you get in here?" There was a long silence while he gathered his words. "It's bad Nando. It's not over. Look out for Rosa. Look out for Luz."

"Why them? What do you mean, look out for them?"

"Find the big one," he croaked.

"The padre?" I asked, but there was no time for more. I could hear the footsteps of several men hurrying down the corridor. I took up my station at the door before they found me out of place.

Anza strode right by me along with two other soldiers. He ignored me completely. The guard resumed his watch and said, "Go home, son."

The door to Sebastian's room closed sharply and I figured I knew where I wasn't welcome. I walked home in confusion. Rosa and Luz weren't soldiers of the presidio. Sebastian definitely had fallen on his head! But he had made an effort with his words and they had been clear.

When I passed Rosa's house, I was reassured by the tightly shuttered windows and gated doorway. I looked at the win-

269

dows of the upstairs rooms and saw no lights. Chimneys poked against the starry sky. It was utterly still and silent.

At home I looked in on Luz. She was asleep on her bed with her mouth partly open and a light snore coming from her. The three girls slept on sheepskins on the floor beside her. No one stirred when I opened the door and looked around. I dragged my own sleeping mat out under the portál and laid it across the doorway. I wish I could say I slept like a log in the fresh air under benevolent stars, but my clamoring thoughts were even worse than the dogs that barked until dawn.

Although Sebastian was an officer at the presidio, he was also clearly the link to Anza's civilian informants. In those few words to me he had warned of a threat to the secret circle of helpers around the governor. Even Luz? What a crafty woman she was. I lay there wishing I hadn't lost my father's beautiful pistol, or turned Ramón's over to Sebastian, because I reckoned that by now my name, too, was associated with that group.

I must have finally fallen asleep, because I dreamed of Father Buzzard riding across the plains with flowing hair in various colors, stolen from different scalps, glued with lumps of pitch onto his tonsured head.

There was no news of any importance in the morning. I dropped Carlos off at the palacio and lingered in the market stalls longer than usual. The town apparently wasn't aware yet of what had befallen Sebastian. Our villa hummed about its morning work, uninformed and unperturbed.

After a while I couldn't stand the inaction any longer, so I rode back over the hill toward the Tesuque pueblo to see if I could find Benito's pistol. It was too valuable a weapon to leave lying in an arroyo. I wasn't eager to revisit the place where Ramón had ignominiously bested me, but getting the gun mattered.

It was there too, kicked under a clump of chamisa, with its barrel sucking in sand. The rainstorm had gummed up the mechanism, turning the powder to muck. I checked it carefully and decided it could be put back in order. Shame washed through me as I realized that on that incredibly violent journey north I never fired a shot. Was I not man enough for my father's gun? I had excuses, but I didn't like any of them.

I was surprised at what a short distance we had been driven by Ramón. Under the torment of chains and the lashings of his quirt, it had seemed like miles, but from where we started it only took me half an hour to get to the road, cross it and find where he had died. Someone had put a little cairn there and stuck a crude cross of juniper sticks into the rocks. The sticks were held together with long grasses, and a flower had been worked into the tie. I pulled the cross from the stones and broke it in two, flinging it into the woods. Then I kicked over the cairn, scattered the stones, and left.

I'd only been away three hours, but there was news now. A family who lived beside the road to La Ciénega had been attacked in the night. Apaches had come in, torched their barn and taken their horses. We heard, too, that roving Indians had killed a Pueblo shepherd down near Santa Domingo, and then stolen his herd, driving the animals into the mountains behind Cochiti. It was all too close to town, and a clear warning.

I was eating fried meat from a vendor on the plaza, when a boy galloped in on the road from Pecos. Comanches had been seen, hundreds of them, massing along the Pecos River a little south and east of the pueblo out there. Well, that one I knew the explanation for, but the rest of the world wouldn't. The palacio started to buzz and mounted soldiers left rapidly in small cadres with much flash and flair, responding to the reports. I tried to enter the palacio by the back courtyard and the stables, but I was stopped short at the wagon gates. I'd hoped for another glimpse of Sebastian, but there was a wartime air now and entry was denied. I wondered who would contact me if I were needed, now that Sebastian was down?

Stories of natives massing changed the mood in the plaza and women hurried to close their stalls. The town was shutting down, so I headed home. On the way, there was another piece of bad news, something Anza needed to know. Padre Baldonado had made his way back to Santa Fe. I saw him striding down the steps of the military church. I changed my route so we wouldn't come face to face.

Carlos came home early too, this time leaning on Francisco. He shared what he'd learned. The Apaches had been seen arriving in droves on the west bank of the Rio Grande. They had by-passed the westernmost pueblos of Jemez, Zia and Santa Ana, just darting in to steal what food they needed. There was rumor of more Indios moving down from the north, as well. Had Anza's scout had time to approach the Utes? An old man at the palacio said the buildup reminded him of the stories about the Pueblo revolt, when hundreds of Spanish were murdered and the survivors fled with just the clothes on their backs, walking all the way down to Mexico.

I thought of the governor's defensive measures, how he had strengthened the citizen's militia, and made people build protective ramparts and towers in their villages. But could a few quickly built walls of stone and dirt really hold back thousands of angry, whipped-up Apaches? And just how long could a fledgling treaty with the Comanches hold, after seventy years of war against them, during which we relentlessly crushed their strongest leaders? Had our governor maybe bitten off more than he could chew?

Later that afternoon, I stood behind Marisol while she sat beside the river. She dangled her feet in the water, but I was unable to relax.

"How good are you with a gun?" I asked her abruptly.

"Arsenio used to have a musket. Before he lost it, I fired it a couple of times. I blew the head off a turkey once, but Nando, I learned back in Medanales that I'm not much good at killing a person."

"You may have to get over that," I snapped. "Carlos can shoot, but he can't run or fight hand-to-hand. Luz is plenty tough, but she's over fifty and likely to take on something she can't handle." Marisol looked at me wide-eyed.

"You might get some help out of Estrella and Feliz, but you'll probably have to knock some sense into them first. You'll be the one I'll count on here, Marisol."

"What about you? What about Francisco?" she asked in alarm.

"Odds are we won't be here. The presidio's horribly short-handed. The Apaches are stronger and better armed than they've ever been. We'd be no better than common deserters if we didn't go and fight."

"And the Comanches? Are they really out there too?"

I equivocated here because I wasn't allowed to tell her the truth. "Yes, just over there." I pointed toward Pecos. "You may be half Indio, but you're a woman and you don't want to be picked up by a Comanche war party." She knew what I meant.

"It'll be up to you, Marisol, and it's possible there will be an attempt on Carlos again, or maybe even Luz. We have at least that much standing left to us in this villa," I added bitterly.

"Of course I'll fight," she said quickly, " but you'd better teach me a few things."

That wasn't a bad idea. So with Luz watching, I had Marisol help me oil my old gun first, and then we cleaned Benito's gun and went over its parts. I showed her how to prepare the charge and load it. I taught her how to stand, and how to bring the gun up with both hands, how to let her breath out. It was beginner's stuff, and we couldn't waste shot in practice, but we had to start somewhere.

Then we went into the yard, and with charcoal sticks I showed her what I knew about fighting with a knife. The serving girls watched and joined in too. We circled round each other, teasing, sparring, and when we got our chance, lunged in with our sticks. A charcoal mark on either of us was a strike. Neck or face thrusts were considered fatal. She had a nimbleness that bested me more than once. I was thinking, as I wiped a black streak off my chin, that it wouldn't be hard to train timidity out of her. With practice, Marisol could learn to kill.

We were all marking time at home, waiting for a summons, or for news of any kind. Dinner was slim. I realized that no one was cooking much today, and that in fact for days we'd all been neglecting the garden. We would pay for that in endless meals of nothing but dried corn, or the dread toasted cowhide. I was just turning to discuss this with Luz, when we heard the dogs barking in the lane and Francisco went out to the yard to look. He came back in with Rosa.

This time there was no sweet pudding. Her face was dark with worry, and heavy, not beautiful now. She had a mannish look about her, which I took for determination.

"Excuse me, girls."

By her look we knew she meant the three young women, who took the hint and disappeared into the back bedroom. It was strange to see a madam bossing us around, but Luz was matter of fact about it.

"Rosa, have wine with us."

"No time. There's much to do tonight. Carlos, you're supposed to take your kit and reside in the governor's quarters as temporary chief of the palacio while the governor is in the field. You are also instructed to guard Sebastian and make sure his needs are provided for. The governor moves out within the hour. If the town is attacked, your family is to be removed to the palacio and Luz is asked to see to the care of Sebastian."

Luz nodded with uncharacteristic meekness. This was one hell of an authoritarian woman we were listening to. I could tell Carlos was wondering why his orders happened to be coming from her.

Rosa anticipated that and handed him a sealed letter, presumably from Anza. Then she turned to me.

"Nando, you're to travel by the southern road with Francisco, to the picture rock above the Galisteo. He's to be the signalman on the hill there. You're to move east until you're in Galisteo, on the hogback above the pueblo, if you can get that far before daylight. Wait until you see Francisco's fire; then start yours to tell the Comanches it's time. They'll be riding across the mesa over from Pecos, down through the old San Cristobal pueblo. You two are essential links on the line, to let the allies know when to come in. Nando, when you're done, you're to pick up Francisco and get to the rear of the governor's lines, to the rear and on the south, he specified. He may need to find you for further work."

"When do we go?" I asked.

"Within the hour. He figures, riding hard, it takes at least six hours to get out there. He wants you in place and hidden before first light. It may start tomorrow, or possibly the day after. That's up to the Apaches."

"Rosa," I said, "Padre Baldonado's back in Santa Fe. Anza needs to know."

"That's old news," she snapped. "He got back two days ago."

We were on our feet and starting to move. Rosa was saying a few words to Luz, who looked worried, though she nodded her head. Carlos was reading his letter. I could tell that he hated having to stay behind, but sitting in the governor's chair provided some consolation.

"Rosa," he said, "I don't understand. How is it that you . . ?"

"The governor apologizes, Carlos. Officers in the regular army are normally given their orders by him, but under the circumstances and because of the rush, he asked me to deliver these orders to you at the same time I addressed his 'Irregulars'."

Carlos seemed to accept that. Rosa turned toward Luz, Francisco and me. "He's asking this of the rest of you because he desperately needs your help."

She went out quickly into the gathering night.

"Rosa comes into her own," I muttered, looking after her. What other business was she hurrying to?

"I had no idea," said Luz, shaking her head. "The governor must hold Rosa in high esteem."

"Stop ruminating, ma, and get some food together." Francisco looked eager to have a job with purpose. I went to roust the girls and the household got ready for war.

V

The Madam

In the Villa of Santa Fe

*B*ack in her bedroom, Rosa slipped her white linen nightgown over the man's head, arranging its folds neatly around
his masculine form. They burst out laughing, because it fell
short, revealing his hairy ankles and his rough leather moccasins.

"This won't do!" Rosa leaned over a boxy trunk and pulled
out a gleaming satin skirt, shaking it loose from the gauzy fabric it had been wrapped in all these years. She unfastened the
waistband and held it so the man could step into it. Tied low on
his hips, it fell far enough below the nightgown to cover his big
feet. Altogether, it looked like a wedding dress, with its bil-
lowy, tiered effect.

She leaned back with her hands on her face and chuckled.
The man stood there awkwardly, looking chagrined.

"Have a peek, my friend!" The looking glass she held up
wasn't nearly big enough to encompass his whole form, but he
could tell that he was a fright.

Next, Rosa picked up soft, black charcoal from the hearth and went to work, thoroughly blackening his face. "Open up. I have to do your teeth."

"Ugh!"

"This won't last. I wish I had pitch." She rubbed the stick on his lips and teeth.

His smile became a fixed, gaping grin as he tried not to close his mouth over the blacking.

Rosa then took a long silk shawl, with glittering silver threads shot through the white fabric, and wound it over his head and shoulders. "Exactly!" she exclaimed.

There before her stood a white-clad, black-faced harbinger of death, a ghostly specter.

"How do you plan to get me across town?" he asked stiffly.

"Juanillo. He's got the water cart. I heard it pull up a minute ago."

"Mary, sweet mother of God, but this is ridiculous!"

Rosa unwrapped the tall, gangly man from the silk shawl. "You'll suffocate in this. Hang onto it until you get there, but lie low and pull this over you while you cross town." She handed him a rough, brown sheet. Rosa giggled, watching him grapple with the long skirts that tripped him as Juanillo led him out to the street. There was a snort of masculine laughter from under the blanket, as the ghoul was packed onto the floor of the cart.

Matter of factly, she handed in a grotesque assemblage of white bones, two candle lanterns, a long reed flute, and on top of the cart, she and Juanillo placed a wooden chair. The groom hadn't relied on the usual small burro to pull the load, but had a strong mule in the traces. He would ride his own horse alongside. Rosa stood in her doorway, excited, laughing, and scared.

A lot depended on this silly masquerade. The moon wasn't up yet, so the rumbly cart was out of sight within minutes.

She went back into the kitchen and washed the charcoal off her hands, thinking that it was less than twenty minutes to the junction where the Apaches' guides would expect to pick up the men coming in from the north, to lead them out to the caballada. The death cart would be there, waiting for them, ominously manned by the black-faced phantom sitting on the high-backed chair. The wispy white gown, lit by candles, would glow eerily in the windless night. There would be a clanking of old bones and strange music in the air from a low and breathy flute. She predicted there wasn't a human in the colony, either Christian or pagan, who would continue along that road. She could almost hear their hoof beats clattering in retreat. There would be no one there to connect the incoming Utes, whom the little Indian woman had warned her about, to the Apaches who awaited them.

"Ma'am?"

Rosa looked over her shoulder at the short, pretty girl standing in the door.

"There's a gentleman here, ma'am. Waiting in the back room."

Rosa cocked her head in question.

"It's him ma'am. I know you told me to be very discreet when he came."

Rosa was embarrassed to have the girl see hot color flood her face and shoulders. She bent over the washbasin and splashed herself with cold water. He had come! Thank God she'd finished her work for Anza, because she wasn't sure which would take precedence if she hadn't. She gathered herself together.

"Come with me. I'll need your help. Has he been given refreshment?" They sped down the back hall and into her room, where the girl began to unhook Rosa's dress.

"Make sure no one bothers us. I know he can't stay long, he never can. I don't want what little time we have to be spoiled by any interruption."

The girl fastened her into the green velvet dress that Rosa knew became her perfectly. Her eyes sparkled when she said, "Bring him in!"

No Indication of Breath

*A*nza's letter to Carlos specified that Francisco and I were to pick out mounts from the presidio's stock for the trip out to the Galisteo, so a couple of hours after dark we headed up to the palacio, helping Carlos along and carrying what he'd need for the next few days. I'd received a formal handshake and a wink from Marisol to send me off to war. Oh well, God, Luz and the whole family had been looking on.

The streets were dark and hazardous with ruts and debris. The small, old houses seemed to lean over the road, shutting off any light from the sky. We tried to hurry, but Carlos wasn't exactly fleet of foot yet. We'd rounded the corner out of our lane and were nearing the plaza when a blood-curdling scream pierced the night.

By my guess, it came from Rosa's. I dropped Carlos' kit and sprinted down the main street. Francisco must have propped Carlos against a post, because I heard him come running behind me. A second scream, and then another, rose into that horrid siren-sound of women wailing. We reached Rosa's doorway. Paulina, inside, clung to the wooden gate that barred the house at night, shaking it, trying to force it open without a key. Behind her, Rosa's crowd of girls keened and shrieked in waves of fear.

"Paulina! Where's the key?" I asked.

"It's on her. She has it somewhere. Rosa's hurt!"

I was yanking on the grill now too. "Get the key, get it off of her. The devil!" I stepped back and took a running kick at the lock on the gate. It didn't budge. Francisco came plowing in after me at a dead run, hit it just right, and the wood around the lock splintered. We pushed our way in while the girls scurried back. The door to Rosa's room was ajar. Smoke billowed out of it in greenish, acrid swirls. She lay on her big bed, in a dark velvet dress, asleep, except there wasn't the slightest indication of breath.

Francisco and I tried to pick her up. She was so limp it was impossible to carry her. Indecorously, we pulled her by her legs off the bed and out of the room, into her courtyard, well away from the poisonous smoke. A half-dozen women and some young men, Indian servants, stood too close around her as we turned her over, pounded on her back, breathed air into her lungs and did whatever we could think of not to yield to what we all knew. Unbelievably, Rosa, capable madam, secret agent of the governor, was dead.

Carlos came into the dark courtyard walking slowly and painfully with his stick. He saw the situation at a glance. He made a gesture to Francisco who left by the door through the back rooms.

"You," he said to the young men, "Wrap her and carry her to the palacio. The governor will want an investigation. No one else is to leave the premises. All of you," he indicated with his stick, "wait in the sala. I will meet each of you in Rosa's office. Nando, inspect her room." Just two hours ago, Carlos had been made aware of Rosa's true role in the colony. Her death, if murder, was an act of treason.

I was supposed to be on the road already, and I had hoped to talk to Sebastian for a few minutes before I left, to find out if he knew who had brought him down. Now the higher priority was for the governor to have exacting details of Rosa's death.

I lit all the candles in her room. I pulled back the bedcovers and then examined the items on her table. I found a nearly empty wine cup, her usual bedtime drink, no doubt. Scattered on the floor over by the wall were some coins that I scooped into my pocket. The room was still thick with stinging smoke. Curled in the corner fireplace were black wisps of something like grass. I went to open the shutters to let in fresh air. They were jammed shut, and not from the inside. I raced out to the back of her house and found a solid oak stick pinning the shutters into place. Could that be left over from winter? It had been warm for a month now.

I bumped into Francisco as he descended a ladder. His hands were filthy. "The chimney's blocked! Not just covered over, but sealed tightly with mud. Fresh, wet mud."

I looked at him, biting at my lip, and then added my evidence to his. "Someone locked the shutters too, and burned something green and wet in her fireplace."

"It sounds like murder for sure, but why was she even in bed? She said she was busy. She practically ran out of our house to get on with her business after she was through instructing us."

I was opening my mouth to agree when a yell came from the sala. "Francisco! Nando! Come here!" Carlos called from inside. We found him in a chair, staring at the cup of wine in his hand. He pointed at a dazed Paulina, who sat slumped on a bench.

"I turned it down because I needed my wits about me, but I let them have some before talking, since they're all a wreck on account of Rosa. That woman's barely breathing!"

I sniffed the cup. "It stinks. I don't know what's in there, but it's way off. Let's get her outside." I gestured toward the dozing woman and two young men picked her up and carefully carried her outdoors.

Carlos demanded, "Who else drank some?" I looked around the room, taking the measure of the several women who stood there. They all shook their heads. The cups stood ready on a tray. Carlos had planned to pour each of them a measure just before they talked with him. Paulina had been first.

Francisco came out of the kitchen with a stone grinding bowl in his hand. There was brown shell-like material still in the mortar. "Does anyone know about this?" he asked. Everyone denied it vehemently. The smell of the wine in the cup, the grass in the fireplace, a sealed chimney and locked shutters: this smacked of women's work, and it had to be an inside job.

"Save it as evidence. Someone will know what it is," Carlos ordered. Then he turned and spoke only to Francisco and me. "Nando, get up to the palacio. Bring soldiers. Everyone here is going into a cell, except Paulina, who we'll put in the infirmary. Francisco, stay here with your pistol and guard this door." He was making sense. He was acting like a commander.

I sprinted toward the palacio. I hoped there were some soldiers left there who were worth a damn. I could still feel Rosa's cold ankles in my grasp, our lovely, lively Rosa! There was no longer any doubt that even though Ramón and Perea were dead, people serving Anza were still under attack. First

Sebastian, now Rosa. There was someone else here in Santa Fe, someone at work right under our noses. But right now there was no time to figure out who.

We were going to run out of darkness. Francisco and I had to be in place twenty-five miles from here in a little over six hours. What I desperately needed to know was what else had Rosa been assigned to do tonight? What was left unfinished? The messages she delivered to our family were critical to the governor's plans. What more had she been asked to arrange? And who made sure that it didn't get done?

Francisco and I rode so fast and carelessly that if anyone was following us they were regretting it. Our horses were probably the leftovers after everyone else had taken his pick, but I was glad in a way that they were old veterans. They knew how to travel at night, and they knew when to hunker down and get the job done. Francisco and I barely spoke, there wasn't time to slow down to make ourselves heard, but once when we were picking through a stony section, Francisco said,

"Nando, I think that was mescal bean in there."

"What on earth are you talking about?" My mind was on the night riding, and how to find Anza when he didn't want me to find him, and how to get wood together fast to build a signal fire, and what if I got it wrong and signaled the Comanches to ride in before Anza wanted them there?

"Remember when we were kids and we got those little necklaces from the trader? Nan snatched them away from us, and you cried and stayed mad for the rest of the day? She said they were poison, they'd make you crazy."

I was beginning to remember. It was the first pretty thing I'd ever had, and this trader from the south just handed them to us, one to each child, and there was my mother, being finicky and taking them away.

Francisco mimicked Nan's voice. "'Eat just one of these and you'll sleep for two days. Eat three and you're dead . . .' That's what she said. They were shiny and had those crackly shells, kind of like beetles. The stuff in the mortar looked like that, at least a little."

"We don't have those around here; they're from the desert I think."

"It's not all that far from here."

Maybe, I thought, but there were a dozen herbs that everybody here knew would dull your senses, or knock you into sudden sleep when you really needed to be off about serious business. What difference did it make whether it was mescal bean, or wild hemlock, or whatever? They'd doped her wine and then they'd lit a fire.

I remembered something, something about a woman's voice in the next room at Rosa's, cajoling, teasing, luring. Someone who obviously liked Perea, who wanted to know when he'd be coming back; someone he talked to freely. I would look for her when I got back. Would I recognize her daytime voice? Or would I have to take her into bed to know if she had just the right tone?

We got a chance to let the horses run again and that ended our conversation for a while.

In Sacred Rocks

*S*un blazed down on the jagged rocks. A shock of ripe corn rose as high as my chest. Snakes twisted behind me. Lightning zigzagged through the sky and a blue bear swaggered under stars. I sat on the ancient peoples' paintings that were chiseled everywhere into the black stone. I had been among them all day. When the heat and the brightness became unbearable, I crawled under a dark overhang that faced north. No one steals horses or fights when it's hot like this, so I slept.

My brother and I had really pushed it, so I managed to get to the Galisteo creek just before it was light. I watered my horse and found a grove to hide it in, hobbled it loosely with a piece of twisted rope, then filled my water gourd. As dawn broke, I was lugging an armful of wood up to the crest of the hogback so I'd be ready when I saw Francisco's fire.

My lava pile was the ideal place for snakes to warm up their skinny bodies after the long winter, but the only ones I saw that day were pecked into the rocks by someone's hand hundreds of years ago. Everywhere I perched was crawling with drawings. I sat on them, oblivious, bothered with the thought that even though Ramón and Perea were dead, that hadn't done it. Now Rosa had been murdered and Sebastian's life hung by a thread. Because of the rush to get out to this place, I hadn't gotten back into the palacio see him. I had no idea if he survived his injuries that had been compounded by a whole day of lying unconscious under the hot sun. Today's heat was frying my own brain and I was in the shade.

Maybe Ramón and Perea were just ordinary slave traders after all and hadn't been involved in the systematic attacks on the colony. Maybe I had completely misinterpreted this thing, for even with them gone someone was still out there, someone ruthless and relentless. Not just the governor's officers, but also members of his information network were being brought down, and clearly by premeditated action.

I woke up soggy from heat, with worries picking at me like the gnats that had started to swarm. Luz and Marisol were at home alone, and where was Baz? Stumbling along through the sand hills east of Abiquiú, or tied to the back of a Comanche pony? I certainly didn't feel good about Padre Baldonado being back in Santa Fe either, but right now I needed to get off this rock, check on my horse, sluice my face in the creek and drink some cold water.

After the sun finished its long, slanting descent and the light turned lavender and dim, I came off the hill. I needed to be quick; it was time for signal fires. I couldn't find the horse at first, so I followed a trail of crushed grasses on a meandering route that took me closer to the river. Through the evening forest's gloom I thought I made out the white patch on his flanks. I moved cautiously so as not to spook the animal, my eyes on the path he'd made through the dense cottonwoods.

I stopped and squinted through the darkening leaves and stepped ahead into a small glade choked with tall, dusky flowers, unaware of the seven men who sat patiently there, each with a rifle pointed at me.

Heat flashed over my skin and my heart pounded like a running horse. My legs wouldn't move. I couldn't see, think, or even hear. I shook my head violently, trying to snap myself out of it. Slowly I put my hands in the air, then stood still and looked at the dark-skinned men who surrounded me. I took a breath and spoke.

"Hello," I said in Ute. "I am Nando, son of Nan, grandson of Cedro."

There was so much silence in the grove I could hear the stream sliding over stones and a cooing of doves in the woods. For a long time no one moved. Then in a sudden burst they rushed me. Before I could grab my knife they were on top of me. I brought my hands up to protect my face. The Indians were grabbing, pulling me apart, tugging on my hair. We were hugging and laughing. One of them even kissed me on the cheek. I was finally experiencing the good side of being a half-breed.

Together we climbed to the top of the hill and sat on the rocks, searching for a sign of Francisco's fire. It would be hard to see, burning against the last pale yellow light in the western sky.

"No one met us," my cousin complained. "Someone was supposed to be there, at the junction just north of Santa Fe. When no one showed up, we didn't know which way to go." What he was telling me was that they were just plain lost.

"Earlier, at Tesuque," another one added, "we'd been told there were Indios massing out by Pecos. We were pretty sure we could find them. We'd ridden a long way just to give up in the last mile."

"Who are you looking for?" I asked, knowing their answer was going to tell me a lot.

"Apaches. Chief Big Hands and his brothers told us to go find them and join up. There was to be a big raid, a whole summer of raids. I wasn't too sure about it. I've never felt good about fighting alongside Apaches."

"So what did Big Hands tell you, to make you change your mind?"

"Lots of fighting, good loot, plenty of slaves to be taken. He said the Apaches were the strong ones now. Big Hands' men carried the best guns I've ever seen. That was all the convincing I needed." However sophisticated the plot was that Ramón had hatched, by the time it got down to the horse-soldier level it had come to this, the thrill of a new rifle.

"The Indios over there, where you were heading," I gestured to the northeast, "aren't Apaches, they're Comanches." I let this sink in.

"No kidding?" My cousin looked at his friends and laughed nervously. "The Comanches would kill us before breakfast, but only after their women had tortured us all night." There was a lot of quick, earnest talk among them, and one man smacked my cousin's arm not all that gently. He ignored it. "What are you doing out here, Nando?"

I'd been waiting for that one, wondering how I'd answer when it came. I decided at the last minute to tell it straight. "I'm waiting for the signal that will trigger the Comanches to come in and fight alongside the Spanish. Against the Apaches. It's a trap, set up to snare the Apaches and whatever idiots elected to join them. Fortunately my friends, you were too lost to fall into it." There was snickering and an edgy shuffling of feet among the boys. My cousin got it though.

"Comanches and Spanish together? That could make anyone, even Apaches, run." He turned to his friends and was almost gleeful when he said, "Lucky for us we fucked up!"

"Did any of the Utes go over to the Apaches?" I asked. They looked at each other for the answer.

My cousin spoke. "When nobody showed up to meet us outside Santa Fe, that left about fifty Utes milling around in the road not knowing what to do. Some of our men got mad and turned around. A few drifted out to the west thinking the Apaches were out there. No more than five or six. You know, nobody was really too eager for this."

"Nando! Look!"

A small fire, just a pinprick of flame, was visible from the hump where Francisco sat in the dark four miles southwest of us. You couldn't really tell it was fire. It was just a speck of white brilliance on the rim of the hill.

"Here's your chance to pick the right side," I said, as I struck my flint and launched a spark into a ball of dry grass. The tinder caught and I maneuvered it under the piled brush. My friends and cousin watched me steadily as though it was a mysterious ritual. Flames jumped into the dry branches and I piled on bigger pieces of wood.

We stood on the knife-edge of the hogback, looking out in all directions for an answering flame. Not even I knew where it would appear, though I suspected it would be in the northeast. Sure enough, in a minute, a responding fire rose against the eastern sky.

"Message received!" my cousin said.

I turned to my clansmen. "Will you ride with me? With us? There's going to be a horrendous fight, but if you join it you don't want to be with the Apaches. You'll want to make sure to stay on the Spanish side." I stood apart while they talked rapidly to each other. Clearly there was hesitation.

At last my cousin said with reluctance in his voice, "Nando, we would need permission from our elders to take part in a fight like this one. We've decided to head for home."

I was impressed that my grandfather's rules still held, and that these men would live by them. We climbed off the rocks together, a line of young men silhouetted against the sky. We didn't talk until we reached the horses. Then I spoke, embracing my friends in the dark; "When you get back, give my greetings to my mother. Tell her I miss her."

"We would, but she's not there now," one of them said.

"What do you mean? Where is she?"

They shrugged, but didn't have an answer. My cousin tried to reassure me, "She was fine last time I saw her. She sat at Cedro's side and practically ran our last meeting. But then a few days later she left." That was all he could tell me, but at least it let me know that quite recently she was alive.

For my friends' part, it was enough for them that they'd avoided getting caught in the move against the Apaches. It felt good to confirm their instincts that fighting alongside their old enemy wasn't right, but they weren't ready yet to make an alliance with Comanches. They knew it wasn't something they could do without long consultations within the tribe.

Even though these men were my friends, even family, the sound of their horses cantering off to the north was a relief. I wasn't sure I could have kept seven fired-up Utes under wraps, even if they were clansmen. I worked for Anza and my job wasn't finished yet.

The Shaking Ground

$\mathcal{F}$rancisco was supposed to meet me along the cart track just north of the picture rock. We planned to ride west and pick up Anza's army together, but when I got to the place my brother wasn't there. I had seen his flare just an hour ago. Francisco could be scatter-brained, but surely he could ride half a mile, or even walk it, in the time it had taken me to travel four. I waited there in the dark longer than I wanted and even started to ride toward the rock. Then I decided that was dumb. No doubt I'd find Francisco with the army west of here. There wasn't time to waste and his disappearance was making me cross, because I had only a vague idea of where I was heading, and if I had to be lost in the night I'd much rather do it alongside my brother.

Anza's letter to Carlos had spelled out approximately where the huge horse herd would be. When I thought I might be getting close, I left the trail and traveled along the sloping hills. I was off any track and the ground was rough with chunks of stone. I came to a lookout point over the valley. On foot now,

I climbed over boulders to the edge of a cliff and stared down into the grassy plains on either side of the Galisteo.

Under the starry sky, the herd, a thousand of the colony's mules and horses, grazed beside the river. The horses' long necks were bent into the grass; their tails swished. I could make out a guard on a horse near a small flickering fire that burned against the cliff wall to the north. It was a lovely, peaceful sight, with a cool wind blowing toward me, so that I could hear the gentle whickering of the animals.

Then from the south, just beyond a low rim of hills, came a dark rider, then another, then gradually I made out a long, sinuous file of Apaches moving up a wide fan of arroyo. From down in the valley, the men guarding the herd couldn't see them. I dropped to my belly and stayed silent and still on the cold rock. Where the hell was the governor? Where was his army?

Helpless, I watched the raiders circle the herd. The action was subtle and slow and started a long way off, but from where I lay I could watch dark detachments move in and out of the gentle hills. I saw an Apache crest a knoll and wait there. I hoped to God I wasn't in someone's appointed place. I decided that it was dangerous to be crawling on the ground. I stood up, so the Apaches would see my form against the sky and think that as part of their plan one of their own had already moved into position here.

I wished I had some way to get into the valley and warn the men on watch. Below, I could see the moving shape of a soldier building up the fire, making the flames jump and spew sparks, but he was a long way from me. I knew Anza, and I was pretty sure there was a plan here, but what in the name of heaven was it?

The horses on the farthest edges started to move. They could tell something was out there. They raised their heads and took a few steps, then began to amble toward the center of the herd, coming in from the periphery. The motion was unhurried, gradual, but the whole caballada began to drift to the west. Under subtle pressure from the edges of the circle, the herd compacted and aligned. Then the pace picked up.

A shot rang off the rocks and echoed through stone hills. Two more crisp rounds were fired. 'Here we go!' I thought, hitting the ground, but there were no answering shots. Instead a thousand animals thundered over the earth. Dust boiled up in a cloud, blotting out the valley as the herd passed beneath me. I could still see the stars, but not the ground. I lay on shaking earth.

In ten minutes it was over. Every last mount for the government's army had been driven out to the west, into the craggy cliffs and down a sandy arroyo toward the vast plains ruled by the Navajos and Apaches beyond the great river.

As the dust settled back onto the empty land, I knew the colony was lost because, on top of everything else, losing the caballada would be insurmountable. Our fire signals had not reached the Comanches, or else these supposed allies had decided not to respond. I had to admit that the governor, whom I had admired so much, had misjudged it. Someone had thwarted Anza's final plan. Whoever had been undermining the colony had just won. After almost two hundred years of beating our heads against the impossibly hard life in this miserable kingdom, we had failed. It was back to El Paso again for the Spanish.

Despondent, I led the horse down a rock-fall into the valley to see what had happened to the men on watch. A quiet knife in the throat? Bodies bristling with arrows? The whole maneuver had been undertaken in silence except for those few shots. I rode openly over the flattened grass that still reeked of a thousand animals, not giving a damn that someone might hear or see me. The action had moved on. Too bad Rosa had to die for this mess, but then again, maybe it was best not to be around for what was going to happen to Santa Fe now. I wondered whether I'd go north and become a Ute, or straggle back to Mexico with the other side of my family.

The fire was a heap of embers, rapidly fading to nothing. I sat beside it and uncorked my flask. The burn of the brandy going down did nothing for me. I was sunk in total gloom.

A rock fell with a thud into the dust beside me. Another smaller one whanged against my shoulder. I whirled onto my feet to face whomever was out there. I gripped Benito's pistol, pointing it at nothing but darkness.

A man's voice called out, low but strong, "Get out of there!"

I turned and raised my cocked pistol toward the voice.

"Move it you idiot, you're going to fuck everything up!" Well, he spoke my language and his message was clear, so I climbed on the horse and headed toward the backdrop of hills.

"Get down, you asshole! Walk it!" Surely this was a friend talking.

I jumped off the horse. I knew when my knees gave way that Luz's fine brandy was already working. Who was disturbing my misery?

He met me in the huge boulders that had accumulated at the bottom of the rimrock. I could tell from his uniform and his demeanor that he was a regular in the presidio army. He looked a little familiar, maybe from Rosa's? "Get your horse tied," he ordered. "It's going to have to stay down here. We're climbing. Hurry up."

Hand over hand, I pulled myself after him up the rock face. It was the shortest way out of the valley. I was breathing hard and the brandy was misinterpreting my steps, but the soldier knew his way. On top he led me to a stacked cairn. We leaned back on it, our forms merging with the black rock.

"Got any more of that?" he asked.

"Of what?"

"That brandy you're reeking of."

Sheepishly I handed him the flask. I was beginning to re-member him. This was the man who had beaten up Arsenio at Rosa's. We should be best friends, except it didn't matter any more. "Go easy. It's strong stuff," I warned. The exertion on the rocks was starting to clear my head.

"Where in the devil did you come from?"

"East, by Galisteo," I said.

"Do you have any clue at all?" he asked impatiently. "I al-most shot you. Then I saw your pistol. No Indian would have a pistol like that one."

I wasn't sure how to take this. This soldier was not only rude, but was also finishing off my brandy. Still, I wasn't up to picking a fight. "I was a signal man. Then I lost my partner. And the army. I'm supposed to be somewhere in the rear on the left, but as you can see, they didn't arrive in time. Somehow the signals got mixed up."

The soldier must have sympathized with my dejection because he generously passed back my flask that still had a couple of swallows in it. I corked it and shoved it into my pocket.

"Listen!" he said.

Was it thunder or guns? There was an explosion down-wind of us. Gunfire boomed. We were on our feet yelling over the noise. From the way the screams and rifle fire rico-cheted and echoed, I could tell there was a burst of fighting down in the deep rock canyons, the perfect place to ambush a large party of raiders who had just rustled your horses. Both the battle and the stolen herd came rushing back toward us. A contingent of Apaches broke out of the canyon, driving fran-tic horses across the grassland below.

That's when the Comanches came on, hundreds of them with their ponies at a dead run, traveling west across the val-ley toward the crackling gun fire and the escaping raiders. These were hard-riding, lance-waving Comanches, and they were out to prove their worth.

Their ponies trampled the ground by the bonfire where I had so recently been sitting. They couldn't just shoot down the Apaches, because they were all mixed up with the army's horses. The enemy had to be encircled and taken one by one as they tried to flee the trap and get to the protection of open country.

The soldier and I watched, mesmerized, from our bird's eye view. Anza's army ran the rest of the maddened herd out of the canyon, driving the Apaches into the hands of their lifelong enemies. It was a night fight, the moon just cracking the horizon, so mostly what we saw was dust, and what we knew came from sounds.

"Rosa! You'd love this!" I cried out as the battle roared beneath me. On the west end of the field the presidio sol-diers fought hand to hand with resisting Apaches, and the Comanches, wise enough not to ride right into the face of the advancing Spanish, turned in one motion and chased a troop of Apaches on horseback, who raced toward the river with a chunk of the army's herd.

A little to the west of where we stood I could just make out a ribbon of dark-haired men filing cautiously along the bottom of the cliff. I nudged the soldier and when he started to say something I gripped his arm to quiet him. In one motion we both slid to the ground, prone on the bristly grass, and watched them come on. We didn't need to discuss it. We both knew what to do. I led out over the boulders and we slithered snake-like between the giant stones and down over their edges, lowering ourselves slowly toward the valley floor and the oncoming line of quietly escaping Apaches. They weren't traveling as fast as I would have thought, seeming more concerned about concealing themselves and moving carefully through the chunks of rubble that provided their protection. At the far end of the line, there was a bunched-up knot, as though they were guarding something, pushing it along. I suspected they were making for the dense foliage along the river and would follow the valley's edge until it siphoned them into the narrow bosque, dense with willow and cottonwood.

The soldier and I took our time, careful not to rattle stones or kick down loose dirt. Toward the bottom, we slid out onto a low ledge just a few feet above the ground. I crouched on my haunches in a ball, ready to spring, but my companion motioned me down. I eased myself onto the cold stone. A thin stream of armed Apaches began to pass beneath us and I caught the hot, horsy smell of them as they sneaked by. Then the larger knot of men emerged from a little bay in the rocks and moved toward our perch. I wondered if they had a prisoner or were rescuing one of their wounded, someone important, apparently.

There was just enough light from the half moon for me to see what they were guarding. Two determined Apaches clutched a short, stocky Spaniard, forcing him to run. The gleaming silver braid on his hat made identification easy. It was our alcalde they were manhandling, Tomás Duran, and they were stealing him away from the battlefield. Presumably they would carry him off to the craggy mountains south of us, and then? Again I realized that the Apaches had changed their tactics. Relying on strategy now, they had taken a valuable hostage. The Indios held him close, pushing him over the rough ground. Duran looked terrified.

I dropped back into a crouch, with Benito's gun ready to fire, but a single gunshot wasn't going to affect much down there. The soldier knew it too. He clutched one pistol in his right hand, a second in his left, and a knife was clenched between his teeth. The men gripping Duran were almost under us. I took careful aim at an older man who walked in the lead. Then I stopped and looked again. What was a gray-haired Spaniard doing with these Apaches? The soldier beside me sucked in his breath and held it.

In the same second we rose and fired at the leader, then I shoved off the ledge with all my strength. The soldier flew through the air beside me. We landed on top of two men who had turned, startled by our shots. Furiously I banged the butt of my gun on someone's head, dropped him, and shifting my knife into my right hand, I slashed the thigh of a man who leapt at me. A swift upward cut left him screaming. Duran's head shot up, and I saw a gleam in his eye as he twisted and fought against his captors' hold. They let go their grip and rushed me, but I rolled under them, and rolled a second time, coming to my feet.

My soldier-friend covered for me, getting off one more round while I scrambled to stand upright.

I ran fast toward the alcalde in the darkness, jumping over the bodies of the men we had just shot, because a huge Apache with flowing hair was racing me to Duran's side. Our portly mayor, catching on, dropped to the ground to get out of my way, and I tucked my shoulder and hit the giant Indian in his gut with everything I had. On the rebound, I saw my new friend struggling with a dark, sturdy man, so I got a solid grip on my knife and sent it flying into the shoulder of his attacker. The man let out a howl and, stumbling toward the cliff, reached back with his left arm and dragged my blade out of his flesh.

Backing up fast, I bumped into Duran, who pulled his own knife from his boot and placed it in my hand. I dropped to a crouch beside him and held the narrow blade up in front of me, ready for the last and biggest of the Indios, who moved slowly toward us across the boulder-strewn ground. The tall man stood still then, glaring at me, both of us armed and taut. I heard the quiet sounds of the soldier reloading his pistol. There was a click. The Apache heard it too. He took a giant backward step and seemed to melt into the cliff, disappearing into the darkness of a crack. I heard a rock tumble as he climbed. I rose to run toward the noise, but the alcalde seized my manta and held me back. Gunfire rang out as the soldier searched for the Apache with a bullet. We heard another small scattering of falling rocks, then there was silence.

The soldier and I took hold of the alcalde by his sturdy shoulders and lifted him off the ground. All three of us ran back into the deep shadow under the cliff to hide from whoever else was out there, and to put distance between ourselves and the dying Indios on our small piece of the battle-ground.

"I'll get their weapons," the soldier said, catching his breath for a moment leaning against the rocks.

"No you won't," I said. "We need to find our horses and get the hell away from here. We've got to keep the alcalde safe and get him back to Anza."

"That's an order!" Duran added, so we changed direction and crept back to the little alcove where I'd left my mount about a lifetime ago. The animal still stood there half asleep, with a boulder pinning its reins to the ground. I bent over to roll the rock off and nearly passed out. Keeping my head down, I tried to even out my breath and slow my thudding heart. I had finally killed. I had bludgeoned and knifed. My whole body shook, as much from excitement as disgust. I spat something vile into the dirt, stood up with the reins in my hand, and cast a quick look at the stars. "Thanks for the gun, dad."

Throughout our own skirmish there had been a constant background din, the noise of the wider battle. Now it was almost quiet. We heard distant hoof beats, a shout, one last blast from a musket and then total silence. From the furtive way the Apaches had been leaving the field, we knew they had not prevailed.

The alcalde was wiping his face with a handkerchief and brushing dirt off his coat sleeves. I handed him the reins, and said, "Here, sir. Take this horse. Anza will be worried about you." It was the first chance he'd had to take specific notice of me.

"Nando, is that you?" He reached out and took my hand with a shaky grasp.

I was embarrassed by his discomposure, but I could understand it. The man had just been through a lot, including the loss of his son. "None other, sir, and meet my friend here whose name I've never learned," I said turning to the soldier, who couldn't doff his hat because it was gone, but who bowed anyway.

"Corporal Bernal, sir. At your service."

Duran looked at us both, shook his head, and sighed. "Only a fool would have gotten himself into that predicament. An old retainer, someone who's been on my hacienda for years, who's done everything I ever asked of him, told me I was needed over at a spot behind the battle. He led me right into their hands. Passed me off to them as though they'd all planned it long ago. The bastard even spat on me!" Then Duran turned and pointed back the way we'd come. "He's lying over there on the ground. One of you shot him."

"What was his name?" I asked.

"Lorenzo." He looked directly at us and very quietly said, "It's amazing who your real friends turn out to be."

"Praise the perfection of the gods' universe!" I added under my breath.

It was a humbling moment for our mayor, but somehow he still sounded like he was making a speech. I pulled the horse's reins over its head and stood there waiting to help Duran mount. "But this is your horse, Nando. I can't leave you on foot," he said, swinging into the saddle anyway.

"There's no choice, sir. Bernal has an animal hidden somewhere here. Maybe he can give me a ride back in."

The alcalde sat up high on my horse, outlined by the light of the moon, in some measure of control again. Then, out of the corner of my eye, I caught a movement. On a jutting outcrop of the black cliff I could make out the tall form of a man standing sideways to us, drawing back the string of his bow.

"Alcalde!" I yelled, but the arrow was zinging through the air directly at the bull's eye of the mayor's chest. It struck with a thud and the alcalde arched back, his arms flailing above his head. I grabbed the horse as it started to rear, and the soldier reached up to break Duran's fall, but it wasn't necessary. The alcalde swung forward over the horse's neck, lay still there a second, and then to our amazement, sat up straight, gathered the reins, and quietly said,

"Pull this damn thing out, will you?"

I ignored his order, because I was hauling on the horse, moving us as fast as I could to the protection of the cliff, so we wouldn't be such a target. Then the alcalde dismounted, and he and Bernal yanked on the arrow, pulling it out of the thick leather of his buff coat.

"Seven layers quilted together by the presidio's armorer. Everyone should wear one!" Duran fingered the tear where the arrow had entered. The point had stopped just before penetrating the last layer. "I'll have a bruise from it, but I can live with a bruise," he said, almost jovial again. "Once, Anza, wearing a coat like this, caught ten arrows and not one pierced him."

Let the alcalde boast if he needed to, but it would be a long time before I could afford leather armor. I was ready for a drink. I pulled the flask out from my shirt, shaking it to see how much was left. Not much. I had a quick nip, then passed it to Duran. He did likewise and magnanimously handed the dregs to Bernal.

"We'd better stay low and stick together," I said, so, cautiously, we headed back on foot toward the center of things, keeping to cover beneath the cliffs. We approached the flurry of the camp that was forming as the presidio army regrouped. At the outskirts the alcalde halted.

"Come in with me, let me tell the governor what you two did tonight," Duran said. Corporal Bernal was all for it, but I held back.

"Have to leave you here, sir."

"Why's that?" he called to me as I started to walk toward the cliff.

"I'm not supposed to be here," I said, "but thanks anyway."

Did the whole battle last even an hour? I don't think so. Maybe altogether it did, from when I drank beside the embers of the fire, until this quiet end. I sat apart and watched the recovered herd settle down and the many campfires of the victorious army of New Mexico light up the night sky, lending a suddenly civilized air to the valley.

My perch above it all wasn't far from the main fire where the governor walked purposefully among his men. I kept scanning the field, looking for my brother. Surely he should have turned up by now? Then several Comanches rode in, pushing bleeding and dirty prisoners ahead of them. Watching them was like the stories Luz told from old Spain, of being in the uppermost seats at a play, with a well-lit stage, characters waving their arms, and actors moving on and off. I couldn't hear them, but I enjoyed the spectacle.

The Spanish had triumphed. The Apaches were scattered for now. From what I'd seen, though, they didn't fare too badly. I had watched a couple of bands race away with a fair portion of the government's stock, but what mattered more than anything was that the Comanches had come through for us, performing perfectly according to plan. We'd made an alliance that would most likely save our hides.

Below, I saw the alcalde, in only slightly marred dress leathers, still handsome and agreeable, strut over to Anza and clasp his shoulder. The more disheveled governor threw an arm over the mayor's shoulder and moved forward with him to stand beside the fire. Before long, the Comanches drew off and made their own hasty camp farther along the cliff line. Our soldiers staked their personal mounts and bedded down.

Anza and Duran were the last men up, throwing wood on the fire themselves, and only when there was none left in the gathered pile did they too go off to their tents. Except for the movement of the watch and the nervous twitching of the herd, the night became still and I slept.

Muddy Fingers

$\mathcal{A}$s the army rode back to Santa Fe, I found I had no patience for regimented life. After less than twenty minutes gagging on the dust of hundreds of horses and mules, I pulled back and waited until they were out of sight. Then I pointed my horse cross-country and came in over the lower Arroyo Hondo. I got to town in time to soak up some of the cheering and good will of the people who were in the streets to welcome back their men. Few realized the importance of last night's encounter, but everyone likes to win.

Anza made a great show of those Comanche leaders who had agreed to make peace with us. The next day, on the sunny plaza, there were speeches and the passing of a silver-headed baton. Sitting nearly upright in the shade under the portál, watching, was a somewhat diminished Sebastian. His head was still wrapped, but the bandage was a small neat thing, not the lumpish turban of four days ago.

"God man, it's fine to see you." I squatted beside him.

"Likewise. Good work, Nando!"

"I can't say I did much myself, but at least I got a chance to see why that man's our governor. Did you know the Utes actually did come down and were trying to join?"

"Join whom?" Sebastian seemed only mildly concerned.

"Not us, that's for sure, but no one showed up to lead them to the Apaches, so most of them went home."

"I wonder if that was just a routine blunder or if God was really on our side?" Sebastian winked.

"Rosa was working awfully hard that night. She might have had a hand. Anyhow, I ran into a bunch of my Ute cousins stumbling around in the woods looking for Apaches to hook up with. They almost turned themselves over to the Comanches by mistake."

"And?" Now Sebastian, in his typical fashion, wanted to hear all of it.

"Once I told them how close they had come to suicide, they felt so dumb they just went home. But I think they got the picture of which side they'd better ride with now. Sebastian," I asked, "did you really fall off your horse, or did something else happen?"

"Something else happened, but I never saw it. My horse threw me and I went down; haven't done that since I was a kid. The horse was so spooked it took off and it still hasn't come in. They say they found footprints around me. Someone dropped by to make certain I was hurt badly enough."

Sebastian delivered this quietly while watching the hastily put together ceremony involving Comanches, Governor Anza the Commander, our alcalde in all his shining silver, both priests, and sacristans carrying the big crosses. I thought the governor's aide was barely aware of me, but I had forgotten that I shouldn't underestimate Sebastian.

"Who killed Rosa?" he asked abruptly.

"I've got just one idea and I hope she's still locked up."

"I don't think Carlos turned anyone loose, though Paulina's only under house arrest. Who have you got in mind?" Sebastian asked.

I told him I wouldn't be sure unless I heard the woman whisper, and through a wall, if possible.

"We can arrange that, but it won't be solid evidence."

"I agree, but it would be an indication. Sebastian, do you know where Francisco is? I couldn't find him after we set the signal fires. I've asked everyone and I still haven't found him."

Turning his head to acknowledge this must have hurt, but Sebastian looked right at me and said, "I didn't know he was missing. I don't like that." I felt the same way.

Even though it was the middle of the week, a special Mass of thanksgiving was held after the ceremony. I left Sebastian in his chair and dutifully trooped in the procession to the church with the rest of my family. The people of Santa Fe were dressed in their scrappiest best, which ranged from ancient silks and rotting parasols, to clean, rough linen, to homespun woolens died with local weeds. It didn't matter which; the enthusiasm was infectious. Carlos was walking fairly well on his own now and managed not to use his stick while he was up in front of everybody.

Late that same night, after the whole town was asleep, some of us returned to the church. Inside, twenty real candles lit up the brightly painted plaster walls. Men in full dress uniform stood in an orderly circle around a coffin that was handsomely made of freshly adzed planks. Another dozen candles created a warm circle of light right in front of the altar. Father Miera presided at Rosa's funeral, and the governor, who had bought the candles and paid for the ceremony, stood with his hand on her casket.

It was a strange assembly in the middle of the night with Anza, a lieutenant, two sergeants, and Luz de Gracia with her household. There were other men there whose faces I recognized, but whom I didn't know. Juanillo, from the stables at Santa Cruz, assisted the priest and then played quietly on a flute. The half dozen girls who used to work for Rosa stood inside the circle, flanked by guards. They had been let out of prison long enough to attend. After all, there was probably just one of them who didn't love her. The governor had a heart and there had been too much death. I was thinking, too, it would give him a chance to scrutinize their faces, in search of clues as to which one killed her.

The ceremony was hushed and not hurried. Everyone understood you wouldn't normally extend the holy sacraments to the madam of a house of prostitution, nor bury her in holy ground, but the people present tonight knew what else Rosa was, and there was nothing about the ceremony that slighted her. We carried her casket ourselves, and in the dark buried her in church ground in a grave Anza had ordered dug.

In the end, I did what everyone else there wanted to do but was afraid of. I climbed up the tower ladder, seized the bell rope, and pulled it steadily for five slow minutes. Never mind that we had to be furtive, Rosa's soul was going to climb to heaven on those long, deep notes. Let the people awaken in their beds and wonder. Rosa had worked to save their lives.

I was worried when I saw Anza waiting for me at the bottom of the ladder, but he did not look displeased. He shook my hand and thanked me. It confused me; what had I done? I hadn't gotten near him since before the battle on the Galisteo, so I reached into my pocket and pulled out the coins I'd found in Rosa's room the night she'd been murdered.

"More of these," I said, putting them into his hand. "The same as the one Ramón dropped, but he wasn't alive anymore to toss these in Rosa's direction."

"Where exactly were they?" he asked, turning one over on his palm.

"Scattered, thrown maybe, on the floor by the far wall of her bedroom." Anza looked up at me, saddened, then once again said, "Thank you, Nando. There's still another job, one not quite finished. Stay nearby, because I'm afraid I'll be summoning you again soon." He sounded almost apologetic.

I told him I would, then after thanking him for honoring Rosa with Christian burial, I headed for home. I'd forgotten to ask if he knew anything about Francisco, but it sounded like I'd get a chance tomorrow if my brother hadn't turned up by then.

I lingered on the church steps, letting my family go ahead of me. A tall, lean man strode rapidly across the dirt, scowling, not looking at anyone as he raced toward the church. The bells had awakened him, caught him off guard. What was happening within his church? Father Baldonado ascended the stairs and faced Father Miera challengingly. Father Miera deliberately turned his back on him, inserted the brass key and locked the doors. Then Miera circled my shoulders with his arm, and under his protection, I descended to the street, leaving the mad friar standing alone at the top of the steps, his dark garments held tight about him, looking like a dismal bird of prey.

I slept in, but finally awoke when Sebastian sent word that I should come to the palacio. As I walked up to town, I saw

315

towers of monsoon clouds piling on top of the Sangre de Cristos, though it was barely past noon. It wouldn't be long until the summer rains started. So much had been overlooked, the garden, my fields up north in Abiquiú. I'd never gotten that new seed corn up to Diego. I had no idea where my mother was, and no one had mentioned Baz in a week, much less had time to look for him. Francisco still hadn't come home and no one had heard anything of him. What the hell, did he fall off the cliffs that night? I'd have to go back out there and look for him, but the governor wanted me here, so here I was. As I crossed the plaza, the sunlight faded and dust started blowing through the streets again. Tree limbs, heavy with thick summer leaves, rose and fell on the wind that spun off the building thunderheads.

At the palacio, a man led me to Sebastian, who promptly took me to jail. I was ushered into a cell at the end of a short hallway. "Wait here." Sebastian ordered me inside, then closed the door behind him as he left. I was surprised at the relief I felt when he didn't turn the key. I wondered if there really was a dungeon underneath the palacio? We had always heard rumors of damp cells just wide enough for a man to lie in miserably.

I heard footsteps in the hall, then another door shut. Two men were talking in the room next door. Francisco! I could hear them well enough, maybe not every word, but most of what they said. Then Sebastian's bandaged head appeared in my doorway. "How's the sound?"

I got it now. "It's close. A little more muffled than before, but let's try. By the blessed saints, Sebastian, when did Francisco get here?"

"Just an hour ago. He's been helping with this. I'll send him in when we get a chance."

Been helping out, I muttered crossly, and why couldn't he even bother to let me know he's alive? Sebastian left and after a few minutes I heard lighter footsteps alongside his in the hall. The door to the adjoining cell closed.

My brother is a good-looking man, with dark curly hair, high color in his cheeks, and the women they brought to him one by one were trained professionals, easy with men. It didn't take long for them to start up conversation and while they talked I listened at the wall. Of course the women were scared and subdued, but Francisco acted like it was a lucky thing that they'd been moved into his cell and got them laughing and forgetting where they were. Twice he let his voice get husky, and I could easily guess at the game he was playing, but as a result I heard whispers and playful badinage.

Sebastian brought in first one girl, and then each of the rest in turn, pretending he had made a mistake, 'sorry to have put you in the wrong cell' sort of thing. Pretty obvious, but I got what I needed. By the end of the exercise, there were two candidates, both of them girls with voices of a deeper timbre than the others.

When we had gone through all six of them, Sebastian and Francisco came and got me. "Which one?"

"Two of them."

"What do you mean?" Sebastian growled.

"Number two and number five sound exactly like the girl with Perea. I recognized Paulina as number six. That was dumb to include her, because she was in bed with me that night." Sebastian let that go.

"Francisco, bring me Angie and Bernadette," he ordered.

I tried to give my brother a loaded look during this short exchange, but he dodged it. He came back in a minute with two very bedraggled prostitutes. One was mulatto and probably beautiful, but hadn't used a comb in five days. The other had a pretty face, but was too plump for my taste. She'd been eating well somewhere in this territory.

"Say something," I prompted each in turn. They stood there stupidly, not having a clue as to what to say on command, so I started them off on the Hail Mary, the only thing I'd ever memorized. Still there was no appreciable difference between them.

Francisco spoke up. "I've got an idea. Sebastian, can you serve as escort?"

"I'd better get someone stronger than I am right now. Wait. I'll be back." Sebastian left us for a few minutes, but Francisco kept talking to the girls and made himself unavailable to any cross or inquiring looks from me.

Accompanied by two soldiers, we all marched in the rising wind over to Rosa's and entered her courtyard. Francisco leaned the tall pine-pole ladder against the wall beside the chimney and indicated the girls should start up it. It was a long climb to the second story and they both held back until the guard poked the fat one and said, "You first." She hitched up her skirts and climbed, almost gaily, up to the parapet. She looked down at the men below her with a smirk, then swung her leg over the roof's edge showing us ankle, calf, and a slice of thigh. We yielded no quarter with our eyes.

The mulatto hesitated at the ladder until prodded. Then she climbed slowly, clutching her skirts against her legs. On top she did a decorous little sidesaddle move over the parapet. The two guards, my brother, and I, joined the women on the roof.

Francisco walked around the chimney that had been sealed shut to insure Rosa's death, until he found what he wanted: perfect casts of human fingers dried into the mud. He took hold of the mulatto, Angie, and held her hand over the prints. Her fingers were way too long and narrow for them.

We all turned and looked at Bernadette. Francisco reached for her hand, but she yanked it away from him. She took a lunging step onto the parapet and balanced there on the narrow edge, her skirts fanned out in the wind and her angry eyes defying us to prevent her from flinging herself into the courtyard below.

A gust from the summer storm snapped her skirt toward me and I clutched it, catching some of the bright cotton between my fingers. I twisted a handful of the material around my fist and yanked. She fell hard on her bottom, squarely onto the roof. The prostitute screamed and kicked at me, but both guards jumped her, pinning her flat. Even so, she whipped her head from side to side trying to bite their arms. Rain began to fall in fat, hard drops. Sebastian had caught up with us by then and had slowly ascended the ladder. Just his sore head was visible over the parapet, as he pronounced, "Madam, I must place you under arrest, under suspicion of murder."

We dragged her to her feet. Francisco clamped one hand around her upper arm, the other over her yelling mouth, and led her to the chimney. He held her right hand firmly, and with great seriousness brought it down into the prints in the mud on the chimney. They fit perfectly. In the now driving rain, the soldiers guided her down the ladder and led her away. I don't know what they did to that woman, but her kind of spunk wouldn't last long once the government decided to make a poor whore talk.

My elusive brother stuck close to the soldiers who led Bernadette away, and disappeared into the palacio without another word to me. Carlos must be in there somewhere too. Clearly something was up, and it didn't include me.

I figured I'd go tell Luz that Francisco was back safely and then get the hell out of here. I was sick of the whole business, and dog-tired. I wondered if I could spring Marisol from Luz's guard. I'd like to spend a couple of hours alone in the hills with her, but trailing vertical clouds of gray were moving toward town, ready to drop more sheets of rain. A nap at home seemed like the next best thing.

I didn't want to be in this crowded town. I didn't want to sleep in a house next door to eighteen other houses. I particularly did not want to take any more of Francisco's mysterious rudeness. At home there was no place to put my bedroll down and hold my girl. I needed to get out of Santa Fe. I wanted to be up at the ranch. In the mood I was in, I needed all the room I could get.

Francisco did come home that evening and was as tired and cross as I. Luz caught the currents, fed us, then went to bed. I tried to be friendly, though I wasn't all right yet about him ditching me out on the Galisteo.

"Francisco, what's up with you?"

He turned on me like I'd slugged him. "I just can't talk right now. Do you understand?" He looked terrible. His face lacked its usual strong color. His hair was flat and dirty. There were dark circles under his eyes.

"Jesus, man, you look awful."

With that he banged his cup down, walked into the room we shared and slammed the door. It looked like I'd be sleeping out in the sala tonight. It had to be about Luisa. Nothing else but a woman could get a man so twisted.

I fiddled around with my gun for a while, cleaning and oiling it. Then Marisol came into the room. For once no one was around. I took her in my arms and held her in a long, slow hug. Under the pretense of taking care of the animals, we went out to the barn and with the rain pattering on the roof, we made love on the clean hay. She was beautiful, and her skin lovely to touch. It seemed like there had never been any horror at all.

In the Name of the King

The next morning was bright and sunny with every bird in town delighted by last night's rain. The battle was over; the news for once was good. Rosa was decently buried, her assailant captured, the scourge of Ramón and Perea had been eliminated, and I'd gotten to snuggle with my girl.

We all worked in the garden, thinning the new growth, planting more rows of corn, beans, melons, everything we'd need. Now that we were sure the last frost had passed we didn't hold back, but got all our remaining seed into the ground.

Yet there was a sense of waiting, that this wasn't over yet. Carlos hadn't come home from the palacio last night. Something intense must be going on up there, and Francisco's gloom hadn't lifted, although he'd adopted a more civilized way of handling it. I felt better, but I too was waiting.

After just an hour in the field, Francisco got up, rinsed his hands in the river and left without a word to any of us. Not much later, I, too, conveniently remembered I had another job and decided to go have a look around. A half-day of stoop labor in the sun was plenty for me.

I drifted up to the plaza on a different street than usual, not feeling like taking the route past Rosa's yet. In the harsh sunlight of the main square, I noticed a small crowd gathered over at the alcalde's mansion, across from the palacio. He was out there, cordial to everyone, though a little more subdued since his son had been buried just the week before. As testament to his resilience, he stood solid and agreeable as ever, giving advice to the carpenter. The little man and his assistant began to insert newly fashioned windows, careful of the real glass in them, into two openings cut through the adobe wall at either side of the alcalde's front door. So that was the big job that was in line before ours. Luz would be furious.

These windows, the first ever in town except those few at the palacio, were tall and gracious, with twelve panes in each, two wide and six high. The carpenter had done a fine job of building the frames. There was even scrollwork on the lintels that the men installed now at the top of the openings. A fair-sized crowd had gathered to see this wonder, certainly everyone who was on the plaza that day. The alcalde's attention was on the workmen up on low scaffolds, wielding mallets and wedges. Duran's wife stood just inside the door, her sad face looking out at all of us. An assistant dropped his mallet, just missing the alcalde's foot, but the mayor graciously bent to retrieve it. Everyone was laughing at the embarrassed worker when the governor came up.

Anza wore his dress uniform. Four officers, including Sebastian, flanked him. His manner was not light.

I scanned the plaza and noticed soldiers deployed discreetly through it. There were two armed men on the palacio roof. As if to underscore the governor's serious purpose, the tall clouds building above the mountains had flattened and now leaned over the town, blotting out the sun.

"Tomás Duran, in the name of King Carlos of Spain, you are under arrest, for assault on a King's officer, kidnapping a citizen of the colony, illegal trafficking in slaves, conspiracy to murder, and murder." A lieutenant read the charges while the governor stood at his side, his face as dark as the sky.

Duran let the mallet drop to the ground. His wife disappeared into the darkness inside. He turned and looked at his friend, Anza. The governor held himself stone-still.

A lieutenant passed the document bearing the charges to Duran. The alcalde stood there reading it meticulously while everyone watched. Warily, he looked up at his friend, the governor, and at the soldiers posted at every possible point of escape. Then slowly, sadly, he lifted the warrant in both hands and held it above his head, signifying that he submitted to the rule of his king. Two armed soldiers stepped forward, seized Duran by his arms and began pushing him through the crowd toward the jail. Anza didn't move as his friend was taken away. Then he turned to the carpenter.

"Seal the holes. Wrap the windows in sheepskin to protect them. Deliver them to the palacio as soon as you are done. These windows are subpoenaed as evidence in the ensuing trial of the alcalde." Then he walked off, still with a military air, but obviously bearing a burden the likes of which none of us could understand.

I watched as he returned to his office through the crowd that parted to make way for him. I realized my mouth was still hanging open, so I clamped my hand over it and started to run.

I raced down the street to deliver the news to Luz. I wondered if Carlos already knew? A dog ran at me snarling. I knew this little runt and gave him an ineffective kick. Dashing over the potholes at a dead run I wasn't being subtle any more, but everyone in town was rushing with the news.

I burst through the door and stopped abruptly. Marisol put up her hand to warn me. Luz had a guest. Whoever it was sat in our best chair. A woman's back was to me. A boy sat on her lap. They were at our table, talking rapidly. Then Luz looked up and smiled. The woman turned slowly in her seat and the boy dropped to the floor and rushed at me.

"Ma! Baz!" And I already was out of breath.

I almost tripped on the child in my haste to embrace Nan. It was a three-way hug and I wasn't the only person with tears in my eyes. Nan was finally forced back by Baz's importuning voice. The boy was skinny and all bones, his eyes huge in his head.

"Why did you hide from me, Nando? I saw you and that girl. I was coming after you as fast as I could!"

What in God's name? "Baz, where?"

"Up by the two rivers. You rode right by me! I was sure it was you. I didn't have a horse, so I borrowed one. I knew I was right behind you, and then below that town I looked and looked along the river, I saw where you crossed . . ."

"Baz! Slow down! That was you? The day we were hiding in the bosque? By the ford below Santa Cruz?"

The kid had tears of frustration streaming down his face. "You hid from me and I was hungry!"

"Baz! I am sorry!" I wrapped him in a hug and held his squirming body so tight he couldn't move. "Who stole you, Baz?"

"A stinky old man on a horse and some Indians. And then they gave me to a really mean man who I had to bite, so I got away, but that wasn't so good, because then I was all by myself and I had to eat a dead fish!"

I was wiping at that nose again. "You're back, Baz. You're all right! Does your granny know?"

"Uh, Uh. We just got here. I had to show Nan where you lived."

I looked up at my mother from where I knelt on the floor. "How did you find our Baz?"

She talked to me in Ute. I guess she wasn't sure of her Spanish yet. "He was picked up by a group of our men, probably just in time, too. They came down here because Chief Big Hands told them to. I traveled with them part way, to visit you."

"Come on mother, you're not going to tell me Cedro let you come down here in the middle of a war, just to pay a call?"

She raised her pretty face toward me with a smile that covered the sharp look in her eyes. I read it as, "Careful, my son. We'll talk later."

My mother went on, in halting Spanish now, with the public version of her story. "After I left Abiquiú, I met up with men who were already returning north and they had Baz. I talked them into handing him over to me. It wasn't hard." She looked at Baz and the two of them laughed.

"I gotta go see granny!" Baz lit out of there so fast we couldn't catch him. That old woman was going to be knocked flat. Luz knew it and started after him, but I stopped her.

"Luz, wait! She'll survive. No one dies of happiness. There's news." Luz sat down again. From the look on her face I realized she expected this to be bad.

I took Nan's hand and sat beside her as I poured out the events of the last half hour. I watched Nan's face to make sure she was getting it. She was. The language was still in her after all.

Luz was as dumbfounded as everyone by the alcalde's arrest. "He was such a nice man! Always a friend to us. It wasn't his fault his son was a bad one! " She shook her head as she let the evidence sink in. "How did Anza know? When did he figure it out?" she asked.

"I've got no idea at all," I lied, trying to buy enough time to sort this out. "After the battle, they looked like best friends, sitting up half the night talking together, but now that I've had five minutes to think about this, it's seems that we overlooked the obvious. Ramón couldn't have been stashing slaves and arming Apaches without his father knowing about it." I felt really dumb, remembering that I had fought to save this notorious alcalde, when even his own men had turned on him out by the Galisteo.

"Duran's always been far richer than any of the rest of us. I sometimes wondered how he managed it." Luz was thinking it through. "Do you know if they'll try him here or in Mexico?"

"They always try the big cases in Mexico, but he could cool his heels in prison here for years." I thought of the sassy prostitute. How long had it taken to break her?

"Why do you suppose they subpoenaed his windows? The carpenter dropped ours off, by the way, with some nice scroll work on the wood." She gestured to the neatly framed windowpane placed gently on top of a sheepskin.

I was thinking that windows were indeed strange evidence, when there was a tapping on the doorframe. A presidio soldier stood there, too polite to come in through the already open door.

"With your permission please."

"Come in."

"Nando is supposed to come to the palacio at once. Governor's orders."

I was on my feet. I bent over and hugged Nan again to make sure she was real. "I'll be back."

He Couldn't Resist

The governor was in a blistering rage. His voice boomed out terse instructions to those waiting on him and when he saw me come in he yelled so loudly that he drowned out the thunder that roared on the mountains. It was muggy, the rain just couldn't get itself going, and the atmosphere in his office was poisonously hot.

Carlos, usually in the forefront, had placed himself behind the row of men who were taking the heat. It was clear he didn't want any attention from the governor in this mood. The look my brother gave me read, "Look out!"

"Aguilar!" Carlos jumped to his battered feet and I stood up straighter. We didn't know which one of us he was after.

"Why the hell has Francisco abducted the prisoner's niece?"

Carlos caught my eye to ask what I knew about this. I managed to signal that I hadn't a clue.

"Sir?" Carlos dared to ask for more information. The governor obliged, still roaring.

"He left while we were on the plaza, and took Duran's wife too! Horses all set up behind their house, even enough for servants. Absolutely against the law. He's tampering with witnesses, kidnapping, as far as I'm concerned!"

"Couldn't he just be escorting them back to their hacienda down south?" I managed to ask.

"Do you take me for a fool?" he bellowed. "I'd already sent men down to their ranch when the tracker discovered they went north! They were heading toward Santa Cruz at a dead run. We just got a report they were seen at the bottom of the hill by the turnoff to Tesuque."

"North?" Carlos and I asked in unison.

"Get your asses moving. I don't have any spare men or time to hunt him down. It's up to you two to rein in that stupid idiot, and Nando," he turned to me glowering, but at least for the moment lowering his voice to speak to me privately, "when you bring your brother back, you'd better be ready with your story on why it was your knife in Ramón Duran's spinal cord! Get moving!"

Carlos was braver than I. "Sir, please, may I have a word? In private?" he begged.

"No!"

So we left, with the eyes of most of the colony's officers watching our ignominious departure. Carlos limped beside me as fast as he could.

"What's this about a knife?" he whispered.

"He's got me there."

My knife? That one really puzzled me. I hadn't had my own knife since I'd handed it to the woman in Ramón's slave caravan. Any knife I'd used this past month had been begged or borrowed and who would recognize Nando's knife anyway? Even I hadn't.

329

"I don't know if I can ride yet," said my brother, "but I can put together men and horses to back you up. What's going on with Francisco?"

"He's in love," I blurted. "Which is also why he stood me up in Galisteo, worried me to death for two days, and shut me out of my own room last night. Now I'm supposed to do what? Arrest him? Shoot him? Talk reason into his befuddled skull?" In frustration I asked, "Carlos, do you think you can ride at all?"

"Well, I think, probably, if I cling to the saddle horn and keep to a slow walk." He was almost whining.

"That'll be good enough. Just come behind me. Look for signs in case I turn off. They aren't going to get far with an older woman and a bunch of servants. The sky's about to open up and it'll be god-awful muddy when it does. I think I can find them, but you're the man with the authority to bring him in."

"Even if Francisco won't come back, we'll have to deliver the women to Anza," he said.

"My guess is Francisco has already figured out how stupid he's been, and I doubt he'll let himself be separated from Luisa."

We were in the stables behind the palacio. I helped myself to two horses, hoping no one had any time to notice today. "I'm out of here. Go home, get some food and ponchos, and keep your eyes open for where I leave the road. I'll mark the place with a little pile of rocks, or a god-damn flower arrangement or something."

I had saddled both horses, and was about to get up on mine, a hooked nose, awkward-looking mare who had seen many miles. I was betting on her long legs. Just as I pulled her through the gate, a thunder boomer exploded sideways into snakes of lightning and she reared up and bolted, leaving me holding a thin piece of broken rein in my hand. The clouds broke wide open then and seemed to dump all the water in them at once.

"Take mine!" Carlos yelled through the storm. "I'll work something out!"

We parted in the street and I was off. It wasn't even suppertime, but the furious clouds made everything dark. The road was slick as grease and neither the horse nor I liked it. As soon as we cleared the houses though, I was able to find enough grass on the verge to hold the mud in place, so we picked up to a canter and were off in pursuit of my handsome brother and the lovely lady in his life.

I couldn't count on Carlos. He'd probably be relegated to Luz's mule now that the horse I'd chosen was careening loose around town. I kept practicing what I'd say when I found Francisco. If he was crazy enough to pull this stunt, he wasn't about to be impressed by his kid brother's attempts at persuasion.

The storm took a breather when I crossed the place where they had been spotted near the Tesuque pueblo. A silvery sun actually shone sideways from under the clouds, brightening the streaming land. Another league down the road, the rain came on again in earnest and made me sorry I was wearing boots. I had to keep lifting my legs to tip the water out of them. Bolts of driller lightning two feet wide slammed into the earth. For some unknown reason none of them hit us and my purloined horse kept running.

I bet Francisco had been planning this all along. He'd dumped me during the battle and run off to go get Luisa at the hacienda. He was back in Santa Fe, avoiding our house at the time the alcalde's family came in from the country. He couldn't talk to me because he knew what he was planning and he knew I worked for Anza. Damn!

The rain was a drum on my back, the horse's hooves a contrapuntal beat. We went on and on. How long would this creature hold up? Just before true dark there was another dazzling shot of lightning, turning the low clouds lavender. Its light lingered in the air and by some miracle flared off the silver rosettes on a fancy bridle, thirty yards to the west at the far side of a full and racing arroyo. If the rain did what it usually does and quit in a few minutes, the water would roll away and leave only a gooey crossing. Right now, with the arroyo two feet deep and sporting standing waves, I couldn't attempt it.

I rode along on my side of the freshet until I was directly across from a solitary stand of young cottonwoods. Water swirled around the roots, and a sodden party, mostly female, huddled under the leaky protection of the leaves.

"Get out from under the trees, you ignorant fool!" I yelled across the arroyo.

Silence for a long while, and then, finally, "Nando?"

"Yup."

"Can you give me a hand?" Francisco's voice calling to me had an uncharacteristically meek note to it. He must have come to his senses and remembered about standing under trees in lightning, because his party filed out from the copse and sat on the edges of a side gully, sopping wet and miserable. My brother was clearly in over his head.

"It's only water!" I yelled. "Not nearly as threatening as the governor right now. You've got to go back to Santa Fe!"

"I know." He was subdued. "We were already coming back when we got stuck here."

"Listen up! Carlos is coming. He'll have food and blankets. I'll leave him a sign at the turnoff and maybe even run into him on the way. He can haul you in. I've got to go calm the governor down and try to keep you out of jail."

Francisco was attempting to turn a wet square of blanket into an insufficient tent for two ladies, but he gave me a resigned wave that looked a lot like "Don't waste your time with an idiot like me."

So I'd found them and now I got to ride all the way back, six or seven miles in the dark, and go face Anza. I could try to get to him through Sebastian. I could pray to find him alone in his office and be able to stand up to his fury without half the garrison watching me. I hoped Francisco's exhausted and love-struck demeanor would convince the governor not to put him in prison and throw away the key. Maybe our commander would be in a slightly more tractable mood, now that a few hours had passed since he'd had to arrest his best friend for treason.

They let me into the palacio through the back gate to return their blown and muddy horse. It was no surprise that Sebastian showed up while I was wrestling with the slimy cinch.

"Francisco and the ladies will take a couple of hours to get here, weighed down by mud and chagrin, I'd say."

"Good thing," Sebastian grunted. "The longer they wait the better his mood will be."

"I figured that," I said. "Carlos was ambling down there on a mule with ponchos and instructions to bring them in. Francisco was beat. I think this is more about love than criminality." Somehow Anza's other charge seemed more pressing to me. "It might have been my knife, Sebastian. To tell the truth,

333

when I saw it I was too terrified to take notice, but I didn't bring Ramón down. I'm not that good."

"I know you're not, but it's still a matter for inquiry. The knife has your initials on it, 'F. A.' "

I remembered when my father gave me the knife. The letters he'd had engraved on it were small and very ornate. I could barely make them out, but I had been pleased nonetheless. In the frenzy of helping the slave women I had forgotten entirely that my initials were on the blade. It was only a badly needed tool.

Was it one of them, then, who saved Marisol and me in the forest? Paying me back for helping them? I hoped so. That felt good.

"So is the governor going to believe me? And how deep is the sling Francisco's ass is in?" I looked to Sebastian for reassurance if any was available.

"Jesus, Mary and Joseph! Your brother solved the mystery. He's got nine fresh new lives with the governor." I stood there speechless.

Here was justice! For a month, I crawled on my belly all over the territory for the governor, tracking down the colony's miscreants and then my brother, fresh from flunking out of school in Mexico City, is the hero? Sebastian read my expression.

"He was able to finger the alcalde."

"Come on! Francisco?"

"The windows, Nando. Francisco knew for a fact that the Apaches had stolen all the glass in the wagons, way below Socorro. When he spotted it at the carpenter's shop, Francisco became suspicious. The only way that glass could have survived and gotten up here was if the alcalde had an Apache friend. Or maybe a whole nation of Apache friends."

I turned from my work and looked at him, making sure that he wasn't making up this fantasy, but Sebastian's face was serious and worn with fatigue.

"So proof of the alcalde's guilt didn't come from the prostitute?" I asked.

"What we got out of her helped; everything all of us did helped. In the end, her confession was useful, but the windows are the hard evidence. Francisco pieced it together and told the governor yesterday."

I stopped shaking out the saddle blanket. "Duran couldn't resist," I said, "being the big shot, being the fanciest man in town. He took the risk and retrieved his window panes."

"Yes," said Sebastian, adding, "and not by fighting Apaches to win them back. He was partners with those people; they'd been cutting deals for years. Remember when the soldiers had the skirmish and rounded up some of the goods stolen from the caravan? There were still several wagons unaccounted for."

I nodded, then finished out the thought for him. "So the Indios screwed up and stole their patrón's wagons as well." I grimaced at the implications. Duran? The magnanimous Alcalde of Santa Fe, in cahoots with the Apaches? Raiding our colony's vital supply train? "I suppose he's the reason the guard was half of normal."

"Strange he would do that when his own niece was in the caravan," Sebastian said.

"Maybe he didn't know?"

Sebastian shrugged at that, then to get the downcast look off my face said, "You're the one who caught his son red-handed, supplying rifles to the Apaches, making a deal with the Utes, and running slaves."

That's not much to feel good about, I thought, since it was Francisco's evidence that had mattered in the end. Maybe they'll pay *him* my thirty pesos!

"Sebastian," I asked, "did they find out what kept the Utes from joining the Apaches at the Galisteo raid? The Apaches would never admit it, but that probably left them way too short-handed to pull it off."

The corporal shrugged. "Something didn't go right for the alcalde about then. Nobody suspected him yet, but maybe without Ramón and Perea he just couldn't do it all. Somehow we had a piece of good luck that night when the Utes turned back. It was the first time that the alcalde didn't carry out his plans effectively."

"He actually got the Utes to come all the way to the edge of Santa Fe, but that was where something went wrong," I said. "Fifty armed warriors added to the Apache force could have tipped the balance."

Sebastian shrugged again. "The prostitutes told us that a Ute woman showed up at Rosa's house, but wouldn't come inside. She waited in the road until Rosa came out to talk to her in person. They think she could have delivered a warning, because Rosa left quickly, as though she had a job to do. But we'll never know, now that Rosa's dead."

An Indian woman? Could this have been what my mother had been up to, and why Cedro let her come down here despite the danger? Knowing Nan, I'd probably never be certain.

"And there's more about that," Sebastian went on, "Duran paid a personal call on Rosa the night she died. The girl we've got was only an accessory. Why do you think he went to all the trouble of using imported poison and green smoke? He was just using her. He needed to make it look like the kind of murder a woman would commit. The girl went along with him. She wasn't smart enough to protect herself."

I looked at Sebastian, horrified, as the meaning of this sank in. I pictured the alcalde approaching Rosa, making it look like love, using her that way, and then handing her the standard payment. I was furious when I said, "If he was cruel enough to kill Rosa, then he must also be the one who arranged to have you knocked out and left for dead."

"He had quite an operation going on at his ranch," Sebastian explained. "There was one man in particular, on old fellow, white, but more Apache than most Apaches, who carried out a lot of his dirty work."

"Probably the one Baz called the 'stinky old man.' The late Lorenzo, most likely."

"There's no longer any doubt that same man is the one who battered Carlos and stole the boy, using a few sidekicks of course, all of them definitely in the pay of the alcalde. I'd say one of them probably spooked my horse. The *late* Lorenzo, you said?"

"I'm pretty sure that son of a bitch is dead. I think I killed him out by the Galisteo." I was surprised at the satisfaction saying those words gave me. "Though judging from what Duran told us about a trusted employee betraying him, I think even Lorenzo finally had enough of his patrón."

"Duran seemed to be the best of fellows, until he wanted something out of you."

A zillion thoughts streamed through my brain. Duran's Apaches dressed as Comanches raiding Medanales. Militiamen driven off by the murders of two of their comrades, right in the middle of Santa Fe. Carlos, an important officer and heir to a huge land grant, not wounded enough for Duran's purposes, attacked again and thrown in the river. The child who witnessed that, kidnapped. The alcalde had done everything he could to destroy the colony. He sabotaged all the governor's attempts at forming an alliance with the Comanches, and feathered his own nest while he was at it.

"How does it figure?" I asked. "The man had it made in New Mexico."

What Sebastian said next knocked my moccasins off. "Alcalde Duran was working for the British. Today we found proof that he's been in their pay for the last five years."

"The British!" I sank down onto the hay, letting a whistle out from between my teeth. England, perennial enemy of Spain, always at war with us somewhere in the world, and trying to assert herself in North America as aggressively as the Spanish. "No one ever suspected?"

Sebastian shook his head.

Slowly I asked, "Perea's accent, was that English?"

"Probably. We'd have to resurrect him to prove it though."

An unlikely proposition, but it was coming together neatly, all of it: Perea, in Duran's pay, purposely telling Valdez it was Apaches on the mountain, so that the army attacked its own allies. Which meant that it was Duran, himself, who came close to ruining the critical Comanche alliance, as well as causing the death of a commanding officer and the injury to my brother.

"But didn't the British lose their colonies on the Atlantic seaboard last fall? Didn't we clobber them in the Mediterranean too? I'd say the clever Señor Duran picked the wrong side."

Sebastian was leaning on a rail now, rolling himself a smoke. "Apparently he was beginning to realize that he'd been backing the wrong side, but he hated the viceroy, hated the stranglehold the Chihuahua traders had on our commerce, and hated the Spanish government that permitted it. He was undermining the colony every chance he got, determined to weaken it to the point where another European power could acquire a foothold. He worked hard for the British and was definitely in their pay. They provided the guns he used to entice the Apaches. To him, anything was better than government by King Carlos and the viceroy in Mexico, each thousands of miles away. Besides, he was having a lot of fun with the Apaches, and getting rich while he was at it. Imagine, having first pick of all the goods coming up the trail. All he had to do was send his friends down from the passes to intercept the caravans."

"You found all this out this afternoon?" I was amazed.

"Remember the iron garrote that was used to hang the soldier?"

I nodded. "The inquisition relic left over from Oñate's day."

"It's not only an instrument of death. It's an effective instrument of torture as well." I could see the rusty round circle of iron being screwed tighter and tighter into the well-fed flesh of the alcalde's neck. I imagined it wouldn't take long.

"At first the governor didn't trust Francisco's story about the windows. He said your brother would be the main person to profit by the alcalde's arrest, since he was planning on marrying Duran's niece. He was about to throw Francisco in jail for treachery and defamation. After all, this was Anza's best friend your brother was implicating. But then you wrapped it up."

"What!" I couldn't believe any of this.

"Those coins you gave him. Good thing you didn't keep them tucked in your pocket, Nando." Sebastian managed a smile. "It didn't take long to get it out of the prostitute that Duran had been in Rosa's room. Not many men here pay for things with English crowns."

339

English money? In God's name! I imagined Rosa, humiliated to the core, hurling his payment against her wall.

"And the coin that I kicked up where Ramón was sitting at the rendezvous?"

"The same."

I was stunned silent, but Sebastian went on assembling pieces. "The British had to be subtle in our part of the world. Getting the alcalde must have been a big score for them. A few years ago, when they realized they might lose their colonies on the Atlantic, I think they began to eye New Spain's territories with their access to the Pacific. It's a known fact they've been arming the Comanches since as early as the sixties."

I heard his words, but frankly, the British didn't seem all that important to me. I was reeling from the fact that the alcalde would not have been caught, and that Francisco would have been jailed for accusing the governor's friend, if I hadn't relinquished the coins.

Sebastian was still talking. "It would be helpful to have Apaches as friends," he said, "if a man wanted to insure his wealth, something very important to Alcalde Duran. And keeping the Apaches strong and stirred up would create constant warfare among the different tribes, providing more opportunities for Duran and his son to acquire slaves, another unpleasant facet of the alcalde's business. Frankly, Nando, I think it wasn't so much his preference for one country over another that put him up to this, but the man's love for luxuries and power."

It was beyond figuring. "If he wanted those," I wondered out loud, "then why the hell did he live in New Mexico?"

Primo!

The earth and air were damp, but the worst of the storm had cleared. Before going home, I needed a few minutes walking alone in the dark streets to come to grips with the revelations of the day.

It was late, but some of the family surely would be up. Carlos undoubtedly had told them where he was going, and I would be inundated with questions. I still had plenty of my own. Did the fact that Ramón cast fond eyes on our ranch as a hiding place for his slave enterprise explain why the Aguilars had been under attack? And what about the mad friar? Surely he was some sort of accomplice to the alcalde. Did the Franciscans, too, have an interest in undermining the current government? I also kept coming back to the memory of the alcalde and the governor sitting up late beside the campfire out by the Galisteo. It's the Spanish side of me that likes to believe good and evil are distinct entities. As a Ute I know better. They are always rolled up together, never quite independent of each other.

341

When the row of houses opened up near our small fields, I could see the long wall of the Jemez mountains still illuminated by horizontal webs of lightning. There was more storm out to the west. I thought of Carlos riding through it, bringing in Francisco and his party. I hoped Carlos was holding up, but Francisco surely would take care of him. For damn certain it was his responsibility, having sucked us all into his mess.

My only remaining job was to find myself food and a dry bed, so I was glad to see there was still light coming from the house. I stumbled over a pile of rubble near the front door. Someone had started knocking a hole through the adobe for the new window; probably the women, restless, needing something to do while they waited.

They were all up, Nan, Luz, and Marisol, sitting on the rolled-up sleeping mats that they'd dragged in front of the fireplace. I was glad to see there was still a pot on the trivet in the coals. The women were all over me at once, probing with questioning looks, fussing over my wet clothes.

"Feed me. Then I'll talk." Luz didn't like my tone, but maybe it reminded her of someone from earlier in her life, because she started ordering everyone around. Then I relented enough to say, "Everyone's safe. They'll be back soon." The women lit the tallow lamps and stirred up the fire. They set my dinner on the table and I fell to. Through the chopped-out opening in the wall I could see lightning flash again in a huge cloudbank that had rumbled in from the Jemez. Nan went to the door and propped it open.

"Here we go again," she said. The wind was starting to turn the leaves upside down and thunder, rolling like artillery fire, split the heavens as I ate. I was all nerves, too tired really for food. I pulled up my own bundle of skins and sat beside the

women, smoking punché, occasionally passing my rolled ciga-
rette to one or another of them. I told them the story, all of it.

"Is this serious for Francisco?" Luz asked.

"I don't think so, not really, but it would have been better
if he'd just made off with Luisa. Anza can't have much interest in her, but taking the Señora along makes it more compli-
cated. You can see he has every reason to forgive Francisco
though."

"Young people always try to ditch the duenna before they
go night riding. I'll bet she pushed her way into his plan," Luz
sniffed, understanding these things.

"She could certainly have been an accomplice in this. Her
life was made considerably easier . . ."

A terrific blast of lightning struck something not thirty feet
from the house. We smelled smoke and tangy sulfur in the air.
Rain slammed onto the dirt roof and a leak started, drooling
wet mud onto the floor. Marisol put a bowl under it while the
rest of us stood in the doorway watching the trees bend in
the wind and an instant river of rainwater gush across our
yard.

A man hurtled through the water toward us from the street.
Lightning lit up his scared and anguished face. He ran straight
to our open doorway and stood there, scowling at us, hands
outstretched and clutching, as though now he finally had us in
his grasp. Rain glittered on his robes. Padre Baldonado glared
at us and then forced his way into our home.

I snapped. It had all gone on too long. I seized Benito's
pistol, cocked the hammer and pointed it at him.

"Get out!" I shouted above the storm. Luz sucked in her
breath. One didn't treat a priest like this, no matter who he
was.

"Get out!" I shouted again, panic altering my voice to something high and unrecognizable.

His eyes were frantic; whatever madness lived in him must be on him now. His face, lit up by firelight, was fierce and difficult to fathom. Was that rain, or were those tears, all over his angular cheekbones?

"Get your Bible," he commanded, in a strangely quiet voice.

I lifted the pistol, realigning it better with the center of his face. "Leave!"

Ignoring the gun, he insisted. "Open your Bible! The one from the ranch." The ranch? What was this man up to?

Mystified, Luz took her tattered Bible down from its place on the shelf next to the statue of the Virgin. She handed it to him. With the book in his hands, the man seemed to calm down. He opened it to the flyleaf. His fingers sought words that were made invisible by dark. The women yielded their places by the fire and he held the book to the light until he found it. The list of names.

"Don Pedro Aguilar," he read. "Under Don Pedro, his two sons, Francisco Aguilar, and right beside him, Benito Aguilar. Under your father Benito, all of you, Carlos, the next Francisco, Fernando, and the rest. Here's where I belong." His long dirty finger pointed to the space under our father's brother, the first Francisco, the elder son of Don Pedro.

Luz scrutinized his face. I kept the pistol pointed at it. This priest was madder than ever we'd thought.

"Benito's brother in Mexico?" she asked, looking up at him curiously.

"My father. Sent out of the colony. Brother to your husband, whom they also exiled, but only to the dangerous lands of the north."

"Nando, put down that gun," Luz snapped at me. She was the boss here, so I lowered it a little. *Cousin* Buzzard? My primo?

"You have been here three whole years and you have never told us?" Luz's voice was high-pitched too.

"No, I couldn't. I apologize deeply and with many regrets for what you must think of me, but there were reasons. I was caught in this plot almost the first day I arrived off the Camino Real."

"Sit down." She looked at Marisol and Nan. "Is there any more food? We'll need to make more, because Carlos and Francisco surely will be coming in too." The women rose and started to work at the fire and the table. Luz wrapped a large blanket around the wet friar and passed him the little that was left of the hot food in the pot. "Eat, and then you can talk," she said softly.

To hell with that, I thought, and moved in to confront him. "If you're my cousin, why did you attack me in front of the church?" I was still angry and I didn't trust this man at all.

Padre Baldonado looked at me and said, almost sadly, "I had to. The alcalde was watching. It was the only way I could deflect his suspicion."

He caught my dubious look, but dared to smile at me. "Perhaps you will believe I'm your cousin when I tell you how ridiculous you looked hiding behind that sprig of cottonwood in a ditch up on the Chama?"

"You what? Wait a minute! You saw me, but . . ."

"But I kept my mouth shut."

"Yes, but I saw you handing arms to the Apaches, rifles of the latest design." My interrogation was far from over.

"I did, all of them slightly altered, so that the firing mechanisms would fail almost immediately." He kept his eyes steadfastly on mine.

"What was so funny up on the hill, under the Cross of the Martyr's?" I was mainly just curious about that one.

"Watching Perea get beat up. He so deserved that!"

I still wasn't done. "I saw you buying captive children in Taos, you, a Franciscan, bound by vows of poverty!"

"It was the only way to get them out of the slavers' hands. The children were back with their tribes before you got to Santa Fe. I always have money with me for that."

I was silent, thinking, watching him steadily, and he kept his gaze level, looking right back at me. "And always you were angry with Rosa! You attacked her house. You were furious that she was buried in the church."

"I was miserable that I had not been able to attend her funeral. Rosa and I had worked together for two years." The padre's face was somber as he whispered, mostly to himself, "That was a person I loved."

I stared at him, frankly stupefied, breaking out of it only when I noticed the doorway was blocked by my two brothers, Carlos and Francisco. Francisco clutched the hand of a tall, tired-looking woman. A pueblo girl stood beside them.

"May we come in? We're under house arrest." Francisco had recovered his airiness, but he gaped when he saw the mad friar, sitting peaceably among us, spooning stew into his mouth from Francisco's own bowl.

"Padre?" Francisco inquired. Carlos and Luisa were inside now too, watching intently.

"Cousin, more like," I said, and Luz started in on the story. The sala, which I had always thought was fairly large, was packed. It was like Christmas, or lambing at the ranch. More candles were brought out, food disappeared as fast as it was prepared. Questions flew.

"Where's the Señora Duran?" Luz asked.

"Under guard at her home, which is where we are too. Carlos is guarding us." We looked over at the lieutenant who had his eyes closed and was leaning back on a pile of sheepskins, snoring lightly.

"And how did you ever become so stupid that you absconded with the alcalde's wife?" His mother peered up at him intending to have an answer.

Francisco took a deep breath. "The Señora had a difficult life with the alcalde, mother. She begged me not to leave her behind when I came for Luisa." He turned to look at the pueblo girl whom Nan had taken to a seat in a dark corner of the room. "Perhaps in the morning you will talk to this girl and then you will understand. She needs your help, and she's eager to get back to her family in the Pueblo, but the governor wants to hear her testimony before she goes. Giving details of her abduction and rape will be hard for her, even though Anza will surely conduct a delicate interview. Her grandfather is a cacique."

I didn't see how Luz took that, because I was still warily watching Baldonado, who had settled down to his supper amidst our chaotic family as though he belonged here. Perhaps he had always wanted to? But he had held back all this time, waiting until the alcalde could be convicted.

"Francisco," I asked, quietly enough that everyone stopped talking so they could overhear me, "did Anza say any more about my knife?"

"You're supposed to be there right after lunch tomorrow. There will be questions."

Padre Baldonado looked up from his supper and said, "I'll attend with you."

"What good would that do?" I charged. "You think I need a priest?" This was too much. Was he going to try to move in and become the new *pater familias*?

Baldonado's voice quavered just a little when he said, "I threw the knife." All eyes turned toward the enigmatic man.

"Like a good primo," I said, nearly in a whisper. "How on earth did you get my knife? No priest could throw like that!"

"One of the Comanche women you helped down by La Ciénega gave it to me. She told me what happened and asked me to try to get it back to the owner, but we didn't have any idea who it belonged to. I was holding onto it, hoping to discover who else was working with us against the enslavement of humans." He regarded me steadily and I returned his look.

Incredulous, I asked, "How did you possibly manage to find us, in the storm, in the woods?"

"I had been on Ramón's trail for two days, desperately trying to stay with him because I suspected he was hunting you. Then that last night, I lost all trace of him. It was dark and I was beyond exhaustion. I slept between two old logs somewhere just above the Tesuque cutoff. Rain hitting my face woke me up, and just at that moment I saw your dim shapes hurrying across the road. There was no question in my mind about what to do next."

"Why did you kill him?" I dared to ask out loud.

He answered without hesitation. "Ramón had captured a member of my family. It was clear to me that he was about to murder you and leave with only the woman. Besides wanting to save your life, I have always detested slavers." Then, sounding ashamed, he added, "Despite my vocation, it was easy."

Everyone had already stopped the tasks they'd been doing. Now we all moved over near the padre. He shifted uncomfortably at the attention fixed on him.

"Tell us, please," Luz said. The man put down his bowl and spoon and told a short and simple story.

"I was less than five when my parents left me at a monastery. The only people who befriended me were the workers in the kitchen. Slaves, mostly, one of them a Ute from New Mexico. He saved my life over and over again, seeing that I didn't lack for food, a blanket, or for kindness. The Franciscans hardly knew I existed until later in my life. To them I was just an urchin, left behind when my parents were arrested. I suppose they died in jail, in Spain, I think.

"Living by the mercy of the kitchen help, I saw their lot as slaves. I learned their language and about their earlier ways. My Ute uncle, for uncle I called him, taught me how to defend myself, and when I got a little bigger we threw kitchen knives together out in the laundry yard until I could do it well. One day a priest watched me as I buried a knife in a wooden cross out in the garden, from twenty feet. That put a quick end to my boyhood! I never talked to my uncle again. I was in robes in the seminary within two days, but I never forgot the stories he told me, and what being forced into slavery had done to his life.

"When I was called to go to New Mexico, I was overjoyed. I would see you and reclaim my family. I would find my Ute uncle's people, his parents and his wife, and I would find a way to stop the slavers who ravaged the people of this territory.

"My second week in Santa Fe, I encountered Tomás Duran. He seemed to be befriending me, and before I knew it, I was in his trust and gradually included in parts of the family's scheme. I recognized the opportunity, and while I am sure it violated every one of my vows, my confessor forgave me and protected my effort to bring their long-standing treachery into the light."

"Your confessor?" asked Luz.

"Father Miera. I know it sometimes pained him, but he helped me see it through. Nevertheless, I will have to return to Mexico soon, to the Mother House, the Convento Grande, and do the penances necessary to absolve this sin."

Luz and I exchanged a long look. She refilled the padre's cup, and told him he was welcome to make his home with us as long as his Order would let him stay.

That night there was so little room on the dirt floors of our house that I couldn't walk between the mats. The rain was a quiet drizzle now, mostly over, but it was way too wet to sleep outside. I gave my own bundle of sheepskins to my mother, who went to the bedroom with Luz, Luisa and all the girls. Both my brothers crowded onto Carlos's bed, because Baldonado had accepted Francisco's mat. When they had all found their places and gone to sleep, I was surprised to see the padre pull from his bundle a long, white, woman's nightgown, and drape it over himself like a sheet. Always odd, this cousin of ours.

All that was left was a saddle blanket. I lay down on it, grateful that it was dry, and pulled my manta over me. I started planning how we would add not one, not two, but three more rooms, and was falling asleep when I heard someone walking on tiptoe across the floor.

Marisol slipped down beside me, hiding herself between me and the wall.

Quickly, I pulled my manta over her. She rolled against me and whispered in my ear, "Nando, I think you have made me a baby."

A smile formed on my lips. I drew her closer and as a wave of happiness rose in me, I found a dozen places to drop kisses on her lovely face. I had an excited feeling that our colony was going to live.

A Glance At The Times

1763 – The end of the French and Indian War essentially splits the North American continent in two, giving Britain possession of the east, while Spain retains the vast region from the Mississippi to the Pacific ocean. France keeps only two small islands in the Caribbean.

1776 – Americans upset the Europeans' tidy equation by signing the Declaration of Independence and the American Revolutionary War begins.

1776 – Spain's King Carlos III creates a special military command in New Spain to protect Mexico's silver mines from Apaches and other tribes attacking from the north.

1776 – Juan Bautista de Anza leads the first group of Spanish settlers cross-country from Mexico to San Francisco.

1777 – King Carlos III appoints Anza as Governor of New Mexico.

1779 – Spain and England declare war against each other and engage in battles throughout the world.

1779 – In New Spain, Governor Anza wins a critical campaign against the formidable Comanche Chief, Cuerno Verde.

1781 – Americans, aided by French and Spanish allies, defeat the British at Yorktown.

1783 – The Treaty of Paris officially ends the American Revolutionary War, as well as the war between England and Spain.

1786 – Governor Anza successfully negotiates a treaty between Spain and the Comanche nation.

1788 – Relieved of the governorship, Anza returns to Sonora and dies shortly thereafter. King Carlos III of Spain dies within that same month, December 1788.

New Mexican Spanish

Acéquia — an irrigation ditch

Adobe — mud bricks

Alcalde — or *Alcalde Mayor*, the headman of a district, equivalent in ways to Mayor

Así fué — thus it was

Bosque — the dense cottonwood forest that grows only along rivers

Caballada — a horse herd, in this story the huge herd of animals held in reserve for the soldiers of the garrison

Cacique — a religious leader of a Pueblo

Chamisa — a yellow brushy weed sometimes known as rabbit brush

Cojones — balls

Cuerno Verde
— the Comanche leader who was killed in battle by Governor Anza's troops in 1779. He was recognized by the headdress he wore which had a green horn on it.

En años pasados
— in years past, or "Once upon a time"

Hacienda — a large house, or country estate

Manta — a woven cape, like a poncho, usually made of wool, also a blanket

Palacio — the Palace of the Governors, the earliest government building built in the United States, still standing and in use in Santa Fe

Patrón — the landowner, the boss

Piedra Lumbre
  - literally translated: shining stone, the name of a large valley above Abiquiú, which is rimmed with colorful sandstone cliffs

Piñon
  - a pine tree whose wood makes an aromatic fire, and which produces edible nuts

Plazuela
  - an adobe house or group of houses, usually constructed around courtyards to provide defense

Portál
  - pronounced "por-TAL", a covered porch

Posole
  - a stew made with dried corn

Presidio
  - a Spanish garrison; in Santa Fe in 1782, The Palace of the Governors

Primo
  - cousin

Punché
  - a locally grown, rough tobacco substitute

Rico
  - a rich man

Sala
  - the main room, or living room, of a home

Sangre de Cristo
  - Blood of Christ, the principle mountains of northern New Mexico. This name did not come into use until after the time of this story, but I allow it here as it will be familiar to the reader.

Teniente
  - the mayor's assistant

Historical Sources

Bailey, L.R. *The Indian Slave Trade in the Southwest*. Los Angeles: Westernlore Press, 1973.

Bowman, J.N. and Heizer, R. F. *Anza and the Northwest Frontier of New Spain*, Southwest Museum, Highland Park, Los Angeles, California, Southland Press, 1967.

Brooks, James, F. *Captives and Cousins*, University of North Carolina Press, 2002.

Chávez, Fray Angélico. *My Penitente Land, Reflections on Spanish New Mexico*. Museum of New Mexico Press, 1974.

Chávez, Thomas E. *Spain and the Independence of the United States*. University of New Mexico Press, 2002.

Domínguez, Fray Francisco Atanasio and Fray Francisco Silvestre Vélez de Escalante. *The Domínguez-Escalante Journal*. Edited by Ted J. Warner, translated by Fray Angelico Chavez. University of Utah Press, 1995.

Domínguez, Fray Francisco Atanasio. *The Missions of New Mexico, 1776*. Translated and annotated by Eleanor B. Adams and Fray Angelico Chavez. The University of New Mexico Press, 1956 and 1975.

Gutiérrez, Ramón A. *When Jesus Came, the Corn Mothers Went Away, Marriage, Sexuality, and Power in New Mexico, 1500-1846*. Stanford University Press, 1991.

Herrera, Carlos R. *The King's Governor, Juan Bautista de Anza and Bourbon New Mexico in The Era of Imperial Reform, 1778-1788*, A Dissertation for his Doctor of History Degree, University of New Mexico, Albuquerque, 2000.

Horgan, Paul. *The Centuries of Santa Fe.* E.P. Dutton and Company, Inc. New York, 1956.

Jefferson, James, Delaney, Robert W. and Thompson, Gregory C. *The Southern Utes, A Tribal History*. Southern Ute Tribe, Ignacio, Colorado.

Kessell, John L. *Kiva, Cross, and Crown, The Pecos Indians and New Mexico 1540-1840*. University of New Mexico Press, 1979.

Kessler, Ron. *Anza's 1779 Comanche Campaign*. Adobe Village Press, Monte Vista, Colorado, 2001. Second Edition.

La Pierre, Yvette. *Welcome to Josefina's World, 1824*. The American Girls Collection, Pleasant Company Publications, Wisconsin, 1999.

Marriott, Alice. *The Ten Grandmothers. Epic of the Kiowas*. University of Oklahoma Press, 1945.

Martinez, Wilfred O. *Anza and Cuerno Verde, Decisive Battle*. El Escritorio. Pueblo, Colorado, 2001.

Noble, David Grant. *Santa Fe, History of an Ancient City*. School of American Research Press Santa Fe, 1989.

Noyes, Stanley. *Los Comanches, The Horse People, 1751-1845*. University of New Mexico Press, 1993.

Poling-Kempes, Lesley. *Valley of Shining Stone, The Story of Abiquiu*. The University of Arizona Press, Tucson, 1997.

Preston, Douglas, Preston, Christine and Esquibel, José Antonio. *The Royal Road, El Camino Real from Mexico City to Santa Fe*. University of New Mexico Press, 1998.

Quintana, Frances Leon. *Pobladores, Hispanic Americans of the Ute Frontier*. University of Notre Dame Press, Indiana, 1991.

Sánchez, Joseph P. *The Rio Abajo Frontier, 1540-1692, A History of Early Colonial new Mexico.* The Albuquerque Museum, 1987. Second Edition 1996.

Schmutz, Ervin M. and Hamilton, Lucretia Breazeale. *Plants That Poison, An Illustrated Guide for the American Southwest.* Northland Press, Flagstaff, Arizona 1979.

Simmons, Marc. "Trail Dust", regular historical news articles in the Santa Fe New Mexican, Saturdays 2001-2003

Simmons, Marc. *Spanish Government in New Mexico.* University of New Mexico Press 1968 and 1990.

Simmons, Marc. *Coronado's Land, Essays on Daily Life in Colonial New Mexico.* University of New Mexico Press, 1991. Included therein: Father Juan Agustín de Morfí's *Account of Disorders in New Mexico, 1778.*

Simmons, Marc. *Yesterday in Santa Fe, Episodes in a Turbulent History.* Sunstone Press, 1989.

Simmons, Marc. *Witchcraft in the Southwest. Spanish and Indian Supernaturalism on the Rio Grande.* University of Nebraska Press, 1974.

Simmons, Marc. *New Mexico, An Interpretive History.* University of New Mexico Press, 1988.

Simmons, Virginia McConnell. *The Ute Indians of Utah, Colorado and New Mexico.* University Press of Colorado, 2000.

Sonnichsen, C.L. *The Mescalero Apaches.* Second Edition, University of Oklahoma Press, Norman, OK, 1958.

Swan-Jackson. *The Apaches and Pueblo Peoples of the Southwest.* Heineman Children's Reference, Great Britain, 1996.

~Publication of Taos Historic Museums, "Hacienda de los Martinez circa 1804".

~Publications of the Museum of New Mexico Museum of International Folk Art: The Royal Road, The Colonial Home, and Adobe Architecture of New Mexico, all by Robin Farwell Gavin, Curator of Spanish Colonial Collections.

~Lecture Series by Southwest Seminars, including an eight lecture series by Alan Osborne, Golden Threads: New Mexico's Early History, and subsequent series offered in 2001 and 2002 as a benefit for the Palace of the Governors. One hour lectures by, among others, José Antonio Esquibel, Orlando Romero, Dr. Stanley Hordes, David Grant Noble, Dr. John Kessell, Dr. Joseph Sánchez, Dr. Thomas E. Chávez, Joe S. Sando, Dr. Fran Levine, Dr. Robert Himmerich y Valencia, Dr. Estévan Rael-Gálvez, and Skip Keith Miller.

~Sixth Annual Anza World Conference, lecture series held in Pueblo, Colorado August 31- September 2, 2001, including talks by Don Garate, Anza biographer with the National Park Service at Tumacacori, Wilfred Martinez, Ron Kessler, Jack Williams of the Center for Spanish Colonial Research at the San Diego Presidio, Roland McCook, the Head Commissioner of the Northern Ute Tribe, Jimmy Atterbury, Comanche spokesman, and Carrie Knight of the Kiowa tribe.

~Exhibits and Festivals at El Rancho de Las Golondrinas, a living history museum south of Santa Fe

The maps in this book were adapted from the original which was drawn in 1779 by the surveyor Don Bernardo de Miera y Pacheco.

Acknowledgements

My friends have been a delight to me in this process and amazingly generous. I thank all of you who read early drafts, encouraged, taught, and kept me in the game. I am especially grateful to Jim Danneskiold (first flight), Rick Shore and Cynthia Marshall, Ken Brody (mentoring at Higgins), Cleone and Alf Stoloff, Marc Simmons, our esteemed historian, my son Jack Dant (your fight scenes need more Jackie Chan, mom), Luis Juarez (loving Apache), expert editors Ardeth Baxter and Dick McCord, Bob and Cat Break (you've got the wrong mule!), Mark Kaltenbach who added sweetness, and of course, Bill Baxter, who with intelligence and humor, finally birthed the baby. The making of this book belongs to all of us.

Thank you!

Pamela Christie received her education at the Catlin Gabel School in Oregon, Bryn Mawr College, Pitzer College, and the University of California at Berkeley. She has lived and worked in New Mexico for over thirty years, in both a remote mountain village and in Santa Fe. She hikes and explores the countryside she writes about, immersing herself in the history and culture of the region.